# I'm the Bomb

Morgan Hobbs was born in Tidewater, Virginia and graduated from the University of Wisconsin – Madison with a degree in English and History. He has worked as a day laborer in Austin, Texas, a commercial fisherman in Kodiak, Alaska, and a reader and story editor for several motion picture production companies in Los Angeles, California. He currently lives in Tokyo, Las Vegas and Washington, D.C.

Rumble Strip Media, Las Vegas 89109
©2015 by Morgan Hobbs
All rights reserved. Published 2015
Printed in the United States of America

ISBN 9781515312123

Thanks to: Lesley Hobbs, Andrew Jackson and David Retzlaff

To Lesley

# CHAPTER 1

The man stepped out of the glass elevator. He approached the receptionist's desk.

"Richard Blow. I have an 11:30 with Heller and Nero."

"Good morning, Mr. Blow. Please have a seat. I'll let Mr. Heller know that you've arrived."

Blow nodded and took a seat under the Rothko. Magazines were lined up neatly on the table—*Variety, Vanity Fair, People* and its Australian sibling *Who, Premiere, National Geographic, Hollywood Reporter, Harper's, The Atlantic Monthly*. He sat in the chair with a hint of a smile, looking focused but relaxed. The receptionist offered a cup of coffee. He politely declined. He picked up a magazine, the latest issue of *Vanity Fair*, and opened it to an interview with the actor Tony Billings. At first glance, it looked like the usual puff piece.

After a time, Heller appeared. Blow stood up, and the two shook hands. They'd met before, in previous meetings and on conference calls. They'd run into each other at parties. They had a mutual friend in Fern Zeller, talent agent at Creative Artists. That was how this meeting got put together. Heller mentioned over drinks at the Peninsula that they were looking for some fresh material. Zeller passed on the name of Richard Blow, a super creative guy stuck churning out sitcoms, trying to break into features. He'd written three or four scripts that got some serious looks. Anyway, give him a meeting, said Zeller. He's developing a story that sounds right up your alley. Sort of a romantic thriller. I don't want to give too much away.

Heller set up the meeting through Blow's manager Patti Tenenbaum after watching several episodes of the sitcom—one, credits to Blow alone, the other two to the team of Blow, O'Hara, and Hanrahan. Heller recalled having seen one of the episodes when it aired on television. The writing was pretty good—smart and funny. The story had a few good surprises, but nothing that suggested Blow could handle an original feature. Sitcom writing was formula writing. Features followed a formula, too, but the lack of strict conventions, established characters, running storyline, often presented a daunting task for writers accustomed to the series format. For a number of reasons, it could be difficult for TV writers, so established, to cross over to features where the real money was at. Pen a sitcom or movie-of-the-week and there was a danger of being typecast. Still, Nero wanted fresh material and fresh faces. Heller was more inclined toward adapting a novel when it came to thrillers. He harbored some doubts about Blow's romantic thriller, but Patti assured him it worked on the level of a comedy, too. Maybe Blow would pull it off. If the pitch generated some laughs, who knew, maybe Blow would get himself a deal. It had been ages since a truly funny spec script came across his desk, and Lord knew, you couldn't rely on the book market. There were a few funny books that came out every year—mainly crack pot memoirs—but not many had a movie sized story.

Blow had some comic chops, and the fact that he'd made it as far as he had in the sitcom grind was proof that he could deliver a conventional set up and punch line, a lost art for the current crop of writers that were all over late night television. Some of those kids—like the kid who crawled out from under the seats on the Letterman show years back—wouldn't have lasted 5 minutes on *Welcome Back Kotter*, and it had been all down hill since then. Thrillers were another matter. The best usually started out as books—*The Maltese Falcon* was a book. *Strangers on a Train* came from a book. *L.A. Confidential.* There were some exceptions, like *Chinatown.* The first draft was as long as a book. Heller was feeling all right about the comedy, less sure about the thriller. The romantic would work itself out. It was mainly a matter of casting. What movie wasn't romantic? They were always about boys and girls. Heller seemed to recall that Blow's real name was Head. Richard Head. Not bad, but Blow was good, too, had a nice ring to it. It stuck with you.

Heller led Blow back to the conference room.

"Nero and the others will join us in a moment."

When they entered the conference room, Jerry was already seated. He stood up, and Heller introduced him to Blow. The two men shook hands.

"I enjoyed your work on *Pen Pals*," Jerry said.

"They made it easy," said Blow. "Billy and Jack and the other writers—Jim and Nancy. It helps when you start out with great characters, when you have Tom Grace and Cindy DeAngeles walking around in a Manhattan apartment in your head."

"The balloon episode was your idea?" said Jerry.

"It came to him in a dream," said Heller.

"Not exactly," said Blow, smiling. "I was nodding off after the *Late Show*. I heard a loud pop. It sounded like an explosion."

"The Nixon balloon."

"On the stucco ceiling."

"My wife loved that scene," said Jerry.

"My daughter in college loved it," said Heller. "We're looking forward to hearing what you've got."

"Terry and Nick will be joining us in a few minutes. Bax and Tina said they wanted to sit in."

A man and a woman entered the room and shook hands with Blow.

"Bax...Richard Blow...Richard, you know Tina," said Heller.

"Great to see you again," said Tina, a young black woman with tortoise shell glasses. "I ran into Richard at the screening last weekend...What did you think?"

"Beautifully shot," said Blow. "Great action sequences. I almost forgot it wasn't Brad and Angie up there."

"*Almost*," said Tina, tilting her head. "Trying to please the bean counters, squeeze those above-the-line costs. No offense, Bax."

"The trailer's pretty hot," said Bax.

"With Brad and Angie, it's hot. Without Brad and Angie, it's got a pulse, maybe," said Nero, the charismatic president of the company.

With jet black hair drawn back in a short ponytail, Nero was of medium stature but was immensely self-possessed, giving the impression of a physical mastery gained from years of intensive training in yoga and transcendental meditation. He had the quality of immediately putting one at ease and was both admired and feared by colleagues in the industry. Nero had the uncanny ability to take any pitch, any proposal, any would-be deal, and break it down, size it up on the spot, rendering a judgment so disarming in its candor and obvious truth that one couldn't help but graciously accept it. It was a talent that he had honed to perfection over the years. Heller had sat in hundreds of these meetings and watched Nero eviscerate almost as many carefully crafted pitches with such speed and ruthless precision the writers had gotten up, shaken hands, and driven halfway home before even realizing they were dead. The feeling was described as peaceful, oceanic. It would hit while talking on the cell phone or stopped at a traffic light, and then the light would turn, and the world rushed by like a cool breeze is how one writer described it.

The group sat down around the table. Heller sat next to Blow, and Nero sat directly across from them. They shot the shit for a few minutes until Terry and Nick arrived from their meeting with the people from Imagica.

"How'd it go?" said Heller.

"Pretty unreal. Pretty soon you're not even going to need actors," said Terry.

"Always need a writer, though. Right, Blow?" said Bax.

"They haven't figured out how to cut out the writer yet," said Blow.

"Forget the writer. You can put 'em in a room full of typewriters like back in the day. Now if you could cut out the *director*...I long for the day Alan Smithee takes a bullet for Hal 9000," said Heller.

"It won't be today," said Tina. "Hal 9000 doesn't have a union."

"They can play chess," said Blow.

"My five-year-old can play chess," said Heller.

"No way a computer could come up with that *Balloon Man* idea," said Jerry. "These days I'm thinking about video games. Blow, you ever try to write a video game?"

"They use writers?"

"They've got to have some kind of script, right? You open the door to the left, this happens. The door to the right, you're fighting 20 ninjas and a hundred flying turtles."

"Blow, would you call that writing? I call it programming.

The player's supposed to be the writer. It's participatory," said Terry.

"It's a revolution," said Blow. "Overthrow the tyranny of the author, liberate the reader-slash-consumer. I took a course on it at Brown."

"Video games are big, but the movies aren't going anywhere. 50 billion dollars worldwide last year," said Heller.

"Blow, have you written anything for 3-D?" said Terry.

"Not yet. I've been working mainly in TV. I have a few ideas. There are some interesting possibilities."

"I've got an Imax thing going. A feature. The whole thing takes place under the sea," said Terry. "The first scene you're following this diver down into this unbelievable aquatic world—amazing rainbow colored fish, porpoises, manta rays, spectacular neon coral reefs, and then the diver turns and suddenly you're sinking through this huge cloud of bubbles, rushing past you, thousands and thousands of them so close that you can practically feel them."

Terry paused, savoring the description of the scene.

"That's beautiful," said Blow. "What happens next?"

"That's all he's got," said Nick. "That's why we're talking to writers."

"Shouldn't be too difficult," said Terry. "Lots of underwater shots. You could probably write the whole thing on the back of a match book."

"I'll see what I can come up with."

"We'll do lunch," said Nick.

"Lunch," said Terry. "My assistant will set it up."

"Now about that feature," said Heller. "What age group are we talking about?"

"The leads are in their late 20s, early 30s," said Blow.

"Young but not too young," said Terry.

"Just the right age," said Nick.

"Adults, young and hot," said Bax.

Nero put his hands behind his head and leaned back in his chair.

"I took the early bird out of La Guardia this morning," he said. "The driver picked me up in front of the hotel, the Mercer. The bell hop gave my bags to the driver, the driver loaded them into the trunk. I only had two bags—both were small enough to fit in the overhead. Over the years I've learned how to travel light, to pack only what is necessary, and to pack very quickly and in such a way that my belongings do not encumber me, so that they provide the bare minimum resistance, and my passage from hotel to car to ticket window to destination is an essay in pure fluid motion—seamless, effortless, like a breeze. And on that flight, while I enjoyed a glass of cool water and gazed out the window at the infinite blue, my mind clear, weightless, a thought came to me, less a thought really than a picture, a picture of a face, male or female doesn't matter, the face was young, with clear eyes and smooth skin, the hair was blonde but it could have just as easily been brown or red—what was more important was that it was a face I'd never seen before, an unknown, young and clear eyed, unmarked by time or experience or the impressions of the world, like a fresh breeze blowing across the desert, a breeze that could almost by itself quench your thirst. A movie was playing. The stewardess had given me a set of plastic headphones. I hadn't opened the plastic bag. I didn't know what movie it was, and I didn't want to know. As I looked out the window, I opened the blind just a crack out of respect for the other passengers—they were all wearing their headphones or were asleep. I didn't want to know what movie was playing. What I wanted, more than anything, as I gazed out that sliver of window, was that—"

At that instant Terry Banner's head exploded. It happened so suddenly and unexpectedly that the first sensation was an awareness of an uncomfortable pause in the conversation, an odd kind of embarrassment at reaching this impasse, the graphic nature of which was only now beginning to register with those seated around the table, in the picture of Terry's headless body posed with legs crossed in cream chino slacks, one hand draped casually across a knee, the other still holding a brandy colored Mont Blanc pen at the termination of an elaborate geometric doodle on the yellow legal pad. The event was surprisingly bloodless, especially at first, and transpired so seamlessly and without forewarning that no one noticed when during the interval between the explosion and the realization, Nero calmly rose to his feet, pushed out his chair and left the conference room. When this detail emerged under hypnosis, Heller was reluctant to dwell on the matter but had to admit that he couldn't recall Nero being present at the moment Bax reached across the table, dialed the receptionist on speaker phone, and asked her to call 911.

# CHAPTER 2

Richard Blow and an actor friend Teddy Cruz were having lunch at the fashionable West Hollywood restaurant The Ivy. They were drinking white wine when the salads arrived. They were seated out on the terrace, which faced a fairly busy street at the intersection of Alden and North Robertson. The sunny terrace was packed; in spite of the fact that L.A. had nice weather year round there always seemed to be a shortage of good outdoor seating. The restaurant didn't take reservations at lunch, and it was next to impossible to get a table unless you knew the waiter or the *maitre d'*. Richard knew several of the waiters, and they were usually able to get him a table if he showed up a little ahead of the lunch rush. He tended to eat lunch there two or three times a week, and sometimes he would meet Teddy if Teddy had to stop in at Castaway around the corner on Beverly. The waiter set down the salad and cracked some pepper.

"Enough about bit parts on daytime soaps, what's this about a head exploding?" said Cruz.

"I was at Morpheus pitching the hit man idea to Heller and Nero. There were a few others there—Bax, Terry, Nick, Tina. It was Terry's head that exploded."

"You've been talking about that idea for a long time. That's the one about the hit man, a young guy, late 20s, something like that. He's engaged to this beautiful socialite, an heiress to a hotel fortune, right? And she's also a model and an actress, and she's got a record contract. She has everything she wants, daddy's little girl. You were telling us about it a couple weeks ago."

"I've been developing the idea for a couple months now. I've got most of the major points of the story worked out. It's the basic opposite sides of the track attract. He's from the inner city, a broken home, his mother was a crack whore, Caucasian. She's the Park Avenue princess drawn to this dark mysterious wildness inside him that she can't tame—he's the only thing in her life she can't have on her own terms."

"Who set it up? Gloria?"

"Fern was talking to Heller. Heller called Gloria."

"So you got a meeting. That's pretty cool. I thought nobody was buying off a pitch anymore, especially from a writer."

"It's picking up. That's what I've been hearing. I got some good feedback."

"They must have seen something they liked."

"I got a lot of good comments on the *Balloon Man* episode."

"That's my sister's favorite episode, when the balloon hits the ceiling, that rough stucco ceiling..."

"I had that pitch down. I stayed up half the night giving it to the mirror. I taped myself and played it back and made changes. I gave it to Dalva on the phone, I called Steve and Jack, I met Ray at Swingers and went through the whole thing A to Z two times over that morning and gave it to Shelley on the phone on the drive over. I could give it forward and backwards and not miss a beat. They took me into the room, and we sat around shooting the shit, the usual repartee. I was hanging back, playing it cool, waiting for an opening."

"And then that guy's head exploded."

"Terry Banner's head—he was wearing this black banded collar shirt, and cream pants. He was giving a whole rap about this underwater 3-D thing."

"I keep hoping it'll go away, like it did after *Jaws 3*. There was that brief renaissance in the 80s: *Jaws 3*, *Friday the 13th* part whatever, *Amityville 3-D*, then nothing for 20 or 30 years."

"I don't think it's going anywhere. I remember seeing *T-Rex* in 3-D at the Museum of Natural History, way back when. That was the first time I'd seen the new generation. I knew it was going to blow up."

"The Museum of Natural History?" he said, taking out a cigarette and rolling it between his fingers. "I must have missed that. Can you smoke out here?"

"Technically we're inside because we're under an awning."

He put the cigarette behind his hear.

"I don't see anybody else smoking."

"People only smoke at parties now. You rarely even see people smoke while they're driving."

"It ruins the resale value."

Teddy made eye contact with the waiter and pointed at his water glass.

"It used to be it was just a few things popping out at you," said Cruz. "I remember sitting there for two hours with those stupid glasses and maybe six things popped out at me, like a spear, then a yo-yo, some popcorn, and juggling."

"The technology has come a long way, but they still gotta get rid of the glasses," said Blow, as the waiter arrived. "I had the duck."

The waiter set down the plate in front of him. Teddy had the fettuccine with scallops and prawns.

"I'll be right back with the Cab," said the waiter.

"I'll have one, too," said Teddy. "Pinot."

"The thing I like about this place, they're not afraid to serve pommes frites," said Blow. "Usually with any kind of meat, all I want are pommes frites."

The music piped into the terrace was a catchy pop number with electro-African beats and icy cool vocals from a Scandinavian sounding female singer.

"Did you see her on the Late Show?" asked Blow. "Gwynn? She sounds nothing like this."

"They don't let them lip sync on that show."

"It's all studio tricks these days. Nobody really knows how to sing."

"That Milli Vanilli guy shouldn't have offed himself. They were ahead of their time," said Cruz.

"They even let them lip sync now on *Saturday Night Live*. That never would have happened in 1979."

"Did you ever see *El Mariachi*?"

"I saw it."

"Everybody made a big deal out of it because it was halfway

decent, and it cost seven thousand dollars to make," said Cruz. "What they don't tell you is Columbia paid almost half a million dollars in post-production. Even with an expensive A-list type of movie, you look at the raw footage, before the post-production, and it looks like shit. So whether you pay seven thousand or seven hundred million, before the post-production, it's going to look like shit. That's to be expected when you're talking about sound, editing, the special visual patina of cinema, but what really surprised me, even when it's A-list soup to nuts, lock, stock, and two smoking barrels, before the post-production even the acting sucks. A friend of mine showed me the dailies for Pacino's scenes from *Heat*, a movie that's practically a monument to unbelievable post-production and hot shot mano-a-mano acting, De Niro versus Pacino, scenes so intensely dramatic they give me goose bumps—in the dailies it's like watching a couple insurance agents from Newark arguing over the last piece of ziti. I refuse to watch myself in dailies. And now I prefer to watch other actors almost exclusively in dailies."

"That kind of lowers the bar," said Blow, cutting into the duck.

"I'm more inspired by mediocrity. You watch the performances in *Godfather, Taxi Driver, Scarface*, any of the usual tours de force of powerhouse acting and you wonder why even get out of bed. It's already been done."

"I find bad writing is contagious. I read bad writing it pollutes my system. A writer is a function machine. Garbage in, garbage out. Words are like gasoline. You read jet fuel, you fly like a jet."

"Don't tell me somebody shows you something, you hope it's going to be great?"

"That's completely different. I'm not talking about peers. I'm talking about Faulkner, F. Scott."

"You should read their screenplays. I heard they weren't so great."

"They're not bad," said Blow.

"F. Scott drank himself to death because he couldn't make it in this business."

"There was more to it than that, but it didn't help."

"This town has killed the careers of a lot of great writers."

"Script writing is a totally different game. Great writers are lured by the promise of easy money."

"They score once or twice, just enough to give them a taste, and then they spend the rest of their lives trying to get back that feeling," said Cruz.

"The business is like a big casino."

"There are casinos everywhere you look now. One day it's going to be an Indian casino."

"Or a Chinese casino. I hear Macau is the next Vegas."

"It may be the next Vegas if you're Chinese. You think people in this town are going to fly to China for the weekend?"

"The film business in Asia is growing by the second. Hong Kong could be the next Hollywood. Or Beijing, or Seoul," said Blow.

"Hollywood isn't going anywhere. They've been predicting the death of this town for a hundred years. It's never going to die because it's already dead. It's a desert, a zombie, a walking corpse with a cell phone and shades. It's like something out of the Bible. It's like the Jerusalem of the entertainment world. Even after the famine, the locusts, the earthquakes, the tidal waves, we'll still be sitting here having this conversation."

"Except by then it'll all be 3-D."

"Or holography, or virtual reality, or scratch-and-sniff. When I first heard the story, I thought maybe it was your pitch that made his head explode. Sounds like you really hadn't even gotten into it."

"There was definitely a tension. I was very aware of it. The anticipation of giving the pitch, when to give it, replaying it over and over in my head. There was definitely a pressure that was building up."

"It wasn't your head that exploded."

"It was Terry's." He shook his head. "I can't think of anything that was that unusual. He's one of these high energy types, always trying to bounce ideas off you. This 3-D thing."

"Do you think I should put 3-D in my reel?"

"You should explore it. Remember what the talkies did to Valentino."

"Are you saying you don't think I'll look good in 3-D?"

"I've only seen you in flat screen. I'm just saying."

"I'm going to a System thing tonight," said Cruz. "At the Star Center."

"Don't sign anything. Or take any oaths," said Blow. "I hear once they get their hands on you, they never let you go."

15

"Don't believe the hype. It's not that bad. And you'd be surprised at who shows up. It's a great networking opportunity."

"It's like a cult, or a religion or something."

"At least it's not a pyramid scheme. Some mother fucker gave me the rap just the other day. Tried to get me to buy $800 worth of vitamins."

"I'm pretty sure it's exactly like a pyramid scheme."

"You know what I mean. I'm willing to try almost anything at this point. The window's still open, but it's closing fast."

"I wish I'd ordered the chicken. They were serving it right on the bone, with brown butter sauce and garlic mashed potatoes with crisped fennel on the top. See, that chick over there had it. It would have gone great with a Riesling."

"I think I'm going to have another glass."

Cruz raised his hand to signal the waiter.

"Espresso for me," said Blow, signing in the air. "And the check."

# CHAPTER 3
*FREDERICK M. BARCLAY*

I came in through the front door, carrying my digital recorder, mike and notepad, dressed in a rumpled black suit and wearing a fedora. I was let in by a huge mustached manservant who I recognized as an off duty member of the Santa Monica police department. I recognized the man because he had once—while working part time as a bouncer—thrown me out of a popular late night dive frequented by campy dyed-blonde widows in their 40s and a handful of rugged longshoremen who mistook these emotionally imbalanced creatures for off-duty transsexual prostitutes. I was there doing a piece about the piano man who had studied—quite literally—under the great Liberace and still had the emotional contusions to prove it. I fell into disfavor with the proprietor of the establishment—a tiny Leprechaun of a man dressed head-to-toe in green velour—when I insisted, after nine or ten shots of Drambuie, on arm wrestling his eight year old daughter, a toxic little vixen who sat perched on a ledge like some great golden haired parakeet hurling taunts and insults at the patrons while rendering our likenesses in obscene crayon caricatures that she hung at an astonishing rate on the wall behind the bar—my own depiction, the straw that broke the camel's back, so to speak, portrayed me as a hippopotamus wearing a tutu and a fedora and thick horn rimmed glasses—the child's artistic acumen was without question—lying on the floor of a toilet stall with a huge pair of elephant testicles descendant upon my chest. Had I been given the opportunity to lock arms with the impudent little moll I would have squeezed her tiny bird hand in my meaty vise like grip until her beady little eyes burst with saccharine crocodile tears. On that night, the mustached bouncer had treated me roughly, using my forehead to open the emergency exit and depositing me in the back seat of a grand old Rolls Royce convertible parked in the alley. I regained consciousness as the Rolls whirred along a windy canyon road. I was sitting upright, holding a gold flask decorated with a winged serpent. In the front seat was a smartly dressed young black couple. When the man turned around—I recognized him as the Grammy Award winning hip hop performer Q—I handed him back the gold flask, from which he took a hearty swig before passing it on to the woman, whose face I never saw. When I next gained consciousness, the car was parked at the edge of a cliff looking out over a moon washed ocean. I got out and followed a narrow trail down the side of the bluff. On a particularly steep stretch, I lost my footing and tumbled head over heel until ultimately coming to rest in a pocket of rock and scrub at the base of the cliff. I was bruised and bleeding, but nothing appeared to be broken. I saw a figure moving along the cliff face and called out to him. I thought he hadn't heard me because I quickly lost sight of him but then a short time later he was right in front of me. I spoke to him, asking for help. He seemed to not hear me or to not understand what I was saying. He crouched down so that our faces were less than half a foot apart. There was just enough moonlight to make him out. I recognized him immediately as the legendary movie mogul Nero. A thousand questions teemed behind my lips, but the only sound that came out was an arid gasp. Nero poured a cup of water from a canteen and fed it into my parched lips. Then he rose and disappeared into the darkness. Beyond where he had stood I caught a glimpse of something burning down on the beach below, a bonfire perhaps, the sound of drumming, chanting; as the flames danced and lashed at the night I was left with the impression not of a bonfire but of a burning cross. After a time, the flames softened and mouldered into a vague marmalade of orange light, and I thought I could hear the sound of a woman screaming far away, but it was only the gentle wail of the surf in a conch shell lying broken inches from my bleeding head. In the morning, I crawled back up the cliff face and hitchhiked to Beverly Hills, where I enjoyed a gigantic three martini brunch at the Peninsula Hotel. I gave the whole sequence of events not another thought, when three weeks later I was summoned, through my agent on behalf of *Vanity Fair* magazine, to Nero's secluded Bel Air lair. If the mustached doorman recognized me now his professionalism prevented him from letting on and he escorted me without ado down a winding hallway that led to a large high ceilinged chamber deep within the house. Nero was seated on a throne of sorts within what could only be described as a kind of upright shoe box structure with a metallic silver lining. A smartly dressed young woman with red hair and glasses sat just outside the shoe box operating a conference phone that was lit up like the alien spacecraft from *Close Encounters of the Third Kind.* She pressed the buttons with one hand, opening and closing lines, merging lines, transferring calls to distant area codes, to distant lands, to outer space, playing the instrument like a concert pianist, by feel, without looking at the keys. I waited in the wings, playing the part of the fly on the wall as I indulged this rare opportunity to observe the maestro at work, conducting a kaleidoscopic symphony of voices and ideas in this ham radio cathedral of invention. To the untrained ear, the sound that came from this performance would have been indistinguishable from the unholy din at any big production company or agency where an army of self-important tone-deaf hacks rolled call after call in a brute force ham-fisted attempt to throw a million gallons of shit at the wall and see what stuck. To my ears, to the ears of a connoisseur, the sound was Beethoven's *9th Symphony,* Miles Davis's *Bitch's Brew,* John Cage's pregnant silences. In the span of a few minutes I witnessed a dozen films born, the master tossing together the critical elements— directors, writers, actors, locations, producers, budget, second act cliffhangers—as quickly and deftly as Picasso struck his palimpsests of Cubist black magic onto those virgin canvasses.

A brief sample of the performance:

The redhead presses the flashing button, opening line 2. A man's voice crackles from the speaker – urgent, with a fast New York clip.

Man on Line 2: We're ten days behind schedule. The rain is killing us.

Nero: Shut it down. Shoot the whole thing on a sound stage. Right on the lot.

Man on Line 2: These are desert scenes! What about the sand?

Nero: We'll bring in so much sand you'll think you were in Death Valley. Fill it with tumbleweeds, scorpions, gila monsters. You can even drill for oil.

Man on Line 2: All right, all right, we'll be there in two days.

The redhead opens line 6: voice of a woman in her forties.

Woman on Line 6: Sandy's booked through till Thanksgiving. Ally's still holding out for that part in the Blacky Effingham project. Jess is available but Tino hates Jess.

Nero: Call Kevin in the morning. Ally's about to suddenly become available.

Woman on Line 6: She's serious about this.

Nero: I'm about to make Blacky an offer he can't refuse. I just bought the rights to the *Figure 8* franchise. Shooting won't start for another six months.

Woman on Line 6: You dear dear man. Dante's gonna flip. Ciao.

The redhead opens Line 1.

Man on Line 1: We need to send a print to Cannes in two days and we don't even have an ending. Morty and Patrick are going at it tooth and nail. The thing is, they're both depressing as hell so who gives a shit?

Nero: Send Morty's version to Cannes and Patrick's to Montreal. Then have them shoot an alternate ending in which the village is destroyed by a volcano. Tell them it's fodder for the trailer. There's a loophole that gives me final cut. That's the scene that's going to distribution state side.

Line 1: What about Asia?

Nero: Asia gets Patrick's version.

Line 1: And what about Morty's version?

Nero: Fuck Morty. Burn it. He can have it back for the ten year director's cut.

With much aplomb, and perfect posture, her eyes never leaving the computer screen, the redhead opens line 8. It's a man's voice, seasoned, a West Coast voice.

Man on Line 8: The West Coast financing is pulling out. The Texas money is hung up in the Suez. The French fuckers are getting fairy feet. Charlie Chan thinks he's gonna be left holding the bag, thinks he's about to take a big Hollywood hot tub-type bath.

Nero: I'm sending Sue to Hong Kong to hold Charlie's hand.

Man on Line 8: Gonna take more than hand holding at this point.

Nero: Hold his balls, hold his dong. Stick a pinky up his ass. Sue will keep Charlie on the hook until Bax and Theo wrap up the South American money and Nick pulls that whale out of Lake Tahoe. Then we reel the suckers in—I pull my skin out of the game and double down on the Scorched Earth project.

Man on Line 8: The Ukrainian money is solid. And they're willing to put up raw materials, I'm talking about shit that glows in the dark, like, you know, from the *mines*.

Then he saw me. Perhaps he'd been aware of my presence the entire time and was simply putting on a show for my benefit. Men like Nero were preternaturally self-aware and in total control of every aspect of their environment. And Nero was not the typical

Hollywood creature, born in the bubble of Tinseltown unreality, insulated from the ugliness of life. He was a man of the world and had walked on the wild side in places like San Juan, Marseilles and Phnom Penh. Before washing up on these bloodless shores, a castaway with nothing but grit and guile, a man who lived by his wits, fueled by blinding ambition and, once upon a time, frequently sabotaged by violent passions, he was now the picture of Zen calm and detachment.

"Mr. Barclay, I've been expecting you. Please, do not be shy," he said. "Regina, hold my calls."

Without looking, Regina pressed a button, plunging the phone's display into darkness and sending the sparkling Christmas tree of orbiting calls off to God knew where.

"May I get you something from the bar?" she said.

"Two fingers of LaPhroig," I said without hesitation.

I learned over the years that it did not pay to be coy with a man like Nero. The slightest indecision, even basic politesse, was considered a weakness, and so was bad taste. Requesting some exotic mineral water would have been the safe choice, but I had to assume Nero knew I was no mineral water man and that the choice would simply have been a calculated attempt to gain his approval. Lesser men were flattered by these crude attempts to mirror their preferences and habits. A man like Nero admired authenticity above all things and could only respect another man who was at all times the embodiment of his own fully realized personal *weltaunschuang*. In many respects Nero and I were—with the exception of our steadfast authenticity—like night and day, he the apostate *bon vivant*, having renounced the pleasures of dust and dice for the discipline of purity and self-control (although he retained a well known taste for the fairer sex) while I continued to pursue the rogue's life of strong drink, impulsive wagers, random encounters (the occasional dalliance with an anxious divorcee or hard luck barfly), lost memory, lost money and lost time, forever slipping through the looking glass and crawling out of rabbit holes with my head a spider web of bits and pieces. Nero had withdrawn into himself in order to master the universe while I continued spinning out of orbit on a head trip to the far-out parties of the solar system, like a spaceman of the modern metropolis, planting my flag in all the hot tubs, Cadillac Escalade limousines and VIP areas that dot the star-maps of my celestial beat.

Regina returned from the bar bearing my drink, two fingers of LaPhroig single malt Scotch in a cut crystal snifter. I swirled the amber liquid around the glass and brought it to my nose so that I could take in the intoxicating fumes. I lost myself for a moment—a snifter of good Scotch was like a woman and could swallow a man body and soul—and came back to find my hosts staring at me with keen interest. I had assumed that Nero was the subject and I the observer but I got the distinct impression that I was what was on the menu, a realization that buoyed my ego while filling me with unease, and for a wobbly moment I was unsure whether he was in my story or I in his. I was not accustomed to having the tables turned—most of my subjects were more than happy to submit to my authorial dictation and allow me to serve as the vessel to their immortalization in the holy scripture of *Vanity Fair, Esquire, GQ, Rolling Stone* or whatever publication I was killing for at the moment—and quickly recovered, drawing on my observations waiting in the wings to construct a poignant, entirely improvised theory about the current state of the art.

"The story is about the new super-creatives," I said.

"The story is always about you, Mr. Barclay," said Nero. "That is why you are here. I read your piece about Tony Billings with great interest."

"I am afraid that piece won me few admirers."

"It set tongues wagging. You gave them a gift. What else would they have to get all hot under the collar about?"

"I was accused by my peers of stepping on my subject."

"The great man must inevitably step on his subject. We are not mirrors. We impose ourselves on the world. The ego is the engine of time. The bigger the ego the bigger the bang. To the victor goes the fossil record. We are slaves to our enthusiasms."

"It has been said that my enthusiasm sometimes gets the better of me," I said.

"You had your story before we'd even said a word. What have you discovered about your subject in the span of a camera flash? What do you have to say about Nero now?"

"That he is the exemplar of a new type of artist, a super-creative who sits at the top of the pyramid, seeing everything through an all-seeing eye and conjuring entire worlds through a wireless headset, destroying the universe through a speaker phone."

23

"Your characterization is flattering, but what separates this new super-creative from the Irving Thalbergs and Louis B. Mayers? They micro-managed the creative process long before I came on the scene."

"Excuse the irreverence, but these men, though great orchestrators of money and talent, though shrewd stewards of story and bellwethers of popular taste, were but tadpoles, caterpillars, walking catfish, middle species filling the gap between an evolutionary leap ..."

"The studio head has always sat at the top of the totem pole. It is not, essentially, a creative position," said Nero. "I am a businessman. I have a talent for making money. No matter what the era, selling a story is no different than selling a tractor or a Barbie doll. It is about making the right decisions. The die was cast with Thalberg and Mayer and we're all still trying to fit the mold."

"The gods created man then gave him fire. We are none of us without debt to the long ladder of time, all the shoulders that we stand upon, but you're being bashful if you deny your special place in history. Fires are burning all around us. It takes the great man to breathe them in and turn into a rocket. Louis B. Mayer, Irving Thalberg, these men were prototypes, you are the apotheosis. Their world trafficked in trolley cars and switchboard operators. Our world moves at the speed of light. You have taken it to the ultimate level. The entire organism of filmmaking runs through your central nervous system. You are an artist of the highest order. You are illuminated."

"I almost want to believe you. But that would allow me to rest on my laurels and might prevent me from doing what I have to do, because, and I say this with absolute certainty, we are not quite there yet. The true messiah—the true creative event—is still to come."

"I hope you do not consider me rude if I inquire about this curious metallic booth that you have taken for your throne."

"It is an orgone accumulator. Thoroughly discredited by the *New England Journal of Medicine*, of course. But who needs longitudinal studies when you can literally feel it in your bones."

"*In your bones?*" I said.

"I have had an erection the entire time we've been talking. Please do not be alarmed."

"I am never squeamish about science."

"Rest assured, my current state has nothing to do with any intimacy between us. It is, rather, a pure expression of orgone energy, detached from any prurient thoughts or external stimulation."

"May I ask how long you have had this erection?" said Barclay.

"It is difficult to tell, because it is not my habit to pay attention to the time, but it would be safe to say over three hours."

My attention was drawn to an ornate red velvet couch in the corner where two comely young aspiring starlets sat patiently, wearing somewhat distracted blasé expressions and, other than the brightly patterned silk negligees, little else, and were presumably waiting for their moment to be draped over our host's ritual altar and receive his patented revitalizing orgone injection.

"I understand that these details are strictly off the record," I said.

Nero showed a faint smile.

"I trust you to use your judgment. Being in a state of bliss, I can suffer no embarrassment and come to no harm. My body conducts the prime evil of the universe while my mind floats freely, sorting through the flotsam of our commerce. And sometimes it is the reverse, my body taking over the mundane affairs and freeing the mind to wander the dark corridors."

"You have me at a disadvantage, I'm afraid. I have always been just one person and frequently only a fraction of that."

"You should really let go sometime. Not submerge your brain in booze and pills, but really let go."

Of course, the exploding head hung over our discourse like a burning air ship, coating everything in sparks and glowing shrapnel and flames, impregnating every exchange between us. He knew that I knew that the matter simply would never come up. I also knew better than to bring up Nero's controversial involvement with the System. This was a topic that no mainstream publication dared to broach. The consequences could be quite cataclysmic, for the journalist as well as the publication. There were no rewards to justify such a risk. The reward was always access, to the set, to the star. And without that access, which could vanish at any time like a specter, one was nothing. Despite my missteps of late, I was still a professional and maintained a healthy respect for the boundaries. Discussing the

System was taboo. That much I still knew.

"What is your current position within the System?" I said, quite involuntarily, feeling the words escape my lips like plumes of opium smoke. I tried with some urgency to will them back into my body, but it was too late, they were gone forever, hovering out there like weaponized trial balloons. I sat there slack-jawed, waiting for the ax to fall. There was a pause, a very pregnant one, during which our eyes performed a dance full of dark intrigue, and then he answered in an entirely disarming way.

"What I would say to a question such as that," he said, as if it had after all been composed of smoke, "is that how can one have a position, as you say, within something that lacks any kind of formal establishment? There is no membership, no hierarchy in the traditional sense, and therefore no position. It is not a church or a cult as some have claimed, only a system of best practices. So if you ask me what my position is I can only respond by saying how can I hold a position in something that does not actually exist, at least in the conventional sense? These practices and knowledge are continually evolving and being elaborated upon by the community. There is no price of admission and there is no price to pay for not following the recommendations, there is no exclusion or excommunication. There is no origin story, only the story of what is possible tomorrow."

"Is it true, as some claim, that the System advocates the use of hypnosis to treat psychological and medical conditions?" I asked.

"The only thing I will say about that is that I am willing to use the available Technology to the fullest," said Nero. "In general, these techniques are primarily used to enhance the performance of athletes, or in some cases, to help an actor prepare for a role."

"Tony Billings being one prominent example," I said.

"One of several notable examples," he said.

"A number of observers have expressed concern that these techniques could be used for mind control."

"I suppose they could be, in the wrong hands. Of course, our concern is primarily with unlocking human, and in some cases *superhuman*, potential."

"To that point, it is said that within the community, you are known as Mr. Fantastic, an appellation that stuck with you following the studio's legendary superhero franchise of the same name."

"We all have names, those we are born with and those that we earn."

I dared not press the issue any further.

"Your current marquee project is a film about pool hustlers being shot on the studio lot. May I applaud you on your choice of Tony Billings for the lead role? There was a chorus of dissenting voices that claimed he lacked the grit and gravitas required for the part."

"Yes, well, I have all the confidence in the world in him. He is one of my finest creations. The project itself was, as you surely know, a bone for the studio's parent company. It was deemed considerably safer than our previous project."

"You are of course referring to *Fire Devil*," I said. "Shot on location in the Australian Outback, at huge expense, suffering numerous weather related setbacks, and, ultimately, loss of life."

"In this Industry we are accustomed to such setbacks, even when, as is sometimes the case, there is loss of life. We know how to roll with the punches. If you're going for the knock out, you have to be prepared to weather the storm. The board is averse to risk. These people are, essentially, aliens from another world. They are not of this place. They don't know our customs or our business. To extend the metaphor, they don't know how to stay alive until the later rounds."

"This suggests that you are simply biding your time until staging the next spectacle."

"The time may come sooner than everyone thinks. What they forget—the press, the wagging tongues, even the so-called board of directors—is that when it comes down to it I'm still calling the shots. While I'm still sitting in this chair, mine is the only decision that truly counts."

"Are you suggesting that there might be a sudden shift in direction?"

"At risk of tipping my hand, I can only say that the time for the climactic statement may be sooner than anyone would have expected. Surely you've heard the rumors?"

"I must admit, there has been some talk about a changing of the guard. I of course dismissed it as idle hearsay."

"The wind of change is blowing. I can feel it like a diseased harlot's breath, making the hair stand up on the back of my neck."

"Certainly they wouldn't consider unseating a legend over

one unfortunate incident. These things happen all the time in this business."

They will say it is one thing, or many things, but it's more than any of that. It's more than any man or number of men can decide. It's a course of destiny mapped out in the stars."

"Even with the failure of that film, the studio still made money, won multiple Oscars, Golden Globes. In the end it was still an enviable year."

"When the tide turns against you, your history is erased. The idea itself seizes us, all of us, like a madness, a tsunami that sweeps away everything in its path."

"At some point, every great man contemplates his final statement to the world, his swan song."

"More and more, I have come to believe that the ultimate creative act is the destruction of one's creations. For unto dust thou shalt return."

"Considering a turn toward a more subversive art?" I suggested.

"In a manner of speaking," he said. "But what I find myself contemplating more than anything is life after. This is what gives me peace, what sets my mind free."

"Might I inquire about what will certainly be a formidable second act?"

"Ballooning," he said, with almost childish innocence. "I've taken a great interest in it of late. It's an avocation with a rich history, full of colorful characters, feats of daring, inventions of the most breathtaking ingenuity."

"And some horrible accidents," I said, quite off handedly.

"And some notable mysteries," he said.

"True, many balloonists simply float off into the sunset and are never heard from again."

"It is romantic," he said. "The danger is one of the things that thrills me the most. And the technology, of course. As we speak, there's a whole team of scientists doing R&D out in the desert."

"To build your balloon?"

"It is my intention to reach heretofore undreamed of heights."

"Shades of Icarus," I said, my id now fully on display.

"An admirable character in every respect. If we don't

ultimately burn up, we haven't strived enough.

"Much like Edna St. Vincent Millay's candle," I offered.

"My own candle is more the Roman variety, burning at one end and throwing up a great many sparks."

"The metaphor presents an intriguing visual," I said.

"Now, I really must return to the business at hand. Jeeves will show you out."

"I had actually prepared some more questions," I said.

"See, you're still sticking to the script," he said. "Just close your eyes and listen."

He closed his eyes and seemed to withdraw into himself, and not wanting to be the odd man out, I closed mine as well, the way a casual churchgoer might do at a holiday service, closing the eyes and letting the mind run wild, looking up now and then to see if it was safe to come out of it. I wanted to hear whatever it was that he was alluding to but all I heard was the idle chatter of the girls on the couch and the soft clack of Ms. Regina's fingers on the keyboard. I opened my eyes and shot a glance at Nero.

"It's okay. It will come to you in time," he said, his eyes still closed. He opened them. I felt naked, as if he could see straight through me.

"That will be all for today. I trust you have enough for your story."

"The interview," I said. "I feel like we've barely scratched the surface."

"Don't worry, you did fine. The job is yours."

"I am afraid you have me at a disadvantage, yet again."

"The details will be revealed in time. I really must get back to my work. There are a million balls in the air. I'm sure you understand."

"But, where do I begin?"

"Follow Tony," he said. "He is the key to everything."

"There is a certain matter of a restraining order," I said.

"Never mind that. You are to write the story that shows the world the authentic Tony Billings, that lays him bare in every sense. What I am talking about is true investigative journalism. You will have to dig deeper than you've ever gone before."

"It is unlikely that I will get an assignment from any respectable publication," I pointed out. "Under the circumstances."

29

"Don't worry about the respectable publications," said Nero. "They do what I tell them. I'll make sure the money is there. All I ask is that you pursue this story to the end, take it as deep as it will go, all the way to the bottom, to the heart of it. Become your subject. Only then will you reveal the truth."

"This sounds like an offer that cannot be refused."

"It is more than that," he said. "It is your destiny."

"I don't know what to say," I found myself saying, perhaps for the first time in my life.

"I'll give you a head start. There is a party at my house this Saturday. Tony will be there."

"That is very generous of you. I'll be on the guest list, I assume?"

"Not exactly. But I trust you'll find your way in."

I found myself bowing like an ancient Chinese mystic, in spite of myself, and drifting back into the shadows, where the huge manservant fell in behind me and silently escorted me from the room.

As I walked away, I heard Regina talking on the phone. "Add another zero to the policy," she said.

I discovered once I was in the sunlight that I was still holding the snifter of LaPhroig, which I sipped judiciously on the drive to wherever I happened to be going next.

# CHAPTER 4
*DON*

"I'm still drinking my coffee," said Juan.

"It's time," I said, standing in the doorway.

The waitress gave me a disapproving look as she took the order of a truck driver sitting at the counter.

"You don't understand. This coffee, I think it's the best coffee I've ever had. I think I'm going sit here awhile and, you know, finish it."

"There's a bottle of Tequila in the car," I said.

"No, you are mistaken," he said, shaking his head. "I don't drink Tequila."

"What about last night?"

"It could have been somebody else."

"You chewed off the top of the bottle with your teeth."

"I know, I know, I've been trying to cut back."

"What do you say we go find those girls?"

"We have to leave the state?"

I did not answer.

"Why we have to leave?"

"Last night? The girls? The game with the matches?" I said. "The raid at the hotel?"

"Last *night?* I thought that was last *year.*"

"You haven't even gone to bed yet. And your lips are bleeding."

He dabbed his lips with the napkin, then showed it to me.

"It's probably just lipstick."

Then he noticed the dark red smear on his collar.

"That's iodine," I said. "From the clinic."

"We better stop at a Chinese laundry," he said. "You know what I'm saying?"

He finished the coffee—throwing it back with a wince—and dropped a dollar on the counter.

"Too hot?"

"Too *black*," he said.

He dropped a quarter on the counter for the tip, and we left the restaurant.

"So where's this Tequila?" he said, sinking back in the passenger seat, checking things out from behind his sunglasses. "I don't see it."

"It's in the glove compartment," I said.

I started the engine.

"Oh yeah?" he said, nodding his head. Then after a time, "So, man, you know, this glove compartment, like where is it?"

"Here," I said, opening it and removing the bottle, which had a conical reservoir and a long slender neck.

I handed it to him, and he began to study the label.

"I don't see any date."

"The date?"

"Yeah, like, what if it's past the expiration date?"

"This isn't a bottle of milk, you know. It's liquor. It gets *better* with age."

"Hey, man, I think you're trying to get me to drink some ancient shit. Maybe this Tequila, you know, maybe it's got some kind of ancient *bacteria.*"

"We'll save it for tonight," I said. "You'll feel different then."

"So this is a fast car," he said.

"It's pretty fast, all right."

"How fast?"

32

"It's fast," I said.

"That's something else, man. That's far out."

I put it in reverse and eased out of the parking lot. As I pulled out onto the road I noticed Juan staring at the bottle.

"Are you sure this is Tequila?"

"Sure ... Mezcal actually, if you want to get specific."

"What is this?"

"That's what I've been saying. It's -"

"No, man ... *this*," he said.

I leaned over to take a look. There was a small white worm at the bottom of the bottle—a standard addition in a lot of Mezcals, what made it seem the genuine article so to speak—but this worm had eyes, that looked somehow human, and I too wondered what it was doing in our bottle.

"Hey, what is that thing?" said Juan. "What's it doing in there?"

"I don't know," I said. "But I'm not sure we should drink this Mezcal."

He gave it some thought.

"It looks strong."

"All Mezcal is strong. It's hard liquor."

"Not like this," he said. "With this, one drink and you black out."

"Do what you want," I said, "I think there's something wrong with it."

"I think this is good Mezcal," he said. "You know, like real premium shit."

"It's your scene," I said.

I took out a cigar. As I held it to my nose, I could sense him watching me.

"I'm going to have one, too," he said.

"Help yourself," I said. "They're in the glove compartment."

For several minutes he stared straight into space.

"So where'd you put it, man, like under my seat?"

I reached over, opened the glove compartment, and took out a cigar.

"Man, where did you get these?"

"Like I was saying, they were in the glove compartment," I said.

"No, man," he said, staring at his cigar in disbelief.

I looked at my own cigar, seeing nothing at first, then all of a sudden realizing what he was talking about. The tobacco, which smelled like the usual very good tobacco you found out here, in from Cuba, was rolled in some kind of—not paper or leaves—but skin. I turned to Juan.

He looked from the cigar to the Mezcal.

"This is too weird," he said, eyes widening. "It's too much, man."

"Yes," I had to admit, trying to maintain my composure, "This is pretty far out."

"What's that dot?" said Juan. "That red dot?"

"What dot?" I said.

"That red dot on your forehead," said Juan.

"There's no dot," I said, checking myself in the rearview mirror.

Sure enough there was a red dot on my forehead. My first thought was that I'd been shot. I took a handkerchief out of my pocket and wiped at the dot, which came off easily.

"Must have been lipstick," I said.

"Sure, whatever you say, man," said Juan.

We drove all night without talking. The sun came up. A short time after, we reached the exit for the town of Papagallo.

"Do you want to get something to eat?" I asked.

"Eat?" he said. "What're we going to eat around here? Some fucking lizard?"

"I could go for a plate of bacon and eggs," I said. "Cup of coffee. Bloody Mary. Puerto Rican screwdriver."

We passed a sign for The Institute of Piscatorial Science.

"Man, I don't like museums."

I kept watching for the turn.

"Museums have coffee shops," I said.

"It's like too early for science," he said. "You know what I'm saying?"

Suddenly the car started to shake violently. Blow out. A short time later, we rolled to a stop in front of the museum.

# CHAPTER 5
*DON*

The Institute appeared to be less roadside attraction than high security compound. At the gate a guard motioned for us to step out of the car. I nodded to Juan, signaling that it was okay to comply. These men weren't police and were probably only looking for alien species. Not our kind of contraband.

I opened the door, putting one foot on the ground and leaning out of the car, then turned my head to see if Juan was following suit. He hadn't moved.

"These gentlemen would like to search the car."

He didn't seem to be paying any attention, and as I got fully out of the car, intending to press the matter, I could tell, because his head was so close to the radio, the lines around his eyes furrowed in concentration, that he was into a completely different scene.

"Please excuse my friend," I said. "He is tired from the journey. He hasn't slept for many nights."

The guards nodded to each other, tilting their heads and exchanging impenetrable glances, hands resting on the barrels of automatic weapons. I looked into the car. Juan still had his head down by the radio, adjusting the knobs and talking to himself in his odd voiceless way.

"I assure you, this vehicle is clean."

"Hold on ... just a moment," said one of the guards before

lowering his head and speaking in a modulated tone into a CB transmitter attached to his shoulder. He put his ear down to the device, said a few words, then straightened up and motioned to the other guards. They backed off the car, leaving us surrounded. In the distance, out of the hot, rippling air, I could make out an old black Cadillac heading toward us. An instant later it arrived. The driver, wearing a black cap and chauffeur's uniform, got out, then walked around and opened the door. The man who stepped out had dark curly hair. He had on black pants and a black button-down shirt with a white banded collar. He wore a large gold and diamond studded ring.

"Hello there. Welcome to the Institute. Please. Excuse the formalities. This is just a precaution. You can never be too careful in the desert. There are a lot of ... drifters out there. But the Institute is open to all good people. Please. Gentlemen." He addressed the guards. "There will be no further need to search this vehicle. These men are in my company now."

"We had a blow out."

He looked over to observe the damage, then snapped his fingers. Two of the guards set to our vehicle with a jack and tire iron.

"You seem to be prepared for anything," I said.

He lowered his head a bit, twirling his fingers by his ear in the manner of a Royal. A guard walked over to the Cadillac and popped the trunk, taking out a black card table and a couple chairs and setting them up next to the car.

"Please, have a seat."

He extended his hand in the direction of the table, a patent smile on his face. I held back, for a second, but clearly I couldn't refuse. I would have to play along. The heavy armed presence had me concerned. These people had a lot of guns. I rarely carried one. Juan usually had one or two around, but he traded the last one for a bag of marijuana some time back. I was getting close to losing my cool. I didn't like the odds. As we took our seats, and the man began to speak, I became increasingly aware of a massive silvery protrusion rising from the top of the Institute. I was fairly well fixated on it when the sound of the man's voice brought me back.

"So what's your game?"

"What do you mean?"

I wasn't being disingenuous. I looked around, from one blank face to the next. Then one of the guards reached over and set down a bottle.

"Thank you," the man in black said. He turned back to me. "I mean, what's your game? You've been to Reno. Vegas. Maybe Atlantic City." He hunched his shoulders, palms facing each other and fingers shooting down at the table. "Come on, what's your poison? Jacks? Marbles? *Dice?*"

"How'd you guess?"

I had to give him that. I was a dice man.

"You look like the kind of man who likes to get right to the point."

He gave the signal and one of the guards promptly dropped a small velvet bag on the table. The man in black shook his hands over it with an amused smile and as he turned it over out tumbled a pair of oversized dice.

"Do you have a bottle?"

"A bottle of what?" I said.

"I don't mean to be presumptuous, but a bottle, if I may, of whatever might be found in the car of a man such as yourself." He hid behind his hands playfully. "No offense."

"None taken."

I looked over to the car to see if Juan was getting any of this, but he was slouched down in his seat, muttering to himself and shaking his head.

"I better go consult with my friend," I said, getting up from the chair.

"Why don't you have him join us?"

I let my eyes go from one face to the next.

"What's with the guns?"

"Please. I would hesitate to even call them guns. Think of them as conductors."

"Conductors of what?"

He raised his hands to the sky.

"Of the light."

"The light?"

He hunched his shoulders, palms up, and looked to the heavens.

"The light of man."

"I see."

I walked over to the car and knocked on the window as one of the guards pried off the hub cap. Juan reached over and rolled it down a crack.

"What do you want, man?"

"If it's the guns I have the man's word. They're more symbolic than anything."

What was I saying? I realized the moment I opened my mouth that it wouldn't make any sense to him. He shook his head and rolled the window back up, sinking back down into the seat and muttering to himself distractedly. I knocked once more and again he rolled down the window.

"Can you give me the Mezcal?"

"What?"

"You know, the Mezcal?"

No response.

"With the worm?"

He looked around the car.

"I don't see it, man. I don't know where it is."

"It's in the ... never mind."

I walked behind the car, stepping around the two guards kneeling on the sand, and opened the trunk, removing a dusty old bottle of fire brandy, a highly volatile libation that you rarely drank unless you had something to prove. I returned with the bottle and set it down on the table.

# CHAPTER 6
*DON*

"Good," the man said. "Now the rule of the game is, if you lose, you have to take a drink from the other man's bottle." He must have sensed my hesitation, and smiled. "Two glasses, please."

As the guard went into the Cadillac to procure the glasses, the man held his smile.

When the glasses were placed on the table, he stretched out his arms.

"Let's begin the game. Your roll."

"I don't know what we're playing."

"What difference does it make?"

"I'm not sure I follow."

"I mean, what difference does it make? You roll what you roll. Like role playing, see. Like life."

"And just maybe you'll let me beat the house."

"Think of it as a morality play. I'll tell you if you've won or not." He laughed. "Don't you trust me? Have some faith."

I sat back and waited for him to get to the point.

"It's simple. The high roll wins."

"That's it?"

"That's it."

"That sounds like some game."

He shrugged.

I threw the dice first. I lost, which is to say I won a glass of the stranger's drink. He poured it out, and I tossed it back. I rolled again: a miserable three. He poured me another…and then another. We continued like this for quite some time. Truth be told he seemed distracted, patiently waiting to refill my glass. As simple as it was, I was starting to take to this game. I have a weakness for strong drink, and soon my eyes were starting to glaze.

"Your roll," I said, slurring a bit now.

He threw. Predictably high. Something like a ten or eleven. I threw mine, a two. The stranger poured out another glass and raised his eyebrows in a kind of token offering of good will, though his mind seemed elsewhere.

"I can't help noticing," I said. "That I lose every time."

"I guess you're just unlucky."

"I'm not trying to sound like a sore loser or anything, but I've never seen a run like this. It's not … natural."

He shrugged.

"It's statistically possible, of course."

"But I've never seen it," I said. "I can't really believe this is purely by chance."

"What are you driving at?"

His dark eyes pierced right through me.

"All I'm saying is, I've seen funny dice before, dice that will do things they wouldn't normally do."

"Well you're right on the money. These are funny dice all right."

He rolled one over his knuckles then dropped it on the table.

"Have you noticed any kind of pattern?"

"I lose."

"I'm referring to the dice."

I concentrated on the dice, trying to get a bead on what he was saying.

"Almost every time I roll low."

He shook his head.

"That's beside the point."

I leaned back in the chair and took in the scene. Something hit me that hadn't been apparent before. The edges of the dice were aligned with the edges of the table. That's not the kind of thing I would have noticed right off the bat. And then, leaning back even further, panning my gaze to take in the whole scene, I noticed that the edges of the table were aligned with the edges of the institute itself. I was no stranger to dice tricks, and I immediately grasped the meaning.

"What direction is the Institute?"

"The same direction as those cattle bones," said the man, shooting his eyes at the sand.

"It's magnetic north, isn't it? These dice are just some kind of compass."

He showed the same smug grin.

"They're more than that. They're transformers. So whatever you roll, it might come up the reverse."

"A gag gift. Like trick birthday candles."

The man gave a polite smile.

I pointed to the car where Juan could be made out ducking down and swatting at something in the air, like a fly or mosquito. We were too far away to tell, and I alone knew there was most likely nothing there, only the persistent, barely audible thrum of fear. Giving up on the prospect of receiving any help from my friend, I folded my arms, resigned. I couldn't help noticing, though, once more, over the stranger's shoulder, the strange silvery antenna that rose salaciously toward the heavens. Once again I was transfixed by the curving machine-tooled sleekness, flaring out like a trident and caressing the sun at the tip. That same instant the man lowered his head to mine confidentially.

"Max," the man said, extending his hand.

"I'm Don," I said.

We shook hands.

"What kind of whiskey is this?" I asked.

"Peyote based. It's a sacrament in this region."

"It hasn't affected me," I said. "I don't feel a thing."

Suddenly the heat became almost unbearable, and as I rose from the table, squinting under the burning glare of the sun, I was faced with a very grotesque scene: instead of guns the security guards were now carrying around live rattle snakes, their chorus of forked tongues flickering out at me like the rays of the sun itself. An ounce more of the stranger's whiskey and I would have vomited all over the hot red sand. I reached down and grabbed the neck of my bottle. The stranger, no smiles now, placed a business card on the table and leaned back. I read the bold imprint: "MAX PRIEST – your lips to God's ears."

"So God rolls loaded dice," I said.

"Now how about you put the real bottle on the table?" he said.

"What bottle is that?" I said.

"The one that everybody is making such a fuss about, the one with the little worm in it," he said.

"The Mezcal? Well, oddly enough, can't seem to find it all of a sudden. No doubt Juan tossed it out the window somewhere along the line, or dropped it down a hole."

"Down a hole?" said Priest.

"Somewhere out in the desert," I said, my gaze turning to the distant horizon.

Priest shrugged and folded his arms.

"So that's the way you want to play it," he said.

"I wish I could help you," I said.

I got into the car and fired up the engine, peeling out on the sand as the two guards working on the tire dove out of the way, the hub cap rolling off to the side. I threw the pair of over-sized dice down on the dash in front of Juan.

"I pinched these from the hip priest," I said.

"What's a hip priest?" said Juan.

"A bad medicine man," I said.

As the tires found their purchase on the ground, digging furiously into the sand, one of the guards, receiving a nod and the two fingered signal from Priest, ran after the car and managed to slip a brochure through the passenger side window. Juan held it just long enough so that I could read what was printed across the front—*Jesus was a fisher of men*—before tossing it back out the window.

# CHAPTER 7

The two men were seated in the office. Nick sat behind his desk, leaning back in his chair, hands behind his head. The large picture window behind him showed the midday traffic on North Robertson. Q sat across from him sprawled out in the black leather and stainless steel chair. He had on a tight black t-shirt and black silk pants. A tattoo of a winged serpent climbed up from the collar of the shirt and wrapped around his neck. He had a gold front tooth and wore a large gold chain. He had on a number of large, expensive rings. His eyes were hidden behind mirrored sunglasses.

"Did you see the way Train threw down on him?" said Nick. "My boy Melo looked like he got hit by an Amtrak."

Q smiled behind the sunglasses, nodding.

"And then at the other end of the court, my man Earl the Pearl had a clean breakaway, straight to the hoop, he lays the ball up, why finish strong, right, this is a gimme, from out of nowhere Train sends it practically into the upper deck. And I'm talking we had seats couldn't have been more than two, three rows back. I could smell Dyan Cannon's hairspray. Train: coast to coast. Ended up winning by like 30. My man Jack never even broke a sweat."

Nick brought his hands down and shifted in his chair, taking a glance out the window behind him. Two young women were walking by on the sidewalk outside. A blonde in a black skirt and a shapely Latina in a short green dress.

"It's like an aquarium full of women," said Nick. "If my desk faced the window I'd never get any work done."

"I prefer a petting zoo myself," said Q. "If you know what I mean."

"Castaway, one door down," said Nick. "It's like a pageant, all day long. Like a fucking parade."

"Throw me some candy."

He licked his lips.

"I didn't see you the other night," said Nick. "I heard what happened at the pimp'n'ho thing. That's pretty fucked up."

"Like my man said, everything gonna get worked out. It always get worked out, if you know what I mean."

"When you go with Donnaway, courtside, am I right?"

"Strictly courtside. No other way to do it."

"Courtside, when Train throws down, you can feel the earth shake."

"Know the best thing about courtside? Laker girl titties jiggling in your face. I don't need no brother sweatin' on me, know what I'm saying? Ball goes out of bounds, brother knows better than to try to jump my way. Brother better watch that line. I gotta have my personal space. Laker girls are a whole other matter entirely. Basketball is a meal ticket for a lot of brothers, don't get me wrong, it's nice to see and be seen."

"Especially courtside," said Nick.

"*Especially* courtside," said Q. "There's really no other way. Like I was saying, basketball is about the numbers. Train get his numbers. I gotta get my numbers, too. After a game I like to have a little party. Now after that game last night me and my boys are chillin' in the back of the limo, I'm talkin' full stretch Hum-Vee, pouring rounds of Courvoisier. By the time we get back to the house my robe is laid out by the hot tub and there's a bottle of Champagne on ice and three Laker girls in bikinis. Those are the kinds of numbers I'm talking about."

"That's what I'm talking about."

The voice came from the far corner of the office. It was a skinny white dude with spiky bleach blonde hair and yellow tinted wrap around sunglasses. The white dude had followed Q in. Nick had never bothered to get his name. Until then the white dude hadn't said

44

anything. He was sitting very erect in a chair by the door. Nick had forgotten he was there. He turned his attention back to Q.

"Those are the numbers that *I'm* talking about," Nick said.

"Two's company, three's rub-a-dub-dub, know what I'm sayin'? Shit happens in threes. Know what I'm sayin'?"

"Three is definitely one of the numbers that you have to take seriously," said Nick. "What is it, celebrities die in threes? First you had what's his name, then the pope, then that other guy."

"There is a very *strong connection* between sex and death," said Q. "That's what I'm talkin' about in my songs."

"Like Shakespeare," said Nick. "The Elizabethan poets, they used to write *I died* when they meant *I came.*"

"Kind of like, I died all over those big double D titties."

Nick could make out the blonde dude nodding in the corner, a very rapid, persistent nod that resembled the flapping of a hummingbird's wings.

"I died, and then I rolled over and went to sleep," said Q.

"If you died," said Nick. "The ladies can't give you grief."

"I'd die a whole lot happier," said Q, "if the bitch didn't have so many damn teeth."

"What are you carrying?" said Nick.

Q bent over, lifted up his pant leg, and unholstered a small automatic pistol. He held it up, looked down the barrel, pointing first at Nick then at the blonde dude sitting by the door. He set the gun on the desk.

"Nine millimeter?" said Nick.

"She's small but she's fine," said Q. "And she packs a lot of heat."

"Fuckin' beautiful piece," said Nick, leaning back in his chair.

Q picked up the gun and sighted down the barrel one more time, moving from Nick to two sexy blondes passing by outside the window. He lowered the gun, turning it over and smiling.

"She's my baby," he said, raising the pant leg and tucking the piece away. "Not as loyal as a pit, maybe, but take a man's face off from fifteen feet."

"Just like a lady," said Nick.

"All cherished things are women," said Q. "Cadillacs. Lincolns. Even big-dicks and AKs, know what I'm sayin'? Laid one of these bitches on your homeboy Bax just the other day. Everybody comes to Q cuz Q can get everything the heart desires."

"That piece you laid on Bax, can you get a few more?" said Nick.

"How many is a few?" said Q.

"A hundred, give or take," said Nick.

"Take a phone call or two, give or take. What you boys need with all that hardware?" said Q.

"Props," said Nick. "For the film."

"Aint no prop guns we're talkin' about," said Q. "This shit we're talkin' about, this shit is for real. So tell me again why you gotta have a hundred units, give or take, if you don't mind my asking?"

"Authenticity," said Nick.

"Then I'm assuming, the way it works, one thing for another, that I got that part," said Q.

"Locked and loaded," said Nick.

Two men in dark sunglasses stood out on the sidewalk in front of the window. It was difficult to make out their features exactly, the way they were standing, with the sun coming straight into the window and casting them in silhouette, but enough to see that it was a white guy and a Mexican guy, both in their mid-30s. The Mexican wore a linen suit and a broad-brimmed hat and carried a briefcase. In spite of the heat, the white guy had on a calf skin jacket and black jeans. They were shifting around on their feet, looking up and down the boulevard, looking everywhere except at the window, like they were on a movie screen. After a time they passed by the window and out of sight and then a few seconds later the same figures could be seen inside the building just on the other side of the smoked glass walls of Nick's office. They were talking to Nick's assistant Dahlia. The Mexican handed her the briefcase.

The office door opened and Dahlia came in with the briefcase.

"Sorry to interrupt. There's a delivery for Q," she said.

She handed Q the briefcase. Once he took it, Nick observed the two men behind smoked glass turn and leave the office.

"I'm guessing those aren't girl scout cookies," said Nick.

"Aint girl scout cookies. Aint nothing you've ever seen the likes. This a straight boutique head trip. That Mexican is one freaky cook. Usually you never see him, but lately he's been coming along on the rounds. The cat he was with? That mother fucker got some serious problems. I'm talking visions, hallucinations, thinking he's dying and seeing the light. Something wrong with that boy's brain, you know what I'm saying?"

"I noticed that you had them deliver it to my office," said Nick.

"I don't want those trippy mother fuckers coming by *my* house," said Q. "They roll like that. Any time, any place. You could give those mother fuckers your GPS coordinates, I'm talking moving target, like in a car and shit, they'll roll up next to you, two in the morning out on the Santa Monica freeway."

"Yeah I was noticing that," said Nick. "The way they just rolled on in here."

"That's a mother fuckin' distribution *system*, know what I'm saying?" said Q.

"My man Stevie said he saw you at the car show," said Nick.

"He saw me? He must be mistaken. That's one scene I don't make. You talkin' about those cars that hop around like jumping beans? Bunch a niggas drinking Colt 45. I'm triple platinum, baby. Maybe next time your man Stevie better take a picture before he starts talkin' smack."

"Said Huggie was there, too. That whole crew from the Bay Area."

"There's no denying Huggie and I go way back. At one time we were like this…" He crossed his fingers. "And when you're my brother, I'll do anything for you. Blood runs deep. No denying he helped me out of a few scrapes, and I did the same thing for him. Sometimes in life the situation changes."

"You going to make it to that thing at the Lux?"

"No, gotta go to the Palisades, homeboy's Bar Mitzvah."

"Heard he's dropping a couple a hundred G's," said Nick.

"Couple hundred *at least*. Homeboy told me when all's said and done, we're talkin' half a mill."

A cell phone rang. Q removed the phone from his pants pocket and checked the number on the screen. A big smile appeared on his face.

"What's up, G?" he said, holding the phone to his ear. "You don't say…You don't say…Lemons, uh-huh, ice…cubes, not crushed…He had to do it, he had to do it…special delivery, be here by later this week, hand made in Italy, from the pistons to the leather

47

seats…458 bhp, you know what I'm saying? …accelerate, 100% pedal to the metal…flowers on the table, in the vase that she gave me for Valentine's Day … don't need no water in it…drain it…you hear what I'm sayin', drain it, then clean it…that's 22,000 gallons, can't clean 22,000 gallons with a little bit of chlorine…face down, you know what I'm sayin'?…at the bottom of the deep end…clear as day…what am I, Quincy, M.E.? … Hard head, thick skin, had to be … need to be drained and *then* cleaned … what does he know about pools? … 22,000 gallons is all I'm sayin' … Got to be ready by end of this week … You don't got to say anything. How they supposed to know? Just tell them to drain it, scrub it down—you know how I like, freaky clean … and the pinball machine, slots, silver dollars … me I'm partial to *Centipede* myself … pool tables mint … uh-huh, speakers on the deck … not him … him either … she's fine and any of her fine feathered friends, you know what I'm saying? … One of them disco balls, not strobe lights, get out … get out … I already talked to him about it…it's cool…later."

Q slipped the phone back into his front pocket.

"Like I was saying, that's one scene I don't make."

"Have you seen it yet?" said Nick.

"You mean…?"

"I got a hold of the prototype, talked to the merchandise guy yesterday. It looks pretty fuckin' great."

"You don't say."

A big smile from Q.

Nick opened a desk drawer and sets it on the table, an 11 inch action figure of Q—gold chains, tattoos, holding a cell phone and an AK-47.

Q leaned forward in his chair, surveying intently, eye-to-eye with the action figure.

"They did a nice job with the details," said Nick. "They did gang busters with the groups. Not just 12 to 15, but 16 to 20, 21 to 26, and check this, chicks 27 to 34. I gave one to Shelley. She flipped. It's standing on her night stand. The trick is … it's the character, right, but it's also Q."

"No trick," said Q. "The character is me. That's the real deal up there on that screen. Larger than life, you know what I'm sayin'."

"Shelley thinks it's cool as shit. She wasn't even really into dolls as a kid."

"Shelley's a fine looking lady," said Q.

"We were hanging out last night, smoked a little weed, you know, to set the mood, first thing."

"What was she wearing?" said Q. "...when you were smokin' that weed?"

"She had on this tight t-shirt, the color was mocha or java or something like that, and she's got this tan skin, bare midriff, and a pair of satin running shorts that go up to here. We were sitting on her bed, in her apartment. The stereo's on, turned down kind of low, drum and bass. She lights this joint, not chronic exactly, but close— she takes a hit then hands it to me. I take a hit. I'm instantly stoned. We're both stoned, sitting back, listening to the drum and bass, passing the joint back and forth. We're talking about MTV or something—one of these shows with a bunch of nobodies and a bunch of sort of famous people in a house together—and the whole time I'm checking out those tan legs, my eyes going over every inch, and those nips pressing up under the tee. I'm wearing sunglasses so she can't see my eyes, but I know she knows I'm looking."

"At least you're being discreet."

"She's used to being looked at. She likes to be looked at."

"She's been looked at by a hundred million tiny eyes," said Q.

"She's lying back with her head against the pillow, her legs are kind of spread apart, and she's playing with the telephone cord, wrapping it around her toes."

"Land line," said Q.

"And she looks over at the doll on the night stand, the Q, and she says, *I always thought it would be cool to get high with Q.*"

"She don't know the half of it," said Q, smiling and leaning forward intently in his chair.

"So she swings her legs around, real slow, and stands up on her knees. She holds the joint to her lips and lights it and takes this real long drag...then she puts the joint in the ash tray and gets on her hands and knees with her ass up like this, and walks on hands and knees until she's got her lips like this close to the Q. She purses her lips, opening them slightly, and slowly blows this long stream of smoke into the Q's face...And that's when I knew the deal was sealed. She turned her head and she had that look."

Q leaned back in his chair and let the smile ride, seeming to savor the idea.

"Cool," he said, nodding slowly. "Cool."

"It's going to be hot."

"I can taste that smoke," said Q. "Tastes like victory."

"With a capital V," said Nick.

For no particular reason, Nick turned to look at the blonde dude. The dude was looking right back at him. Nick turned back to Q and followed Q's eye to the window where two very foxy Chinese looking girls were walking by.

"Like a petting *zoo*," said Q. "'cept I'm the one in the cage. Need to open that window and catch you some breeze."

"If I jump out, it's no big deal, right? I'm down on the street."

Q had his head cocked to one side. He seemed to be zeroing in on something, like a telephoto lens turning slowly to zoom in on its prey.

"I heard about that head," said Q.

Nick fixed him right back.

"What head?"

"That's what I'm saying," said Q. "That's what I'm saying."

They sat there for some time, nobody saying anything. Q set the gun on the desk.

"All I'm saying is when that hardware comes in, you tell your boy Nero where it came from, *capiche*?"

Three young women passed by the window, all tanned with long legs. Everybody watched the girls walk, except for the blonde dude, who was staring straight ahead, straight into space.

# CHAPTER 8
*FREDERICK M. BARCLAY*

Tony lived in a sprawling Spanish style white stucco mansion in the hills of Los Feliz. His handlers had done a more or less exemplary job of keeping it out of the star maps, but I found it rather easily, following Tony home after a typically boozy evening at the Viper Room and have since spent many a night parked out front in a darkened 1978 Cadillac Seville, smoking herb cigarettes and observing my quarry through a pair of World War I field glasses, stubbing out one cigarette after another in the tin coffee cup that sat next to me in the passenger seat. I did not include myself in that abhorrent lot called the paparazzi and had no intention of sneaking any of those abhorred peeping tom shots that degrade the entire entertainment journalistic profession. I was studying my subject to gain a broader, more in-depth understanding of his psyche and habits, in the manner of a Dian Fossey or Margaret Mead observing their gorillas and island savages. I observed with the penetrating eye of the naturalist, the anthropologist, the cryptologist unlocking the riddle of the Sphinx. I slaked my thirst with smoke and hunger, my private eye ever zeroing in to crack the unsolvable code, the unknowable true self that was Tony. I observed him now, through the dark tunnel of the field glasses. Tony and the girl spilled out of the Maserati, falling all over each other, laughing like a pair of hyenas in heat. Tony dropped something and was all at once on hands and knees searching the car park screaming like a child while the girl leaned over to offer soothing words of condolence, all of which I was able to make out perfectly without being able to hear a thing. And then he found it and waved his arms frantically at the girl. She handed him a bill—what denomination I am not sure—which he quickly rolled into a kind of improvised straw, lowering his nose to the asphalt and seeming to snort up the found substance. When he came up his eyes were on fire and he was breathing heavily; he ran his fingers through his hair then grabbed the girl and pulled her to the ground, forcing her head into his lap. I quickly recognized the bobbing head as that of Sherill Sutcliffe, an actress whose beauty was so radiant and talent so awe inspiring that the sudden realization of our proximity was enough to make my legs go numb and my heart skip so many beats I was sure that, just for a second, I had left my body and was looking down at the roof of the car as I floated up toward the black heavens. Sherill and I had once been quite close, back when she was a struggling actress barely able to pay the rent, and she frequently enlisted me to drive her to the homes of her well-heeled "dates" in Bel-Air and Beverly Hills. I would sit patiently in the car smoking cigarette after cigarette, catching the occasional glimpse of a dropped garter or skirt hiked to heaven through a half-open blind. Those moments of intimacy in the car afterward, sharing a cigarette or passing the brandy so she could wash away the taste— were memories that I would cherish forever. We drifted apart over the years, as her stock continued its meteoric rise while mine was bought and sold a thousand times over in a thousand two-bit East River brokerage houses, split into half-pennies, packaged into junk bonds, my value line racing from spike to dagger like the EKG of a cardiac case in the throes of a crystal-meth binge. It was no secret that Sherrill had been in love with Tony for years—while he ostentatiously chased every party dress from Sunset to Pico, trotting her out for a quick fix whenever whimsy overcame him—and she countenanced these debasements with her customary aplomb and the stiff, and frequently glazed, upper lip of a Royal. Mercifully, I missed the money shot as Tony grabbed Sherrill's hair, jerking her head from his lap and furiously servicing himself, her raised knee obscuring my view of the climactic, face-distorting expurgation. What came next was rather predictable, a standard part of Tony's debauched after-hours repertoire, and no surprise to any who, like myself, lurked with prying eyes in the dark shadows at the perimeter of his star kissed life. From behind the glass of the windshield, within the muted automotive observatory of steel and glass, I watched his lips exhorting his vile instructions, his finger pointing heatedly toward the ground and watched as Sherrill lowered her face to the asphalt, extended her tongue and lapped at the ground like a kitten at a saucer of milk. I recognized in this performance the quality that made her one of the leading actresses of our time, this total effacement of the ego, this ability to prostrate oneself before the god of Thespis and suffer whatever debasement the role demanded. She had scarcely completed these ministrations when Tony grabbed her by the arm and, laughing like the proverbial demonic child from countless films, dragged her down the driveway, she just gaining her footing and then conspicuously losing a heel, as he opened the door and shoved her inside the house while he remained outside on the stoop and made a call on his cell phone. I quickly pulled out a surveillance device about the size of a transistor radio I'd picked up at a store for private dicks and tuned into the phone's frequency. Although there was a fair amount of static, I was able to make out the conversation.

"Live pineal gland," said Tony into the phone.

I could hear super-agent Mort Klondike's rasp on the other end of the line.

"Live pineal gland? At this hour? What are you talking about?"

"I want it. I have to have it."

"Tony, be reasonable. What you're asking for ... you know I'd do anything for you."

"You *said* you could get me whatever I want."

"I'll see what I can do. In the morning, I'll send Rathburn out to the morgues."

"It has to be *live*."

"Live pineal? You want me to go out and murder somebody so you can get high?"

"The book said it has to be from a living person."

"What book? Have you been reading Burroughs again? Kid, you can't believe everything you read. What are you going to do with it?"

"Eat it."

"You want to eat glands, order the sweet breads at Spago."

"I'm not stupid. It's not the same thing. Besides, they give me heartburn."

"Let's talk about it tomorrow."

"I know what I want. Don't try to change my mind."

"It's three o'clock in the morning. How about a valium?"

Tony hung up the phone and went into the house.

I waited until I had finished my cigarette then left the car, gently closing the door behind me. I walked in an inconspicuous, though suave, manner along the moonlit street, lighting another cigarette before proceeding down Tony's drive. I stuck the cigarette in my mouth and crouched to the ground to pick up the abandoned high heel shoe. I held it in my hands, admiring the sleek curved form and caressing the polished black leather. I raised the shoe to my nose and inhaled deeply, closing my eyes and losing myself in the bouquet. The familiar smell, like the taste of Proust's madeleines, unleashed a flood of memories ... of polishing a pair of thigh high black leather boots—with Sherrill in them—as Sherrill primped for a date with a married studio head who was notable for having webbed feet and being in the incipient stages of leprosy ... working the calluses on the soles of her feet with a pumice stone while she, her hair in curlers, emptied a pint of cottage cheese and talked on the phone with her then boyfriend, a certain dwarfish and garishly hirsute Las Vegas magician ... lacquering her toenails on a hair raising drive along the rugged seaside cliffs of the Pacific Coast Highway (I also happened to be driving) to visit the Malibu studio of a notorious gigolo hair stylist ... massaging her instep with expert fingers after a particularly arduous day on the Paramount casting couch. And, finally, at one particularly memorable wrap party, stealing a sip of Cristal from a baby blue Prada pump as she—spent from delivering a career-defining performance in a period romantic comedy featuring a loveable Irish wolfhound the size of a small horse, the title of which currently escaped me—drifted into a Champagne and barbiturate induced sleep. I dropped the shoe into my satchel and continued down the drive to the back of the house. To the anthropologist, to the passionate observer of human nature, there was no stone too mired to turn, no limits to the depths one might stoop, to realize the truth about one's subject. These garbage cans weren't mere receptacles of kitchen trash, beer cans, hairspray, pill bottles and used condoms—although these artifacts were in no short supply—they were goldmines of anthropological data, tunnels into the dark recesses of Tony's inconceivably vast, cavernous psyche. I sifted through the detritus of Tony's life – energy drinks, face creams, aerosol body sprays, reams of unopened fan mail, several dozen pairs of girls' panties, my hands poring over the soiled contents with a mounting sense of urgency, certain that I was about to find it, whatever *it* was. I was so close I could taste it, like a dab of raunchy French perfume on a woman's pulsing jugular vein. I tossed aside a banana peel, plunged my hands past an adult diaper, a smashed half-full bucket of Kentucky Fried Chicken, a soggy copy of *In Style*—curiously, there was an assortment of cheap retail clothing: a t-shirt with a print of a howling wolf, off-brand cargo shorts several sizes too large for Tony's narrow waist, pair after pair of gray knee-high tube socks, with the security tags still on them—my hands plunging ever deeper into the filth, until, yes, could it be? I withdrew my hands and held it up to the glare of the motion lights. But of course. It was so obvious I never would have guessed it in a million years. I realized at once this changed everything, this blew the whole thing wide open. It couldn't be more profound, really—a naked lady playing card, the Queen of Spades to be specific. The model was a sultry Latina whose decadent come-hither pout and succulent aureolae no doubt caused many a stone cold poker face to dissolve into hot pools of molten lust. I thrust the playing card into my satchel, along with the dampened magazine and several half-eaten pieces of fried chicken, and stole away into the night.

55

# CHAPTER 9
*DON*

I could see Juan nodding to himself and gazing out into the distance.

"Jesus," he said, pronouncing it *haysoos* and shrinking down into his seat. "Yeah, Jesus." He shook his head distastefully—"...very bad greaser"—and continued shaking his head like that for some time, deep in contemplation.

We drove for several hours, Juan maintaining an air of quiet detachment, though over time he had obviously become very interested in the dice. He tried to play it off at first, tossing them distractedly against the dash and waiting long beats before deigning to see what had come up. But before long the guarded curiosity had given way to unabashed obsession, almost uncomfortable to observe. I saw the quick furtive glances out of the corner of his eye. I knew that it would eventually prove to be too much. His hand reached out toward the dice.

I reached over and very calmly grabbed the dice and squeezed them for an interval of several seconds, saying, "Better cool it for awhile."

This seemed to snap him out of it and he looked over at me as one whose madness has been cast in a painfully revealing light, like the point at which a fever turns, before sinking back in his seat in a daze. I knew, though, that very soon he would forget what had just happened and reach out to pick up the dice, and when it happened—out of the corner of my eye I saw the hand moving across the dash—I extended my own hand and pressed it down upon his. He turned to me with a look of mild astonishment and retracted the hand, turning his head front and center and staring out into space, which really wasn't his style at all. And within a matter of minutes he was back to his old self, glancing now and again out of the passenger side window, showing the telltale bob of the head and song on the lips that gave the impression of a non-stop internal soundtrack, the reason those of his ilk seemed to be always moving, bobbing, grooving, swaggering, and swaying, all the while appearing chillingly unmoved. I had a suspicion that the only reason he ever bothered to glance out of the window at all was to see the reflection of his own sunglasses. This is one of the reasons I did all the driving. I rarely bothered to delve too deeply into his psyche, perhaps out of suspicion that it might consist of no more than a limitless black void. I had no desire to gaze into the abyss, so I respected whatever dark surface tension held together the shadowy fabric of his being.

It was then that I became fully aware of something that Juan had been going on about that was happening down the road, tuning in to it like background music. Oh yeah, that, I thought to myself as the vague gesturing and scattershot commentary suddenly meshed with the scene that lay ahead.

Several *federales* were pulled over on the shoulder of the road, their roof lights going round and round in noiseless strobe, resonating with the twisted, heavy metal aftermath of vehicular trauma. It looked to be the scene of a very bad accident, and I slowed to a crawl and finally a stop as one of the *federales* turned around and waved me down. The wreckage was strewn all over the road, and as we drew close I could tell by the still warm afterglow, the air saturated with the energy received at the moment of impact, that it was still relatively fresh.

The condition of the road made it unlikely that we would be able to get by any time soon. I climbed out of the car and went over to take a look. The *federale* who had waved us down was now bent forward with his head inserted through the twisted window casing of the driver side door. I stood behind him and tried to get a glimpse of the carnage inside but the man had a large build and I wasn't able to make anything out.

"What happened here?" I asked him. "Que pasó?"

But the *federale* leaned even further into the car as I said this, and I was about to put a hand on his shoulder when he began to twist out of the crushed opening. As he turned around very slowly I saw that he had the soft impassive face and slightly sad eyes of a certain kind of unexcitable Mexican. Even though it was midday and the sun shone down hot and bright, the devil's burning eye, his skin looked cool and dry, his uniform spotless and neatly pressed.

"What can I do for you, sir?" he asked in his quaint provincial accent.

"I was wondering if you could tell me what happened here."

"It is very unfortunate," he said, lowering his head slightly. "The warning, it was on the screen that block out the sun, in big black letters. It was right in front of his eyes. I don't know. Maybe he don't read it. Or maybe he read it and he don't do what it say. Maybe he think nothing happens to him. Even though it say never to have nothing between you and the airbag."

He moved his head to consider the wreckage.

"Well, what did he have?" I said.

He turned fully back around, pausing gravely, before saying, "A knife."

This was a bad omen.

I thanked him for the information and left him standing there. I climbed into the car, firing it up without a word.

"Hey, what that fat greaser say?" asked Juan.

"I'd rather not talk about it," I said, as the tires squealed.

I cranked the wheel and burned a hard U-turn on the narrow slip of asphalt that passed for a road, as the intoxicating smell of scorched rubber filled the car.

"There was another road back there. I think we'd better go on that one for awhile. This one is too full of death."

# CHAPTER 10
*DON*

It was then, driving like that, looking for this other road, that I became aware of the presence of an irresistible weight bearing down upon me. I knew what this presence was, this feeling of an unbearable weight pressing down, knew now that he was not far behind, maybe had even been lying in wait down the road ahead, behind the accident, like an intense, unbearable pressure very heavy upon my brain, the proximal weight, the fevered score of my nemesis. It would be only a matter of time before he was dangerously close. The burden of his pursuit I had carried with me for some time, and I suffered under a persistent foreboding, an imminent sense of the ever diminishing space between us. Contact became sensually real, like whiskey that you can taste the moment before it touches your lips. I had seen a sign, a very bad omen. And because of that I knew. We would be consumed in flames. It wasn't so much a headache as a burning pressure, a thickening of the blood vessels and a swelling of the brain. For once it was hotter inside than out.

I moved to strike a match, and looked around for a flint. Almost immediately my eyes settled on a quartz figurine of the Virgin Mary on the center of the dash. I extended my hand, and with a flick of the wrist, struck it off her.

"Hey, don't mess the Virgin," Juan objected, the burning

match arrested midway to the cigarette in my lips. "It's bad luck."

I brought the flame to the tip of the cigarette, then shook out the match and let it go out the window. I couldn't even quite remember how she had come to be there in the first place, as neither of us was particularly religious. I held the smoke in for the duration of several breaths then let it go slowly out. The first drag was always the best. I usually only smoked while driving. Juan liked the occasional cigar, but it seemed he usually wouldn't even light it, just carry it around and jab it in your face to make a point.

He claimed to be from Argentina, the usual gaucho fantasy, fairly prevalent in this part of the country, everyone maintaining that they were from somewhere else, the farther away the better. But I was not unsympathetic. When you're headed toward the land of fire you need all the mental armor you can put on. I had my fair share.

I pulled in by a small strip of shops. We stepped from the car and walked over to the Chinese laundry. I couldn't help but notice the striking figures we cut, Juan and I, in the shimmering reflection of the shop door. Whereas Juan wore black wrap-around sunglasses, my own were classic aviator glasses with a semi-opaque sepia tint that, however murkily, still showed the eyes. Dark sunglasses like Juan's created a sense of detachment from other eyes. They not only made you look cool but made you feel that way too.

I opened the door, and our shadows preceded us inside. As we stepped out of silhouette and into the light of the shop, I removed my sunglasses and put them in my breast pocket. The proprietor was a small elderly Chinese man who greeted me with a persistent frantic grin.

"Can I help you find something?" he said.

"The back," I said.

He gave a slight nod of the head, smile widening.

"Yes, yes," he said, ushering us inside.

I saw that Juan had already found his way to the passage. I moved to catch up. Behind the door we ducked through strings of hanging beads and into a narrow hallway cast in a garishly soft red light. At the end of the hall we went through another door into a small room that glowed with the red light. An Asian pop song played on the radio on a table in the corner. Standing beside the massage tables were a pair of nearly identical Chinese girls in matching flower print bikinis.

I sat down on one of the tables and took off my shoes.

The girls giggled.

"I need a towel," said Juan. "So I'm not, you know, too naked."

A good massage was just what the doctor ordered, to relieve the tension. I needed to melt into the soothing calm of a woman's hands. As I lay on the table—I had removed my sunglasses; Juan still wore his—I had a very intense reverie. Juan and I were driving down the highway, lying back and enjoying the ride, when a huge golden horse with no rider materialized on the road before us. I tried to brake but it was too late. As we plowed irresistibly forward, the prow of the car made contact, and the golden horse, so peaceful and statuesque, exploded, an instant, it seemed, before the inevitable impact in my mind's eye.

I woke with a start. I looked over at Juan, but he was into his own scene. Just turn over and let her work her magic. I put my hands behind my head and let my eyes go to the ceiling.

"Looks like a big toadstool," she giggled, her tiny hands expertly caressing.

Toadstool? What the hell was she talking about? This was cactus country. A completely different type of mind.

After the big bang, she cleaned me up with a hot towel. I slipped into a silk dragon robe hanging nearby—it may have been one of the girls' but it fit well enough—and reclined on the table, my head resting against the pillow. I fished a Thai stick out of my pants on the floor and lit up, sharing some with the girl. The marijuana went straight to my head, legs, neck, arms, feet. I was instantly gone and felt in a very odd jocular way, letting loose small bursts of incomprehensible babble and spontaneous fits of laughter, absurd stops and starts, groundless smiles of intimate connection, that whole beatific glow—I was completely stoned. I laid back and enjoyed the supernal smile. My date danced giddily around the room, changing her pose in time with the music.

I thought now of Fanta, my nemesis. I saw his shaved head and narrow razor edged face. His one beady eye black and soulless, the other socket covered by a black wrap-around patch. He drove a black Rolls Royce and wore an obsidian pendant that hung from his neck over a loose shirt with sleeves that flared out and hung down menacingly whenever he crossed his arms, each hand covering an elbow, showing an excess of large rings. He wore two small gold hoop earrings and carried a black magnum at his side.

I was forever wary of letting him get close enough to use this weapon on me. I wasn't afraid of dying. It was the bullet. A gunshot wound was something you never fully recovered from, the splintering of bone, the severing of nerves and tendons, exploded flesh. I could not allow him to leave his mark on me, as I had done to him. The missing eye. I had done that. And he vowed to one day put a bullet through mine. This implied a certain intimacy at the moment of impact. One couldn't reliably put a bullet through a man's eye from a distance. If I stayed a moving target, if his eye never met mine, he couldn't get a lock.

I planned to have him at my back and strung out far behind, kept comfortably at bay until the final downward spiral, delivered at last into the burning aperture of the desert. Until then, every moment was stolen time, and would never seem real. I felt the weight of his pursuit pressing irresistibly down, making contact palpable and inevitable, a sensation that was perceptibly real. But I still believed in one thing, steal all the time that you can. I don't know why, but I felt secure here, basking in girlish giggles and the lewd red light. As if we had temporarily stepped out of bounds. Still, he was in my head, he was out there somewhere. This invasion, of one man into another man's head, never seemed to affect Juan. Evidently those shades were too dark to let in any of the wrong kind of light. It was at times like this that I doubted my own wisdom. I had a blind side. There was at least one man to whom I would never again turn the white of my eye.

We took leave of the place the same way we came in, giving the girls a fat tip. They gave us one, too. The way to golden horse. Just down the road, they said, waving good-bye. Apparently I'd spoken aloud and at some length during that fevered vision.

We passed through the hallway and ducked through the hanging beads that led back to the front of the shop. The old Chinese proprietor stood there with the same hysterical grin, nodding as if to inquire of our satisfaction. I wanted to punch him in the neck. I noticed Juan handling a Chinese dragon lighter on display by the register. With each flick, a flame rose from the dragon's mouth.

"Look at this weird lizard, man. I really dig it. It breathes fire. I never seen nothing like that before. The lizard that breathes fire. See, it's like he's smoking, man."

Juan had a weakness for novelty items, anything shaped like cars, animals, famous people. But his fascination rarely lasted for more than those first few delirious burns. One or two more thoughtless strikes, and it would inevitably be tossed in the back with the rest of the junk.

# CHAPTER 11

On a desolate street in Watts, a midnight blue stretch Mercedes pulled up in front of The Moneymaker, a nondescript one story stucco building, the only distinguishing feature the bulbous neon outline of a woman's derriere above the cherry red door. There were bars on the windows and behind the bars, panels of cardboard taped to the inside of the glass so that it was not possible to see inside from the sidewalk. Nero emerged from the car first. The driver got out and opened the passenger door. Three well dressed Japanese businessmen stepped out of the car, followed by a young woman in glasses and a grey skirt suit. The Japanese looked around the neighborhood curiously while smoking their cigarettes. A burgundy Maxima with tinted windows rolled by super-slow with huge thudding base shaking the glass. Down the block, three black kids on bicycles rode around in circles. Across the street a slender middle aged black man in a purple tank top suddenly ducked through a break in a chain link fence and walked down the middle of a basketball court. The driver walked around and opened the red door. Inside the club vague forms moved about languidly in the shadow light. Rather than the sun illuminating the scene inside, it seemed, just for an instant, that the opposite was happening and the gloom from the club was spilling out onto the sun drenched street. The Japanese dropped their cigarettes on the sidewalk and entered the club, followed by Nero and the girl, the door closing shut behind them, sealing in the gloom. Several of the patrons were casually smoking cigarettes, and one man sat at a table by the stage smoking marijuana from a small metal pipe. The Japanese immediately took out fresh cigarettes, lighting each other up, while Nero scanned the room for the hostess, identifying a likely candidate, a youngish black woman with huge eyes, thick thighs and long wavy black hair, and waved her over with a five dollar bill.

She took the money.

"You want change?" she said.

"Your best table," said Nero.

The place was empty but for a handful of hard looking black men, most in their 40s and 50s, who sat spread out in the dark at their individual tables, quietly watching the performance on the stage with icy cool intent.

"You can sit anywhere," she said, walking off and delivering a bottle of Bud Light to the man nearest the stage.

Nero led the group to a three sided booth about twenty feet back from the stage. Nero slid into the center position, stretching his arms out over the back of the banquette. The girl moved into the booth, just to his left, while the Japanese took seats across the table, with their backs to the stage.

Except for Nero, the young female translator and the Japanese, everyone in the club was black—the patrons, the bouncer, the emcee, the cocktail waitress, the two dancers. In talking up the club to the Japanese, Nero had promised them something special, some real local color, off the beaten path, far away from the tourists, far away from the show business insiders even. The truth was that Nero had never visited the establishment before, had never heard of it for that matter. The plan had been to simply drive around Watts and South Central until they found something that looked promising. It hadn't taken long. There was no way to go wrong really. These days, Nero rarely ventured south of Pico and was just as much out of his element as the visitors from the East.

The girl on stage was long and surprisingly slender with small natural breasts and *café au lait* skin. She had straight black hair, green eyes and wore a stud in her belly button and had another through the tip of her tongue that she flickered at the audience like a serpent from the edge of the stage. She was mostly black, with a good mix of white and maybe a note of Korean or Chinese. Her eyes were hollows, and her face was all lines and angles, all the smoothness burned away. She had the high wire body of a speed freak. In a well rehearsed move, she turned away and bent at the waist until her cheek grazed her ankle and her hair brushed the floor, her eyes looking back. She gave her ass a measured smack then grabbed a pound of flesh, held it for a long beat then came up and swung around the pole.

The Japanese talked among themselves, oblivious to the spectacle on the stage. The young translator sank down in her seat, her eyes nervously searching the room and finding, out there in the dark, sets of yellowed bloodshot eyes searching right back. She came back to find one of the Japanese leering at the stretch of bare thigh that showed beneath her hemline as he rolled a cigarette between thumb and index finger, letting the smoke curl up and consume his eyes. She crossed her legs and turned away.

Nero gave her a nudge.

"Now straighten up and give us a smile. You know how important it is to be polite to the Japs."

The girl forced a smile, thrusting out her chest and throwing her shoulders back. Yukio, the senior most of the three, smiled and nodded, then resumed talking with his compatriots.

"Body language is very important to the Japanese. They pick up on the subtlest cues and are sensitive to even the most imperceptible slight," said Nero. "Every interaction is a minefield of unintentional and potentially lethal offenses."

"I taught in Kyoto for two years after college," said the girl.

"These men eat Kyoto for breakfast," he said. "These men are a giant three headed monster from Planet Zero. You don't have to fuck them, of course. That's not really what it's about, just smile and bow, and at the end of the day, send them off with a little token of appreciation, a cocktail napkin with a kiss of lipstick, say, or a pair of soiled panties. The Japanese are constitutionally indirect. If you threw your feet up on the table right now and spread your legs, all they'd do is take a picture."

"Do you want to know what they're talking about?" she said.

"I haven't the slightest interest," he said. "All I want is their Yen. They've already made up their minds, or they wouldn't be here. This visit is strictly pro forma, dotting i's and crossing t's. If they return home empty handed, there'll be a lot of wagging heads."

66

"They're disappointed there isn't more violence," she said.

"Tell them I'm ready to discuss business," he said.

The girl bowed with prayer hands and leaned forward, saying in Japanese, "Mr. Nero wishes to discuss the opportunity."

Yukio turned to Nero and nodded.

"We are ready to discuss the matter," he said in Japanese.

The girl translated for Nero.

"Tell them we need forty million," Nero said.

The girl translated.

Yukio conferred with his colleagues then addressed Nero.

"We've already given you twenty million," he said. "And we have yet to see a script. We have yet to see a budget, market projections or commitments from big names."

The girl translated.

"Can you do sixty million?" said Nero. "Sixty million is optimal. That way we don't have to answer to the Koreans."

Yukio glowered.

"What can you promise?" said Yukio. "What commitments can you make?"

The girl translated.

"What I offer you is not just box office," said Nero. "But *revenge.*"

The girl looked from Nero to the Japanese, then back to Nero.

"There is a well known writer doing a piece on me for *Vanity Fair* magazine," Nero continued. "In the article this writer pronounced me the exemplar of a new breed of super-creative. I resisted the idea—we both knew this was false modesty, because what I am is much more than a mere super-creative, whatever exactly that is. What I am, gentlemen, as I am sure you have all heard the story by now, what I am … *is super-human.*"

The translator swallowed hard, turning to the Japanese and saying, "These girls sure are pretty."

The Japanese huddled together, appearing to give the matter serious discussion.

"This head thing has gone to his head. He thinks he has supernatural powers," said Kenjiro.

"The coroner's report said it was spontaneous combustion," said Hitomi.

"It is considered a sign of status here to conduct oneself as a functioning psychotic," said Yukio. "Still, this picture could do a lot of box office. It is safer to give him the money."

Yukio addressed Nero.

"We ask for a new completion bond," said Yukio. "With adequate reserves."

The girl translated.

Nero smiled, giving a little bow with prayer hands, then hailed the waitress.

"A bottle of your finest Champagne," he said.

When she returned, she set a bottle of Cook's and five plastic Champagne glasses on the table. Nero slipped her a C-note, which she slipped into her brassiere as casually as if it were a book of matches. The bottle sat untouched for a long moment, until Nero shot the translator a glance.

"Of course," she said, bowing, then picking up the bottle and filling the glasses.

Everybody took a glass and raised it in a toast.

"To the Scorched Earth project," said Nero.

The Japanese smiled and nodded. Nero smiled and nodded.

"To revenge," he said, smiling so intently that he bared his teeth.

Everybody tipped their glasses and took a drink.

"You know you can get this at Ralphs for four dollars a bottle," said the translator.

"Money is no object," said Nero.

In the background, the dancer was making her rounds, inviting each of the patrons to stuff a dollar or two under her garter. By the time she reached their table, she had six rumpled dollar bills strapped to her leg. She turned around, bent away slightly and jiggled her ass, then turned back around, setting a high heel on the table and snapping the garter against her thigh. Nero stuffed two crisp clean dollar bills—B-grade counterfeits he produced himself at great personal expense—under the garter, then licked the tips of his fingers and gave her an affectionate two-fingered smack right on the hock. The dancer looked to the Japanese, but they just stared back with amused and inscrutable grins. She took her heel off the table and began to walk away. Nero grabbed her by the arm. Her eyes lit up like Roman candles.

68

"Not so fast, sweetheart. As I am sure you are aware, when we came in, I gave the hostess strict instructions that you were to approach the table just as we raised our glasses to have our toast. You were to place your foot on the table, remove your shoe, fill it with Champagne, then feed the Champagne to, first, the Japanese, beginning with the most senior of the three and proceeding to the youngest, followed by our lovely translator, and, ultimately, yourself. Not only were you several steps too late, visiting the table after we'd completed our toast, but your shoes are completely inadequate for serving Champagne, lacking a reservoir capable even of capturing more than a thimbleful of this delectable libation."

"They can suck my toes for fifteen dollars," she said.

"That will not be necessary," said Nero. "From now on, you must keep your feet soft, pedicured and completely clean. After soaking them in Epsom salts, you may buff them with a pumice stone. In the future, I will send somebody around to inspect them before we arrive. The Japanese are exceptionally hygienic. Wear shoes that are sanitary and that contain backs and sides capable of holding three or more ounces of ceremonial spirits. While you are performing on stage, pay attention so that you time your arrival to precede the consummation of the toast."

"Do you know Rick?" she said, her eyes as wide as saucers.

"Certainly not," said Nero. "Do I look like I'm from around here?"

He peeled off three more counterfeit dollar bills and stuffed them under her garter.

"Next time, I expect you to be prepared," he said, as he wheeled around and headed for the door.

"You know Leon?" she said, her voice trailing off in the gloom.

Nero pushed open the door and the group followed him into the jarring light of the afternoon.

In the car, the three Japanese sat next to each other in the back. Nero and the translator sat across from them. Nero looked at the Japanese, smiling. The Japanese bowed their heads and smiled back. The translator looked from Nero to the Japanese then back to Nero, he smiling and the Japanese smiling back again, as the cycle continued to repeat itself. The car slowed to a stop, and the translator craned her head around to see what was going on. A homeless man was lying face down in the middle of the road. The girl immediately opened the door, got out and went over to the man. She shook him until he regained consciousness then helped him to his feet. She was escorting the man to the far sidewalk when he pulled a gun and shot her, taking her purse and sprinting down the middle of the street as her body fell in a heap. Nero and the Japanese stared down at the body as the driver checked her pulse.

He shook his head.

"It is a pity," said Yukio, in English. "So young. And I never even got her name."

"She was from the agency," Nero said.

# CHAPTER 12

*DON*

As we left the shop I became aware of an odd kind of electric crackle. I thought to ask the proprietor what it was, but I had no desire to go back inside. Once we were under way I pulled out a cigarette and turned to Juan for a light.

"Light? What you talking about, man?"

"That lighter you just got. The dragon."

I saw a vague glint of recognition, then he shook his head.

"I don't got that anymore. It's gone, I think. Yeah, I don't know where that thing is, man."

"What are you trying to tell me?"

"It's gone, you know, like I don't know where it is anymore."

He shook his head at the mystery of it and turned to stare out the window. Watching him closely, I slowly brought the match forward—I knew he was observing me out of the corner of his eye—the unmistakable beginnings of a painful wince showing in the lines around his eyes, until, scant inches away, I struck it against the white quartz of the Virgin. I brought the flame to the cigarette then shook it out. Juan shook his head.

"I think it's no good, man. It's bad luck."

I took a long drag on the cigarette, holding it in, savoring the arid flavor, then let the smoke slowly stream out my nostrils until the car was filled with it. I rolled up the window, and the smoke hung almost still in the air.

"See, I'm the dragon," I said.

"You ain't no lizard, man. You're a snake. You're gonna get us kicked out the fucking garden."

"That's just an old wive's tale," I said.

We received a jolt as we passed over some old railroad tracks. I turned my head and followed them to the horizon, where they disappeared in the dissolving light. Leading nowhere, I thought. They probably hadn't been used in quite some time. Almost spectral now. The traces of a bygone age.

We drove like this for some time, as day turned to gloaming and then the blackest of nights. A dust storm was brewing up around us, and before long we were driving blind. We pushed ahead and soon were being whipped about by an incredibly strong wind, seemingly from every direction at once. It felt as if the road was crumbling away beneath us.

"One twenty-five," I said to Juan, after a glance at the digital display.

"No shit, eh? That's pretty fast," he said, seeming not a little impressed.

Without even really thinking about it I held off for a moment, just maintaining, as it were, so that our bodies lost their resistance to the increase in speed and just kind of floated through the rapidly passing night, shielded by a protective bubble of low-octane motorized sound.

"How fast we going now?" asked Juan, looking at me over his sunglasses.

"Two twenty-five."

"Holy shit. This is some car, man." He whistled and nodded his head. "Pretty fast for a ... for a *car*." He whistled again, then turned solemn. "Do you understand what I'm saying? Like I think we're gonna catch on fire."

I watched with mounting fascination as our speed continued to climb inexplicably higher, leaving me oddly detached, a spectator to our fate.

"Two sixty-five," I said, my voice gone flat, a dead tone.

We had reached the point where speed no longer even seemed like speed. We were enveloped in a cocoon of motorized sound, the night's scenes and shadowy depths becoming the undifferentiated blur of a single black mass. Even the bumps and jolts of the road had gone quiet. We were completely disconnected from any sensation of road, or wind, or any of the violent frictions that one relied upon when traveling night blind.

I hesitated to look at the speedometer.

It was with utmost calm and equanimity that I finally turned to Juan and said, "Three hundred."

"No shit, eh?" he said in the quiet voice of one about to lay low for awhile, and indeed he sank way down in his seat, not saying anything, just observing from behind dark sunglasses.

"We're in the air," I said. "It's ... some kind of tornado."

Juan got down even lower in his seat and took out a cigarette. His hands were shaking so badly it took several attempts to get it lit.

"I think we're near the hotel," he said, nodding to himself.

"Hold on," I said, very calmly. "This may be very violent when we come back down."

# CHAPTER 13
*DON*

I remember something very traumatic when we finally landed, the sound of two tons of metal and glass crashing against the earth with catastrophic impact and tumbling over the hard black sand. When I awoke, rather than it being morning as I expected, the start of a brand new day, sun up and the nightmare ended, it was still pitch black. I shook Juan, but he was deeply unconscious, perhaps fatally.

"Wake up," I said, giving him another good shake.

I lifted his sunglasses and searched for signs of life in his eyes, but they were just as black and unfathomable as his still beating heart. Apparently he was, technically, still alive. A beating heart was one thing, but it remained to be seen whether another word would ever pass those dark lips. Well, there was nothing I could do for him now. I turned my attention to the road ahead, or rather the lack of one. It was difficult to see through the web of crushed glass, so I leaned back and kicked out what remained of the windshield. Turning the key I was pleasantly surprised when the big engine fired right up, not a bit reluctant. I eased down on the accelerator and with a wobbling rear wheel and badly traumatized suspension began a slow crawl over the rough terrain. The shocks, naturally, were completely shot. The steering, too, was a bit loose, and it was all I could do to keep a reasonably straight course as the car meandered like a sleepwalker into the orange light of the moon. The headlights were smashed to bits, which made the moon's watery trail the only road to travel. The moon as both head lamp and guiding light.

After a time we came upon a large encampment—a colony of tents of all shapes and sizes festooned with lanterns that suggested a roving band of some kind, civilized nomads. There were signs of great industry, glimpses of forms moving about as they passed under the lights. I stopped at the edge of the ravine and killed the engine.

Upon arriving at the encampment, Juan had begun to make some sounds and was now mumbling unintelligibly. I got out of the car and stood before the ravine. Down below there were scores of tiny forms moving around dreamily in the darkness, illuminated by the lanterns like fireflies. At the center of this activity, staked out by a yellow glow-in-the-dark ribbon that rippled languidly in the wind, was the outline of a truly gigantic cross.

A dark complected woman (I could tell this even away from the light) approached wearing a U of M sweatshirt, her hair in a ponytail.

"Do you speak Spanish?" I asked her as she drew near. "We were in a car accident, and my friend, he was unconscious. Now it sounds like he's speaking in tongues."

"*Tongues*," she said, as if she'd never heard the word before. "Let me see him."

I opened the passenger side door and let her have a look. Juan lay back with lips slowly moving, giving voice to those strange foreign sounds.

"I don't think he's speaking Spanish." She listened intently now, head turned down. "I think, unless I am mistaken, I have only heard it spoken a few times, I think he is speaking an ancient dialect of Aztecan."

"That's a dead language."

"Maybe your friend is a linguist."

"Can you tell what he's saying?"

"I only know a few words, but I believe he is saying, repeating over and over again, *the ring of fire, the ring of fire*."

"That's his favorite Johnny Cash song," I said. "He'll come out of it any time now. Thank you for your help."

I closed the door.

"What's going on down in the ravine, is it a dig of some

kind?" I said.

"We are looking for a cross that was supposed to have been used in the crucifixion of a giant. We have found traces of iron in a configuration that corresponds with the cross of the legend."

"How old is it?"

"We do not know. For some reason the carbon dating does not work. The isotopes, they do not decay."

I looked back down into the ravine, at the gigantic cross demarcated by the rippling yellow outline. The image of the crucified giant flashed in my mind, like a glimpse, a fated impression—the violent gasping death of the last of the Titans, the energy released at that moment greater than a thousand shrieks of lightning.

"Where's the nearest service station? Our vehicle is in need of repair."

She looked over the wreckage of our car.

"I think it is better to walk."

"She's still got a little life left in her," I said, giving the trunk a pat.

"Follow the light of the moon. In the morning you will pass Dead Man's Cactus. You can make an offering if you wish. It's up to you. I recommend it. From there you veer right and go between the two boulders. Eventually you will arrive at Temato Rock. You will know this rock when you see it. There is no other one like it. Climb on top and look to where the sun sets. You will see a small mountain with a lake of fire on top. What you are looking for is on the other side."

"Do I have to go over the mountain and through the lake of fire?"

"No, you would be killed. You must drive around it. You will see it. It's the only service station in the area."

"Thank you again for your help," I said. "How do we get back to the road?"

"Oh no, I'm sorry if you do not understand. There are no roads here. Only desert."

"I was on one just a little while ago. We got lost in a storm."

"Maybe it was longer ago than you think. Maybe you lost track of the time. I assure you there are no roads anywhere around here. Not for a hundred miles or more. This is devil's country. You must find your own way."

"Are there any maps of the area?"

"There are many maps, but they are made only to find specific things. I'll give you my binoculars. The desert is mostly flat. Just follow the moon until daylight, then look for the cactus and the big rock."

"Thank you for your advice."

"Good luck on your journey."

She handed me the binoculars and walked away. As she disappeared into the encampment I spotted a couple ten gallon gas cans on the back of a jeep. They were full. I lifted them off and put them in the trunk. Juan was still in a mumbling stupor when I got in the car, his head lolling about drowsily. I turned over the engine and eased away from the edge of the ravine, driving slowly through the maze of tents and temporary structures, doing my best to heed the girl's advice and follow the receding light of the moon. For now, that was the best we could do. Once we had gotten out of the encampment, I relaxed and settled in for the drive ahead. I couldn't have burned it if I wanted to. The entire body of the car was held together in a very tenuous way, and I felt that any undue stress might cause it to go to pieces beneath me, leaving me stranded upon the vast desert with my unconscious babbling companion.

I maintained a slow steady speed, smoking the occasional cigarette and trying to make out meaningful shapes in the barrenness of the night. Even though I couldn't pick up any stations out here, I neglected to turn off the radio, being content with the strange unearthly sounds reaching me from God knew where, maybe outer space, that ever fluctuating high frequency pitch, that other worldly whine and hiss. Nothing could make you feel so profoundly alone, out in the middle of nowhere with the eerie music of all those souls screaming through your radio like a haunted transmission of the whole night time mind.

I thought back to that long ago event that turned friend to foe. My partner back then was Fanta. We were an elite team, the first choice for the most damnable assignments. We found missing persons and tracked down the rarest substances, having the keenest sense for all lost things. And then I witnessed something I was never supposed to see. Orren, the shadowy figure who led our tong, always appeared before our table in silhouette, the blinding light shining from behind, his voice electronically modulated so that it sounded something like Donald Duck. What I chanced one day to see, and the one unforgivable crime in the land of second chances, was the exact nature of Orren's identity. I happened to discover this while wandering through an area of his compound where I wasn't supposed to be, compulsively lighting an old World War II lighter I liked to carry around, playing with fire as was my habit then. Unaware of where I was, of how far I had gone, I looked up from the lighter, having just capped the lid over the flame, and found myself passing a door that showed the finest hairline crack of light. The corridor was dark, and I had been using the lighter as a strobe to guide me. I was curious to a fault then, always needing to know what was going on behind the scenes. Without hesitation I pressed my eye to the sliver of light. I recognized Orren's form instinctively, so many times had I seen it etched out of that blinding light. I moved closer, anticipating the revelation of true identity

Slowly, by degrees, he turned to face me, and I tell you, what I saw there I was in no way prepared to see, because, and even now I shudder to think of it, I tell you, HE HAD NO FACE. Where a face should have been there was nothing, absolutely nothing. He was having a conversation on speaker phone, something about a drop in the desert—"down in Tierra del Fuego … a phaeton with junk in the trunk hitched to the golden triangle pony express." The conversation was conducted in code, of course, but from those fragments I determined that there was a lost shipment of Golden Triangle heroin being transported in the trunk of a Phaeton. So absorbed in what I was hearing, I dropped the lighter, and it clanged against the floor. His head turned ever so slowly in my direction. A more monstrous vision I couldn't imagine, and I left that place as fast as my hot breath would take me.

It was unfortunate that Fanta would suffer for my crime. The whole sequence of events unraveled so quickly I hadn't a chance to warn him. I could never again show my face on the old scene. The punishment for a crime of the eye was eye for an eye. So now Fanta was half-blind, even though he had seen nothing, knew nothing, the lost eye held ransom until the day he delivered my head, a bullet hole in place of my wandering eye. It was too late to turn back the clock. He was my nemesis, and I would have to do him in. The stakes were high on all sides. He would pursue me to the ends of the earth, and we were a good way there now.

And of course by the time I found it, a '57 Mercury Phaeton abandoned in the desert with the key in the ignition, and popped the trunk, there was nothing inside but a dusty old bottle of Mezcal with a worm at the bottom for my troubles.

# CHAPTER 14

Bax and Nick were in the neighborhood and decided to drop by the set, located on a soundstage on the studio lot. They had been having dinner at a new restaurant right down the road, and thought might as well stop in. Bax and the director Jack Dante had worked on several projects together, the last a successful psychological thriller adapted from a British made for television movie. Dante, a Brit, complained bitterly about having to work in Los Angeles, in this arid hell hole, but the sunny climate had brought some color and consistency to a complexion that tended to be alternately flushed red or pasty white. Dante had a house in Malibu and returned to the UK only on rare occasions. He was married to the legendary California blonde bombshell Brigitte Summers and hadn't made one of the smart small movies that had made his reputation in many years. He was a perfectionist on the set, demanding and hot tempered with the crew, but able to turn on the charm with the actors and reliably delivered strong performances. Aeon had purchased the script six years ago and no less than fifteen top writers had touched it since. The story still had some problems but the project was a good showcase and had attracted the interest of some top talent. The story of pool halls, fast money, and dangerous love was enough to lure Britain James and Tony Billings. Right away, Bax had boiled the script down to a mini-soundtrack and a collage of quick-cut images, a 30-second trailer in his head that he turned into a razor sharp pitch.

Nick had heard it so many times that now the trailer lived in his head, too. He could even hear the pulsing beats of the would-be sound track. It was hard to reconcile the dailies, so slow and washed out, with the rapid kaleidoscope of imaginary sights and sounds that had given birth to the movie now being created on the sound stage. Some players had a gift for story, the art of the pitch; it was effortless, like blowing a kiss—three acts in one bite size package. Bax had a talent for trailer. You gave him a script and he immediately saw the entire trailer right in his head. He could blow it up for you like a big neon trial balloon. The best part about it was you could see it and feel it and hear it without even knowing exactly what it was all about. But it didn't matter because the trailer was what you were really selling anyway. That was the economics of opening on 3,000 screens, domestic.

There was a fair amount of traffic on the lot for this time of night. There were several cars ahead of them at the gate. As the guard waved them through, Nick noticed a robust middle aged man in a fedora and hipster glasses being led away by security. It looked like the entertainment journalist Frederick Barclay. Probably had one too many at the screening. Nick found a spot near the set. They recognized Dante's Jaguar, a slick looking 1976 XJ12 with a fresh midnight blue paint job. They came into the building at the south entrance and made their way down the hallway through the clutter of wires and equipment to the sound stage. There was a veritable hush. Scores of crew tended cameras, booms, dollies, and various devices to aid in the capture of light and sound. The general mood was attentive, but there was an attitude of having held this pose for a good part of the evening, the attitude of a crew resigned to riding out the scene until late into the night and beyond. Dante's crew was on a tight schedule for the interior scenes. Nick had built in some slack for the exteriors, especially for the boat chase on the bay. It was the only thing that passed for a big expensive exterior scene in the whole movie. Clouds or rain could wipe out shooting for days. There was a whole stockpile of boats just waiting.

The set was the inside of a smoky, dimly lit pool hall. There were two interior prop walls that joined in a corner with a pool table with a Pabst chandelier hanging over it in the middle of the semi-enclosed space. The chandelier hung from a boom that extended from a metal tower. The focal point of all these elements was the pool table, and what was on it, a single white cue ball set squarely in the middle of the table in the soft glow of the chandelier. A jet black 8 ball was positioned in an almost direct line from the cue ball to the corner pocket. Nick's first thought was that it looked like an easy shot. Tony Billings was standing about ten feet from the table in a white t-shirt and jeans. The t-shirt wasn't model tight, but the sleeves were cut high enough to reveal Tony's sculpted biceps. This was the source of the conspicuous silence that had overtaken the set, and Nick thought in retrospect that he had even caught a whiff of it outside the building and that the silence had gradually intensified into the nullity of the white cue ball burning under the klieg lights. Tony stood somewhat outside the cast of the lights, which accentuated the impression that he was cloaked in shadow. One might have gotten the impression that he was waiting for something to happen, but Nick soon came to understand that Tony was not merely standing by waiting and watching, he was in fact in a state of intense concentration. Who knew how long he had been standing there like that? He gave the impression of not breathing, of slowly turning to stone with the faint glow of his eyes the only part of him that was alive.

Bax said, "This must be some kind of actor thing."

"It's the Method," said Nick. "He's trying to get into character."

"There's Dante."

Across the room, Dante was engaged in a very animated discussion just off to the side of the set with the costume designer Jessica Laine. Dante had wild thinning hair that was matted with sweat. The conversation, barely audible at this distance, was about the only sound in the room, like the sound of someone screaming with the volume turned way down. Dante saw them and waved them over with an emphatic gesture. It was only once they were within a couple feet that they got the gist of the conversation. The jeans Tony had on were designer Japanese denim. There's no way this young hustler from Cleveland would have on a pair of designer Japanese denims. The shirt was not model tight but it was model cut. The thread count was too high. The way it reflected the light it looked like a $500 t-shirt.

"You want more grunge?" said Jessica. "Or straight off the rack? He's going to look like he got his clothes at JC Penney."

"Not JC Penney, for Christ's sake, I want them to look like they were ripped right off James Dean's back."

An assistant handed her a white t-shirt on a hanger. She held it up so the shirt caught the light. It was model cut but looked like it had been worn a few times and tossed in a corner. It was rumpled, stretched, a little threadbare, with dark accents that could have been residue of asphalt, burnt rubber, motor oil.

"Like that?" she said.

"Like *that*," said Dante, pointing to one of the crew, a brawny dark complected young man wearing an electrician's belt. He was in the process of replacing out some of the miniature light bulbs in the control panel. His white t-shirt was threadbare and clung to his torso less from the cut than from good old fashioned sweat. Dante had the AC turned off to get the authentic sheen of sweat. He deplored spray-on.

"You, with the screwdriver," he said, marching over. "Give me that."

The young man looked down at his shirt, uncomprehending.

"He's a Teamster," Bax said to Nick with a nudge and a wink.

"It's not in the contract," the young man said and went back to work.

Dante took a roll out of his pocket and peeled off hundred dollar bills.

"I'll give you three bills," he said.

The young man considered it. He took the money. He pulled the shirt over his head and handed it to Dante. Dante brought it to Jessica.

"This is what I'm talking about. Tell him to put it on."

Jessica explained the situation to the assistant and sent him over with the shirt.

"Don't talk to me," said Tony, from the shadows.

Tony continued to focus on the cue ball. The assistant looked at Jessica and shrugged.

"Maybe tomorrow," she said.

Meanwhile the brawny young Teamster had put on the distressed designer tee that Dante had rejected. Dante had to admit to himself it looked great on him.

"We're not leaving here until this scene is in the can," said Dante. "Too much time has been invested. Does everybody hear me?

83

We're not leaving!"

"Can we smoke in here?" said Nick.

"Only the talent ... and the money men," he said with a wink.

"I can never remember," said Nick. "It's different everywhere you go."

He opened a pack of Marlboro Lights and removed a cigarette.

The Teamster was also having a cigarette, held between his lips while he worked on the wire. Several others were smoking, crew types.

"I don't put up with that California bull shit," said Dante. "There should be real smoke in a pool hall." He turned to address the crew. "Everybody, start smoking!"

Dante turned back to Nick.

"Maybe Tony will find his motivation. He's very serious today. I only smoke after meals now, under strict orders from my chiropractor. These California doctors want you to shit your brains out to cure a cold. There's enough poison in the air here to kill all the vitamins in the solar system."

"I'm taking 20 or 30 pills before I've had my first cup of coffee," said Bax. "They have me on everything, most of it herbal. There's no way to know if it's doing anything unless I make it to a hundred."

"Some of that herbal will put you in the ground if you don't watch it," said Dante. "But not half as fast as all that pharmaceutical crap. If you want to live forever cut your head off and stick it in the ice box for a couple million years."

"How long's he been standing there like that?" said Nick.

"Not quite an hour. Haven't you heard. He's discovered the Method."

"I heard," said Nick.

"There's a rash of it going around."

"I hear Britain's got it," said Nick.

"She got a dose when she did that theatrical bit," said Dante.

"Where is she?" said Bax. "She in this scene?"

"That's her," said Dante. "On the table."

Bax pointed to the table.

"There's a cue ball..."

"That's Britain James," said Dante pointedly.

"How can you tell?" said Nick.

"Red lipstick marks. You can't see from this angle, but they're hers all right. No mistaking that pout."

"Britain James is the cue ball," said Nick.

He blew a stream of smoke toward the set.

"Britain's the cue ball," said Bax. "She turned into it, like a magic trick."

"She wanted a larger role in the scene. It's the pivotal scene in the story really, just Tony and the cue ball, the oldest, most biblical of themes, man versus himself, a wrestling match with the inner demons, a man haunted by his past. He's playing for all the marbles. Everything, his entire bleeding future resting on this shot. Whether he makes it the audience won't even see. It's a cut away, a cliffhanger of sorts, the two-thirds of the iceberg hidden beneath the surface. It's the inner life of the picture, a depth charge for your psyche, it'll kill your shrink. Our lovely girl Britain is deeply involved in this picture; she's made a substantial investment of her inner life; she's laid bare her flesh; she considers it vitally important that she have a presence in this scene, one that is crucial to the culminating drama, though not at the expense of the story. Blessed girl, she stopped short of insisting that her character be written into the scene. She asked for fifteen minutes alone on the soundstage. The crew cleared out, we all cleared out, and left her alone and vulnerable beneath the lights. When the fifteen minutes were over we filed back onto the set—Britain was nowhere to be seen, so it took a little while for the light bulb to turn on—I figured she'd just split, but not Charlie—he remembers the exact placement of every prop, something like a photographic memory, and the first thing he does is point to the cue ball—you see, there hadn't been a cue ball when we'd left. Charlie had sent a bloke out to fetch one, and he hadn't arrived yet. With great sensitivity he rolled the cue ball across the felt with his eye right down on the table, and that's when we knew for sure, though by this time I'd begun to suspect it—the red lipstick mark on the white of the cue ball…"

"She turned into a cue ball," said Bax.

"Not turned into so much," said Dante. "This is quantum physics. This is Heisenberg."

"I thought it was Strasburg, you know, the whole Method thing."

"It's all the same," said Dante.

85

"Cool," said Nick. "That's really going to come through on screen."

"It's going to pay off big time," said Bax, lifting his cell phone to his ear. "Yeah, I'm on the set...Nick and me...Sort of, I can't really explain...I'm not sure yet...Have her drop it off with Eric...she is and she isn't, we'll work something out with the contract...It's going to be a great scene...every penny...later."

Bax hangs up the phone.

"Marty says Aloha."

"Tell Marty to fuck the Virgin Islands," said Dante.

"I thought it was *Tell Marty to fuck the LAPD*," said Nick. "I've been telling him you said to say that all week."

"You won't be saying that when the levee breaks," said Bax.

"Would do this city a fuck load of good," said Dante. "Scrub it clean."

"Baptism by fire," said Nick, taking a drag on the cigarette.

"This is not a good city for honest drink," said Dante. "I had some crap last night–vodka mixed with a Red Bull energy drink. I was jabbering like a bleeding lunatic until five in the morning. It's worse than cocaine."

"We were drinking those the other night, till about five o'clock in the morning. On the way to get breakfast we wound up driving to Vegas."

"We had that meeting with Tenenbaum the next day."

"I had to pay that guy to drive the car back."

"Las Vegas is a good town for drinking," said Dante. "It's bloody awful but good for drink."

"Old Vegas or new Vegas?" said Bax.

"Haven't you heard? They rebuilt old Vegas *in* new Vegas. The real old Vegas is obsolete," said Dante. "Nobody went there anymore anyway. It's been dipped in amber and put out for display."

"I heard it's making a come back," said Bax.

Dante pulled aside the wardrobe assistant.

"Be a dear, run over and see if you can get him to put on that shirt."

The assistant approached Tony with the shirt, holding it out to him on the hanger as if she were holding out a piece of meat to a bear, afraid to get too close for fear of getting her head taken off. Tony was still standing in the outer rim of darkness at the edge of the

86

set, his face showing a look of intense concentration.

"Mr. Billings," said the assistant.

"I'm doing it," said Tony, as he made his move toward the set, leaving the assistant holding the shirt in the half light.

Tony emerged into the glare of the klieg lights. He stood before the pool table, with his head lowered slightly, eyes beaming. He held out his hand, and the prop man walked over briskly and handed him the stick. Tony took it without taking his eyes off the cue ball.

"Wait a minute," he said, handing the cue back to the prop man. "Chalk."

The prop man poured some chalk into Tony's hand. Tony slapped his palms together, sending up a cloud of chalk dust.

"I've seen that before," said Nick. "Who does that?"

"Gymnasts," said Bax. "Right before jumping onto those bars."

Tony took back the cue and began circling the table. The prop man walked briskly from the set. Tony rounded the corner of the table, eyes never leaving the cue ball, and picked up a cube of blue chalk. He spun it on the tip of the cue then blew off the loose chalk.

"Are we rolling?" said Bax.

"We've been rolling the whole time," said Dante. "The advantage of digital—the camera never sleeps. Real peace of mind for the talent. You can rest assured not a single bit of priceless nuance will be missed. It's hell for the editor, but what isn't? The talent hate to waste a breath that doesn't wind up in the can."

It was true, the attitude of the crew hadn't changed noticeably since Tony's entrance on the scene; the attitude had been attentive and business-like the whole time. Nobody yelled action, or said cut. There was no clear line between takes. This could be just another false start, and then Tony would retreat back to the shadows to search for his motivation. The digital was cheap, but the meter was running. Bax did the numbers in his head, out of habit, and then wiped them out. Dante was ace when it came to delivering on the talent. He knew what he was after. What you saw on set never looked like the movie you saw on screen. On the set it looked fake. Between the raw dailies and visits to the set, it was hard to believe that any of this ever amounted to anything. Mountains of money resting on a house of cards–play actors with face paint. Sometimes he yearned for the whiff of pork bellies or the feel of a durable good. And then he slid into the brand new BMW with the top down and caught a flash of the model's bare thighs under a short skirt in the next seat, and the warm California breeze blew the thoughts out of his head. And gradually he learned not to think so much. How many C.P.A.s ever contributed an idea for a crucial third act scene for an international blockbuster seen by millions of people? How many accountants sat in an office with a short megalomaniac in a kimono and said things like "Fly out Britain James" or "Tony gets a thousand dollars a day per diem"?

Tony was rounding the table again. He sized up the shot then switched back and started rounding the table in the other direction. Finally, he put his hand down on the felt and wrapped his index finger around the cue, sighting down the length of the cue with the intense narrowing eyes of a sniper. There was a long breathless pause during which the camera closed in tight on Tony's expression, capturing a taut bead of sweat as it formed on his brow.

The pool cue drew back. Bax watched it on the monitor. Dante never watched the monitor. In fact, he barely seemed to be paying attention. At that moment he was arguing heatedly under his breath with the prop man's second assistant. Bax watched the pool cue complete its backward motion; then the cue slid forward, gently striking the cue ball and sending it rolling over the felt toward the 8 ball. The cue ball struck the 8 ball, knocking it toward the corner pocket. As the 8 ball sank, the cue ball hit the rail, ricocheting out into the middle of the table.

"Fuck me," said Tony. "Did you see that?"

Dante looked up from his conversation.

"Beautiful," he shouted. "That's a wrap."

Tony straightened up and shook his head.

"You saw what happened. I've got to do it over."

"We'll take care of it in the editing. It was a beautiful stroke."

"What about the iceberg?" said Tony. "The way we talked about it. The cue ball should barely kiss the rail."

"Nobody's ever going to see it," said Dante. "Once the balls are rolling we cut-away."

"I've practiced it a thousand times."

"One more time," said Dante. "Just loosen up a bit."

88

Tony leaned forward and set up over the shot. The prop man's assistant returned the balls to their mark. Nick could make out the red lipstick on the cue ball before the assistant spun it away from the camera. Tony replayed the moves from the previous take beat for beat, the muscles in his face tensing through an exact sequence of rehearsed expressions. He released the cue and the cue ball struck the 8 ball, which slid smoothly into the corner pocket. The cue ball hit the rail and rolled out to the middle of the table.

The balls were set up again and the shot was repeated three more times, with the same result. Tony's eyes burned as he stared at the table.

"She's not giving me anything."

"What are you saying?" shouted Dante.

"She's not, you know, giving me anything to work with."

"Britain," said Dante.

"I don't know how I'm supposed to respond. I mean, look…"

He opened his hand, indicating the cue ball. The ball sat squarely on the table, perfectly still.

"How am I supposed to respond to that?"

He lit a cigarette and shook out the match.

"I can't work in these conditions."

"It's about passion," said Dante. "It's about the sweet, tender caress. The last kiss."

"I thought it would be different somehow."

"This is Britain James," said Dante. "Just you and Britain. Let nothing stand between you."

"Maybe that's the problem," said Tony.

"We're talking about Britain," said Dante.

"You saw what happened."

"You're asking a lot of yourself. We'll use an insert and put it together in editing. The stroke, the look on your face, bloody marvelous."

"We agreed no inserts for the pool scenes," said Tony. "I always do my own stunts. It's got to look completely real. The ball's got to stop right at the rail, and then the camera holds on it for two beats, just like we talked about."

"After the cue ball strikes the 8 ball it's a CUT TO," said Dante. "Nobody will ever see it."

"It's about truth," said Tony. "The two-thirds of the iceberg under the sea."

"Where's Curtis?" shouted Dante.

Curtis was the film's subject matter expert. A five time national eight-ball champion and member of the BCA Hall of Fame, he'd been hustling pool since he was nine years old, playing sailors and drunks in the beer hall where his uncle tended bar. He was mid-50s, with a mustache. He had weathered, handsome looks and an easy manner. When he got up from the bar stool at the edge of the set, Nick realized for the first time that there was even anybody there. He made his way across the set, walking with a relaxed stride. When he reached the pool table, he gave Tony a smile and opened his hand to take the cue. Tony gave it to him and backed up a few steps, standing with his hand holding his elbow as he smoked the cigarette.

Curtis surveyed the situation then leaned down over the table to size up the shot. He pulled back the cue.

"Take it nice and easy," he said.

The cue slid forward in a silky smooth motion.

"Just a kiss," he said, as the tip of the cue made contact with the ball.

The cue ball rolled over the felt toward the 8 ball.

"Just like she's a woman," he said, straightening up.

The cue ball touched the 8 ball so softly it sounded like a whisper then went at an angle toward the rail. From where he was standing, Tony could see the red lip marks turning end over end. The 8 ball dropped into the corner pocket. The cue ball continued to roll, finally coming to rest against the rail.

Tony's eyes burned behind the smoke from his cigarette. Curtis handed him back the pool cue, touched him on the shoulder, then walked across the set in that easy stride, returning to his seat in the shadows.

Bax, who had been pacing in the background, having a hushed conversation on his cell, hung up the phone and put it away, maintaining a conspicuously stone cold poker face.

"It was Nero wasn't it? Don't tell me," said Dante.

"There's been a change in plans," said Bax.

"New location," said Nick.

"New location. New project," said Bax.

"Out in the desert," said Nick. "Everything's been arranged."

Dante's face fell.

"What did he say exactly?" said Dante.

"He said pull the plug," said Bax.

"Fucking lunatic," said Dante. "Who does he think he is, God?"

"It's not clear at this point," said Bax.

"It would have to be one of those really old gods that like to fuck with people," said Nick.

"Fuck me," he said. "Picture's half in the goddamn bag."

"Look at it this way," said Bax. "You know how you always dreamed of doing a remake of that old movie about the two kids wandering around the Outback?"

"Wandering around the desert with that little Aborigine," said Nick.

"Yeah, *Walkabout*," said Dante. "That dream was already crushed, if you remember. Drowned in shit."

"You had a shot at it, and then there was that whole thing with the tornado. And the fire?"

"Picture was a zombie by that point anyway, total bastardization," said Dante. "The bean counters fucked it all to hell."

"You still want to finish what you started?" said Bax. "Now's your shot."

"This is that fucking reverse-*Superman* bull shit," said Dante. "It doesn't have anything to do with *Walkabout*."

"I'm talking about a rogue shoot," said Bax. "A hand-held. A couple child actors."

"Wouldn't cost a thing," said Nick.

"Nobody would even notice," said Bax.

"Write a 16 page script," said Nick.

"Write it on the back of a cocktail napkin," said Bax.

"Drive out into the desert and see what happens," said Nick.

"Just like the original," said Bax.

"Where's the drop?" said Dante. "Don't tell me you don't already know."

"Fire Land, New Mexico," said Nick.

Dante's voice rang out over the silence.

"Clear the set!"

Pacing back and forth under the klieg lights, Tony was already on the phone with his agent.

"This is bull shit," he said. "I was nailing it. Fucking killing it."

"Take it easy, kid," said Morty.

"I told you last time. He can't just yank me around like his little puppet. I'm not his little bitch."

"Just ride it out," said Morty. "His days are numbered, but for now we got to play it cool."

In the car heading down Melrose, Bax and Nick talked about how things might have gone with the film. Bax said that the great thing about pool movies was that they rarely went over budget. You didn't have to fill an airplane hangar with water or move a crew to Morocco or go up in an airplane with the cameras. You didn't have to do too much planning for the weather. You didn't have to build a lot of elaborate sets or invest in a lot of special effects. There were a few high speed street races, some orchestrated violence, a pool tournament scene with a couple hundred extras. The A-ratio was almost 50%. Bax believed the greater the percentage of budget that went to the above-the-line costs, especially the lead actors, the greater the chance the project made money. Some of these projects try to get a bargain on the talent and invest in location, stunts, special effects. This usually didn't pay off. Famous faces sold the picture. Nine times out of ten. According to conventional wisdom, the star was the brand. Then special effects were the brand. And now the brand was the brand. But Bax would still take a true star any day of the week.

They continued on Wilshire into Beverly Hills and turned off onto one of the north-south streets. A mutual friend, a big time land developer, Joe Sarkasian, was having a party. Nick had promised to stop by. Bax parked the car around the corner. They walked up to the house and opened the door. There were about thirty people inside. Joe met them as they walked in. He introduced them to several groups of people before excusing himself to take a call. Nick and Bax moved out onto the verandah where Joe's partner Mindy Holloway, a former model in her late twenties, was standing with her husband Jack Mendes. Mindy recently had a baby and had made the move into the land game, where she'd been able to leverage her looks and laundry list of famous potential clients. Jack had produced dozens of blockbusters in the 80s and was still a bit of a player.

Jack cracked a walnut with a pair of steel tongs.

"So, Nick, how's it going with that Scorched Earth project?"

92

# CHAPTER 15
## *FREDERICK M. BARCLAY*

Tuesday, 1:36 PM

I stroll down the boardwalk, past the Santa Monica pier with its aroma of salt water, kelp, guano and ripening fish bait, past the Mexican vendor peddling his wares of hot tamales and Sex Wax t-shirts, past the Jesus on rollerblades with his trench coat overflowing with faux Rolexes and glass pipes, my heels clicking against the wooden slats as I twirl the silver equine handled walking cane I'd picked up from a wino for a pocket full of loose change that literally rained upon his recumbent sleeping form like pennies from heaven. I am a man on a mission, a secret agent of sorts, assaying this surreptitious assignment handed down by a mysterious higher power who inhabited the dark towers and shadowy byways of the popular imagination. I was a natural choice for the assignment, having made the particular subject my own personal cause célèbre over the years, a predilection that had earned me a degree of infamy in certain quarters.

I lift the binoculars to my eyes. It's easy to spot Tony, seated on his surfboard bobbing on the waves, due to the fact that he is surrounded by a retinue of bodyguards who are themselves seated on surfboards—a gigantic mountain of a man with a white beard named Frog, a black ex-con from Queens who can barely swim named

Leroy and a short bowling ball of a man with a bald head who I didn't recognize – their eyes scanning the crowd on the beach while trying to keep up with their charge. The beach is, naturally, filled with paparazzi and screaming teenage girls. After letting several good prospects roll by, Tony finally picks up a short wave, turning his board, kicking furiously then rising to his feet. A local surfer, a scrawny kid with brown skin and long black hair, pivots over the lip and cuts in front of Tony, inciting the bowling ball man to leap from his board and tackle the kid. Both disappear beneath the wave, never to resurface. Meanwhile, Frog and Leroy struggle furiously to keep up with Tony, their arms and legs beating the water to froth. Leroy makes it all the way to his feet before the board flies out from under him and he disappears in the surf. Frog has just made it to his knees when the board suddenly catches an edge, sending him tumbling head first into the chop. The result being that Tony cruises unguarded into the shallows where he is immediately set upon by scores of screaming girls who appear to literally rip him to pieces. When at last he emerges from the scrum he is desperate, frightened and entirely pantless. He immediately breaks into a full sprint, literally streaking down the beach, his bare ass a blur of white with the screaming girls and paparazzi in hot pursuit and the two remaining bodyguards, Frog and Leroy, struggling in vain to catch up. Unfortunately, I am not properly outfitted to join the chase, so I take a seat on a bench vacated by a young professionally attired gentleman (crisp white Oxford, blue-and-red power tie) in the throes of an epileptic fit and enjoy several hot dogs, ultimately making it back to Beverly Hills in plenty of time for happy hour at the Peninsula.

Wednesday, 2: 15 PM

Tony moves through the throng of shoppers surrounded by the ever-present phalanx of body guards. Despite the disguise—dark sunglasses, cargo shorts, do-rag, fake mustache—the young star attracts no small amount of attention from the packs of teenage girls who endlessly circulate the Beverly Center like schools of fish in some vast retail aquarium. Before long the expedition has become a veritable parade as one girl after another falls in behind Tony like so much dust in the tail of a luminous comet tearing headlong through space. A dozen cell phone cameras snap pictures as Tony holds up a pre-ripped t-shirt, tries on a pair of cheap purple sunglasses, winds up a plastic Hannah Montana music box then proceeds to stuff those items into the baggy cargo shorts and duck furtively out of the store. As the crowd moves on to the next store, I observe the hulking Frog pay off the shop clerk then run, with the surprising short-burst speed of a grizzly bear, to catch up. By the time he arrives at the next store, just in time to lay a c-note on the seventeen year old store manager, Tony is already exiting the boutique of affordable home wares with a spatula, a votive candle and a cocktail shaker stuffed down his shorts. Outside the store, Tony unloads the stolen loot on Leroy, who stashes the hot items in a large duffel bag.

It isn't until we reach the pet store that I realize the scope of Tony's avocational ambition. Not content with the nylon leash, the studded collar, the sequined Chihuahua vest or the no-spill dog bowl, he goes on to boost a desiccated pig ear, a Siamese fighting fish and a live chicken, remarkably smuggling out all of these items in the surprisingly capacious cargo shorts. I take leave of the looting party long enough to grab a hot dog, several pretzels and a slice of pizza at the food court. Mercifully, by the time I finish this snack, it's time for happy hour. Saved by the death knell. I walk out of the mall and am confronted by the startling visage of my five o'clock shadow sprawled like a withered giant over the sun bleached pavement.

Thursday, 4:20 PM

The studio audience is full of howling stoutly built homemakers from places like Oklahoma City, Topeka and Sarasota. I'm in there with them, having waited out in the sun for three hours to score a left field seat at the Destiny Show. We leap to our feet, throwing our hands in the air and screaming at the pitch of ecstasy bordering on mass psychosis. Tony is on the couch, bouncing up and down. Destiny holds his hand, which momentarily calms him. She looks into his eyes.

"I want to know what's in Tony Billings' future," she says.

"The universe has a plan for each and every one of us," he says. "I put my faith in the Technology and trust that it will guide me toward my special purpose."

"A lot has been made of your involvement with the System. There are rumors, I won't ask you to say yes or no, there are rumors that you have an exalted status within the community, that you are in a position of power. Do you believe that because of your celebrity you've been given privileged opportunities?"

"The Technology is available to anyone who believes. Because of who I am, because people recognize me and appreciate my work, I'm in a unique position to spread the word and make a difference in peoples' lives, and I've put myself at the service of this mission, the same thing any practitioner would be expected to do. As far as any special treatment, that hasn't been my experience."

"What does your faith do for you?"

"My faith gets me excited."

Again with the bouncing, up and down in his seat like a hyperactive (and especially gifted) child.

"I can see that," says Destiny, leaning back a touch.

As the bounces get higher, the audience goes wilder.

"Sometimes I just want to jump for joy!"

He's up on his feet now, bouncing in a kind of frog crouch. Destiny shoots a glance at her producer, Rodney Tower, who meets her eyes briefly before turning back to the monitor. Tony's standing straight up now, jumping on the sofa cushion as if it were a trampoline. And then he's in the air, chest thrust back, legs rotating over his head. Destiny has gotten up and now stands some distance from the couch. The crowd is going crazy. The backflip, perfectly executed except for the landing (Tony's feet coming down behind, rather than on, the couch), results in Tony crashing to the stage and lying there in a heap. All at once the screams of excitement turn to screams of solicitous terror, as the entire studio audience rushes onto the stage at once, burying the fallen actor under a spastic heap of robust Middle American maidenhead. Of course, I'm right in there with them, wildly clawing through the pile of bodies in an attempt to get to Tony. I barely avoid the first blow, feeling Frog's ham sized fist just graze my beard before demolishing the face of the woman standing next to me. The second blow takes out a rather large brunette who had previously identified herself as a homemaker from Des Moines, Iowa, sending her reeling backward off the stage. A plumply hysterical redhead grabs Tony's ankle and holds on for dear life, wrapping herself around it like flotsam in a storm ravaged sea. Leroy delivers a quick compact punch to the back of the woman's head, knocking her out cold and leaving her slumped unconscious over a tangle of bodies. I immediately hit the floor, first pretending to look for my glasses then, satisfied I have momentarily escaped the focus of the body guards' brutal interdiction, rolling clear across the stage and over the edge, miraculously landing on all fours like a cat (it was easily a two foot drop). I scurry crablike under the apron of a sound table, and it is from this vantage, with the terrified screams of the studio audience building to a bloody crescendo just outside my cold refuge, that I put pen to paper to record the details of these events.

Thursday, 6:30 PM

It is rare that business and pleasure mix as splendidly as they do on this occasion, as I sit in the bar at the Peninsula, nursing a Beefeater martini (stirred, not shaken) and feasting from a snack caddy of delectable Peloponesian olives, Syrian dates and Tuscan almonds, while waiting for a sighting of Tony, who is reputed to be staying in a suite on the uppermost floor. I don't have to wait long. I have barely taken the first exquisite ice-breaking sip when I catch a glimpse of Tony gliding through the lobby flanked by Frog and Leroy. I take leave of my drink and make my way to the lobby, where I lurk about in the wings pretending to talk on my cell phone, all the while keeping one eye on Tony. From the distinct curl of his lip I can tell right away something is up. In his black silk pajama bottoms and white undershirt, Tony marches right up to the guest services desk and begins dressing down the concierge. I ease closer to get a gist of the conversation.

"Now you need to listen to me for a second," says Tony. "I called down here twenty minutes ago and asked for a monogrammed bathrobe."

"It might take a little bit of time," says the concierge, contritely.

"How much time does it take to sew some letters on a goddamn robe?" says Tony, crossing his arms.

"It's not as simple as that," says the concierge. "You see, after business hours -"

"Business hours my ass, you know how much coin I drop at this rat hole?"

"Sir, we value your business, of course, and we're doing the best we can."

"When? When? Just tell me when?"

"An hour, maybe two, it's difficult to say."

"So you expect me to walk around in my goddamn pajamas all day!" he screams. "I want that shit monogrammed, A-S-mother fucking-A-P."

"Sir, please, the other guests? Perhaps we can take this conversation behind closed doors?"

"So now you're telling me to shut up, is that it?"

"Not at all…"

"You little bitch."

"Sir, please."

Tony hands his cell phone to Frog, then crosses his arms and lowers his head. Without hesitation, Frog hurls the cell phone at the concierge, bouncing it off his skull, and sending the man to floor, whimpering and mewling like an infant.

"My eye!" the man squeals, hysterically.

Tony turns around and marches back to the elevator, accompanied by Frog, while Leroy drops a few crisp bills on the body of the whimpering concierge. I turn away as they pass by then quietly slip back into the bar to take some notes and finish my drink.

Saturday, 10:48 AM

I am seated in front of a coffee shop nursing a double espresso and perusing the *Times* Arts & Leisure section when I see Tony's black BMW pull up in front of the Star Center across the quiet tree lined street. Tony hops out, leaving the engine running, then jogs down the walkway and passes through the front door of the stately old brick manor. A homeless man, meandering down the sidewalk, stops and bends down to look inside the window of the car. No sooner has he straightened up to continue on his way than a shiny black Denali screeches to a halt behind the Bimmer, Leroy jumps out and gives the homeless man a vicious beat down. Frog gets out of the Denali and throws the homeless man in the back, while Leroy gets behind the wheel of the BMW. The two vehicles depart in tandem. I look around, but nobody appears to have seen a thing.

I down the rest of my drink, folding the paper and tucking it under my arm, and just as I step into the street I notice an old 50s Mercury parked in the shade of a small tree. The well-dressed Latin American behind the wheel reminds me a little of Carlos Castenada in his prime, the familiar visage from the dust jacket photos. Having crossed the street, I stroll lazily along the wrought iron fence, letting my gaze drift to the entrance Tony had passed through just a moment ago. I know better than to linger. Despite the lack of an obvious security presence, one understands implicitly the repercussions of any unwanted forays onto church grounds. Someone was always watching. Interlopers were dealt with harshly, and with chilling discretion. I continue my stroll along the perimeter, rounding the corner and eventually coming upon a service entrance where a non-descript white delivery truck idles at the gate. Passing behind the truck, I reach out and try the latch, almost without thinking, and find to my surprise that it is unlocked. The door opens and I find myself diving headlong into the back of the truck just as it begins to move forward through the gate. I close the door and stretch out on the floor of the truck, making my body so stiff and still that I barely breathe. The back of the truck is windowless and so dark that I have no idea of the nature of my fellow cargo. Bed linens, office supplies, baked goods, it could have been anything. Finally, the engine stops, I hear the driver's door open and close and then nothing. I begin to sit up when I hear the telltale click of the latch. I immediately lie back down and—grasping for anything with which to cover myself—pull a sheet over my head (apparently the truck was delivering fresh linens). The rear door comes open—I can hear it, can see the light through the sheet. I don't move a muscle, lying there stiff as a board. My heart races as the men enter the truck, and I quietly curse myself for such impulsiveness. A sillier idea I have never had. My goose was undoubtedly cooked and then some. I expect the sheet to be ripped back any second, rendering me fully exposed, as both trespasser and stowaway. I can hear the sounds of their labor. Whatever the cargo is (other than bed linens, that is), it's heavy. I can feel something big sliding away next to me. My curiosity gets the better of me and I pull the sheet back for a quick glimpse, see the two men in crisp white outfits and dark sunglasses stepping down off the back of the truck. The tall man carries one end, the shorter man carries the other. I can tell right away it's a dead body, of that there is no doubt. I turn my head. The truck is full of them, stacked like loaves of bread. I don't have time to think of what to do next. An instant later they're back inside the truck. The tall one has me under the arms. The shorter one takes my legs. I do my best impression of dead weight. It isn't the first time I've played that part. I'm out of the

99

truck. They set me on a gurney then go in for the next body. We're in some kind of loading bay. A fluorescent light flickers overhead. I count at least eight bodies on gurneys. The sheet has slid from my face, so I'm able to make out my surroundings through the blurred vision of half-closed eyes. We're being wheeled down a long dimly lit hallway with brick arches and dull cracked plaster, then the sheet is pulled back over my eyes and everything is dark. When the light comes back on I find myself in a large holding area with around twenty other bodies, all stretched out on gurneys. When the two orderlies in sunglasses return to the room, I quickly lie back down and close my eyes. They wheel me and one of the other bodies through a door at the far end of the room and leave us there in the dark. A few minutes later, the door opens and the light turns on as two men enter. We appear to be in a child's bedroom, with a bunk bed, a toy chest and several scenes from Winnie the Pooh painted on the walls. The first man, bald and chinless, wearing a grey suit and wire frame glasses, waits in the doorway, while the other, whose shock of gray hair and wolfish features I immediately recognize as belonging to veteran network newscaster Jasper Storm, walks fully into the room, staring down at the two bodies (which include myself) with those intense coal black eyes while obsessively massaging his beard.

"Take your time," says the chinless man, with the faintest of smiles, as he closes the door.

The body next to me, I notice, belongs to a huge bloated whale of a man, stripped to the waist. Jasper walks in a circle around us, appraising us with those dark eyes while slowly loosening his tie. At last he casts off the tie, slips off his shoes and begins unbuttoning his shirt, while whistling Wagner's *Flight of the Valkyries*. It is not until, shirt open to the waist, belt hanging unbuckled, he opens a black leather doctor's bag and takes out a variety of elongated, oddly shaped stainless steel instruments (some preposterously bulbous, others twisting like fantastic corkscrews) and lines them up neatly on the bed, that I grasp the true nature of his unconscionable intentions, a realization that fills me with near crippling terror.

"What plans I have for you, my lovelies," he says, flitting over to my bare chested companion, leaning down provocatively, so that his lips press against the cold lifeless skin, and making a thunderous farting sound on the man's enormous stomach.

100

He straightens up, and as he dances toward me holding his vile metallic dildo, turning a pirouette, then waltzing toward me like a toreador, dildo tilted over his forearm in the manner of the matador positioning his sword for the brutal climactic insertion, I barely manage to choke back a scream. The panting satyriac old goat is just about upon me (and more) when there is a knock at the door.

"Just a minute," he responds, peevishly.

He straightens up, closing his shirt and putting away the instruments, before opening the door. The bald chinless man stands in the doorway, wearing an expression of utmost contrition.

"I apologize for the interruption. You're needed in the Consciousness Center," says the chinless man.

"Can it wait?"

"He asked to see you right away."

Reluctantly, Storm tucks in his shirt and follows the bald chinless man out of the room. Without a moment's hesitation I open the side door and push my gurney back into the holding area, or mortuary, for lack of a better term. I find the body of a man whose aspect somewhat resembles my own, being of similar age, girth and beardedness, and wheel him into the child's bedroom next to the bloated bald man. I shut the door and lie down in my gurney just as the door opens and the two sunglass bedizened orderlies appear. The short one walks right up to me and pushes me through another door leading to an altogether different room, parking me next to a table with a metal bucket of ice on it, leaving me to wonder what kind of Champagne-and-caviar horror awaits me next. The two orderlies leave the room and shut the door. The room has the feel of a psychiatrist's office, sparsely decorated with modern furnishings. I am about to get up when I realize there is someone else in the room, two people in fact, lying on hospital beds separated by a table covered with surgical instruments and several sophisticated looking machines adorned with all manner of buttons, levers, lights and graphical displays. Perhaps because the intrusion is so unexpected, it takes me a moment before I realize that one of these individuals is in fact Tony Billings, lying there with his eyes closed, seemingly unconscious, hooked up to an IV. Curiously, a gold ring sits on top of his left eye. The other unconscious individual is a man of similar age and appearance to Tony. And I can't help wondering: is it possible that I am about to enter into a necrophilic three-way with

101

the hottest young actor on the planet? This question lingers as two heretofore unseen men enter the room. The first is dressed as a priest, the black suit having a contemporary fashion forward cut, with a form fitting jacket and tapering pant legs. The priest has thick wavy black hair, full lips and mischievous dark eyes. The second man is, quite unmistakably, Nero.

"Mr. Fantastic, as you can see, everything has been prepared," says the Priest, addressing Nero.

"What's with the gold ring on his eye?" says Nero.

"He has a stye," says the Priest. "Thing was giving him fits."

"How'd he get it? Let me guess," says Nero.

"Those twins in craft services?" says the Priest. "The ones with the buck teeth and all that junk in the trunk?"

"The double-wide twins," says Nero.

"Seems they did our friend here the honor of sitting on his face," says the Priest. "At the same time."

"I thought I told him to keep his sunglasses on," says Nero.

"He'll need 'em in the desert," says priest.

"He'll need more than that," says Nero.

"It's going to be off the hook," says priest.

"Got all our ducks in a row," says Nero. "The Swiss Miss money. The Triad money. The Hiroshima money."

"Welcome to Fire Land."

"I'm starting to get that feeling again," says Nero. "Like Atlas."

"Little gold man with the golden globe on his shoulders," says priest. "Moon walking down the red carpet."

"Who's the John Doe?" says Nero, indicating the man in the bed next to Tony.

"Name's Don. Came in complaining of visions, hallucinations, voices in his head, that sort of thing," says the priest. "Wanted us to get the demons out of his head. By any means necessary."

"Like an exorcism," says Nero.

"Like an audit," says the Priest. "He thinks we're accountants."

"It looks like he tried to take matters into his own hands," says Nero, eyeing the hole in the center of the man's forehead.

I hadn't noticed it before—a small hole, encrusted with

102

blood.

"From the looks, I'd say an eighth inch drill bit," says the Priest. "Self-medicating with Black and Decker."

"Should have used a masonry bit," says Nero. "Would have gone straight through, no mess."

"They diagnosed him last night. Overactive pineal gland," says the Priest.

"The third eye," says Nero.

"We've seen it before, but never like this. That thing was wriggling around like a rattle snake. The man's brain was on fire."

"And everything went all right with the extraction?" says Nero.

"Quick and dirty," says the Priest, nodding toward an Erlenmeyer flask on the table with what appeared to be a small worm suspended in an amber serum in the conical reservoir. "Went right through the blow hole there. Very convenient."

"I'm assuming Tony was pleased about the news," says Nero.

"Practically foaming at the mouth," says the Priest. "Kid's been champing at the bit for some fresh pineal. Heard it's the ultimate kick."

"The ultimate mind blow," says Nero.

"Thought we were going to serve it up to him on a silver platter," says the Priest. "I told him it doesn't work like that. You've got to put it on, like a thinking cap."

"He's in for a wild ride," says Nero. "This isn't like all that club shit he's been sniffing. This is the real thing."

"I'm all misty eyed. Our little show pony is about to grow up," says the Priest.

"Into a big old Trojan Horse," says Nero.

"And then one day his head cracks open and we jump out and slit their throats in the night," says the Priest. "Figuratively speaking."

"Ride that unicorn straight into the sun," says Nero. "Knock it out of the sky and set the world on fire, just like Phaeton."

"They'll never know what hit 'em," says Priest.

"I might have to try it out myself once Tony's done with it," says Nero. "It's not every day good fresh pineal walks right through your front door."

"You won't have to wait long. I give the kid a couple days

max," says the Priest. "He'll be screaming to get it out of his head."

"What's with the stiff?" says Nero, looking down at me.

"Another donor...for the sex change in room six," says the Priest. "The surgeons are going to hit it after wrapping up the pineal transplant."

His words strike me like a cold shower, causing my manhood to shrink dramatically inside me. So they're going to carve us up— first Tony's brain, then my ... it's too much to even think about.

"When is the operation?" says Nero. "I want to make sure I'm gone before the surgeons arrive."

"A few minutes still," says the Priest.

"How deep are they?" says Nero, eyeing Tony and his unfortunate donor.

"First stage," says the Priest.

"Are you using any anesthetic?"

"Just hypnosis."

"Make sure you erase my face," says Nero.

"Consider it done," says the Priest, waving his hands like magic wands over the patients' faces.

Nero leaves the room.

Priest moves behind the two men, laying his hands on their heads and whispering.

"You're going deeper, deeper than you've ever gone before. Leaving everything behind. Names. Faces, especially the face of the man who was talking to me. You will not remember this face."

He takes out what appears to be a necklace with a shiny black bullet at the end of it, so lustrous it could be made of glass, and dangles the bullet so that it swings back and forth before their eyes.

"Three ... two ... one ...," he says, before tucking the black bullet back in his pocket.

The Priest moves behind Tony now, placing his fingers on his temples and leaning over so that his lips are just inches from his forehead.

"You're about to go nuclear, baby. You're gonna blow up. Bigger than Fat Man or Little boy combined..."

Just as he says this, Don the donor sits bolt upright in the bed. His eyes shoot open and he pans his head to take in the scene.

"Easy, fella," says the Priest, slowly moving over to him.

In an instant, Don grabs the beaker with the gland in it then

104

jumps from the bed and flies out the door.

The Priest picks up the phone on the wall and dials an extension.

"We've got an escapee," he says, with surprising calm. "Lock it down."

He hangs up the phone and leaves the room.

Surveying the instruments on the table—bone saw, rongeur, rack-and-pinion stainless steel rib spreader, a collection of scalpels with what appear to be zirconium nitride edges—it doesn't take me long to figure out that the nature of the second procedure—to be performed, apparently, on my person—might not be limited to the mere excision of the male organ (a bone chilling prospect in its own right) and might extend to a complete divestment of my anatomy. With mounting terror, I roll off the gurney and run to the door, finding it locked. I search desperately around the room, opening cabinets, pulling at vents, nothing. I'm trapped. And then I see it, staring me straight in the face. The garbage chute. I pull the handle and it opens easily. I enter head first, am stuck for a moment around the area of the midriff but after a few vigorous wriggles I am able to squeeze through, and then it's glorious free fall, down through the dark sliding narrows. At last I burst through the plastic flap at the bottom of the chute and sail out into the light of day, my arms and legs swimming in the air, as I land in a pile of trash and assorted medical waste – coils of rubber tubing, beakers, syringes, plastic bed pans, indeterminate organ meat, etc.. I climb out of the dumpster, sprint to the wrought iron fence and scale it as if it were no more than a subway turnstile. And then I am off, running like a wild animal into the light of this angelic city.

# CHAPTER 16
*DON*

We had been driving like this for some time. Over the highway of dust, blasted out over the desert. Past signs and unnatural wonders, strange outcroppings of rock, and vast absences, the desert floor dropping out abyssmally beneath our feet. The landscape painted from extra-terrestrial hues. Hot winds blowing and swirling with sand. The desert strewn with dried fur and meat, the sloughed carcasses of cars and drivers in weathered pieces—blown out tires, old shoes, burned out radiators, cigarette packs and beer cans, and everywhere the kinds of animals that thrive out of the murky society of slime, all of them jointed, and armored, and crab-like, even the birds. Here and there the solitary scavengers that pick and claw their way through the dead ocean, monadic as grains of sand. The desert hues the hardest, most impenetrable surfaces, the driest shells and scales, the most insoluble shields. I have found here the greatest integrity of form and single minded desire. A man can travel for miles and miles without blinking an eye, anywhere as good as the next to slip away into the blinding light. The only relief the cool siesta of night.

When I came-to we were still driving like this, blasting out of dawn with the orange sun at our backs. Memories from the night before, haunting me now, foreign places, flashes of light, the cries of the women, and the continuous lash of fire. My companion stared straight ahead, head bobbing to his own impenetrable sounds. I took a good look at him over the top of my sunglasses, which didn't register a bit, just more cool dreamy glances out the passenger side window, the lighting of a cigarette, smoke blown insidiously into the membranes of my eyes. What was there to question? I didn't question it a bit. The same dark sounds crackled from the radio, a haunting collage of voices from distant space, blasts of static, music broken into bits or fused outright, fading in and out. There were a million stations like this up and down the dial. The moment you lost one another came on in its place. In the middle of the night was the best time to hear it, as the sun drowned out the most unconscionable sounds. At night the radio was the landscape. I had to remind myself to keep my eyes focused on the path ahead. It was that easy to forget your place. You could lose it in an instant. There were tricks to keeping your head, keep it from bleeding into the light. Disembodiment was a constant temptation. Lack of discipline didn't fly out here. Then you were just meat. In the desert, the individual was only a figment. On a plane of sand, not a mist or cloud to mediate the burning sun in the sky, I could drive a million miles an hour. The police made unexpected appearances, like specters. The ratios made a certain amount of sport guaranteed. We blasted out over the desert, in the dawn light, the sun at our backs like the burning eye, delivering us from the night. The radio sounds died down. Sun up and your brain went quiet, everything turned inside-out.

# CHAPTER 17
*DON*

The strange thing was, as darkness became dawn and the sun rose up on the horizon, taking its place in the morning sky, the moon stayed out right beside it, and nearly as bright. I had never seen this before and couldn't imagine how it could happen. Maybe it was an illusion created by an unusual quality of the air, a rare diffusion of light. The impression was of having two suns, side by side. And then all at once the moon went out like a light. I knew what I had seen was the rarest of signs, an eclipse of the third kind. If I had so much as blinked I'm sure I would have missed it. As the darkness filtered out, up there, somehow the moon lost none of its light. The question was, did it come from the sun, or was there something even bigger looming up behind, even if just for an instant?

Juan had come to during the night but was still a little dazed. He hadn't said a word the entire drive and showed no expression of any kind. When I asked him if he had seen what I had just seen he just looked off into the distance.

"It was really something," I said. "I couldn't believe my eyes."

Finally he turned his head to look at me. I had been staring at him for some time now, and I could tell, even though he wore the same impenetrable dark shades, that his eyes were very wide indeed.

"That's right," I said, more to myself, as I brought my

attention back to the desert. "That's how it is now."

I picked up the binoculars and started scanning the horizon for the cactus the woman had mentioned. There were actually quite a few of them about, this being the desert. I assumed, since the girl hadn't given me any kind of description, it would be obvious when we came across it. I began looking for unusual features, strange tumorous growths, twisted bifurcations, a lizard perched on a shoulder blade, the meaty corsage of the desert flower. Anything that suggested the human form, or corpse for that matter. Maybe it was a cactus that had wilted over, its skin dried and blistered by the sun, vultures forever picking at the decayed flesh.

I handed the binoculars to Juan so that I could get out of my mind for a while. I shut my eyes, pressing my thumb and middle finger up under my sunglasses and massaging the orbs of my eyes. The play of phosphenes behind my eyelids, the easing of tension, served as a welcome relief from the wearying visage of the desert. When at last I opened my eyes, my vision still plagued by lingering sunspots like rings of petrol evaporating on the water, I found Juan handling the binoculars in a curiously disdainful way, holding them out away from himself with a reluctant tilt of the head. At last he held them up to his eyes.

"What the hell, man? I don't see nothing."

"Maybe it's the sunglasses. You might be using too many lenses."

With a shrug he took them off—I had almost forgotten that he had eyes—and made another attempt at peering through the binoculars. Rather nonchalantly, after just a bit, he set them in his lap and put his shades back on. I let it go as long as I could.

"See anything?"

"Yeah, I see it, this fucking cactus. It's smoking a pipe, wearing a big hat."

Before long we came upon the cactus. It must have been the one, because it was wearing a huge sombrero, along with dark sunglasses, a traditional poncho, and a corncob pipe inserted into an obscene looking gash that served as the mouth. I got out of the car and walked over, lowering my sunglasses for a better look. Juan joined me there.

"I was told we're supposed to make an offering."

"You're supposed to give it a drink," said Juan.

109

"What kind of drink?"

"It has to be Mezcal," he said. "Real Mexican Mezcal. But any kind of liquor will do. Just pour it in the pipe then get down on your knees, and wait."

"For what?"

"You know ... *the sign.*"

"How do you know all this? You were pretty far gone when she told us about it."

"Everybody knows it, man."

I was somewhat skeptical, but it seemed harmless enough. After retrieving the Mezcal, I unscrewed the cap and extended it to Juan. He shied away.

"I don't dig that greaser, man."

I shrugged and proceeded to pour about half the bottle down the corn cob pipe. I took a belt for myself then screwed the cap back on. I pulled at my pants and slowly got down on one knee. Just as I was about to remove my sunglasses—I had to squint hard against the intense glare of the sun—I caught a stream of burning liquid dead in the eye. I recognized instantly that it was the very Mezcal I had just poured into this impetuous vegetable. I stood up and wiped the sunglasses on my shirt, and was just about to punch the damned thing in the face when it dawned on me the truly awesome size of the thorns.

"That's a bad sign," said Juan.

"I'm gonna tear the fucking thing apart."

"I don't know, man. I think it might be a bomb."

A bomb? Where the hell did that come from? I turned to him in utter disbelief but the seed had already been planted, the damage had already been done. I patted the dust off the front of my pants, regarding the cactus for a moment, before turning my back on it. The more I thought about it the more sense it made; the fucking thing could be a bomb. Otherwise it would probably have been stripped bare by now.

I returned to the car, but Juan remained, not ready to leave the scene.

"Maybe we should shoot it," he said. "You know, like drive away and shoot it."

"We don't have any guns. And besides, it could be a really big bomb...the car isn't in very good shape. We might not be able to outrun the blast."

"Man, I don't think it's a bomb."

"You're the one who...Forget it. Let's get out of here."

# CHAPTER 18
*DON*


"We need to find a hotel," said Juan. "I want to, you know, lie down and watch TV or something."

We climbed into the car and were soon headed for the two boulders about a half mile away. Limping across the desert like this, in a damaged vehicle, brought to mind the shifting incongruities of a landscape that could seemingly conceal nothing but that never the less couldn't be visualized from one place to the next. Juan kept babbling something about the pearly gates, but there was nothing of the pearl about them, aside from the shape. The two boulders sat upon the desert like huge planetary orbs, not outcroppings so much as distinct specialized organs. We passed between them, measuring ourselves against the timeless, cosmic weight, the hulking forms bearing down on us with the enormity of space, with the colossal weight of the ice age. We spent what seemed an eternity in the eerie calm of their shade, feeling the intensity of the stillness like a pervasive quiet on the brain. At last we traveled beyond them and were once again struck by the light. After a time we came upon a large free standing rock, not appearing unusual at first, until we were right up on it; it was truly a remarkable thing to see, like an image out of the comics, a true colossus, broad at the top and tapering to an impossibly narrow base. I got out of the car and walked up to it.

"Nothing to be afraid of," I said. "A true rock of ages."

"That thing is gonna fucking kill you, man," Juan opined, rolling down his window then rolling it back up again.

"It's a lot safer than you think. It's been standing here like this for eons. You couldn't knock it over with a tank."

But Juan would have none of it and kept pointing agitatedly at something over my head. I looked up, shielding my eyes from the sun, and indeed there appeared to be some letters etched up there above me in the rock. I made out an I, a K, an L, a U, an R, a K. Squinting hard against the sun, I backed up to get a better perspective and read the whole thing out loud—"I ... KILL ... YOU... ROCK"—then turned around to see what Juan made of it, but now he was gesticulating wildly, with a crazed look in his eyes. I turned back around, staring up into the sun, and was overcome with the disorienting, mind altering sense that I was falling over backward, but within an instant I got my bearings and the whole scene came into lightning relief, that it was not I who was falling over but that the great rock was now very rapidly—where at first it must have been only teetering—falling over onto me.

In a desperate lunge, I dove over the hood of the car, feeling myself propelled by the shock waves from the brutal collision of rock and earth that threatened to close the gap for good and forever seal my fate. How long would my luck hold out, I thought, as I tumbled head first over the hood of the car (catching a glimpse of Juan as he regarded with unflinching cool the immense wall of rock mere inches from his face) and going into a shoulder roll through the cloud of dust settling around the car.

Without a moment's hesitation I rose to my feet and climbed onto the roof of the car and then, having found a foothold, mounted the bloated corpse of the rock. This was undoubtedly the rock that was spoken of by the girl at the camp. Following her instructions, I looked to where the sun set over a distant mountain peak.

We navigated through a seemingly endless maze of obstructions before finding open desert. The mountain continued to loom up in the distance, and I couldn't help noticing, as we drew nearer, the thin stream of smoke rising from the peak like a rope from the heavens, and I was reminded of what the girl had said about a lake of fire at the top. At the time, I had dismissed the story out of hand. It was possible the mountain was an active volcano. That would make sense. A crater of molten lava forever breathing its promise of disaster out into the air. A sleeping, destructive giant, this lazy, wispy sign of its heat the only way you knew it was still alive. Best case scenario, it was some kind of hot springs, just good pure steam. A fantasy, I knew. If paradise lay anywhere on my map it was somewhere far behind, no longer even a memory. I knew the lands I was headed for were a hell of a long way down.

# CHAPTER 19
## FREDERICK M. BARCLAY

As I lay down, I remembered thinking that I would only close my eyes for a moment. I was all of a sudden so tired, and no matter which way I turned everything looked the same. No matter how hard I tried, no matter how intensely I stared, I couldn't see my way through the thicket of branches and leaves to the clearing that surely waited beyond. I couldn't even be sure how long I'd been out here—five minutes? five hours?—wandering aimlessly through these dark woods, frustrated, disoriented and suddenly very tired. The path I'd taken on the way in had seemed so ineffable, but even as I attempted to backtrack I discovered that the trail I'd haphazardly navigated through the tall timber and uncommonly thick undergrowth had evaporated like jet vapor. Some time later, I awoke to find myself being molested by a trio of assailants—their hands were all over me, searching every pocket and crease. The one in the paper Burger King crown—a black kid with yellowed dope-glazed eyes—was going through my wallet, while the other two—a white kid with huge furry sunglasses and skin tight jaguar print pants and a slinky Russian woman with unusually prominent canines and a fur coat that made her look like a Siberian husky—searched my pockets.

"There's nothing in here," complained the Burger King hipster bitterly as he folded the wallet and dropped it on my chest.

"Somebody's coming," the girl said, in thick Russian model timbre.

The trio quickly disappeared through the branches, and a moment later I found another face staring down at me, that of renowned filmmaker Jack Dante.

"Jack," he said, reaching down and taking my hand. "Jack Dante."

"Of course I recognize you," I said, as he pulled me to my feet. "You're one of the greatest living filmmakers."

"Am I still alive? I question that," he said. "I question it every day. More and more, I wander around this city like a ghost."

"We actually met, years back, through a mutual friend. Sherrill Sutcliffe."

"Julian?"

"Fred Barclay," I said. "The writer."

"Any friend of Sherrill's," he said, shaking my hand. "Great fun, that one. Easier to spread than I Can't Believe It's Not Butter."

"I wouldn't know," I said. "I was on my way to the party. I must have gotten lost."

"You're lucky I found you. This is the wrong property. Besides, you can't sneak in through the woods anymore. They're patrolled by huge white Dobermans. Everybody knows that."

"How did you find me?" I asked.

"I just came in here to shoot up and heard all the moaning. Another minute or two those kids would have stripped you naked. It happens all the time," he said. "What are you on, if you don't mind my asking?"

"Not a thing," I said. "I had a few glasses of white wine, but that was earlier."

"What establishment?"

"It was an open house. Over in Beverly Hills."

"One of Sarkasian's?" he said.

"How did you know?"

"Recently he's started poisoning the freeloaders who show up for the complimentary wine and canapé sandwiches. Probably slipped you a roophie. Same thing happened to me. I came-to just as a couple kids were throwing my ass into a dumpster behind Ralphs."

"Someone could get killed. Or worse," I said.

"You could have been raped," he said.

"By Sarkasian?" I said.

"You're not his type. He likes the young ones. Don't worry, I got your back. Just try to keep your head straight."

"Where are we going?" I said, as he led me through the woods.

"I know a short cut," he said.

A short time later, we emerged onto a quiet lane that we followed until reaching an imposing iron gate. On the brick wall adjacent to the gate was the gilded inscription: "There are things known, and there are things unknown, and in between are the doors of perception." And then right next to it, spray painted in red: "You know where you are. You're in the jungle baby. You're gonna die! In the jungle. Welcome to the jungle. Watch it bring you to your shun n,n,n,n,n,n,n,n,n,n,n,n -"

"Ominous," I said.

"One 'n' short," he said, tracing the final n. "Still fresh."

"He rubbed the red inky substance between his thumb and forefinger.

"Is that blood?" I said.

"Probably never saw it coming. Black jack to the back of the head, chloroform gag, then hauled away without anybody hearing a thing. It'll be gone by morning, without a trace. A shame, really."

"How do we enter?" I said.

He pushed, and the huge gate swung inward. Dante smiled, then proceeded through. The gate opened onto a vast lawn filled with marble sculpture of the nude, neo-classical variety, elaborate topiary, a Japanese water feature and a surprisingly anxious assortment of would-be revelers. On the crest of the hill, set behind a half-ring of water at the back of the property, was the infamous mansion. We stood next to a modest carriage house that afforded a splendid view of the environs.

"I hadn't thought it would be so easy to get in," I confided.

"We're not there yet," said Dante. "See that raft?"

On the bank of the moat (there was no better word), near the madding revelers, was a full size Venetian gondola. The gondolier, an exceptionally tall African-American in full cap-scarf regalia, stood at the bow, resting against his pole.

"Stick with me and keep your mouth shut," said Dante, as we proceeded toward the house.

As we moved through the throng of party-goers and for the first time got close enough to see their faces, I was struck by the expressions of melancholy and desperation. Although they were uniformly poised and good looking, nattily attired in their laconic Tinseltown night-finery, there was something of the face-pressed-against-the-window look about them. As if they had given up all hope.

Dante addressed the gondolier: "Caron, my man," he said, extending his hand.

The gondolier warily gripped his hand, giving Dante a solid bro shake.

"It's kinda tricky, so I'll spell it out for you—K. A. H. N."

Dante rapped me on the chest with the back of his hand.

"Lot of people think it's CONN or COHN or CAAN. Nobody gets it right."

The gondolier's eyes went up and down the list.

"Mr. Kahn plus one," he said, at last flashing a big smile. "Welcome aboard."

Dante and I took our seats in the gondola, and a moment later, we were gliding across the water.

"I use that one whenever I'm on this side of the pond. Sal Kahn. The name is like a skeleton key to every velvet rope shindig in town. Khan's notorious for getting his name on all the lists and never showing up. Unless you do business with him you probably have no idea what he looks like. These gatekeepers have no clue."

"I'm surprised a director of your stature has trouble with gatekeepers," I said.

"Nobody recognizes me in the states. And Nero makes a point of accidentally leaving me off the guest list. Of course, he understands if I were on the list I'd never bother to show up. It's good sport really."

Back on the shore we'd just left, there was a sudden commotion, as revelers ran and twirled about the lawn, screaming and waving their hands above their heads, as if trying to ward off some invisible attacker.

"Are they possessed?" I asked.

"Bees," said Dante, matter of factly. "Africanized Bees, to be precise."

"The most dangerous kind. They kill dozens of people every

118

year," I said.

"These bees are professionals," said Dante. "They played the killer bees from *Attack of the Drones 3D*. Everybody knows they're harmless."

I looked around to the other faces onboard. They showed no reaction. Interestingly, my fellow passengers seemed even more miserable than those left on shore.

I had no recollection of reaching the other side of the pond. When I woke up, I was lying on an abundant black velour divan with the brim of my hat pulled down over my eyes. In my state of semi-conscious limbo, I watched Dante work the room (adorned with a multitude of black Velvet Elvis paintings), moving from group to group, shaking hands, slapping backs, making introductions and telling loud stories. My recent arousal and transition from a recumbent to a seated position caused nary a raised eyebrow, as one group after another swirled gaily around my leaden form, seemingly oblivious to my unfortunate predicament. So, it was with a welcome lack of self-consciousness that I finally rose to my feet and unobtrusively joined Dante and his circle of acquaintances, who ranged in age from early 20s to middle age and who were all strangely familiar, like youthful photographs of dead relatives.

"As I was telling Fred here earlier," he said, working me seamlessly into the conversation. "You gotta keep hustling. You never know when your time will come. It could be tomorrow. It could be twenty years. In this business there are second acts galore. Third acts. Fourth acts. Even after you kick the bucket, they'll bring your ass back from the dead."

"Has anyone seen Tony Billings?" I said.

"Earlier," said a buxom red headed woman in her 50s.

"He went that way," said the silver haired gent with over-large teeth, nodding toward a doorway across the room.

"You know him?" said a red headed boy-man of indeterminate age.

"We have a bit of a history together," I said.

"To eternal youth," said Dante.

The group raised their glasses to us as Dante and I walked away.

"They were all vaguely familiar," I said. "But I couldn't quite place them."

119

"Former child actors," said Dante. "Doomed from the start."

"What about the doorman?" I said, as we approached the threshold.

A muscular young man in black t-shirt and chinos hovered in front of the doorway. He had a military style hairdo and wore a transmitter in his ear, with the wire running down his neck into the tee.

"This one's easy," said Dante. "Just look straight ahead. Don't make eye contact."

The doorman eye-checked us as we approached. Dante gave him a quick flip-nod and proceeded through the doorway. As instructed, I stared straight ahead, my expression as immutable as stone. Having made it through without issue, we walked down a short spiral staircase then around the corner, ducking our heads as we entered the room, which was brightly lit and done almost entirely in red, from the padded leather walls to the low hanging plaster ceiling to the hardwood floor. Once inside, we were able to straighten up somewhat, but not much due to the low ceiling. In the near corner of the room, a Karaoke machine played the music from the Madonna song *Papa Don't Preach*, while a young Japanese female dressed in a Catholic school girls' uniform of black and white check skirt, white Oxford shirt, sang the lyrics in an exuberant chirpy voice, kicking her bare legs into the air and shaking her petite derriere to the beat. I recognized the girl as an actress from a popular TV show. On the show, she played fourteen or fifteen, although her real age was anyone's guess. Arranged around the girl was a small audience of well dressed Japanese money-men and creative types. From the posture of the men, heads awkwardly twisted, bodies hewing toward the far wall, it appeared as if they had been on their way somewhere else and had just paused a moment to take a look. Not one of the men faced the girl directly, and there was a good half a room of empty space between the performer and her audience. One of the men, the director Takio Kashugiro, dressed in a tapered black jacket and skinny black tie, taut sculpted face framed by black rimmed glasses, stood with his feet and body facing the far door, his head turned sharply in the direction of the girl. He observed her with an almost insidious level of concentration, his eyes never blinking, never straying from the girl. At regular intervals, he raised the cigarette to his lips and took a measured drag, the only outward sign that he was even alive. Dante and I held back for a few minutes to get the lay of the room. The entire time we stood there, nobody moved, nobody talked. Even though they were arranged together in a group, the onlookers appeared to be going in different directions. The room could have been a busy street corner near Shinjuku Station. The only thing that held them together was the girl. The moment she stopped, you got the feeling they'd scatter like shrapnel from a blast. But she never stopped, the song kept repeating in an infinite loop.

As we made our way across the room, toward the far door, we walked over their frozen shadows like engrams from Hiroshima. I could feel the heat of the blast half a world and half a century away. It felt like empty space. Walking past Takio, I stared into his eyes. We'd met a number of times before. I'd even interviewed him for *Premiere Magazine*.

I stopped and took out a cigarette.

"Got a light?" I asked.

No response.

I fished around in my pockets until I found my lighter, then brought the flame to the tip of the cigarette, inhaling deeply.

"Have you seen Tony?" I said. "I think I must have just missed him. Supposedly he's around here somewhere."

Again, nothing. No sign of recognition, no change in expression. The eyes went straight through me. He raised the cigarette to his lips, took a drag, and blew smoke straight into my face.

"I'm doing a piece about the Scorched Earth project," I said. "Very hush hush. Supposedly a lot of Japanese money in it."

Again getting no response, I turned my head to observe the performance. The girl threw her arm up into the air, twirled around and sang (for what seemed like the 90th time) in her perky cheerleader's voice: "I've made up my mind, I'm keeping my baby."

"However this turns out, I want you to know how much I admire your work," I told Dante. "I was disconsolate when I heard the news about the abortion of the *Walkabout* remake."

"Still birth more like it. Picture was dead on the vine. We spent years in development, took a crew all the way down to the Outback. For what? So the bean counters could turn it into a bloody cartoon?"

"I rather liked some of the embellishments, I admit."

"It was a remake of *Walkabout*. Walk. Get it? By the time we started shooting it was Tony fucking Billings and his Aborigine sidekick riding around the Outback in a fucking vintage muscle car looking for an undetonated nuclear bomb from World War 2."

"I understand the school girl from the original was replaced by twin prostitutes," I said.

"It was a fucking joke," muttered Dante, shaking his head.

I looked around at the frozen Japanese faces.

"This isn't my scene," I said. "Besides, it doesn't sound like anyone's seen Tony."

"I heard we just missed him," said Dante.

"From whom?" I said, quickly scanning the statue-like faces.

"I heard," said Dante. "I got my sources. He was just here."

"What happened to him?"

"He already made his way inside."

"Then let's blow this joint," I said.

"Sure, sure," said Dante. "But it's gonna be tricky."

He nodded toward the huge sumo wrestler seated in front of the exit.

"Somehow we've gotta get Tiny away from the door."

Against the far wall, next to the sumo wrestler, was a table with all manner of hors d'oeuvres—smoked eel and flying fish roe sushi, various unrecognizable pickled vegetables, some gelatinous morsels wrapped in seaweed—and several bottles of artisanal American whiskey.

We hung around the table, snacking on the hors d'oeuvres and drinking liberally of the whiskey.

"What's the plan?" I said.

"Eventually he'll have to get up to use the bathroom," said Dante.

"The man looks like he has a bladder the size of a zeppelin," I said.

"You got a better idea?" said Dante.

Suddenly, the room began to shake violently. Chandeliers swayed. Whiskey bottles and rocks glasses leaped from the buffet table and crashed to the floor, followed by a cascade of ice cubes, bouncing on the hard wood. I had to crouch to keep my balance, as wave after wave of solid matter rolled under my feet.

The girl abruptly stopped singing, raised her hands to either side of her face and shrieked: "Godzilla! Godzilla!"

"Sweet Jesus," the wrestler said, in a voice that was surprisingly soft and sweet (for a man of his not inconsiderable size), and not at all Japanese sounding.

As the man dove for cover under the hors d'oeuvres table, his massive shoulders undercut my legs (even as this was happening, I couldn't help notice that the girl's admirers hadn't so much as budged, remaining entirely frozen and transfixed by her terrified display, until, all at once, they collapsed like bowling pins), sending me flying backward through the doorway and tumbling down several flights of stairs. The next thing I remember seeing, as I looked up, were Dante's legs as he stepped over me and into the next room.

"Come on, pull yourself together, Barclay," I heard him say as he sauntered nonchalantly into the room. "This is where it's really happening."

Bodies in jumbles, on love seats, on the floor—everybody in the room was laughing as they tried to pick themselves back up.

"Had to be a 7.0," said record exec Gordon Lane.

"6.7, 6.8 tops," said Ira Newberg, the VP of production over at Reliant.

Talk show host Brenda Toffer looked into the mirror in her compact and blandly patted her cheeks with blush. Up and coming game show host Adam Lesher was still on the floor, his body convulsing with laughter.

"I don't think I can get up," he said.

"What happened to my drink?" said stand up comic Hugh Doyle, on hands and knees feeling blindly around the floor.

"You should be more concerned about your glasses," said veteran publicist Shelley Lang, as she kicked them halfway across the room.

"Of course, why would I want to?" said Lesher. "When I've got this dog's-eye view of Natalie's plum panties."

"Close as you're ever gonna get," said auburn haired soap actress Natalie Hardaway as she crossed her legs, and took a drag on her cigarette. "Unless, of course, you can shoot off your prick."

"Here it is," said Doyle, as he lowered his head and began lapping at the puddle of whiskey on the floor.

"That's what I love about the Irish," said Lane. "Never waste a drop."

"My people have been through famine," said Doyle. "You don't know what it's like to suffer."

"He's not even real Irish," said Natalie. "He's half-Polack or something."

"Can I buy you a drink?" said Lane.

"How bout you let me finish this one first?" she said, applying mascara to her eyelashes.

"I might have sobered up too much by then," said Lane.

"What's a matter, Lane? You run outta little chickens to chase around the copy machine?" said Natalie.

"Every once in a while a man wants something a little more sophisticated."

"One thing nobody ever called me was sophisticated," said Brenda, blowing on her fingernails.

"Who's the kitty kat?" said Natalie.

The girl—a slinky Asian chick with an innocent smile and alert eyes—was perched on the end of the couch, with her legs crossed in a silk party dress, a shiny little red thing that wrapped her like the casing on a stick of dynamite.

"Must be from another planet," said Brenda. "I haven't seen her around."

"Hot as a pistol," said Lane.

The girl had long black bangs that fell into her eyes, and she smoked a thin white cigarette from a long black vintage 1960s cigarette holder, like the one Audrey Hepburn used in *Breakfast At Tiffany's*.

As they talked in front of her, she stared straight at them, with the cigarette holder resting in the corner of her mouth, taking frequent short puffs, and letting the smoke curl from her nostrils like one of those sultry Far East dragons. Lesher picked up an LP, blew the dust off, then flipped it over and set it on the turntable. Cool syncopated sax blew from the sound system.

"I fucking love the sound of vinyl," he said. "It's so goddamn lush, like listening to heroin."

"I'm Suzy," said the girl at last.

"And what do you do, Suzy?" said Natalie.

"I make ceramics," she said, as she licked an orange popsicle.

"With those fine little hands," said Natalie.

"What kind of ceramics?" said Doyle.

124

"Little discs," said Suzy, making a ring with her fingers. "They are called superconductors."

"Oh well," said Natalie.

Suzy's long painted nails clacked a sine-wave along the cigarette holder as she took a puff.

"Do you know any tricks?" said Natalie.

"Don't scare the poor girl," said Lesher.

"One," said Suzy. "I can eat more than a man."

"I bet she hasn't eaten a thing all day," said Brenda. "She's probably starving."

Dante and I were seated in a pair of leather easy chairs in front of the blazing orange artificial fire. I held a cigar in one hand, while slowly swirling a snifter of Grand Marnier in the other.

I took a seat across from the girl. There was nothing between us but the lustrous tiger maple coffee table and an iceberg of tension, which I quickly melted by offering my hand. She settled back into the sofa, slipping her bare foot from the high heel shoe then extending the deliciously arched foot over the table. I took the foot—perfumed and immaculately pedicured—in my comparatively ogreish hand, then leaned over the table and gave it a gentlemanly kiss.

"There's nothing to eat in here except paté," said Lane, setting a couple tins on the table. "What I'd do for a cocktail weiner."

"What haven't you done?" said Natalie.

"I can tell you have a good appetite," Suzy said to me in a delighted tone, rolling the cigarette holder sensually between her lips.

"I must admit to a considerable appetite," I said. "Carnal and otherwise."

"I've heard your name before," she said.

"You've no doubt read my work in the finer pop culture rags—*Esquire, Interview, Vanity Fair* -"

"Frederick Barclay. I remember now," she said. "The name that came to me through the Ouija board."

"I'm afraid that's impossible," I said.

"It was you. I feel same energy," she said.

"I am very much of the here and now, I assure you," I said.

"I think she's calling you a has-been, Barclay," said Lane.

"Some future self? Or maybe just lost soul," she said. "Searching for ... I do not remember. Tony. That was the name. Yes, Tony Billings."

"She's onto you, kid," said Dante.

"Tony B," said Lesher, snapping his fingers. "He was just here a second ago. Hit me up for a smoke."

"Everybody wants Tony," said Brenda, outlining her decadent rictus in in a thick smear of burnt ochre lipstick.

Lesher draped his arm over Natalie's shoulders.

"That better be a mink stole," she said, coolly. "Or Arctic fox."

"Ouch," Lesher said, lifting the arm, then blowing on his hand and shaking it out. "And here I thought you girls needed a little warming up."

"They think because they've been with all those daddy humping little girls they know something about women," said Brenda.

"They know about women like a stock broker knows about pork bellies," said Natalie. "Ticker tape on the killing floor."

"You a ringer, baby?" said Doyle, giving Suzy a nod.

"I am not a bell," said Suzy brightly as she swallowed the rest of the popsicle, leaving a naked stick.

"I bet she's rung a few."

"Look at them slobbering all over her," said Brenda.

"Men think everything's a metaphor for sex," said Natalie. "A girl licks a lollipop they got a hard on."

"I've always had considerable skill in that department, or so I've been told," said Brenda.

"Why don't you give us a little demonstration?" said Lesher, tossing her the ornamental gourd.

She held it with the bulbous end resting in both hands and raised it up to her mouth, where she considered it for a moment before sliding her lips over the small knotted tip. She worked the tip for a while, sliding her lips up and down in a sensual yet dignified manner, letting the tip slip out now and again and curling her tongue around it. I had to admit, I felt my own juices stirring yet again, and not just the ones in my mouth. Finally, she slid her lips all the way down, then withdrew slowly, running her lips back down the shaft and applying them to the bulbous root, applying the most exquisitely wet pressure. And then it was mercifully, achingly over.

There was a kind of swooning, relieved, applause. Brenda bowed her head, smiled elegantly, wiping the gourd on a kerchief and handing it to Suzy.

"I apologize about the lipstick," she said.

"Tastes like tangerine," said Suzy, already darting her tongue over the gourd and smiling favorably.

After a few more exploratory licks, she tilted her head back, lowered the not insubstantial gourd to her mouth and made it disappear.

"All gone," she said.

"You really are talented, aren't you," said Brenda.

I turned to Lane.

"You mentioned you'd seen Tony," I said.

"Through that doorway and down the hall."

My eyes followed his. In front of the door were three massive white Dobermans, sitting side by side, their erect pointed ears twitching alertly.

I strode nonchalantly toward the door and was about to sail through when it stopped me cold, the sound of the three hell hounds growling in unison, like an unholy choir. They were staring right at me, ears lowered, canines bared. Slowly, without making eye contact for fear of provoking an attack, I retreated back into the party.

"What are you gonna do for an encore, baby?" said Lane.

"Dessert," Suzy said, smiling sweetly.

She opened her purse, reached in and began to pull out what I at first mistook for an earth worm—this was revolting enough—and turned out to be the thin naked tail of a very live white rat. She dangled the wriggling vermin over her gaping mouth, lowering in first the head, then the forelegs and before long she'd swallowed the entire animal, slurping down the naked pink tail like a limp noodle.

"I think I'm gonna be sick," said Doyle, clapping vigorously, his face overcome by a wearied nauseated expression.

"I tell ya, I'm in love, really and truly," said Lane. "Chick is a grade A carnival freak."

"Those are Shutzhund-trained attack dogs," said Dante. "You try to go through there, they'll rip you to pieces."

"I have an idea," I said.

I picked up one of the open cans of paté and rolled it out so that it circled around and came to rest right under their noses.

"These animals are in work mode, the only thing they're

gonna eat are your nuts."

For a second it looked like nothing was going to happen, and then all hell broke loose as the dogs pounced on the can at once, their furiously writhing bodies becoming embroiled in a whirlwind of fur, saliva and gnashing teeth.

As we eased past the dogs, out of the corner of my eye I caught sight of Suzy's final trick. She was pulling something from her mouth, it just kept coming and coming, unbelievably, until her arm fully extended over her head and I could see quite clearly the head of a very live snake emerging from her mouth, and stuffed into the snake's own mouth was the white rat, with only the tail and legs visible. Suzy very calmly pried the snake's jaws open, removed the rat, which appeared no worse for wear, and dropped it safely back into her purse.

The onlookers were at first stunned silent, and then practically apoplectic.

"What are you?" said Doyle.

"I am a magic hat." said Suzy.

"What's that mean?" said Lesher.

"It means she's pregnant," I heard Brenda say through the terrifying din of the battling guard dogs.

From the sound, one would have thought the hounds were ripping each other to pieces. Perhaps because of their good training, and despite the exaggerated display, they appeared, at least thus far, to be inflicting no real damage. It was the simplest thing in the world to slip past this violent whirlwind of flying fur and gnashing teeth and out of the room. We were fortunate, I couldn't help thinking, that deep down the dogs were not, despite all their expensive training, true professionals after all.

# CHAPTER 20

Blow sat in the bath. The lights were set low, and a scented candle burned on the faux-marble counter. The scent was Rosemary, with a note of Eucalyptus. Blow had been in the tub for over a half hour. As the water turned lukewarm, he unplugged the drain and let the hot water run until the temperature came back up. Often when he practiced his pitch, he performed it in front of the mirror. The technique allowed him to focus on his expression and body language. He'd also been practicing visualization—seeing himself in the situation and imagining how his audience would respond. He found the practice relaxing and felt that it somehow gave him an element of control over the outcome, as if he were getting into the heads of the agents and moneymen and pulling their strings for once, tinkering with destiny.

The warmth of the water, the low lights, the jazz playing softly in the other room, the feeling of weightlessness, allowed him to sink deeply into these imaginings and to stay there for a long time, running through the script again and again until it had the weight of reality, sometimes for well over an hour, while the candle burned down to a limp flame swaying over a pool of molten wax. His chin rested on the water. His eyes were open. His lips moved, repeating the line over and over. By this point, he had the pitch down cold, and could give a flawless rendering any time, on a moment's notice, without thinking about it. The pitch was like a part in a play learned in grade school and never forgotten, the part of him that ran on autopilot. There were all these characters—versions of Blow—that could be called upon to come out and perform their part while the authentic Blow stepped back and watched it all play out. A lot of actors had scores of these characters, and in some cases Blow had found that the characters were more real than the individual, who frequently seemed withdrawn and neurotic, a hollow shell without a part to play. Blow had his own share of neuroses but was more or less comfortable in his own skin. Lately, he had been touched by an anxiety that at first he had trouble understanding, until he traced it back to the day of the unfortunate supernovaing of Terry Banner's head.

Blow had seen on television that many children who stuttered had mothers who overcorrected their speech. Lately, Blow had had dreams that his voice wouldn't come out and these dreams had begun to haunt him during the waking day. He'd practiced the pitch so thoroughly that there was no question about a perfect delivery. Still, the anxiety remained. That's when he hit upon the idea of developing a way to transition into the pitch. The thing about the pitch, it was so heavy, so ironclad, you dropped it in the middle of a conversation and it sucked the air out of the room. He needed something that would bridge that gap, allowing him to move seamlessly from whatever bull shit they were talking about to the actual pitch the same way you could, apropos of nothing, lean into a woman to remark on her perfume, establishing the closeness that would lead to a kiss and then the fire storm that followed. The answer seemed obvious once he'd thought of it. Just bring up sports. Wait for a break in the conversation and drop a remark about last night's game, like, *did you catch the game last night?* Before anyone has a chance to respond, start describing what happened at the game, only what you're describing, shot-by-shot, is not the game at all, but the first scene of the movie, which happens to be set at the Staples Center at the end of a Lakers game. Once they're hooked, delivering the rest of the pitch is easy: the usual star-crossed lovers from opposite sides of the tracks, with a twist. This was insurance. This was the key to the lock box that was crushing under an ocean of anxiety. The pitch had become a demon that had to be exorcised. He felt the tension in every bone, like an unreachable itch.

Blow continued to run through the entire sequence, connecting the dots in his mind—A to B, B to C...Like the characters recalled from childhood, when the time came he would step back and let the pitch take over. The beauty of it was it could be injected anywhere. It was simply a matter of timing, controlled breathing, measuring the beats of the conversation and picking the right moment to join in, like an improvisational jazz player searching the air for a score that wasn't there.

The phone rang. It was on the side of the tub. Blow let it ring another time and answered it. A man's voice, Teddy Cruz.

"What's up?" said Blow.

"I'm on Ventura Boulevard," said Cruz. "On the way to that restaurant by the theater. That Italian place, Il Piccolo or something. They should be wrapping up now."

"Which one was that again?"

"The Chekov number," said Cruz. "The Seagull. Tara went. Everybody's heading over to the restaurant. Meet up with us. The wine list is killer."

"Not tonight," said Blow.

"What you got going on? Are you going to call that chick from ICM again?"

"I'm working on my pitch," said Blow.

"Tomorrow's the big show—part deux. Now we're talking."

"I've got it all worked out," said Blow.

"Lay it on me," said Cruz. "Let me hear your rap."

"The whole thing?"

"Just the lead-in. Say I'm talkin' up a blue streak, a whole bunch of random shit, and you jump in. I'm Nero and I'm going on about Zen Buddhism, Tai Chi, Transcendental Meditation. This morning I woke up. It was 5:00 am. I went out into the garden as the first light of dawn spilled out over the tops of the hedgerows. I assumed the lotus position, closing my eyes and taking long deep breaths. The gardener came around and poured a bucket of water on my head. I was so at one with the universe, he thought I was a fuckin' plant..."

"I caught the end of the Lakers game last night," said Blow.

"Listen to my homeboy dropping science," said Cruz.

"There was a shot outside the arena, all these people streaming out onto the sidewalk, this mad rush to get out of there,

10,000 people, and in the middle of it there's one guy walking against it, straight toward the camera, and then he passes it by—he's stone cold, in a jacket and sunglasses, and he just passes the camera by, without even a glance. And that's when I got it, I mean, I had the whole arc, three acts and a logline, but that's when it all came together, the opening scene, he's wearing a tan blazer with a black t-shirt underneath, walking against the tide of people, until he's right on top of us, and then the camera flashes forward. He opens the door to the skybox and goes inside. The camera stays on the closed door a beat. Jump cut—the door opens, our man emerges into the river of people; a moment later he's lost, swept away. We're in the middle of the arena; the fans are filing up the aisles on their way to the exits. The camera suddenly zooms on the skybox clear across the arena and then accelerates and freezes on the body, a middle age man with a bald spot wearing a pink designer t-shirt, hanging halfway over the rail, a spot of blood expanding on his back. Someone below looks up and sees him. Suddenly everybody is looking up at the body. Out front, the man gets into a white Mercedes AMG. There's a gorgeous blonde behind the wheel—'So where are you taking me?' The man pulls two tickets out of his breast pocket. 'The Joel Scott gig.' The girl lights up and falls into his arms. As flames leap from the exits, the big white Mercedes is off like a shot...That's it."

"They'll never see it coming," said Cruz. "One minute you're talking about the Lakers game, the next you're right into the pitch."

"It'll get me from point A to point B," said Blow.

"Isn't that what they always say, speed is power?"

"I see the whole thing playing out in my head."

"Like a chess player. You're looking ten moves ahead. Just tell me, why'd he shoot him?"

"The man who dies is a big time land developer, and he's the only one who knows the secret about what's happening out in the desert."

Blow was getting another call.

"Hold on a second."

He pressed the button and took the call.

"Hey."

"What are you doing?"

It was a woman's voice.

"Hold on a second."

He pressed the button.

"I gotta run. Sara."

"Later," said Cruz.

He disconnected from Cuz.

"What are you doing?" she said.

"I'm in the tub."

"That sounds relaxing."

"Not exactly."

"Working?"

"I'm practicing my pitch."

"That thing you were talking about."

"Tomorrow."

"Let me hear it."

"I'm still ironing a few things out."

"Just tell me. Then you can come over and do lines with me. It's your kind of scene."

"I caught the end of the Lakers game last night..."

# CHAPTER 21

An apartment in Beverly Hills, well-appointed with the usual Mid-Century Modern furnishings, Eames chairs, Noguchi glass-kidney coffee table, George Nelson slat benches. The big screen TV is turned to the pre-game for the Super Bowl. The stands are filled with people. The camera cuts to outside the stadium, thousands of fans streaming in through the gates. Then the channel changes: it's the scene in *Walkabout* where the father drives his children out into the Australian Outback and tries to shoot them before turning the gun on himself. The channel changes back to the pre-game. A female reporter pulls aside a kid in his teens and puts the microphone in front of him.

"Where are you from?"

"Concord," the kid says.

"First trip to the Super Bowl?"

"Yeah."

"Who do you like in today's game?"

"Patriots."

"Who's your favorite player?"

"Brady."

"Is there anybody out there you want to say hello to?"

The boy turns to the camera: blank stare.

"Do you realize how many people are watching you right

now?" the reporter says.

"I don't know," the kid says.

"A billion."

The kid's head explodes.

Sitting on the couch watching the television and talking on the phone is a man in his late twenties, Teddy Cruz. He's wearing a dark blue button down shirt from Barneys and a pair of tan slacks. He has black wavy hair, blown back. A recent issue of *Vanity Fair* lies open on his lap.

"Did you see that? What did she say to him? ... I think they call that the law of large numbers... I don't do that. I've got enough to think about... I'll probably have something to eat first. I've got leftovers from the other night... Squab, with some kind of risotto. A crimini mushroom and cilantro risotto. 16. It just opened a couple months ago... Once or twice with Paul and Dianne and the redhead from the Agency, what's her name? ... Karen...I always miss the kick-off. It's like a tradition, wait, *Walkabout* just came back on. I'm flipping back and forth...The commercials haven't been good in years...Similar to pigeon... How the fuck would I know?...I picked up a pair of Bruno Maglis..."

He lifts his feet up onto the coffee table and stretches out his legs, staring at the shine of the black leather shoes.

"...and a belt...She used to be a model...late 20s, 27, 28...I talked to him a couple days ago...not in a long time...Blow, yeah, I heard his rap... for the most part ... his problem is he's got to be more assertive. He wants to play the cool counter puncher. Sometimes you've got to go on the attack ..."

He listens, cradling the phone against his shoulder. He glances up at the screen now and again to catch the player profiles. There's a scene inside the locker room.

"Without the volume, the whole lead-in lacks tension," he says. "It's like watching an aquarium...almost peaceful...The difference is, they're trying to cast out these Thetans, return you to this pure original state of being. With the System, it's not about returning to this mythical purer self, it's about what you need to get to the next level..."

He hears a call coming in on the other line.

"Let me get this," he says.

He takes the call. A man's voice.

"Did you hear, the police defused a bomb at the Superbowl?"

"What kind of bomb?"

"Atomic."

"You're shittin' me."

"That's what people are saying."

"I'm on with Sara. Let me call you back."

He switches back to Sara.

"That was Ralph. He's in the car on the way over…A case of Cristal. As soon as the clock runs out, we're going to pour it all over everything…He has to have whatever they're having on TV….New Year's all over again…yeah, Ciao."

Cruz picks up the magazine on his lap and resumes reading.

# CHAPTER 22

Article published in *Vanity Fair* magazine, titled: *Eye (I) on Tony Billings* by Frederick M Barclay

The first time I interviewed Tony Billings, many years ago at the sparsely decorated Manhattan flat he shared with a certain aspiring young actress named Sherill Sutcliffe, who happened to be a close friend of mine back from our days with Shakespeare in the Park and who served as liaison in setting up my interview with Tony—the official assignation of which was agreed upon and sealed with a kiss (Sherill—then spelled C.h.e.r.y.l) and a handshake (Tony) at the then little known Midtown eatery Chez Guevara—he (Tony) had just starred in a raw, low-budget film about disaffected Italian-American youth called *American Bambino* for first time director Clay Barlow— whom I had previously met at a fund raiser for Hansen's Disease— and there were musings around town, nay, a veritable rumble, about superstar potential.

Tony's fierce acting style—he was given to frequent bursts of raw emotion (some thought *too* frequent, most notably the writer of *American Bambino*, Dirk Minelli, who threatened to kill Tony on more than one occasion) spitting his lines of dialogue like the cobra spits venom—coupled with undeniable good looks, more James Dean cum youthful Marlboro Man than pretty boy, made him a hot commodity overnight. A lush head of brown hair that when cut short

137

stood on end as if being sucked by a vacuum cleaner couldn't have hurt either. My own hair had begun to recede in high school and to this day whenever I tip my hat I am haunted by the past, even though I am, in all other respects, exceedingly comfortable in my own skin. It is no surprise that I long for the days of Henry Miller, when hats were *de rigueur* and the tonsorially challenged fought on equal terms with the hirsute in the garden of connubial delights. Perhaps my time has come and gone, a faded memory like the brave, worldly literature of that more noble age, an era steeped in the incandescent sweat of boxers, bull fighters and earth shattering sex. (If only I could have gone to the rug with Anais Nin...Ah, the sweet nectar of forbidden fruit.)

We stood, Tony and I, in my living room sipping brandy as Tony admired my piece de resistance, a painting I had done under the influence of Miles Davis, herb cigarettes, too much wine, and, of course, da Vinci—it was a reasonably faithful replica of the Mona Lisa, an example of a ritual I performed, and believed in very strongly, in which by reproducing the great work, stroke by stroke, I hoped to inhabit the genius of the master, that, by retracing his steps, I might gain some rare glimpse of the artist's soul, to crawl, as it were, under his very skin. That is, I assumed he was admiring my work but it was difficult to follow the train of his eyes concealed as they were behind the smoke of dark sunglasses, an affectation of celebrity that Tony took to instinctively upon his matriculation into Hollywood's *creme de la creme*. Can one blame him? After all, the sunglasses, the perfect hair, afternoon shadow like a charcoal painting, and the detached, laconic air—even outright haughty disdain—are their right, just as surely as the scepter and crown are a king's and the Mormon patriarch his bounty of fecund brides.

It was then, after raising his shades and staring ponderously into his empty glass, that he said, "Got any coke?"

Of course I obliged him—that, too, was their right—spilling the last of my coke onto a coffee table book of Braques and forming the lines with my platinum card. Tony leaned over and snorted up the blow through the vacuum cleaner nozzle of a rolled fifty dollar bill (actually it was a five-spot but Tony insisted I exaggerate the value) and the interview finally got the proverbial kick in the hindquarters that it required.

Facing each other in identical antique wicker chairs, I posed my first formal question—that is, "for the record," as there is much dirt kicked around when I get together with Tony and his ilk that must never make it into print—for instance, Tony revealed confidentially that legendary mogul Nero is in fact, as has long been rumored, an embryophage—I asked him what makes him tick as an actor. Staring out the window for a moment, as if searching externally for what can only be found within, he lit a Marlboro Light, inhaled deeply then tilted his head back and blew smoke at my ceiling.

I knew what he meant.

And having, too, developed a thirst for smoke, I lit my own cigarette, an unfiltered Pall Mall, and let the silence, which was, after all, the only *true* language, sink in. Matching him cloud for cloud, our expressions contemplative, even relaxed, yet belying the tension that exists just below the surface and which makes for a great interview, I began to formulate my next question. Tamping my cigarette into the mother o'pearl ash tray, I leaned forward, my words poised at the cusp of my lips, then took pause and retracted my advance. Something had been needling me, and I decided to take issue about it with Tony. At the time of our last meeting I had suggested to him that he might switch to Pall Malls. I considered them a superior cigarette and thought I had convinced him of their virtue. Here he was, however, smoking Marlboro Lights.

"I see you're still smoking Marlboro Lights," I said to him.

He shrugged.

"You didn't like the Pall Malls?"

He winced, took a long drag on the Marlboro Light, and exhaled, and I felt my fists clench. I decided to broach the subject of his increasing reputation as a cocksman, as somewhat of a loose cannon, if you will, or lothario, in the sexual arena.

"I've been with a few girls," he said nonchalantly, a trace of humor in his voice.

"But it's really not fair," I insisted, "this reputation, the insistence by the media to chasten. Have we so soon forgotten the lessons of Gargantua and Pantagruel?"

"I never saw their movies," Tony said, wincing again and blowing a cloud of smoke.

I took a drag on my cigarette, blew a ring of smoke, then another, and ground the butt into the mother o'pearl. Flicking the pack of Pall Malls so that a single cigarette emerged, I extended it to

139

Tony, my eyes widened entreatingly. He winced again, and I blinked, then pursed my lips, eyebrows raised in an expression of *laissez faire* disapproval, and leaned back, withdrawing the cigarette with my lips and lighting it.

Our mutual friend Sherill Sutcliffe was in town working on a project with a certain infamously wiry and perfectionistic director whose vault-like secrecy and pathological fastidiousness had long been a thorn in my side, and I casually dropped her name.

"Yeah, I knew her," Tony said.

"You lived with her, Tony," I reminded him.

He shrugged.

"Personally I have always found her to be one of the most talented young actresses on the screen. Her radiance, professionalism and intelligence are arguably nonpareil in this business, particularly among film actresses, who, though they may dazzle on screen, invariably fail to impress in matters of *tete-a-tete*. Sherill's failure to achieve commercial success is nothing but an indication of a non-supportive, non-artistic industry, of a viewing public without taste or scruples, and, I am ashamed to admit, a media that coddles to and perpetuates the criminal wrong-headedness of both. During my stint with Shakespeare in the Park, Sherill was the lone, bright star in my Sirian night. Her freshness and vitality inspired me to persevere, and I always found in her expression a tolerance, one might even go so far as to say warmth, as I labored over my lines. Iambic pentameter had been like a strange taste in my mouth, like a very tough and resilient piece of fat. True, she possessed a solipsistic streak. What I took for tolerance, for understanding, may have been no more than a kind of profound detachment—whereas she would simply stare off into the distance (the outward looking mask) as I committed dramatic *faux pas*, the others tended to go into diatribe or leave the stage in a huff—they were all homosexual—but accuse me of naiveté, considerate is considerate, motivation be damned."

I concluded with a heavy fist on the arm of my chair. Tony blew smoke and smiled.

"I heard she's gettin' jammed by that human coat hanger," he said.

I put the Pall Mall out on my wrist and grinned oppressively. Tony seemed a little taken aback, his mouth hanging somewhat ajar, his breathing suspended. Then he smiled, as if amused, and continued smoking. To reassure him, I lit my own cigarette and was soon matching him cloud for cloud. Tony and I had been friends for some time, and my admiration of him was unreserved. There were few popular actors capable of delivering the fevered, no-holds-barred performances in films about jet-planes, bar tending, affable big foots, little league hockey—as well as a string of cop-canine buddy pictures—that Tony had managed to do time and again, a yen for craft pushed to the limit in his current project, as yet untitled, about an S.S. officer who reinvents himself as a sherpa.

And then there was the matter of his flawless complexion and rippled abdomen. My own significant girth, a thickness of middle that I had carried with me since boyhood, as well as a full beard that I cultivated originally to mask the bad skin that befell me during the teenage years, were, I believed, contributive to an overall look—the fedora, the beard, my substantial midsection, the horn rimmed glasses—that was well suited to my latter day role as chronicler of the *zeitgeist* for the more rarefied organs of pop cultural *digerant*.

I noticed that Tony was becoming increasingly distracted, and, fearing the complete loss of his attention unless decisive action was taken—in many ways the celebrity, no matter what the age, was like a young child or animal—I tightened the reins, appealing to his youthful vigor and need to be in constant motion, and suggested we go for a ride in my BMW.

"What for?" he replied.

"It's the latest model," I told him. "You will really be amazed. The performance is simply world class."

"I know. I've got one," he said, wincing.

"Is it red?"

"Yeah." He blew smoke.

My fist clenched reflexively, my palms were hot with sweat, and he must have sensed, because his expression suddenly betrayed a twinge of nervousness, the undeniability of my silence and intensity of stare. He dropped his cigarette into the empty brandy snifter—a breach of social grace that one learned to accept when traveling in these circles; their whims must be countenanced, for their egos were quite fragile; the rewards of being cast in their star's glow, however, were commensurately great—then rose from his chair with the characteristic wince and intimated, "I gotta take a leak."

Once in the car I dissuaded Tony from putting on his seat

belt (he would buckle it, I would unbuckle it) with the warning that they did more harm than good as well as with the added assurance of a passenger-side air bag. I was none too certain of the overall veracity of this statement but felt justified nonetheless due to the nobility of my desire to hone an atmosphere of Romantic excess and Kerouacean devil-may-care bravado. I set the bottle of Glenfarclas between my thighs, to which Tony reacted with a suspicious side-stare, and turned the key, bringing the engine to a roaring, big cat-like purr.

We proceeded into the night and within an hour, during the course of which I drank heavily from the bottle of Glen, I found myself whirring along just the kind of winding, ill-lighted country road I had had in mind. Heretofore, nary a word had passed between us, so in the spirit of camaraderie and male-bonding I extended the Glenfarclas to him. He declined rather sheepishly, so I splashed some on his coat and pants then turned out the headlights.

Increasing my speed in anticipation of the blind, hairpin curve that lay up ahead, I stole a glance at Tony, and in his expression of muted terror it was clear he had divined—we were so close and understood each other so well that words were seldom necessary; he simply *knew*, telepathically—that I had decided that, by the stroke of midnight, I would be wearing his skin. The skin of his knees on my knees. His scalp on my scalp.

Having come upon the curve I switched into the inside lane, which was designated for oncoming traffic, in order to minimize the inertia that could perhaps cause us to lose traction and fly from the road, and was immediately set upon by a  pair of opposing high-beams. I swerved instinctively, missing the vehicle—I am unsure of the make but was left with a sense of its being something on the order of a Mac Truck—and smashed through the guardrail, finally coming to rest at the bottom of a ravine.

I looked at my companion, who appeared shaken but not stirred, and suggested since we were relatively unhurt that as a finale to a heated evening of matched wits and virility, a meeting of men characterized by the need to destroy, as well as become, the other, we partake in a physical bout along the lines of the unctuous *au naturel* wrestling match between Oliver Reed and Alan Bates in the film version of Lawrence's *Women in Love*.

Tony limped desperately from the car, but I soon overtook

him, and, saying, "I simply must insist," tackled him so that he lay prone and forlorn, my arms wrapped about his legs.

There is a moment aspired to in the career of every interviewer, a consummation of one's spiritual and occupational odyssey, in which the ultimate revelation about one's subject is achieved, a secret wrapped in a code, a golden nugget of truth that lies just beneath the layers of armor and posturing, beyond persona, which is definitive not only about the individual, but about the entire human condition. Pulling down Tony's pants, I found it, there, illuminated by moonlight on the pale arch of his right buttock: A precisely drawn tattoo of the human heart.

# CHAPTER 23

They were seated around the conference table. Nero was there. Tina and Bax were there. Jerry and Heller were there. Blow was seated across from Nero, between Nick and Jerry. As the others talked, he sat back coolly, taking it all in and nonchalantly injecting his own observations, letting it come to him naturally from all across the table. Heller had his arms behind his head. Nero, the coolest of the lot, so cool he was lukewarm, never did that, never had to reach back to appear relaxed. Nick was in the middle of a story about the premiere the other night, the Tom Langley flick about a Colombian drug lord who finds God in vast cargo holds full of cocaine, something about the purity and the whiteness.

"There were protesters outside," said Nick. "Religious types. I guess I always knew they were around because of the Crystal Cathedral, but somehow I thought that was only for TV."

"L.A. is full of spiritual energy," said Jerry. "It's one of the most spiritual cities in the country."

"More spiritual than Salt Lake City?" said Tina.

"As I remember, the formula had to do with the number of deities, the variety of beliefs, the combined income of priests, monks, yogis, rabbis, witch doctors, the prevalence of transcendental meditation, acupuncture, acupressure, chiropractic, herbal remedies, hippies, psychoactives, tattoo parlors, fortune tellers, annual sales of energy drinks, that sort of thing."

"Atlanta is spiritual. So is North Carolina. Pretty much the whole South. They have churches the size of football stadiums," said Tina.

"Mexico is spiritual," said Bax. "Basically any place in Central or South America."

"Basically, anything south of the Mason-Dixon," said Nick.

"I hear Africa is getting spiritual," said Bax. "First animism, then the whole Catholic thing."

"Think those African cats are going to take to the whole celibacy thing?" said Jerry. "No fucking way."

"Basically, any third world nation," said Blow.

"Any place that's hopeless," said Nick.

"Did you hear about that comet?" said Bax. "I saw something about it last night on all the news channels."

"The one that might hit the planet," said Nick.

"Something like a one in a hundred shot. The thing's on its way," said Bax.

"It's a mile in diameter," said Blow. "Solid crystal core."

"I had a dream last night," said Nero.

All eyes shifted to Nero. The room quieted down.

"It was Oscar night. I was wearing a tuxedo, an Armani. I was wearing a black cowboy hat. Sherill was there but for some reason she wasn't with me at that moment. I was standing by myself on the walk-up to the auditorium. The photographers were on the other side of the velvet ropes, flashbulbs going off like a fireworks display. A procession of beautifully dressed men and women moved past, making their way toward the auditorium. They were all people I had known and worked with, actors and actresses, producers, writers and directors, sound editors, composers. The sun was still out and the air was filled with the sound of shouting fans and beseeching photographers. I gradually became aware of a large form at the entrance to the auditorium. It was still a long way off, but there was something momentous in the slow purposeful movement, the gradual unfurling of what was, I could clearly see, as it drew closer, a giant red carpet. It was easily over ten feet in diameter. Either the other people had already gone inside or they had moved out of the way. The velvet ropes framed a broad path that curved out from the doors of the auditorium. I could see the dense spiral slowly turning down the path, and I became aware that darkness had fallen and there was barely any sound. The carpet continued to roll toward me undiminished. It was now almost upon me, ten feet tall, like a tidal wave rolling toward a desolate South Pacific beach, so close that it drowned out all sound, drowned out everything around it, drowning my memories, my sense of identity, and all I could see was the wall of red rolling in the darkness, over and over and ..."

"Check this out," said Jerry. "You heard this?"

The vibe in the room changed immediately, from glass to hot plastic.

Blow let his eyes move inconspicuously to Nero. As usual he was difficult to read.

"This is the rap I was talking about," said Jerry. "It's going all over town. Get this. You're hearing it here for the first time. Carter just gave me the whole spiel about fifteen minutes ago. So here it is, the whole Lois Lane-Superman set up, a monster riff on the Marvel comics bit."

"Superman's hot," said Tina.

"Lois Lane's hot," said Nick.

"Never like this," said Jerry. "The problem is Clark Kent. Lois can't see the rock hard abs under that three piece suit, but he can see what she's got under that neat little skirt suit and it's driving him out of his mind. After work one day, a group from the *Planet* is down at the corner bar for happy hour, and these people like to drink. Lois has had like six Cosmos. She just had this blow out with her billionaire playboy boyfriend Chance Claiborne. It's really over this time, and for once she's vulnerable. She's slurring her speech and starting to hang on Clark, telling him he's such a nice guy and everything. Ever the gentleman, Clark walks her back home. By the time they get up to her apartment she can barely walk, and he has to carry her to her bed. He sits down on the bed beside her and tries to get her to drink the water. Eventually she sits up and has some of the water, and she seems to be doing a little better. Then as he leans over her to set her alarm, his cheek brushes against a bare tit. When he went to get the water, she must have climbed out of the skirt suit. Her body slides down under him until inevitably their lips meet and Clark finds himself in this wild, passionate lip lock with Lois Lane who's writhing half naked beneath him. By the time he gets his head straight and thinks maybe he should cool things down, his pants are

146

open and he's inside her and she's making all these heavy sounds in that smoky voice of hers. When he finally comprehends what's happening it blows his mind because, you know, he's fucking Lois Lane, and it's like a switch has been thrown or something and he's turned into this animal, no longer Clark Kent or Superman exactly, something completely beyond his understanding. Now they're making wild love all over the apartment. Lois is saying 'Oh Clark...Oh Clark', over and over and somehow she starts to feel a change, a quickening in his breath, but it's more than that. There's something different about him, somehow he's too...*hard*. Her head starts to clear a little, and she says *Clark? Clark?* you know, kind of like *where are you?* because his eyes are closed, and from the expression on his face she knows he's lost, out there, I mean, there's no way to reach him now, and it's like she's seeing him for the very first time. She reaches out and ever so slowly removes the glasses, and when she sees him, without the glasses, and sees the face that she's fantasized about all these years, the face of the man she's worshipped, the face of Superman, for a second she's overcome with emotion. She's making love to Superman. But when she sees that look on his face, a look she knows well, she begins to comprehend what's about to happen next. She's been with some studs before but we're talking super human. *Clark, Clark*, she says, trying to get him to snap out of it..."

Blow became aware of a subtle change in the general mood. There was a mounting tension. He could see it in the faces at the table, a rising redness in the pallor, veins bulging in the neck, throbbing temples. For the first time, Nero was leaning forward in his chair, a look on his face of uncharacteristic intensity, his eyes focused on the middle space, and then Nick put his hand to his forehead.

Jerry continued, "...she can feel the tension mounting, his muscles hardening like iron, his eyes are open, and she thinks just maybe he's trying to tell her something. 'I...' he says. 'I...' as the sweat drips from his forehead. *Clark*, she screams. 'I...' he says. 'I...' But she realizes it's too late as his face contorts and his body goes rigid. 'I...I love you, Lois.' And in her eyes at that moment is an expression of horror at what's about to happen next as she feels his heart race and the spasming followed by a growing sense of fullness like a balloon blowing up fuller and fuller until, finally..."

147

There was a pregnant pause. Blow noticed Nero start to rise from the table. Nick was practically doubled over in his chair. The tension was so thick it felt like the air would shatter.

Jerry took out a pack of cigarettes. He removed a cigarette and lit it. He took a long drag and blew.

"Does anybody mind if I smoke?"

He dropped the pack on the table.

"As I was saying," he said, pausing to take another drag on the cigarette. "As I was saying," he paused again to wave out the match.

"You mind if I have one?" said Blow.

"Help yourself."

Jerry pushed the pack over to him. Blow took out a cigarette and rolled it between his fingers.

"I caught the end of that Lakers game the other night," said Blow.

He put the cigarette between his lips.

Nick blinked, his face suddenly gone slack. Nero leaned back in his chair, almost imperceptibly.

"There was a shot outside the arena," said Blow. "...a tide of humanity washing out onto the street..." He lit the cigarette. "And in the middle of it, there's one man, walking against it."

# CHAPTER 24
*DON*

The engine began to falter. The car gradually, then completely, lost power, and we coasted to a stop. I got out and popped the trunk, taking out one of the ten gallon cans of gas and emptying it into the tank. I threw the empty canister out onto the sand.

The sun fell. We smoked silently to carry us through the night, and when finally the sun came up it shone in the distance, pristine and incendiary, a disconnected product of the imagination, like a mirage on the landscape. Soon we were there, and I drove the big car onto an apron of immaculate black asphalt and honked the horn for service as suggested by a sign hanging between two vintage 1950s pumps. A very well dressed man emerged from the station wearing beige khakis and a crisp white button down shirt (with the name Hans stitched in the front pocket), as well as a wide brimmed straw hat with an Indian band wrapped around it. He had pale white skin and a long face, with a white goatee, and looked to be in his late sixties.

"What can I do for you gentlemen?" he said, wiping his hands on a shop towel.

"We were in a car wreck."

"Will you please open the hood?"

"I'm mainly concerned with the body," I said.

"A doctor asks you to open wide and say 'ah,' even though you think it's just a little something with your body. Please indulge me."

I obliged him and popped the hood. As I did so, he began circling the car.

"Do you know what kind of car this is? It is a Phaeton, yes? Do you know that I am one of maybe only a handful of people in the whole world who knows how to work on a car like this? You are very lucky to come here. I am a specialist. I have everything you need in this garage."

"Where are you from?" I asked. "If you don't mind my asking."

"Switzerland, originally. I personally designed and fabricated, by hand, the world's smallest mechanical watch. It nearly drove me insane. Now I live out here. In all this. It *alleviates* the pressure."

"What kind of business do you get out here?"

"I told you that I am a specialist, I may see one, two, three cars a year. But that is enough. It's nice to get a couple of good boys like you. Most of my customers, they are only here for the gas. They are all drug dealers, you see."

I lost sight of him for a moment as he moved in front of the car, disappearing behind the hood, and then I heard him say, "Aha, this is your problem right here," accompanied by the sound of something being forcibly dislodged from the engine. He reappeared by my window holding what looked like a large chunk of quartz. "There, now it will run very much better without this. Now it is a car, you see, in its truest form. It will feel to you like a machine. Not...this." He indicated the quartz contemptuously. "It is, you know, like a tumor."

"Whatever you say," I said, regarding him through my sunglasses. "What about the body?"

"I am afraid there isn't much I can do for that. It is, you know, prohibited to keep glass on the premises. See, you have so many dents, so many parts that are smashed and broken. The one thing that I can do for you is to put the engine into the body of another car."

"I'm kind of attached to this one."

"We have limited resources in the desert, so I am afraid that

150

is out of the question. What I was thinking, about the engine, is I will put it into the body of a Renault. You like Renault? You remember Renault? The Renault *Fuego*?"

"That's not really my style. I was thinking more along the lines of an American car."

"Let me check my book." His finger went down first one page then another. "American...American...American..." He shut the book and looked into my eyes. "It seems I don't even have Renault."

It began to dawn on me where he was going with this.

"It seems I have only Le Car. Do you like Le Car? You see, it takes up very little space here."

"This engine won't fit in a Le Car."

"I agree, certain accommodations will have to be made. Less room, less luxury in the interior. None of the usual frills of Le Car. But in the end I believe it will be quite exceptional."

Juan and I left the car and went into the office for a glass of iced tea. Hans drove the car into the garage and shut the door. I reclined in a chair and set my glass on the desk. I must have closed my eyes. When I awoke it was to the familiar sound of a continuous electric crackle. The mechanic was standing over me cleaning his hands with some kind of petroleum based hand cleaner. The tin of it on the desk said *Goo*.

"The operation has been a success. Your car is now a Le Car. Your friend, I think he is very impressed. Would you like to see?"

I tried to clear my head, following him out the door. It looked like a Le Car. Our big strapping American roadster was now a mini.

"You see," he said. "You see, I was able to make everything fit inside. Now it is perfect, yes? All of it is in Le Car. Of course I had to take certain liberties with the configuration of the engine. Certain modifications. A little nip here, a little tuck there, and drop it into Le Car. Now it is perfect. Voila. Le Car." He kissed his fingers like a cook. "See how beautiful, putting such big things in small packages."

"We need gas."

"I am sorry, there is no gas."

He smiled big as the desert.

I looked at Juan, who appeared somewhat agitated.

"I told you, your friend, he is very impressed."

Juan shook his head. "It's bad, man. Very bad."

"See, you believe me now. It's bad. Hah hah hah. It is a bad car now, yes? Would you like to get inside, experience the look, the feel, of Le Car?"

I squeezed into the driver's seat and fired her up. At least it didn't sound like a Le Car. It still had a little of the big car moan.

"I don't think I can get in, man," said Juan. "I'm too big."

"Just put your head down."

He got in, not a bit impressed.

"We're packed in like those fish, you know, in the *can*?"

"Sardines."

"No, tuna, man."

"Don't worry. Not much further now."

Hans had transferred over the contents of the old car. The Virgin on the dash. I checked the glove compartment. Two cigars. Bottle of Mezcal. Dice on the floor. The back littered with the same tchotchkes, lighters, and cigarette wrappers.

"Before you depart," said Hans, interrupting my mental check list. "I believe there was a man here looking for you, a Turk, or an Egyptian. You know this man?"

"Did he leave his name?"

"I believe he referred to himself as the man named Fanta."

"I've been expecting him."

"He said that he lost you in a storm. He told me, he told me to tell you that he would meet you at the Northern Pike."

He was circling now, like a shark. Closing in. He was out in front for the moment, but it was only a matter of time before he moved in behind.

"Where can I find this Northern Pike?"

"From here one must simply follow the desert down into the valley of fire. There are crop circles down there, you see. You have heard of these? Crop circles, only without the crop. Hah! Sometimes these circles are on fire. Do not ask me how. Perhaps it comes from within the earth. It is truly one of the world's greatest wonders, and I have seen everything."

So that was where it would end, in a land of fire.

"Before we go, answer me one question. Why here?"

He smiled mysteriously.

"There is, how shall I say, a certain natural advantage." He paused and fixed me with his clear blue eyes. "You must promise you will never reveal this to anyone."

"Not while I'm alive."

"You see that mountain? You see the heat?" He lowered his head to mine, speaking in confidential tones. "There is a vast pool up there, perhaps the single greatest reserve of hot bubbling crude oil in the entire hemisphere."

I flicked my cigarette out the window into a pool of petrol, but it failed to ignite.

"Good luck ..." I said putting the car in gear and heading off into the swirl of dust and sand.

# CHAPTER 25
*DON*

We were burning it now, tearing over the desert tarmac. You could really feel the speed in a Le Car. Juan gazed out the window, bobbing his head to the unfathomable music that greased his mind, moving his head in time. I concentrated on the terrain ahead, boulders, rocks, the occasional cactus or patch of wild flowers. I saw a lizard on a rock. A snake slithering just wide of the tires. A tarantula climbing a thread of saliva. A scorpion preying over an open eye. There were vultures up there, circling. I lost them now and again in the sun. I could feel it, a lightness where before there was the unbearable weight of pursuit. Now I felt him as an absence, as if all the noise had culminated in silence. The radio had even gone dead, not a single atmospheric sound. The entire bottom had dropped out, and the desert was as soft as a cloud. For the first time I knew I was searching for something truly heavy, that there was something truly heavy down the line. Then I saw it, in the rear view mirror, like a spark of black it caught my eye. I turned to look. So small now, in the distance, I could tell that he was gaining ground. Fanta's Rolls Royce, that black bullet of motorized spite, streaking toward us through the expanse of sand and light, a dust cloud churned up behind. Though still far off I could feel the velocity of his pursuit and the promise of impact it contained like the violence of a thunderclap.

I could judge by the sun that we were heading north now. Our course was straightening out, leveling off, winding down. We followed the contour of the desert, swept ever downward onto the alluvial expanse of a great plane of sand. So where was this Northern Pike? Had we missed it? And then I saw it, rippling in the heat like a mirage. From a distance it resembled a primitive antenna reaching up to the sky, elusive and shape-shifting in the desert light. From the disrupted sound of the engine, the intermittent loss of power, the faults and starts, the gradual dying down, I knew that we had just about come to the end of the line.

"We're out of gas," I said, looking over at Juan as the engine sputtered and we went into a coast, gradually slowing to a stop. "We're dead in the water."

Juan ignored me and continued to look coolly out the window.

"This fucking car, man, it's too small." He half-heartedly punched the dash. "Not enough power."

I got out of the car and had a look around. The Northern Pike was a gigantic wooden stake, and mounted at the top—I had to squint through the sun to see it—was the head of a bull, impaled so that the tip of the stake erupted out of an eye socket. It was a long way up, and it made me wonder who, or what, had put it there. I looked to the south. That black bullet was getting bigger all the time. No longer a mere speck, it appeared to be moving faster every time I laid eyes on it, blowing up frame by frame, coming at us as from out of a dream.

"I think this used to be a lake," said Juan.

"What makes you say that?"

"All those fucking boats, man."

He was right. There they were. I was surprised I hadn't noticed them before—a veritable ship's graveyard. There were hundreds of them. Their iron carcasses weathering to nothing in the hot sand blasted air.

I walked around the back of the car and popped the trunk. No gas can, it wouldn't have fit. I picked up the bottle of fire brandy, unscrewed the cap and took a long drink. I lowered the bottle and wiped my lips. It really did burn, not a little bit.

"We're fucked," I said, walking over by Juan. I offered him the bottle. "Care for a drink?"

"It's too early for a cocktail," he said, waving me away.

"Come on, drink it," I said. "It'll make you one with the fire."

"Why don't you pour it in the fucking gas."

Why hadn't I thought of that? I went around and unscrewed the gas cap. I took one for myself then turned the bottle upside down, feeding half of it into the tank. Settling back into my seat with the bottle of fire brandy between my knees I could see, as I looked up into the rear view mirror, the dust storm rising up behind. One got the impression that impact from that black bullet would blow us to smithereens. Taking a deep breath I allowed myself a moment of calm, a cleansing of the mind, and turned the key. The engine once more roared to life. Combustion was combustion. It hardly mattered what kind.

I looked out over the landscape with new eyes. I could envision a terminus now, a vanishing point materializing on the horizon. I pressed the accelerator and we were off like a shot, churning up the cattle bones that littered the sand. I had it in high gear, as the plane of sand flew out from beneath us. Even though there was no road, I knew there would be a toll. I took a swig of fire brandy—the gap closing fast—and steeled myself for impact. There were entire skeletons now, of cattle, sunken into the sand. A blinding flash of black back-lit my eyes, my sunglasses heated up with the double image of that dark knight—I could make out his form in the tinted glass. He was directly behind us, looming menacingly in the rear view mirror, the hulking beam of that black beast taking up my entire rear line of sight. I took a last swig of brandy and offered some to Juan—he took a drink and handed the bottle back—feeling my pulse go slack, as if we had plateaued for real, final melt down, ground zero. And then like magic, just as we had been told, a wall of fire rose up in a great circle before our eyes. So this was it, the chance to be burned alive in a ring of fire. Fanta liked to fill-up the Rolls with some kind of super-combustible petrol, like rocket fuel. He did everything to the max. I threw the bottle out the window and watched as it exploded over Fanta's windshield, christening the black Rolls with a spray of liquid fire. An instant more and I had arrested my breath, though I couldn't bring myself to close my eyes, witnessing with pyrotechnic fascination as we plunged through the wall of fire, the flames blown momentarily inward, licking the paint from the Le Car's metallic hide. So imagine my surprise, believing we had broken through, as I was confronted with the vision of yet another ring of fire rising up inside. I steeled myself for this second immersion in flame—even ducked down and closed my eyes, and when I opened them, and only for a moment, all seemed impossibly serene and quiet, as if at last we had reached the melting calm at the center of this infernal ring. Then there was a blinding flash of light, the sensation of paralyzed time. Before us the inner wall of fire blew down. I looked back and saw it, the car of my nemesis consumed in flames, the simmering aftermath of automotive explosion. My ears were traumatized by the violent atmospheric pop that enveloped us now, transporting us through the outer ring of fire, blowing it out and sealing our fate within the prophylactic membrane of evacuated space. The wall of fire rose back up behind us. Unexpungeable, it seemed to issue from a deeper, more primary source, obscuring for good the immolated carcass of my nemesis, a slow burn of core flesh and exo-skeletal remains in red tongues of flame.

As the car slowly coasted to a stop, I looked beside me and discovered that Juan was no longer there. In his place was a thin stream of smoke lazily rising from a charred spot on the seat. I raised my sunglasses. It was hard to believe my eyes. I would miss him. He was a true friend. I got out of the car, and it was then that I realized I was totally fried. My lips were chapped and burned, my face hot and red, not a drop of moisture in my eyes.

# CHAPTER 26
*DON*

I would walk from here and when the sun grew too intense, conjuring visions from my burned out mind, and sapping all the fluid from my spine, I would go down onto my hands and knees and crawl along the desert sand, wringing from my soul every last drop of life I had, until my ravaged body seized up at last and there was nothing more to do but lay down on the hot dusty ground, reaching up to the burning sun ... to ... I had no way of knowing, when I came to, how much time had gone by, or how far I had traveled. Imagine my surprise then, when at last I opened my eyes, to find a large drunken Indian standing over me.

"Can I have this?"

He was holding the quartz figurine of the Virgin that had been on the dash of the car. I looked at my hand and it was open now, lying flat against the sand.

"Help yourself."

"I always wanted a white woman," he said, stringing it on a leather strap and wearing it as a necklace.

"What can I do for you, Chief?" I said, trying to make out his eyes from the sun.

He looked down reflectively.

"I never made Chief."

158

As we regarded each other in silence, I couldn't help but notice the pouch of water the Indian wore around his neck.

"Is that buck skin?" I asked.

He looked down.

"No. Pig. I made it out of a football."

"Do you mind?"

"Sure," he said, taking it off and lowering it down by the strap. I drank from it greedily, losing much of the precious fluid down the side of my mouth. I could see he was interested in something of mine. He nodded to the ground beside me.

"I wouldn't mind having some of that."

The Mezcal.

"Be my guest. You can finish it off. And don't forget the worm."

"You sure?"

"I'm in no condition for strong drink."

"Thanks," he said, shrugging his shoulders and reaching down for the bottle.

He took a seat on the rock next to me and after a moment's contemplation drank deeply.

"Not bad for Mezcal."

"Not a Mezcal man?" I asked.

"Not much." He held up the bottle. "Must be a mestizo thing. I'm a whiskey man."

"I had some of the local batch recently," I said. "Very bad medicine, I think."

"I thought it all came from Tennessee," he said.

"This was a special batch, you know, for use in religious rituals?" I said.

"I don't think Indians take communion," he said.

"It had peyote in it," I said.

"Must have tasted like shit," he said. "Peyote makes me puke. Never could figure out why anybody would want to eat a cactus. Acid's a lot smoother." He took another swig. "Wanna buy some?"

I pulled the charred bills out of my pocket.

"A bit short on cash," I said.

"Me, too. All I got left's a clay house and a dried up creek. I got a few dogs around here somewhere."

He looked off into the distance.

"I must have been hallucinating," I said.

"Worst hallucinations from the DT's. I use the acid to take the edge off. Sometimes I think I'm all covered in fireflies."

"Is there a town nearby?" I asked.

"Yeah, there's a bar, that way," he said, pointing over the hill.

"How far?"

"About twenty miles."

"I don't know if I'm up to it."

"That's too bad. It's a real good one. There's El Cantina. A couple miles from here. I don't know if the water's that good."

"I don't need that much really. Usually hardly ever touch the stuff. The fire took it all out of me. See, I'm already starting to sweat."

"Yeah, you're a white man all right. Red skin stays dry. See mine. I don't lose a drop. I can drink alcohol right out under the sun. All day long. All I got's this hat ... never get sunstroke or anything. Shouldn't be out in the desert without any water. You don't even have a hat."

"I'm wearing sunglasses."

"Anyway, I've seen worse."

"I was lucky to get out with my skin."

"I got a ... tub a Noxcema at the house. Want some?"

"I'm not sure I can make it."

"That's okay. I'll go get it. It's just over there. I'll be back in a minute."

He wandered off. I continued to lie there. It wasn't until later the next day that he finally came back, by which time I had more or less resigned myself to a lingering death.

"I thought you said you lived just over there."

He cocked his head. "About thirty, forty miles."

"How about the Noxcema?"

"Lemme see." He went through his bag. "Yeah, here it is."

He handed it to me, and I unscrewed the lid.

"Jesus, how old is this?" I said, somewhat taken aback. "It's turned to powder."

The Indian leaned over to take a look.

"Oh yeah ... that's even better."

"What the hell is it?"

"Heroin, I think. Yeah, that's what it is. China White."

"Christ, heroin?" I looked down at the powder. "You didn't happen to bring any water did you?"

"Back at the house." He made a turning motion. "I'll go back and get some if you want."

"I'll settle for the heroin. How much do I need?"

"I'd ... take a whole bunch. Just put your nose down there and breathe it in."

I put my nose down into the jar and inhaled as much as I could in one sniff. When I raised my head, my face was covered with white powder. The Indian laughed uproariously.

"Hey, you look like a mime."

I licked the powder from the corner of my mouth.

"Flour."

He shrugged. "I thought it was Noxcema."

"It's a good thing I didn't main-line."

"Turn your blood to dough."

"You live out here with your people?" I said.

"What's left of us. My people are originally from the mountains."

"How did you wind up in the desert?"

"One day, while the children were playing by the caves, they found something, shaped like an egg, only it was blue, the purest most beautiful silver-blue you can imagine."

Cobalt, I thought to myself.

"What was that?" he said.

"Nothing, go on."

"When they returned to camp they brought it to the medicine man. He told them to show it to nobody and to take it back to the caves and bury it deep within where no one will ever find it. The children were disappointed, but they did what was asked. For a long time, everything was the same, the object had been forgotten, and then one by one each of the children got sick. They all died."

"I'm sorry."

"Except for one ... the one who found it and held it in his hands. This child grew into a giant."

"What happened to him?"

"He left. I don't know. No one ever heard from him again, but there are stories he became a professional wrestler, traveling from city to city, continent to continent, all over the world. Hey, do you

161

have any smokes?"

I remembered the cigars. I offered them up to him.

"You sure?"

"I'm completely fried."

"Where you get 'em?" he asked after opening the pouch. "It looks like you only got one left."

"Let me see. Maybe my friend smoked it after all. I don't remember where we got them. Somewhere along the way."

"I know this cigar. It comes from this valley."

I gave him a blank look.

"This cigar I hold in my hand right now is probably wrapped in the skin of my ancestors. It's one of our most sacred objects. An age old tradition. I don't know how a cigar such as this could come into the hands of a white man. But there must be a reason. If you smoke this cigar you will feel no pain and suffer no hardship. You'll have the strength of a wild animal. The courage of a dead man. Nothing in the desert can harm you because you wear the skin of the ancestors. You are one with the spirits."

"It's gonna take more than smoking the skin of some dead Indians," I said.

"And this Mezcal. I know this Mezcal, too."

"Haven't touched it. Don't care for the looks of that worm."

"That's no ordinary worm," he said. "That's the Great Homunculus."

"The great what?"

"A magical creature imbued with all the wisdom of the ancestors. If you eat it you will receive a vision of the moment of death, your spirit sucked into the great hole."

"Where does it come from?"

"They're made by an old woman in the village. She takes the worm, or maybe it's not a worm, maybe it's some kind of larva, you know, or worse, and pickles it in ketamine."

"Special K? You're talking about going into the K-hole?"

The Indian shrugged.

"Are you, by chance, a fisher of men?" I said.

"Nope, not me. Not even a fisher of fish. Rather eat rattle snake."

"What about the cigars?"

"They're laced with PCP."

162

"How old is this tradition?"

"Ten years, maybe."

"PCP's not really my thing. I'm more of a Cognac man, maybe a little bit of weed."

"Some people call it Angel Dust, or Zombie. They use it on elephants, I think. Big game tranquilizer. You take that you won't feel nothing. Yeah, you smoke one of these, you'll just get up ... walk right out of here."

"People tear their arms off on PCP. They gouge their eyes out. It can make you go crazy."

"It makes you super human."

"I guess I don't have much of a choice," I said. "Can I have a light?"

"I don't have any matches," he said, patting himself down.

"Can't you make fire?"

"Not without a match."

I looked at the cigar longingly.

"What if I ate it?"

"I don't think it's gonna work as good. You can try."

"I can't afford to waste it."

And then I had a vision, the moment the match struck off the Virgin's back. What made her any different from the other back seat trash?

"Let me see the Virgin for a minute," I said, holding out my hand.

"Indian giver, eh?"

"I'll give her back," I said, clenching and opening my hand greedily.

"Hey, you'll pull her head off!" he protested, as I tried with all my might to do just that. Finally it flipped back and a flame rose out of her neck.

I smoked the cigar leisurely, taking it out now and again and contemplating the smoke. After a short while I believed I was starting to feel the effects.

"Thank you for your bad medicine," I said, rising potently to my feet.

"No problem. I better go now. In case you go berserk. Good luck."

The Indian departed, and I walked off carrying the Mezcal.

And it was true. I did go crazy at times, interrupted by total paralysis. I stood there, immobilized, with eyes wide open but nothing going on inside. The desert developed a strange resilience. I ran naked through the sand. Then I was clothed again. Where before everything hurt, hard and sharp, burning hot, the rocks under my feet and sand in my eyes, the blazing sun, reptiles and scorpions, birds of carrion circling up high. Now I walked, now I ran like a demon. Speeding up, slowing down, laughing like a mad man. It went on and on like this, so hot inside, hotter inside than out. This was what protected me, made me buoyant, this deutoplasmic pressure expanding from within and blowing out my mortal skin.

Much later, after the effects had more or less worn off, after time had quickened its pace, and the miles that I had walked did not just seem like forever, were stamped by real, physical time that you could hold in your hand, like hours of cold sand, I came upon a team of scientists working on a weather balloon. Only two of the scientists actually worked on the balloon, while the rest sat at a table playing cards. The scientists had dark features and hair and spoke French. There was one woman among them, a real beauty, and she seemed to be carrying on a flirtation with the youngest of the men. They didn't pay any attention to me at first, until I asked if there was anything to drink. One of the men set a glass in front of me and poured out a healthy dose of Cognac. I needed this more than I needed my own blood. I raised the glass to them and nodded appreciatively. There was a strong breeze and the woman had to keep brushing her hair away from her eyes. The young man produced a lighter and lit her cigarette, drawing her close to shelter the flame from the wind. I noticed another man, apart from the others, lying on the ground with his head propped up against a backpack. He had a yellow and black radio on his chest, and he was continually adjusting the dial, but the only sound that came out was static. I finished my drink, setting the empty glass on the table.

"Who's the Yank?" I said.

"He is nothing," said the man who had poured my drink. "A critic."

I walked over to him. He was of medium height with glasses, a thick build and a ragged unkempt beard. He gave the appearance of having been lying there like that for weeks. On the ground next to him was a notebook and a pen, the page that I could see filled with crazed scribbling.

"Are you a journalist?" I said.

He looked up at me with half-dead eyes.

"Once upon a time," he said.

"Where are you from?" I said.

"Los Angeles."

"You look familiar," I said.

"So do you," he said. "Around the eyes."

"I saw you dead."

"You're the John Doe," he said, coming back to life. "You were there. Come closer so I can see you."

I crouched down so that our faces were almost touching. There was a thick fog of dust on his glasses.

"You're a mirage," he said.

Just as he said it there was a great commotion, and I looked up to see the weather balloon skittering across the sand, catching a thermal and lifting off into the air. Another moment and it was practically out of sight.

"I'll come back for you," I said.

"Save yourself," he said. "There's nothing anyone can do for me."

Once the balloon was out of mind, the card game resumed. After a couple more hands, they invited me to join. I politely declined. It was time to be on my way.

"Pick a card," the man said in his heavy accent, fanning out his hand before me. "Any card."

"I'm a sucker for a good card trick," I said.

"This isn't a trick," he said. "Please pick a card."

I noticed for the first time the deck they were playing with had pictures of naked women on it. I tapped a card. The man licked the face of the card and stuck it to his forehead, tits out. The Queen of Spades. The woman looked Mexican. She had pitch black hair and large breasts with nipples that could put your eye out.

"Now what?"

"Souvenir," the man said, as the card tumbled from his forehead onto the table.

He looked around and the table erupted in laughter. I tucked the card in my back pocket.

"There's supposed to be a cantina around here," I said.

The men exchanged doubtful looks and shook their heads. The dealer flicked an ash into the wind. As I watched the ash blow out into the desert, in the same direction as the weather balloon, I couldn't escape the feeling that I'd made this scene before.

# CHAPTER 27
## FREDERICK M. BARCLAY
*...the party continued...*

Dante and I emerged into a small but sumptuously decorated theater with a low ceiling and a collection of Victorian style chairs and divans arranged around a modest dais. The guests lounged about smoking, drinking and chatting idly while the magician—I am assuming he was a magician because he wore the requisite black suit and tall hat—and his female assistant rolled a large cabinet of sorts out into the center of the stage. I quickly recognized the cabinet as the very same orgone accumulator that had encased Nero during our recent interview. We had arrived just in time, as the magician appeared to be about ready to begin the performance. I still loved magic, retaining a child-like enthusiasm for the craft that caused me to momentarily forget about my quest for Tony. I moved along the perimeter, keeping one eye on the magician while the other searched the room for signs of my quarry. The dim lighting on this side of the proscenium—the stage itself was lit up like an interrogation room—made it difficult to make out the faces bobbing in the currents of cigarette smoke, so I moved through the audience as inconspicuously as possible, ducking down and weaving through the tables and chairs like an overly solicitous usher. After nearly crushing a woman's toes and then toppling into her unhappy date's lap I settled into a chair at a table by the stage where I continued to scan the room for any signs of my prey.

As soon as we entered the room, Dante had broken away to schmooze the producers Bax and Nick (I could see him going through the elaborate ballet of his patented junk ball pitch, intended to confuse the target with various forms of misdirection, allowing the saleable idea to just sort of float by, past the flailing defense mechanisms that automatically deploy in these instances, and lodge in the unconscious with the result that the individual barely even realizes they've been pitched at all) who were themselves in the process of schmoozing a couple of blue haired cocktail waitresses, whom they had backed up against the glass wall of an aquarium filled with huge goggle-eyed Black Moors.

By the time my gaze returned to the stage, the show had already begun. The magician held the door open as the female assistant stepped into the cabinet. She gave a small curtsy and a smile before the magician closed the door and locked it tight. He took hold of the cabinet and gradually turned it around so that we got a good look at all sides. Next, he invited a member of the audience to come up for a closer look. When no one volunteered, the second female assistant, who appeared to be a near identical twin of the first, took me by the hand and led me up onto the stage where I performed a cursory inspection of the box, slapping at the sides and listening for the echo of a hidden compartment, shaking the door by the handle. Lastly, I got down onto the floor and slithered underneath on my back so that I could test the bottom, which was the most obvious point of egress. I checked for a hinge or seam of some kind but in my estimation the box was secure. I stood up, signaled my approval to the audience and returned to my seat.

As the magician pronounced his magical incantation, waving his wand at the box and shooting his fingers out like a lightning bolt, I overheard snatches of conversation from a nearby table:

"Nothing is forever. Why should art be any different?" said theater actor Alex Blondell.

"I'll tell you what's forever," said glam rock guitarist Slim Coker. "Those hand prints on Hollywood Boulevard. It'd take a nuclear war to get rid of those things."

"They're going to discover them in a million years under the rubble and think we walked on our hands. They'll say, hey, I guess

168

that's why they didn't make it," said international financier Wayne Chang.

"Hand prints all over the sidewalk, that'll be the only thing left," said Slim, as he bounced a pair of dice off the cocktail waitress's back.

With a theatrical flourish, the magician pranced toward the box and flung open the door. Being the one to vet the box, I was even more astonished than the rest of the audience to discover that the box was completely empty. There was a long round of happy applause. Once more I was led up onto the stage to verify the outcome. I repeated my previous performance, slapping and knocking on the sides of the box, this time also stepping up inside to make sure the girl wasn't curled up in some hidden compartment. The magician jokingly moved to shut the door on me, my involuntary panic eliciting a wave of titters from the audience. My face flushed, I stepped from the box, nodded my approval and returned to my seat.

The magician repeated his spell, waving the wand and shooting his fingers out at the box. With considerable aplomb, he stepped toward the box and threw open the door. Only there was nothing inside. Although the magician tried to play it off with a laugh, from his flustered expression I could tell that this was an unexpected result. He shut the door to the box, then stepped back and cracked a joke about how true magic doesn't always play by the script. Once the perfunctory guffaws died down, he repeated the hocus pocus, stepped forward with a deep breath and threw open the door, with the same result. The cabinet was empty. This time he went white as a ghost. "Mirabel!" he cried as he pushed the box aside and opened the trap door on the stage floor that had previously escaped my detection. I couldn't honestly say if at that moment I was more concerned for the missing girl or my own credibility as an audience participant. I joined a throng of audience members who rushed onto the stage to get a better look. The secret compartment beneath the stage was quite empty save for a bare mattress intended to break the assistant's fall. The magician jumped down into the compartment and pulled up the mattress, then pounded at the walls. The compartment was even more secure than the box had appeared to be.

"What happened to the girl?" said Coker.

The magician was completely at a loss. This had never happened. The audience got up from their chairs and went around the room searching for the girl, turning over tables, pulling up rugs, taking pictures off walls. Most seemed to think this was part of the act, but it was clear from the magician's discomfiture that something had gone wrong with the trick.

And then I saw it, a Champagne flute tipped over on the rug. The flute was empty save for one item, one essential clue. Nestled in the bottom of the glass was the butt of a cigarette. It wasn't just that the cigarette was a Marlboro Light—a number of young actors smoked the same brand—or that the discarded cigarette had been discovered at the bottom of a glass. Many show business brats put out their cigarettes in this manner. But this particular cigarette? In this particular glass? Tony was on a real Mumms kick of late, leaving a trail of smashed and soiled Champagne flutes all over Hollywood. And the attitude of the cigarette itself—only smoked halfway down, the insolent tilt against the convex curve of the crystal, the spent ash muddying the still effervescent (and not insubstantial, for that matter) dregs. I fished the butt out of the glass and pressed it to my lips, inhaling the complex aroma. It was still warm, and redolent of Tony's peculiarly celestial heat with its base of manly charisma and ineffable notes of boyish (some might say bratty) charm.

"Did you happen to see which way he went?" I said.

"As far as I know, there's only one way in or out of here, and that's through that door," said Nick, nodding toward an opening almost completely obscured by two hulking Hells Angels.

"There has to be another way," I insisted.

"This is it," said Dante with a curious wink. "Take it from somebody who knows. You've gone as far as you can go."

"Yep, that's it, pal. No exit," said Bax.

"Word," said Nick.

"What if there's a fire?" I protested.

"Who said there isn't?" said Bax. "Can't you feel the heat?"

I cast my gaze toward Dante, who was once more talking up the cocktail waitress. He held the woman's hand in his, tracing the lines on her palm with his finger. He had taken me as far as he could. I was on my own now, come what may.

Eventually the two brutish Hells Angels guarding the exit were drawn into the hunt for the missing assistant, and I used the opportunity to slip undetected into the even darker passage where I skulked along the wall as quietly and inconspicuously as I could.

Before long I got the sense that I was being followed. I looked over my shoulder and of course there was nothing. Then I looked again and there it was. Even in the dark I could make out from the dorsal fins, reptilian head, the upright body dragging the long tail, that this thing following me in the dark was some kind monster. I quickened my pace but the monster gained ground and was all of a sudden upon me, locking me in a horrific embrace. The fact that the skin was made out of rubber did little to alleviate my sense of terror. In some respects, it was even more abominable to be stalked by a man in a rubber suit than by the genuine article. Who knew what kind of fiendish Japanese perversions the interspecies cross-dresser had in store for me?

Miraculously I escaped from his rubbery embrace, which caused him to trip and lose a step momentarily. I used the opportunity to find a tall cabinet with an unlocked door, easily big enough to fit my robust form. As I opened the door and shut myself inside, it occurred to me that the cabinet appeared, even in the darkness, to be the more typical style used for the disappearing-girl-in-a-box trick, more typical than the odd metallic orgone accumulator anyway. So it was hardly surprising when I felt the bottom of the box give way and found myself in sudden free fall, arms and legs bicycling in slow motion as my body plummeted through an eternity of empty space. A full blood-curdling shriek had just escaped my lips when I suddenly became immersed in death's warm amniotic embrace, no more struggling, no more pain, only a feeling of pure tranquility and bliss. And then (thumb in my mouth, weightless body curled like a fetus) I felt it, a jolt to the reptile part of the brain that caused me to burst from the pool, arms wildly flapping like some strange flightless bird, and take a desperate life-sustaining gulp of air.

Less fortunate the rubber monster who, it turned out, had followed me through the trick cabinet and was now lying in a heap on the white tile that surrounded the pool. From deep within the costume I heard a faint (final?) gasp and then nothing.

I removed my clothes, which were completely soaked, and exchanged them for the white terrycloth robe hanging next to a stack of towels. There were no windows, of course. It occurred to me that I hadn't seen one for some time now. The air was heavy and smelled of humidity and chlorine, a cocktail of sterility that could, under the right circumstances, a lightning strike, perhaps, or a flash of radiation, suddenly burst with florid microscopic life. I draped the wet clothes over a chair and emptied them of the few items that had survived the submersion, transferring them to the pockets of the robe. The Pall Malls were a total loss. The lighter, too. A disappointment considering the vintage Zippo was advertised to have burned down an entire village in Vietnam. I checked the breast pocket of the robe and was pleasantly surprised to find a silver cigarette case and mother o'pearl lighter. I opened the case, removed one of the cigarettes, which appeared to be hand rolled, and struck it with fire, inhaling as if it were my last breath. Sweet Mary Jane. I took another drag then proceeded through the door and down the long dark hallway.

I opened the door and slipped in unnoticed. It was a small room with a low ceiling. The walls were a combination of dark mahogany and leather paneling with long lavender curtains tied back to reveal clam shell sconces that leaked a kind of dead colorless light that crept like ivy up the walls. Compared to the previous room, this was a considerably more low-key affair. The vibe was casual, down-beat. A man in his mid-40s who I recognized as South Carolina senator and presidential candidate Ted Severs was bent over at the waist lining up a putt. The putter came back, then accelerated forward, sending the ball on a slow roll over the wall-to-wall tiger skin carpet, ultimately coming to rest at the bottom of a highball glass tipped on its side.

Clad only in flip flops and the terrycloth robe, I strode right up to Senator Severs and handed him the joint.

"Don't mind if I do," he said, waving the burning cigarette under his nose to take in the aroma before setting it between his lips and taking a big hit.

"Nice shot," I said.

"I just wish I could do it out on the course. I've always been great at parties. If the voters could watch me work a room I'd have been President when I was 35."

"How'd you lose the secret service?" said gossip columnist Pamela Nixon.

"They weren't on the guest list," the Senator said with a wink.

"Sly dog," said Pamela.

Sitting in a chair near gangsta rapper-turned-actor Q was the budding screenwriter Richard Blow. I could tell from his inward expression that his mind was somewhere else.

172

"I know that look," I said. "One writer to another, tell me what's got you hung up."

"I'm stuck on the climactic scene," he said. "I've been working on it for days."

"Stop working on it," I said, sagely. "The answer is always right in front of you."

"Like, feel the force or something," he said.

"Something like that," I said.

Meanwhile, Q rolled up a fat joint with a hundred dollar bill.

"This shit even more chronic than chronic," he said, pressing it to his lips. "Laced with straight PCP."

He flicked the torch, and as the flame burned the paper, I could see the light bulb going on in Blow's head.

It suddenly dawned on me that the imposing block of ice that stood in the middle of the room was not, as I had first thought, just a crude ice sculpture. Those eyes peering out were real. Immured inside the ice was the magician David Blaine, who wore a fixed expression of blasé wonderment and whose hands were raised as if pressing against the walls of an invisible cell.

It was right there in front of me, on the floor: the shattered bottle of Mumms, the empty pack of Marlboro Lights, the droplets of tiger blood.

"Tony?" I said, barely aware I'd spoken aloud.

Severs nodded toward the far corner of the room. That's when I saw the snake coiled up in a wicker basket, an enormous albino anaconda with soulless pink eyes and a prominent lump midway down its considerable length.

"It's too late," I said.

"Don't worry, it's probably just the cleaning lady," said Severs through a mouthful of chips.

"He was here," I said. "The next room, where is it?"

"Follow Mr. White," said Q.

"Who's Mr. White?" I said.

"That old Colonel Sanders looking mother fucker talking to the Godmother," said Q.

The Godmother he referred to was, of course, the one and only Esmeralda Rubio, former cocaine queen-pin of the western hemisphere, looking more than ever the part of the old dragon lady, with long nails that curled down like talons, thick quivering neck,

173

heavy violet liner ringing coal black eyes, and smoking a menthol cigarette from a cartoonishly long cigarette holder. She held court from her perch in the tall Victorian wing back chair, while the man in the white suit displayed an antique gold pocket watch, laying it over the back of his wrist like a salesman at a jewelry store.

Colonel Sanders looked back at us, as if his ears were burning, and put the watch in his pocket.

"You better get going," said Severs, as Colonel Sanders crept along the wall, disappearing behind the curtain.

In an instant, I was in hot pursuit. I went behind the curtain and passed through a narrow doorway, heretofore concealed, that led to a long hallway lit by two rows of Tiffany lamps that hung upside down from the ceiling, which was so low that I had to stoop slightly as I walked. I followed the distinguished gentleman in the white suit until he turned the corner. When I reached the next leg of the hallway, the man was nowhere to be seen.

There were doors all up and down the hall. I tried each in succession, but they were all locked. Next to one of the doors was a small end table upon which sat a crystal decanter, but unfortunately no glasses. Having developed a powerful thirst, I picked up the decanter and took a sip. It wasn't until I'd slaked my thirst and set down the decanter that I realized there was a Mr. Yuck sticker on it. I also noticed an assortment of sponges and rags under the table.

"Who stores cleaning solvents in Christofle crystal decanters?" I wondered aloud.

"The super-rich," said the voice.

I turned to find the man in the white suit, only this time instead of Colonel Sanders, it was Mr. Rourke from the old TV show *Fantasy Island*.

"It actually tasted quite good, reminiscent of a 1978 Chateau Lefitte," I said.

"All of the master's cleaning fluids are of an excellent vintage."

"I'm just looking for someone."

"You just missed him," said the man in white, walking back up the hall and disappearing around the corner.

I continued searching for the door, to no avail. At last I discovered a tiny door behind a Norman Rockwell-style painting of a Playboy bunny that hung near the floor. I got down on all fours and stuck my head through the opening to have a look around and immediately received a scratch across the bridge of my nose. I retreated back into the hallway, and out leaped a three-legged cat. The painting had merely been an artful way to conceal the closet that contained the cat's litter box.

"That's Mr. Glass," said Mr. White, passing me by on his way down the hall.

I followed him this time, around the corner, staying close at his heels, and saw him pass through a door I'd overlooked before because the entire façade of the door was covered by a full length mirror. I approached the door, observing my swelling form in the mirror, overcome by the realization that I was finally at the heart of it. At last, I gripped the handle and pulled the door open.

At first I was so blinded by the blaze of whiteness inside the room I couldn't make out what kind of room it was or who was in it, but as my eyes adjusted to the light I realized that it was in fact a bathroom, spacious and well appointed, but not ostentatiously so. The room was done up in white porcelain, white tile floor and glossy white enamel walls. I spotted Tony right away. He was seated on the side of the tub snorting a line of coke off a lady's hand mirror. There were only a few other people in the room, a lesser actor named Ray Winter, the drummer from Switch Bitch, Mike Dollar, as well as a young man I didn't recognize who had short spikey blond hair and a ferret-like nervous energy that made him appear to be constantly nodding with the rapidity of a hummingbird's wings, a sort of tweaked out Venice Beach surf wigger, if you will.

"Hey Pops, you looking for someone?" said Tony.

All at once I felt my iron resolve crumble like a house of cards. With my ultimate object right in front of me, within arms' reach, staring me in the face even, this holy grail of hair, flesh and bone that I had quested after for so long with the single mindedness of a knight errant, biting and clawing my way through every obstacle *fortuna* laid in my path, I suddenly lost the will to follow through. It was as if I no longer even knew myself, how old I was, where I was from, it was doubtful I could have even answered the question of my own name.

"I'm afraid I may have swallowed some poison," I said without thinking, the words fairly dribbling from my mouth.

"Here she is," said Tony, patting the seat of the toilet. "Don't

175

be shy."

"We've all been there, man," said Winter.

"Just let go," said Dollar, finishing off a line of blow. "Pray to the porcelain god."

The surf wigger just nodded, his head humming a thousand beats per minute.

"Yes, of course," I said, prostrating myself before the bowl.

It should have been so obvious. This is what I had been looking for all along, a magic portal. I had already passed through so many impassable entries, it was time to lift the last veil, take the final plunge.

I lowered my head over the bowl and tried to see my reflection in the perfumed *eau d'toilet*, redolent of lavender, but there was nothing there. And then I attempted to retch, undergoing a series of increasingly histrionic spasms that resulted in no more than a thin line of drool.

"There's nothing inside," I said, more to myself.

"Come again," said Tony.

Realizing at that moment that there was only one way out, I lowered my head into the bowl and baptized my crown in the perfumed water.

"A little help," I said, voice echoing from the porcelain bowl.

"Whatever you say," said Tony, taking the handle and giving it a thorough flush.

What happened next could only be described as the most terrifying and cleansing experience of my life, a kind of brute force swirlie that was equal parts school boy prank and military grade torture. As the water rushed down the drain, sucking my head into the Coriolis vortex, I felt myself transported through the narrowing aperture and delivered into a dimension of pure transcendent bliss.

Of course, I'd gone nowhere. When I looked again at the water that had just filled the bowl, I was surprised to discover a beautiful goldfish fanning its tail. I opened the lid of the tank. There must have been a dozen of them swimming around in there.

"*De rigueur* for the contemporary bath," said Dollar.

"Nice touch," I said. "I have to admit I'd always been curious to see how Nero did his bathrooms. The man has always been somewhat of an enigma."

"He doesn't live here," said Tony, ashing into the toilet bowl.

"I'm sure you're mistaken," I said. "Only recently I visited this very house to discuss an assignment of the highest importance."

"It's a false house," said Tony, smugly. "He has two identical houses on this property. The one he uses for parties, and the one he actually lives in, on the other side of the hill, facing the valley."

"A mirror image," I said.

"That's why they call it Janus House," said Winter. "Everybody knows that."

"I'd be surprised if he was even *at* this party," said Dollar.

"His own mother fucking party," said Tony.

"Nero? No fucking way," said Winter. "Not in a million years."

"Right now, cat's probably sitting on top of a mountain, lotus-style," said Dollar.

"Or meditating, in one of those chambers with the energy and shit," said Tony.

"I was actually just looking for somebody," I said, grasping at a *raison d'etre*.

"That old man in the white suit?" said Tony.

"Did you see where he went?" I said.

"He went that way, dude," said Winter, pointing to the door at the far end of the bathroom.

I pulled myself to my feet and staggered toward the door, swinging it open and hurling myself through it and ... I heard the door shut behind me ... it took a moment for my eyes to adjust to the dark, but once they had, there was no denying what this place was. Not a room, that much was certain. I was no longer even inside the house. I was outside, standing on the front lawn of the estate, in front of the carriage house, right back where I'd started, only the grounds were empty of would-be revelers. All was quiet. There wasn't a single sign of life. And then I saw it. A white coyote, caught in a rivulet of moonlight that streamed down through the smog shrouded night. A dirty brown jack rabbit hung limply from his mouth. The coyote lowered his head, turned away slowly, and trotted off across the lawn. As usual there were more questions than answers but I was none the less much the wiser. I divested myself of the hypodermic, removing it from the pocket of the robe, ejecting its noxious liquid payload in a high urinary arc, then tossing it out into the night. Too, the stainless steel hunting knife (more specifically an

177

SOG knife, of the type favored by Navy Seals, with stacked black leather handle and a groove running down the parkerized seven inch blade) unstrapping it from my leg and hurling it deep into the ashen blackness. I had been so close, yet so far away. How rarely did life play out as conceived in the mind's eye. I lurched forward, staggering out over the lawn as fast as my legs would take me, then bounding like a wild animal across the barren heath.

# CHAPTER 28

Nero and Blow were seated by the pool. The huge Mongolian manservant brought out the tea and set it on the table between them, then poured a cup for each. After Nero took a sip, nodding approvingly, the manservant bowed and retired from their presence. The pool was shaped like the cross-section of a pearl, round with organic undulations. And the water was a perfect teal blue, reflecting the sun like a fun house mirror, alternately compressing and stretching it out, and losing none of the luster. Blow found himself wondering whether, if he dove into it, his body would melt like a wax figurine in a doll house fire or whether it would be cool like a black hole. Blow took a sip of tea then put down the cup.

"So basically, the assassin's lined up his last two jobs, one a high profile underworld figure, the other a politician. He's steps away from retirement, he's leaving the life for good. I'm not saying he's old. I'm thinking mid-30s, somebody like Channing Reese or Tony Billings, but in this business you've got to know when to walk away from the table, or find yourself under it. He takes out the underworld figure. That leaves the politician. Ordinarily he's very cool and detached about the whole thing. He reads the intel, plans it out and does the job. The guy is a mechanic. He doesn't waste a move. But this time he finds himself lurking around, watching through a telescope, showing up at rallies and fund raisers, he even shakes his hand, things he never would have done before. He doesn't even know why he's doing it, whether it's the thrill of it, the thrill of taking a chance, walk the tight rope, or whether it's something deeper and weirder, like maybe with this last one, for just this last one, he's got to know, he's got to get close. So he's at the rally, the politician is walking through the crowd, kissing babies, secret service all over the place, only they don't see the Albanian. Only the assassin makes him, because the assassin understands exactly what the Albanian's doing, he makes him right away, he sees the gun come out of the jacket, nobody else sees a thing, a shot goes off, the crowd scatters, people screaming, the secret service has the politician on the ground, you see, the shot went high, the assassin's all over him, he takes the gun away, he and the Albanian are rolling around on the ground, at each other's throats, and the Albanian suddenly recognizes him, and he smiles, I know you, I know you, he says laughing, and so the assassin chokes him out and kills him. Later, he tries to convince himself he did it for professional reasons, if the Albanian got to the politician first, he wouldn't get the money, but he knows it's not that simple. Something's happening to him, he's changed somehow. And to complicate matters, the politician has a daughter -"

"I was thinking about that Superman idea," said Nero, carefully peeling a blood orange and pulling apart the sections.

"That joke Jerry was telling at the meeting?" said Blow. "The one about Superman hooking up with Lois Lane? All this pressure building up?"

"There's something there," said Nero.

"I used to be a huge fan of the DC series," said Blow. "I still have a lot of my old comics in a box somewhere."

"This is something that interests me."

"You want to make a Superman movie?"

"You remember the plot from the original?" said Nero.

"Lex Luther buys up all this worthless real estate in the desert. Only it's not so worthless because he hijacks some nuclear bombs and sets them to go off right on a major fault line, which would make all of coastal California fall into the ocean, turning all that worthless desert into priceless beach front real estate."

"In effect, bringing the ocean to the desert. Only in my movie, it's the reverse."

"Bring the desert to the ocean?" said Blow.

180

"That's for you to figure out."

"I'll start working on some ideas."

"Just so I'm clear, this isn't a comic book movie," said Nero. "It's not about Superman. It's about THE superman."

"You mean from philosophy, Nietzsche and all that?"

"The way I'm thinking about it, it's set in the desert."

"I can work with that."

"Of course those are just so many details. The central story is an adaption of a chapter from the Mahabharata, about a shared bride. The Mahabharata is of course the central Sanskrit epic of ancient India. To give you some perspective, it is over ten times as long as the Iliad and the Odyssey combined."

"I'm somewhat familiar with it," said Blow. "So it's a fusion of the Mahabharata and Superman."

"You know why I wanted you?" said Nero.

"They didn't say, exactly."

"Because I see myself in you," said Nero. "Because you don't have any qualities of your own."

"I'm flattered," said Blow.

"What have you heard about me?"

"The usual stories," said Blow.

"Do you know what you see in me?" said Nero, pausing for effect. "Exactly what I want you to see. You hear what I want you to hear. You're familiar with Quantum Theory?"

"Photons. Quarks. Schroedinger's Cat," said Blow.

"My image is like the box."

"The box where they put the cat," said Blow.

"They can speculate all they want about what's inside, whether what's in there is dead or alive. The only thing that is certain is that they will never know."

Blow looked at the pool, at the clean arc of the sun on the still water, while the Mongolian manservant picked up the tea set from the table. Blow adjusted his sunglasses and nodded at the manservant, then tilted forward in his seat.

"Do you have any questions for me?" said Nero.

"I've got a lot of ideas," said Blow. "This is a tremendous opportunity."

Nero's phone rang. He picked it up, put it on speaker.

"It's Bax. We're with Bernie…"

On the other end of the line, Bax and Nick were bouncing around the desert in an old camper with the location scout Bernie. A huge squall of static drowned out Bax's voice.

"What on earth was that?" said Nero.

"Picking up some strange sounds on the radio," said Bax.

The camper had stopped now. Bax and Nick were walking around on the sand.

"How does it look?" said Nero.

Bax and Nick stood at the edge of a hole. The opening was just big enough to swallow a Volkswagen. They stared down into the black depths.

"May have a slight problem," said Bax. "Turns out it's some kind of toxic waste dump."

"How toxic?" said Nero.

"Like, nuclear," said Bax.

"Tell me more," said Nero.

# CHAPTER 29

They were just off Laurel Canyon Boulevard, turned up one of those slender little feeder roads tucked in the trees you never noticed if you drove it every day and looked like it went nowhere, quiet and wild and unkempt back here, like what it must have looked like back in the day when it was all dirt roads, kerosene lamps and bungalows, before there were million dollar houses lining every ridge and dotting the hillsides, a constant ooze of glossy European cars snaking up and down the dusty causeway. A quarter mile back and it was like that whole other world just disappeared, and you were swallowed up in a hidden valley of gently swaying eucalyptus, scrub oak, sage brush, elderberry, laurel sumac, preternatural jades and giant aloe, the road turning from pocked and broken pavement to gravel and then dirt as it wound around the pulverized granite hillock and opened up on a vast sunken vale surrounded by undulating embankments.

"The thing that I like about the M5," said Bax, his hands gripping the black leather wheel of the precision roadster. "...is the sport-tuned suspension. Ass-deep in the canyon, taking an S-curve at 75, two o'clock in the morning, flying high on some damn thing, that's when you really appreciate it."

"Those lost twilight-zone hours," said Nick. "Only time you can open the damn thing up. Scare the shit out of the coyotes, watch them scatter like field mice."

The man who came out to meet them was an old German. He was neatly dressed in a crisp white button down shirt and khaki pants and wore a wide brimmed straw hat. He was a collector of sorts. Some would say a hoarder. Down in that shambling old mansion you could find some pretty unusual pieces, including a wide array of vintage watches and clocks from all over the world. Also, wind chimes, Art Deco lamps and chandeliers, deluxe croquet sets, pewter candlesticks, illuminated manuscripts, the whole ball of wax. And out here, swarming over the hillsides like fire ants, in every color, was a veritable battalion of mint condition Le Cars, as far as the eye could see.

"I always wondered what happened to them all," said Bax.

Nick lit a cigarette, then closed the lighter and slipped it back in his pocket. He took a drag on the cigarette then swept his arm out across the vista, glowing end of the cigarette leaving a wispy contrail in the burnt orange firmament.

"We'll take a dozen," he said.

The German started to walk away.

"Oh yeah," said Nick, stopping him in his tracks. "And, like, a shit ton of agricultural grade fertilizer."

"Anything else?" said the German.

Nick thought for a second.

"Helium."

# CHAPTER 30

In the 51st floor conference room of Palomar Holdings' New York headquarters, the board of directors sat around a long oval shaped table surrounded on all sides by glass, one side, a window overlooking the Hudson River, the other three, sound-proof partitions that allowed the eye to travel through the sleek, modern spaces of the limitless open floor plan. Up on the video screen there was a wide angle shot of the Australian desert. Something was moving slowly through the center of the frame. At first glance it looked like an apparition, the specter of a long dead Titan perhaps, looming over the horizon, but as the apparition drew closer, its vague corpus seeming to materialize out of nothing more than wind and air, it took on the distinctly earth-bound form of a tornado, a slender tongue of fury reaching down from the sky to lick the wind ravaged landscape. By degrees the tornado's ghostly hue darkened, until it was almost obscured behind a scrim of dust and sand. At the bottom of the screen, just coming into view, the scrubland blazed under a corona of orange flames. As the twister met the brush fire, the blaze sent plumes of black smoke into the darkening tornado and then, all at once, the flames themselves climbed up through the swirling vortex until the entire tornado was consumed in fire, like a demon come to life, forming out of earth, wind and fire and ripping and burning everything in its path.

Standing just to the side of the screen, Brad, 30ish with short blond hair, perfect tanned skin, crisp white Oxford shirt, blue-and-red striped power tie and teeth that sparkled even in the conference room's dead natural light, pressed the pause button on the remote, freezing the terrifying fire devil in its tracks.

"And that's just exhibit number one," said Brad, turning to face the board. "At Fortress Indemnity, we like to think of ourselves as the unsung heroes of the film business. Now we may never get to walk up on stage at the Oscars. No hot shot actor is going to thank the insurance company in his acceptance speech. We know that. We don't even get one of those tiny little credits at the end that no one ever sees, like set medic or best boy. But that's okay. We know what time it is. Fortress Indemnity isn't about the credit. Fortress is about making money. As you well know, it's Fortress's money that backs up the money that makes these films. So in a way, we're the *real* money men. Without our vote of confidence, the money dries up."

"What is this about?" said Ira Cantor, the board's silver-haired chairman.

"What this is about," said Brad, pausing for dramatic effect. "Is what happens when the money dries up."

"If you think you're going to walk in here and force our hand..." said Ira.

"Nobody's trying to force you to do anything," said Brad, in a reassuring tone.

"This is the head of a major motion picture studio we're talking about," said former RCA head John Paul Davies.

"We're not in the habit of discussing personnel decisions with anyone, much less a bond company. No offense," said Cantor.

"As I said, I'm simply here to present the evidence," said Brad. "And let you draw the conclusions."

"Not that I want to tip my hand," said John Paul. "But why not just sit back, watch how things play out? You must have seen the writing on the wall. Nero's seen it. Everyone's seen it."

"Nero's in the hot seat. It's all over town. Pick up a copy of *Variety*," said Cantor.

"We're past the point of rumors," said Brad. "Or wishing he gets the hint and does the honorable thing."

"These things take time. There are a lot of pieces that need to be put in place," said Cantor.

"Palomar acquired the studio, what, four years ago? We still need to find out where the bodies are buried," said John Paul.

"Figuratively or literally?" said Brad.

"We're all in the same boat," said Cantor. "We lost a lot of money on that *Fire Devil* picture."

"Not as much as Fortress lost when Ray Leo burned up in that tornado. Fortress coughed up thirty million to indemnify the Japanese, to indemnify the Ukrainians, the South Americans..."

"What we're trying to say is, it's not a matter of if, but when," said Cantor.

"Yeah, you're preaching to the choir here," said John Paul. "In the past few years, Nero's dug himself a neat little hole. And no one's more keenly aware than the people in this room, but you can't hold the man personally responsible for a tornado. That caught on fire?"

"And grilled one of the lead actors halfway through principal photography," said Brad.

"It's an Act of God for Christ's sake. It's the weather!" said John Paul.

"As an isolated event, sure. In theory, that could happen to anyone. But look what's happened since. Two months ago, Nero's admin is gunned down in an attempted car-jacking in Watts," said Brad, clicking the remote.

The video screen advanced to show a quiet intersection in South Central Los Angeles, a chalk outline of a body in the middle of the street.

"The driver admitted he got lost," said Cantor.

"I'm not making apologies for him, but it's not like Nero pulled the trigger," said John Paul.

"One month ago, Terry Banner's head exploded during a pitch meeting with the writer Richard Blow," said Brad, advancing to the next image.

The video screen showed the conference room where Terry Banner's head exploded. A chalk outline of a body occupied Terry's swivel chair, the white line forming arms and shoulders and coming together at the neck before mushrooming out where the head should have been and limning a splatter radius on the back wall the size of a hot air balloon.

"I thought they said that was spontaneous combustion," said

187

John Paul.

"Two weeks ago," Brad continued. "Nero throws a party at his house. During the magic show, the magician's assistant disappears in the black box trick. She hasn't been seen since."

"Nero wasn't even at the party," said Cantor. "The magician's story checks out. He's legit. The police never pressed charges. It's a basic missing person's case."

"This video was taken from the security camera in Nero's home," said Brad.

The video screen showed the flustered magician from the party as he attempted for the second time to fling open the door of the cabinet to reveal the vanished assistant, and then pushing the box aside and jumping down into the compartment hidden beneath the trap door.

"Nero didn't even hire the magician. It was that catering company," said John Paul.

"Maybe the girl had a fight with her boyfriend and decided to skip town. Who knows?" said Cantor.

"In isolation, on a case by case basis, these *freak accidents*, they don't necessarily tell us anything. An exploding head—science tells us it can happen to anyone at any time. A car-jacking in a bad part of town. A third rate magic trick that takes a tragic turn. A tornado engulfed in flames. What do they tell us?"

"They don't tell us jack shit," said Cantor.

"What I'm here to tell you," said Brad. "Is that these events are following a disturbing trend."

"Can we be candid here for a second?" said former Treasury Secretary Catherine Keller. "There's a certain matter of a golden parachute."

"Tens of millions for early termination," said Cantor.

"Unless there's a violation…" said Catherine.

"Of the morality clause," said Cantor.

"That shouldn't be too hard to prove," said Brad.

"Harder than you think. He's got lawyers too," said Cantor.

"We've got nothing," said Cantor, shaking his head. "We've got jack shit."

"The fact is he's still got another year on his contract," said Catherine.

"We realize it's going to cost you, initially," said Brad.

"The golden parachute," said Catherine. "You'd rather we pulled the cord."

"Than Fortress eats a hundred million dollar claim?" said Brad. "In so many words."

"What are you proposing?" said John Paul.

"If Nero stays at the helm, the studio's films will be unbondable."

"That sounds like an ultimatum."

"I realize there's no one particular act, no magic bullet. But the pattern is clear. Nero is turning toward decadence, death, darkness. Whatever you want to call it. While there may be no hard proof, no finger prints or forensics, the circumstantial evidence is starting to pile up. I don't know where it's heading exactly, but it's not good."

"Got a hunch, eh? Guess what that and a triple A rating from Standard and Poor gets you," said John Paul.

"Gets you jack shit," said Cantor.

"We have risk models, of course. Computers. Actuarial data. But there's something else. Call it a $6^{th}$ sense. It's my job to know ahead of time when something bad is going to happen. The police can't do that. They're not allowed, don't have the expertise for that matter, to predict when something bad is going to happen. They just clean up the mess. This sixth sense, as I like to call it, is something I've developed over time. Now it's possible I have some God given trait that allowed me to develop this ability, an overactive pineal gland perhaps, an enlarged hypothalamus? Whatever the case, when I see the light go out at the end of that tunnel, I feel it here." He held his fist to his gut. "And I know it here." He touched his finger to his right temple. "And sure as Hell will extinguish the Kingdom of Heaven and night devour day, you better move your chips off that number before the next spin of the wheel."

With his finger cocked gun-like at the board of directors, Brad suddenly dropped to the floor and underwent a series of violent seizures that caused his body to convulse on the geometric patterned carpet like an electric eel. After several minutes of this, during which the board looked on in stunned silence, the seizures just as suddenly stopped.

"Don't worry about me, folks," Brad said, jumping to his feet with preternatural alacrity. "Everything's okay. I'm okay everybody."

189

He raised his arms, eyes moving from one face to the next, then clapped his hands together, bowing his head and, as he raised his chin, flashing a smile so brilliant that Ira Cantor swore he could make out his own crystal clear reflection in the huge bared canines.

Cantor lowered his head toward John Paul, speaking in hushed tones.

"Word is, Tony Billings has developed a taste for fresh pineal," he said. "Keep tabs on this one, in case we need to tap that shit."

"Word is, they had one on the line," said John Paul.

Cantor shook his head sadly. "The fish that got away."

# CHAPTER 31
*FREDERICK M. BARCLAY*

In the back of my mind I realize this was one of those dangerous drunks. Straight whiskey. American whiskey. A mash of corn, rye, different kinds of rat poison and formaldehyde. Aged in oil drums. Bottled in China. The kind that made the Indians go crazy. The kind that wiped out entire civilizations. Pouring it straight into this hole in my head, straight into this hole inside me that can never be filled. And the thing is that I feel stronger and more alive than ever. Certain that I am on the verge of something big, something gigantic. It's at the bottom of this bottle, a huge limitless ocean of possibility. The end of time, the beginning of everything. The manifestation of all my destinies swirling around in a reflecting pool of fermented annihilation. I put my eye to the mouth of the bottle and see my image dancing in the amber vapors like some half-gone genie. I'm sitting on the floor, bare chested with my glasses on, my pallid voluptuous form awash in the oracular light blaring from the television screen. I take a swig of whiskey and set the bottle between my legs. I pick up the revolver, a 38 Special, and spin the chamber. There's one in there if I need it. I put the gun to my head and pull the trigger. Nothing. Just a click. I level the gun at the TV, sighting down the barrel. Tony Billings' face in close-up. Dripping with sweat. The dark shadow on his chin etched from a thousand daggers of light. I squeeze the trigger, by degrees. A blast of powder and fire. A hole the size of a golf ball opens up in the screen, the scene continuing to play out around it, the smoldering black hole moving from Tony's neck to his eye to his temple. I lean forward, walk on my hands and knees toward the television. As I attempt to climb inside, my head butts against the screen. I rear back on my haunches and lunge forward, slamming my forehead against the hard glass. I turn around and walk on hands and knees to the far side of the room. I pick myself up and get down into a three-point stance. Hut one. Hut two. I'm sprinting across the room, head lowered like a charging bull. *I am a bullet*, I say, as my face collides with the screen and everything goes black.

# CHAPTER 32

When the actress arrived, the Champagne was already on the table, in a bucket of ice. The door was unlocked. She opened it and entered. Their eyes hadn't met when Nero raised the bottle and poured out a glass. He handed her the flute then poured one for himself. They raised their glasses.

"I'm glad you were able to make it, on short notice," said Nero. "Do you like the Champagne?"

She smiled.

"This is a very special bottle, one I've had for a long time, brought it up from the cellar. It's one I've been saving for a special occasion."

He took a sip then set the glass down next to the script.

"Oh, how silly of me, would you like some cocaine?"

She took a sip of Champagne, her lips a perfect line.

"Of course, you can have whatever you like," he said. "By the way, call me Mr. Fantastic."

"Whatever you say, Mr. Fantastic."

He picked up the script.

"Some people, they only want to see the reel, or the video of the screen test. I've always found ... it's been my experience, that a reading, a real reading, in an intimate setting, tells me more than I could ever hope to get from a video, or even an audition with a room

193

full of people, a director, a casting agent, too many people, too many distractions. I find that an intimate meeting, at night, when the lights are low, tells me even more than my wildest dreams."

He handed her the second copy of the script. Their eyes met.
"Shall we begin?"
She nodded.
"What was your name again?"
"Marianne," she said.
"Marianne, you will play the part of the actress."
Nero began the count…
"3
2
1
0."

### Marianne
A mirror on the hotel room wall catches the man's reflection. He leaves through an open window, cowboy hat under the sash.

### Nero
Your skin is softer than rose petal.

### Marianne
A woman enters the room, sets down the handbag. She removes her earrings by the mirror, vines on the bedposts, the man's reflection frozen in the head lamps of her eyes.

### Nero
Say goodnight.

### Marianne
A ladder to the window. Plane overhead.

### Nero
Headshots of the starlet float down from the sky. This one signed in lipstick, with a kiss. Blown around the desert highway. A bird falls from the power line. Followed by a sky diver wrapped in silk. The ground comes up to him, naked and alive. Into the cement.

Marianne

Margarita loves you.


Nero

A whisper like wild fire. Lives lost in the mines, searching for Jasmine. They never find her.


Marianne

She's an hour glass, she's quicksand, she'll bury you alive.


Nero

Catalonia by sunset. A boat on the sand. The old harbor at midnight. The stories she tells, her voice a lullaby.


The actress found herself sitting on the floor, by the end of the couch, her dress falling away from her thighs. She looked up at Nero, her lips parting expectantly. He wore an afro wig and a false mustache. He held a gun.

"Put this on your head," he said, handing her a red wig.

She nervously set the wig on top of her head, without taking a breath.

"Don't move," he said, sighting down the barrel. "I'm going to shoot it off. I've done it a thousand times."

Nero pulled the trigger, point blank. An explosion of smoke and sound. When Marianne opened her eyes, she was surprised to find that she was still there. No hot lead, no fire in her guts or her brains. Even the wig was undisturbed, not a hair out of place.

Nero said, "It's all smoke and mirrors, baby. And then one day it's real."

Without taking her eyes from him, she found the pages on the coffee table and slowly rose to her feet. They picked up where they left off.


Marianne

Late summer wedding at seaside, sun on the water, lapped by an orange tide. A man steps out of a black Jaguar. The women covered by long flowing veils of white. He puts a finger to his lips, tracing the outlines with his eyes.

Nero

Pillars of salt. They're gone, they're dust. Blown away like candle light. The temple in a reflection. He lowers his head. A prayer and a ransom. She's breathless, buried, head above the sand. A shadow passes over. She opens her eyes. A match strikes against the sand, sets her necklace on fire. Rafts of vine and flower, the flotillas of twilight.

Marianne

She whispers his name, one last time.

Nero

Armada after Armada into the northern isles. A weather balloon hung up in the power lines, stranded on the inter-continental divide. The clouds move in around him, a lowing from the mines. Starlight outside. Marble statues. Ancient bandages. Skins of wine. Traces of carbon and formaldehyde. Ladder to the balcony. Climbing the vines. The first look—big zero in disguise. Her last gasp petrified.

Marianne

The man tips his cowboy hat, hanging it by the mirror. His lips are black. He puts on a miner's lamp and turns out the lights. I am black time, here for the licking up of the world.

Nero

She smells like roses and Tequila. The smile of a belt buckle. She's as cold as ice. The head lamp fires, strips the night from her eyes.

Marianne

A woman slips into the pool beneath the motel lights. A light turns on in a ground floor room, a man going out for ice. The woman tests the shallows. She glides along on her back, long blond hair a feather boa around air chilled flesh, bare breasts.

Nero

The engine turning over in a Cadillac silences the scream from the upper deck, a Cyclops in the window and a stunner burning under the head light. Floral wreaths, garland, flowered vines from the hillside, star fruit, sliced lemons, and a bucket of ice.

## Marianne

Bottle of gin, elderflower syrup, quinine, and ginger snaps. A man steps up to the edge of the pool, a jug of wine in his hand. He's wearing a white suit. In the middle of his speech, he falls into the water.

## Nero

The woman glides by, eyes open, bare skin cold as ice, she turns over in the water and dives.

Nero set the gun on the table and picked up a glass of water. He took a sip. He lowered the glass to the actress, down on the floor. She took a long drink. She choked on the water, gasping. Water leaked from the sides of her mouth. Nero pulled her to her feet. He pulled her close, and they began a slow dance. He turned her around. She dipped. He let her fall onto the couch. She shook the hair out of her eyes, and the wig fell off.

Nero took the rose stem from between his teeth and tossed it down to the actress. He pressed the handkerchief to his mouth. When he removed it, there was a spot of blood. He tucked the handkerchief back in his breast pocket. He kneeled down next to the actress. She took the pill from his hand. He gave her the glass of wine. Looking into his eyes, she washed it down.

"If there's one thing on which I simply must insist," he said. "It's playing dead."

He pulled the cowboy hat down over his eyes and crossed his arms over his chest.

Marianne came to, as if from a trance.

"Who are you?" she said. "Are you going to kill me?"

"You were dead on arrival."

He led her with his eyes to an envelope of money on the table.

"Take it," he said.

"You don't have to."

"That is your role," he said, folding his arms.

She picked up the envelope.

Nero picked up the red phone and dialed the number.

After a moment, Marianne could hear a man's voice answer.

"Pull the plug on the pool party," Nero said, and then he hung up.

"I just wanted to say how…"

He waved his hand, signaling for her to be quiet.

"The actress said nothing, staring up with starry eyes.

"You got the part. Both of them. I told you I'd take you to heaven," he said. "Now say something in Spanish."

"Yo me llamo Marianas," she said.

"Looks like it's time for you to split."

He took the sword from the wall and lowered it over her head.

"Remember the old trick where the girl gets cut in two?"

"The one where she's in a box," said the actress.

"It's simple, really," he said, leading her to the coffin. "Nothing to worry about."

He opened the coffin and Marianne crawled inside, stretching out in the red quilted interior. He raised the sword and brought it down fast, slicing the box cleanly in half. He pulled the two sections of the box apart, and two girls slithered out, Marianne and another girl who looked just like her.

"Let's party," they said.

# CHAPTER 33

They were seated near the corner in the back, Blow conspicuously wearing sunglasses indoors and carrying himself with the air of one trying to maintain a low profile, in spite of the huge pompadour that caused Teddy to do a double-take when they first met inside the restaurant. Teddy's own sunglasses were hanging from the collar of his t-shirt. Blow poked at the salad distractedly with his fork, looking up now and again as if he expected to see flash bulbs or the importunate eyes of a gossip columnist. Teddy let his eyes wander the room full of posers and players, following the same track as Blow's. Nobody looked back.

"The thing is," said Blow. "An artist must be first and foremost a salesman, or he is like a tree falling in the woods and no one around to hear it."

"I've always believed you've got to love the process. If you love the process, the work will take care of you," said Cruz.

"That's what I always believed, too. But it's not true," said Blow. "It's not a bankable strategy. Ask anybody who's anybody. Leaves too much to chance. You can't just plug away with your nose to the grind stone. The universe will not support you, I don't care what the Buddhists say."

"All I'm saying is, it's all a crap shoot, on some level," said

Cruz. "I mean, we all come out here with the same dreams, thousands of young hungry talented people, all after the same thing. One out of a thousand is chosen, by some divine hand, and the rest fall through the cracks. That's why it's got to be about the work, about the journey itself, there's no guarantee where you're going to wind up."

"I don't agree," said Blow. "There's no magic involved, no mystery. You get what you deserve. It's a perfect system, really. The market allocates resources with ruthless efficiency, rewarding the winners and punishing the losers. There's too much at stake for social engineering."

"Then how come half the clowns who make it are somebody's nephew?" said Cruz.

"Pure Lamarckian evolution. The ones who grew up out here, it's in their DNA. They just have something. I can't explain it."

"So what's it like working with Nero? I heard he's a big league control freak."

"He's very specific and demanding, of course. He has to get what he wants. He's got a lot of balls in the air, worlds on his shoulders. I've learned a lot."

The waiter walked up to the table.

"You guys need anything?"

Cruz looked up, nodded. "I'm good."

The waiter looked to Blow, who seemed not to see him.

"Just wave if you need anything," said the waiter, before leaving the table.

"We were in acting class together," said Cruz. "James or Gerald or something."

"The thing is, if you want to make it in this business," said Blow. "You need to think ten moves ahead, like chess. That's what makes him what he is. He has the vision. The focus. He sees the whole board, every possible combination of moves."

"We're all just pawns," said Cruz. "In some elaborate game. Is that it?"

"You're lucky if you're a pawn," said Blow. "You're lucky if you're on the board."

"Word is this whole house of cards he's built? It's about to come crashing down. The feds are building a case. IRS. FBI. Even the insurance companies."

"They're just rumors," said Blow.

"That whole thing about the Church? Sham corporations and secret Swiss bank accounts. Running dirty money through the Virgin Island laundromat. Word is he's the man behind the man behind the man, the big fish, top of the food chain."

"He's got a lot to lose. He practically built this town. He's a made man. What's the motivation?"

"Consider this, maybe he's after something bigger than the movies. Let's face it, the movies aren't getting any bigger, and he isn't getting any younger. Nero's a showman and the movies are no longer the greatest show on earth. Dude might be looking for a bigger stage."

"Bigger than the movies?" said Blow. "He's already at the top of the mountain."

"Maybe he wants to climb a different mountain. Or go down into the Valley."

"So now he's some kind of high stakes shaman?" Blow shook his head. "I'm not seeing it."

"Everybody knows he killed his own twin. In the womb," said Cruz. "Strangled him with the umbilical cord."

"That's just a myth," said Blow, rising. "Nobody ever took that seriously."

"A friend of mine read the case study in med school."

"Anyway, I gotta split," said Blow.

"It's been real, brother. See you next week."

"Why don't we play it by ear," said Blow. "Things are getting a little crazy."

"I'll call you."

"Talk to my assistant," said Blow.

"Your assistant?" said Cruz.

"Let's keep in touch," said Blow, walking away.

"Later," said Cruz.

# CHAPTER 34

They were parked under the basketball hoop, right next to the bent and rusted chain link that surrounded the derelict playground, holes in the fence big enough to let in packs of coyotes, the asphalt cratered and buckled with scrub growing out of the long spidering cracks. Here and there on the other side of the fence were large brick buildings scarred with graffiti and broken glass. Factories? Warehouses? Schools? It was anyone's guess. From the looks, even the squatters were long gone. Bax watched a tumbleweed come rolling down the street, only it wasn't a tumbleweed, he realized, it was just an empty plastic bag blowing in the wind. And when the wind died down the bag collapsed on the pavement, deflated.

Q sat behind them, in the center seat, with his legs spread out on either side, his arms sprawled across the adjacent seat backs. He had on a purple bowler hat, the brim angled low over black sunglasses, the kind with the lenses that bulged out like giant bug eyes. His fingers were a showcase of heavy gold rings. Bax leaned forward slightly, his eyes methodically scanning the horizon, hands gripping the wheel. Nick had the cell phone to his ear, listening to a string of messages and then, when the messages ran out, to the infinite loop of the electric female voice listing his options, two to save, three to repeat, over and over.

On the way in, they'd encountered a man lying in the middle

of the street. Initially, Bax stopped the car and started to get out, but Q told him to pay no mind and keep right on rolling. Down at the end of the block there was a kid on a bike riding around in circles in the middle of the road. Across the court a ragged looking dog with no collar sniffed at a lamp post, raised its leg then kept right on going.

"Maybe I shouldn't have brought the M5," said Bax, eyeing a rusted out 85 Olds with no hubcaps parked across the street.

"Better to roll up in a set of primo wheels," said Q. "Nigger see you roll up in a bad ride like this, know you rollin' heavy, go the other way. Roll up in a brand new Camry, Accord, *Volvo*, well, that's a whole nother story. Look like a cup cake on wheels, with birthday candles and everything, nigger make a wish and blow your ass the fuck away."

"I can never get this GPS to work," said Bax, ineffectually stabbing at the touch screen.

"I should have brought something," said Nick. "I've got a .44 in my night stand. Locked and loaded."

"It says we're in the middle of a … bay or something," said Bax. "…like in the, you know, ocean?"

"A lot of shit go down in the ocean," said Q.

"Go-fast boats," said Nick.

"Go-fast boat, shrimp boat, tug boat, all kind of boat," said Q.

A car passed by, a beige mid-90s Maxima. Bax jerked his head toward the car, spilling what was left of his coffee.

"I just got these back from the cleaners," he said.

"Cream and sugar?" said Q.

"Black."

"Black on black. Like it never happened," said Q.

"Once it dries, you'll never even notice it," said Nick.

"I have another pair in the trunk," said Bax, opening the door and starting to get out.

He felt a hand on his shoulder, Q holding him down. Q nodded. In the distance, the prow of a big red Mercedes Benz 560 SEC AMG nosed around the corner of the outer most building. The car turned and faced them, then stopped, idling for what seemed like several minutes. Bax watched the car, taking short, slow, quiet breaths. Nick leaned over and changed the channel on the radio,

203

found a country station, some old song by Hank Williams.

"Any requests?" he said, raising his head.

Then the Mercedes was moving again, rolling slowly over the cracked asphalt. They watched the prow of the car advancing toward them, blowing up frame by frame.

"So the way this works, we hand them the briefcase," said Nick, clutching the handle. "And then they transfer the merchandise, I mean the, you know, the *assault weapons*, like, into the trunk?"

"Something like that," said Q.

"They probably have to count the money first," said Bax. "I'm assuming."

"Explain to me again," said Q. "…why He makin' you buy all this *real* hardware?"

Bax checked his teeth in the rearview mirror.

"Authenticity."

# CHAPTER 35
*DON*

When I arrived at the cantina I felt like I had walked around the world, like a man arriving from another time. It had to be the cantina the Indian spoke of; there was nothing else for miles.

I opened the door and went inside. The muted lighting of the bar once more played havoc with my eyes, and everything was a haze until my pupils dilated enough to let the defining light inside. Still now, it looked like the aftermath of a very wild scene, empty bottles all over the tables, half-eaten platters of food, party favors, a forgotten sombrero. I took a seat at the bar. It was then that a familiar sound emerged from the gloom, the same dancing electric crackle I had heard so many times down the line.

"What's that?" I asked the bartender, a very serious looking Mexican. "Some dead air radio station?"

"It's a Geiger counter," he said, pointing to a device behind the bar. "It measures radiation."

"Radiation, is that a problem around here?"

"You should have heard it the other day. Thing went crazy. Sometimes I think it's the people, you know."

He set a glass of Mezcal down in front of me.

"This is from your friend."

"I think you must be mistaken."

"There was a man here looking for you."

"How do you know it's me he was looking for? You don't know my name."

"He said I will know this man when he comes. He is unlike other men. He is a man with no name."

"Everyone has a name," I told him, throwing back the Mezacal.

"A Christian name? A man like you?" He narrowed his eyes at me. "I ask you then. What is your name?"

"I'd tell you but it's still on the tip of my tongue. A few more of these might loosen it up." I raised the glass and he poured me another. "I'm sure you understand. My mouth is still dry from the desert. It makes conversation a burden."

He nodded and backed away from the bar, leaning against the wall with his arms folded and occasionally working on a cigarette that burned slowly in an ashtray by the register. In the man's easy hands, smoking took on the quality of a deeply profound and ritualistic act, and I became entranced as I watched him, the way he held it using more fingers than I had seen other men, the way he watched it into his mouth, savoring the smoke, the time he spent tamping it into the ashtray, the smoke slowly rising from deep within his lungs and letting from his mouth in a silky stream. He had the ease and composure, the comfort and sureness in his every movement, of men who do only one thing at a time and think only of what they do. Men like these lived in a perfectly smooth world, free from the disorienting shock of objects rearranging themselves with the blink of an eye.

There was a fish mounted on the wall, with small scales and a small round mouth. Though I had once been a sportsman I couldn't identify it. It was easily as long as a man.

"What kind is it?" I asked over my drink.

"Bonefish," he said nonchalantly as he dried a glass with a dish towel.

It couldn't be. I strained to make out what was inscribed on the plaque beneath it.

"*Bimini*? Are you sure about that? I know this fish. In the Bahamas they call it the grey ghost. It's a flats fish. You can take them on a fly, in water as thin as glass over pure white sand. A trophy is ten pounds. The Bahamas are a top spot, but I've never heard of one over twenty-five."

"Bikini," he said, watching the cigarette as he artfully snuffed it out in the ashtray then raising his eyes to meet mine. "Not many people realize the largest bonefish in the world are found in the islands of the Pacific, in deep water. Not as glamorous for a sportsman such as yourself. You can't catch them so easily on the fly. But the size can be truly amazing."

I still hadn't gotten over the first part.

"Bikini *Atoll?*" I said.

"Everything's grown back," he said. "There are some true giants down there. Leviathans. You can't imagine. My cousin found this one washed up on the beach."

"Where are they now?"

He paused to light another cigarette, then shook out the match.

"Some people say they're moving deeper all the time, down into the Marianas Trench, their flesh getting heavier, more compact, condensed by the unbelievable pressure of the deep. But also gaining in size, expanding out into the vast space beneath the sea. One day they will probably come up for air, their eyes sewn shut, or big as globes, because there was no light. In the meantime, we get only a glimpse."

"I'd like to get a better look."

He set his cigarette on the ledge of the ashtray then lifted the great fish off the wall and set it in front of me. I ran my fingers along the scales.

"It's not real."

"No one does skin mounts anymore. Taxidermy is a dead art. But this is an exact replica. It cost my cousin a lot of money. I'll show you the photo."

He picked it up off the shelf behind him, a sun-bleached Polaroid of a dark man in sunglasses on the beach standing over a big fish that resembled the one before me now.

"The same?"

"I assure you it is. My cousin is not a liar."

He picked up the bonefish mount and hung it back on the wall.

"Do you have any water?"

"There's a well out back."

207

He nodded toward a door at the other end of the bar.

"Thanks for the tip," I said, dropping a few coins on the counter by my glass.

I got up and crossed the dimly lit room, picking an uneaten chicken leg off a plate before reaching the door. I opened it to the usual blinding light, my eyes slowly focusing on the source of a fury of barks and growls, a muscular little dog kicking up a whirlwind of dust as it went around and around chasing its tail. I watched for a time, but there appeared to be no end in sight.

"How long's it been doing that?" I said.

"About an hour. I think it's fuckin' crazy, man," said Juan.

I tossed the leg of chicken on the ground, and the dog grabbed it and ran off.

"Hey, man, you're not supposed to give a dog a chicken bone. It could fucking choke," he said.

"I thought you were dead."

"I got abducted. I was in a flying plate. Then I don't know what happened. When I woke up I was playing dice. All these fucking greasers, they were cheering for me, you know. I was winning everything, and I didn't even know what fucking game we're playing. And then I lost everything, even though in the first place I didn't have nothing, and I'm thinking, man, those fucking greasers are gonna kill me. So I roll the dice, and I'm looking at them and starting to back up, because I think I'm gonna have to run away, and then I see their faces. Nobody's saying anything. I look at the table and these fucking dice, they're right on top of each other."

"So what?"

"They split," he said, lighting a cigarette. "In this big greaser limousine."

"Low rider?"

"Yeah, man, with like thirty people in it. Everybody's shaking their fists and laughing."

"That sounds like a pretty tense scene. Who were they?"

"Extras, I think."

"Extras?" I said.

"They're shooting a film, out in the desert."

"Who's shooting a film?"

"I don't know, man. These greasers, they say they're cousins of Quetzalcoatl."

"Who's that?"

"He's like the *god of illegal shit*, you know what I'm saying?"

"You mean *crime lord?*"

"Yeah that's what I'm saying, man. Guns. Drugs. Women. You name it."

I followed his eyes to the horizon, but all I could see was smoke coming off the land.

"What about you, man?" he said.

"I was stranded in the desert ..."

"Yeah, and then what?"

"I was found by an Indian."

"Medicine man, eh? Those greasers can get anything."

"Not this one," I said.

"I got a surprise for you, man."

We turned around together.

"I won that car."

It was a beautiful old American muscle car, same 1950s lines as the original one, except it was black, with tinted glass.

"...and everything in it."

"Stereo?"

"Take a look inside."

He smiled, and I could see, even through those impenetrable sunglasses, the knowing glint in his eye. I went over and stuck my head in, leaning through the passenger side window and taking in the scene. Cherry leather. State-of-the-art dash displays, liquid crystal everything. Stick shift. The infamous pair of dice. They hung from the rear view mirror, over the space where the Virgin had been.

Stereo.

"Hola."

I turned my head to find two voluptuous senoritas in the back seat.

"Hello, ladies," I said, being charming. "What are your names?"

"Maria."

"Ana."

"Care to go for a ride?" I asked.

"Si."

"Si."

Both were extremely desirable, in flimsy summer dresses

showing ripe breasts and bare brown thighs. But there was something about her eyes, the rosebud swell of her lips, the hourglass curve of her hips. The one on the right caught my eye. I withdrew from the car and turned to Juan.

"See, I win everything," he raved. "Even these fine looking ladies."

"Let's blow this joint," I said.

"Where to, man?"

I looked out at the desert.

"It doesn't matter."

We drove off, catching the last light of dusk in the rear view mirror. As night fell, Juan and I didn't say a word. The girls talked continuously in their foreign tongue, drowning out the silence of this lonely hour. I thought back to the day I deserted my wife and child, now barely a memory. Her pregnant, containing all the promise that lay behind. It was late, and a full moon was out. I brought the car to a stop and shut off the lights. I turned to Maria, my lovely girl on the right.

# CHAPTER 36

Usually Bax picked the location. The location scout sent him the list, and he made the call. First he'd think about time, cost, logistics. Those sorts of things. Then he thought about where he'd rather hang out during the inevitable visit to the set. Vancouver or Detroit. Austin or Wilmington. The High Sierras or the Swiss Alps. Sometimes Nick made the call, if he happened to get to the list first. This time Nero set up the whole thing, had it all arranged in advance. Somewhere in the American South West. It wasn't Death Valley, but it felt like it. It was the Death Valley of New Mexico. Red rocks and burnt orange sand. Trailers, prop trucks, cranes, generators and booms. Porta-potties and misting tents. The sun hanging in the sky like a naked bulb in a cinderblock room. Impossible to escape. Impossible to get out of your head. In the background, an enormous Raja's palace rose up from the temporary settlement like an ancient monument, the way the pyramids stood over the low-rise sprawl of contemporary Egypt. With its domed chhatris and bracketed chhajjas that spread out from the structure like wings, light spiraling in hypnotic patterns through perforated stone jalis, the palace had the appearance of a mirage. Constructed in only three weeks, it looked like it had stood for centuries and would stand for centuries more, long after the colony of tents, trailers, campers, busses and trucks took flight, leaving the whole scene covered in epochal drifts of sand.

This time, Nick had gotten to the girl first. The new actress. He'd found her standing behind the misting tent having a cigarette. She was wearing ripped cut-off jeans and a faded pink tank top. She had long chestnut hair, and while they were talking she kept piling her hair on top of her head to cool her neck then letting it fall back over her shoulders. She had a tattoo of a Chinese symbol on her upper arm and another one on her hip that looked like the rings of Saturn rising up from the waist of the cut-offs. Her gold sunglasses had large tea colored lenses that allowed you to see the reflection of your own sunglasses and through the reflection into the pools of amber that held her eyes, that made the eyes seem to go wherever it was you had in mind. It had only taken Bax a second to catch up to them, hitting up Nick about some very urgent matter that affected the schedule or the budget or the union contracts or something.

"When the Japanese get wind of this," he said. "They're going to shit."

Then he pretended to just notice the girl and extended his hand.

"I'm Bax."

"Hi," said Marianne, shaking his hand.

"We loved your reel," said Bax.

"Ron put it together," she said.

"That scene, with the watermelon, tripped us out," said Nick.

"That was like take 29," she said. "I had watermelon juice all over me. They kept having to change my dress and sponge me down."

"Twenty-nine takes, they could have planted an entire watermelon patch with all those seeds," said Nick

"I think I swallowed half of them," she said.

"Now you've got all those little watermelons growing inside you," said Bax.

"And it didn't even make it in," she said.

"Looked great on the reel," said Nick.

In the middle distance, traversing the stretch of desert between the Raja's palace and the misting tent where they were standing came a seemingly endless procession of long shapely yachts, high masted sailboats, cigarette boats, pontoon boats, sparkling bass boats and Boston whalers being hauled across the sand on trailers.

"Is there a water scene?" she said.

212

"Not exactly," said Nick.

"Nothing's set in stone," said Bax. "You know, the whole thing with the script."

"I didn't think there was any water within a thousand miles of here," she said. "Where did they come from?"

"Like magic," said Bax, snapping his fingers.

"You'd better believe they cost a pretty penny," said Nick.

"So what do you do for fun around here?" said Bax.

"Hang out in my trailer," she said. "I've got satellite."

"Killer," said Bax.

Nick's eyes had already gone past them, scoping down the lane between the tents. A girl was stepping down from the running board of a white cargo van. Nick gave a little flip of the head, like a kill-shot from a sniper at long range. She turned, smiled and disappeared around the bend.

# CHAPTER 37

The tent was larger than the others, with a high ceiling. It was tricked out with all the amenities—full bar of artisanal waters, air conditioning, state of the art sound system, high-definition projector and big screen. But it was still a tent. It reminded Blow of the tents from the old show MASH. It could have been the tent used for the operating room or the chapel, only a lot nicer, with designer fold-up chairs and an assortment of high-end collapsible furnishings. On the big video screen, against a back drop of open desert, was the frozen image of Tony in a white linen suit holding a gun.

The real Tony was seated off to the side. He was in a t-shirt and cargo shorts, wearing sunglasses in the dim light and talking on his cell phone. Blow and Dante sat in front of the screen with loose pages of script spread out on the table between them.

"In the Mahabharata myth, the two clans prepare to go to war over a dice game," said Blow.

"The one clan lost all this valuable real estate and a shared bride who all seven brothers were banging and now they want the whole lot back," said Dante.

Tony (on phone): "Come on, baby. Listen ... We've got another three weeks down here, I'm already going out of my mind."

"So they're about to declare war on their cousins," said Blow.

"And the whole time, the leader's being egged on by one of

214

his charioteers, who's really Krishna in human form. The leader's starting to have second thoughts about sending all these men, who are his extended family, to slaughter. And that's when Krishna shows his true face," said Dante.

Tony (on phone): "She's all right, she can't remember her lines for shit ... just on set, I've been keeping to myself. There's a lot of spiritual energy out here. I'm trying to turn down all the noise in my head, take a journey inside myself, discover who I am."

"The script is a reference to the myth," said Blow.

"I got that. I'm fine with that," said Dante. "Have to throw a bone to the critics. Give 'em something to go on about. I still want to fire bomb that fucking Raja's palace."

"The palace ties the script to the myth," said Blow. "It's the visual anchor of the scene."

"It's a bloody abomination," said Dante. "It's so goddamn on-the-nose when I look in the mirror I can't see my bloody face. It's like a big giant black wart that blots out the sun. It's a fucking joke."

"He was very clear about the vision..."

Tony (on phone): "You can't get good shit out here... Come on, baby. Don't leave me hanging like this. Bring me a little doggie bag, just enough to get me through the shoot. I promise, I'll make it worth your while."

"I can't believe you're going along with this shit. Supposedly you've done a few goddamn decent things," said Dante.

"If you'd been there when Nero explained it -"

"I've heard plenty, believe me. I've been going around and around with that lunatic since before you learned to drool in front of the telly," said Dante.

Tony (on phone): "Of course not like the last time, I was an asshole then, I realize that, things are different now."

"I'm probably older than you think," said Blow.

"Aren't we all. I'm as old as Moses and you'd never guess I was a day over 63. The way he acts you'd think he'd been around from the beginning of time, but he came out of nowhere just like everybody else, just popped out of thin air one day. And then one day, just as suddenly, it'll be just like none of this ever happened," said Dante.

Tony (on phone): "It's you I want to see. I'm just saying, pick up a few things on the way out, you know what I'm saying?"

215

"One thing he was saying was that his character, the Driver, AKA the warrior chauffeur, had to have the confrontation with Tony's character out in the open, in front of everybody, but when the change happens, when he turns into the monster-god, Tony is the only one who can see it. I'm trying to figure out how to make it believable, something that could really happen, while staying true to the myth," said Blow.

"You better think quick. We're shooting this nonsense tomorrow," said Dante.

Tony (on phone): "How should I know? Somewhere in Mexico, I think. Have Karen set it up."

"I have a pretty good idea. I'll have to run it by him, of course," said Blow.

"You're the writer, aren't you. Tell him to keep his nosy prick out of our goddamn story," said Dante.

"I'm trying to stay true to his vision," said Blow.

"His vision? He's not the one in here writing till four in the morning. In fact, I've never seen a single thing written by his own hand. I bet he's never even signed a check. He's constructed this maze around himself, built layer upon layer of handlers, proxies and shell companies between him and the rest of the world. Has he ever even shaken your hand? He never touches a goddamn thing. And I'm not talking about all these little blow jobs at gun point. He's a fucking hologram."

Tony (on phone): "You know what I like, a little of everything: reds, greens, yellows, blues, buttons, tabs, tincture of this, powder of that, a few tools: pipe, spoon, dropper, torch, maybe throw in a syringe for good measure. The usual thing."

"The script is in his head," said Blow. "We're like midwives, helping him give birth to this thing inside his head."

"Everybody's got something inside their head. In my head, I'm fucking two 19 year old Chinese girls," said Dante.

"Chinese girls. Good. We can use that," said Blow, as he started to type.

A woman came into the tent with a wooden spatula and a bucket of pink goo. The woman, Ramona, wore pigtails and retro glasses with thick black rims.

"Oh God not that," said Dante, grimacing.

"I'll make it quick and painless," said Ramona, immediately

216

setting about pouring the pink goo over Dante's face. She used the wooden spatula to slather the goo over his eyes and mouth.

"I can't believe I agreed to this," said Dante, voice burbling up through the pink goo.

"Stop being such a baby," said Ramona. "The alginate cures in five minutes."

"Why him? He's not even in the movie?" said Tony, lowering the phone for a second.

"Because in the climactic shoot-em-up scene, it's going to be our bloody faces on all the plaster corpses. Me. Jerzy. Bax. Nick. Even Blow over there. All the behind-the-scenes talent, and I use that word loosely."

"It's huge for the fan sites," said Blow. "Somebody spots the director's face or the writer's face or the cinematographer's in the background among the corpses at the whatever minute mark, it's all over the blogs."

"You think Hitchcock would have put up with this?" said Dante. "Or Nick Roeg?"

With one last flourish of the spatula, Ramona sealed his lips with the goo. "That'll shut him up." She looked to Blow. "Who's next?"

# CHAPTER 38
*FREDERICK M. BARCLAY*

I had mixed feelings about the trip to the desert. I was a city person, a citizen of the universal cosmopolis. And it was a long drive from Los Angeles. Out in the West there was always distance, more distance than anything. On this occasion, the story was worth chasing. A major film project, cloaked in secrecy. Nobody seemed to know anything about it. Most of all it was a chance to reunite with my favorite subject (and *bête noire*), the vastly underrated actor Tony Billings, and take care of unfinished business. The mission was not yet accomplished. There was more yet to discover, substantially more, an objective that could only be realized through the most intimate and penetrating journalistic investigation. There had already been several near misses. The truth was out there to be found, in the nothingness of the desert. It was dark, and there were few other cars on the road. I turned the dial of the radio in search of an AM station, listening acutely as the tuner leaped over bands of hiss and static. I zeroed in on a blip of articulate noise, slowly twisting the knob back and forth until the noise cohered into a distinct voice, the reception teetering on the head of a pin. The signal broke up then came back, just long enough for me to hear it. It was Tony's voice, rising up out of the static, as if he were trapped in another world. It was difficult to make out what he was saying, but there was one word that I understood for certain because he was repeating it like a warning, or a mantra: *Fire ... Fire.* And then the voice was gone.

218

# CHAPTER 39

The one thing that stood out about the trailer right away—despite the idle bodies strewn about, many in various stages of undress, and the constant haze of marijuana smoke hanging in the air—was how incredibly neat it was. Spent blunts and empty liquor bottles were immediately thrown out. No food was allowed inside. The trailer had a bathroom, but no one was allowed to use it. Not even Q himself. Six times a day, Tommy Boy went over every surface with a damp cloth. Twice a day he vacuumed the place top to bottom, front to back, with a vacuum that had a special HEPA filter. Q allowed the smoke to linger because he believed it had a sterilizing property.

Q stood in the middle of the bodies, staring at his reflection in a full length mirror. Behind him, Erica, a sultry mocha skinned young woman in a silk leopard print dress with a large afro and a coppery gloss on her lips, raised her arm, turned her hand over in a mote of light and smoke projecting from an opening in the blinds, then let the hand fall languidly to her thigh, while DJ Trix, wearing wraparound shades and a fat gold chain that hung out of the purple and yellow Lakers jersey, the yin-and-yang medallion at the end of the chain resting on his chest like an armor plated heart, sank back between plush red velvet pillows, taking a monster hit off a bong that resembled a sawed off double barrel shot gun. Q waded through the haze of smoke, closing in on the mirror. He stopped about four feet from the reflection. The man in the mirror met his cold hard gaze.

He took off his sunglasses, hanging them on the collar of his shirt, and stared fiercely into the reflection of his eyes.

His face moved through a series of intensely intimidating expressions (snarled lip, narrowing eye brows), each one met in kind by the man in the mirror, like two equally matched opponents facing off in the center of the ring before touching gloves. Neither man giving an inch or showing the slightest sign of weakness.

"I know who you are," he said, staring into his eyes. "Yeah, I know all about you, you dirty mother fucker. You cock sucker. Little faggot. Punk bitch. I'll rip your fuckin' heart out, show it to you, make you go blind with fear."

He tilted his head to the side, flashing crazy eyes.

"I'll stab your eyeballs," he said. "Cut off your head and drink your blood. Wear your skin like a bathrobe. Slam your nuts with a Nike five iron, straight into outer space. Turn your hands into ash trays."

Gradually, the face relaxed, the jaw going slack, eyes softening.

"I know who you are," he said. "You're just a scared little boy, scared little boy who wants his mama. Go on, run to your mama, little boy. You can't hide no more. Be a man and show yourself. Be a man and come out into the light. Show your hurt to the world."

And then he started to cry. Just a trickle at first, eyes moistening, followed by great heaving sobs.

"I'm lost, mama," he sobbed. "I'm lost and I'm all alone."

Then the face in the mirror melted like celluloid, before undergoing a rapid series of changes, metamorphosing from happiness to pity to sorrow, followed by petulance, embarrassment, fear, indifference, hatred, disgust, paranoia and homosexual lust.

"Hey Bro, what's all that?" said Antoine, settled into the cushions with Tammy's bare leg draped over his lap. "That the Method or some shit?"

"Not *the* method. A method. My method," said Q, without breaking concentration. "Whole lot of different methods. Can't learn this in some workshop. Can't buy it on TV. This one's all mine. Part of my flesh. In the marrow of my bones."

Q leaned forward slightly, slanting his head toward the glass.

"To be...or not to be. That's the mother fucking question," he said, as he slammed his fist into the mirror, shattering the glass.

220

# CHAPTER 40
*FREDERICK M. BARCLAY*


The ground was harder than I expected, not the billowy sands of the Sahara but a hard-packed carapace that already, at this impossibly early hour, reflected the intense burning heat of the just risen sun into my cracked lips and bleary eyes. Lying on my belly, stretched out behind a cactus, I squinted through the field glasses, spying Tony in the distance perched on the smooth misshapen red rock, one knee raised up level with his hips, with the palms of his hands pressed together in front of his chest, the fingers forming a temple—what I immediately recognized as the classic praying mantis pose of Tai Chi. As Tony moved fluidly from one pose to the next, I marveled at the animal grace of the natural athlete and the poise of one of the world's premiere thespians, both qualities on full display under the glare of the huge red spotlight slowly rising toward the proscenium of this incandescent theater in the round. What marveled even more was discovering the young wild cat actor practicing this most spiritual art at this early hour while his cohorts continued to slumber on into the afternoon—this after burning the midnight oil in a marathon tour of the camp's burgeoning after-hours scene of cocktail parties, card games, drug fetes, cock fights and garden variety orgies, the expression of a manic creative energy that must be exorcised anywhere and everywhere at once. I had been observing this stupendous display for nearly five minutes, attempting to peer through and around the assistant holding the large screen that shielded Tony from the sun, the assistant waving the fan and the assistant who alternately wetted him with a portable mister and squeezed a plastic water bottle that squirted a liquid into his mouth I later identified as a mixture of green tea, ginseng, Ketel One vodka and Red Bull energy drink, when Tony suddenly hopped down from the rock, toweled off, climbed onto the Harley Davidson idling nearby, and sped off toward the encampment, kicking up a trail of dust behind him. Considering the encampment was only a stone's throw away, I had no trouble tracking him down, finding the Harley discarded next to an assembly of dumpsters on the outskirts of the set. As I crept along the blue iron wall of the dumpster, the carnal sounds emanating from behind the container and the pungent aroma of the overflowing refuse combined into a single multi-sensory brew that induced in me a mild but decidedly disorienting sense of nausea. I steeled myself, firm in my resolve to face this test of my journalistic mettle, and peered around the corner to witness Tony being blown by one of the girls from craft services, who, with the knees of her fine little legs reddening against the sand, sucked and slurped at his immaculate veinless member as if it was some life sustaining popsicle quickly melting away in the kitchens of Hell.

Tony shouted encouragements, in his usual way. "Hold it," he said. "Now use your throat muscles to squeeze the head. That's it. Don't let go until I tell you ... Now tickle the underside of the shaft with the tip of your tongue. Lighter! More playfully!" he shouted. "That's it, that's it. Now breathe in some air ... not too much, just enough to cool the head a little while you tug on the balls. There, lips slowly sliding up the shaft—slow the fuck down! Don't you know how to suck a dick? All right, that's it, now when you get to the tip, spin your head around nine times and puke on my cock." He adjusted his sunglasses. "You know, like that bitch from the Exorcist."

The girl coughed out Tony's glistening member and paused to remove a hair from her mouth.

"Sorry," she said.

"That's not mine," he said, pointing indignantly at the hair. "This shit is trimmed and coiffed by the same fag that does Wally Zane's chest hair."

"You really want me to spin my head?" she said. "How does that work exactly?"

"You're the one who's supposed to be so great at sucking cocks. I thought you said you gave the best head in camp."

"If you had a rope, or a swing or something," she said.

"Christ, just finish me off already," he said. "Do I have to figure everything out myself? I told you I can't take a decent shit until I've had my pole smoked."

She held the member at the base, slapping it against her cheek a few times before taking it all in.

"Now hammer me with your face," said Tony.

I knew what was coming next—had seen it many times before in even less distinguished circumstances, images that still lingered—and so excused myself from the grand finale, retreating to a safe position near Tony's motorcycle where I enjoyed several herb cigarettes as the wind muffled the bestial sounds signaling the crescendo of Tony's peculiar morning ritual.

When Tony emerged from behind the dumpster he was zipping up his pants with a cell phone cradled between his shoulder and ear. He walked right by me without showing the slightest sign of recognition

"I thought you were going to be here today," he said into the phone.

Even in the wind I was sure I recognized Sherrill's voice on the other end of the line.

"I've got to see you," he said. "I can't wait any longer. It's making me crazy."

He had been alternately walking and running and now broke into a full trot in the direction of a stand of porta-potty latrines. He hopped from one latrine to the next, unsuccessfully trying door after door. Finally, he squeezed into an open latrine, the phone still pressed to his ear, and as the door closed behind him I glimpsed his pants drop to his knees and his rear descend toward the seat in one single deftly executed motion. The porta-potties were situated in such a way that I was able to easily maneuver unseen between them and establish a vantage whereby I could conduct surveillance of Tony's conversation with Sherrill. Lying on my back with my head wedged through the narrow vent at the base of the latrine, affording me an up-close view of Tony's dirty feet in pristine Salvatore Ferragamo sandals. I will not bother to describe in detail the onslaught of disgusting noises and aromas that overwhelmed my senses, but will only point out that my subject did nothing to shield said noises from his interlocutor during the course of the romantic phone conversation, which went as follows:

"I need you here now. Now get on a plane, or a bus, or a fucking cab, and get your ass out here," said Tony.

"I know why you want me out there. You don't love me," said Sherrill. "You never have."

"Of course I love you."

"Don't say it if it isn't true."

"Do you think I'd ask you to come all this way if I didn't love you?"

Explosion.

"I see you found somebody to loosen you up," said Sherrill.

"Just the local cuisine. Goddamn jalapenos. They put em in everything. You know I have a sensitive stomach."

"And a Teflon heart."

"Don't be like that. You know how I feel. I told you my shrink says I have self-esteem issues, none of this shit is my fault. I'll give you his number. You can call him yourself."

"It's always the same story. I don't feel like I can trust you anymore. Not after that stunt you pulled with those skanky circus freaks. *In my bed.*"

"To be fair, baby, that was Cirque de Soleil."

"It was hardly the first time, Tony."

"That was just some weird shit I had to get out of my system before I could learn to love myself, on account of losing my virginity when I was eleven to those sweet little Tanzanian foreign exchange students."

"You expect me to believe that you've changed?"

"Come on, I'm down on my knees, baby."

"I bet you're not the only one."

"You know my rule. No blumpkins before 11:00 AM."

"You're disgusting."

"I'm clean, baby. My body is a temple."

"Your soul's in the gutter. Sometimes I don't think I know you at all."

"I'm trying to be strong. I've been focusing on my spirituality.

224

I've been meditating, doing yoga, Tai Chi, all that Oriental shit we used to do back in LA, but I have needs. I'm so close, baby. I just need you here with me to take that next step."

(silence)

(mild explosion)

"You there?"

"I'll be out tomorrow."

"I love you so much, baby. I'm gonna be really good to you."

"You better be."

"Don't forget my shit. Love you."

He closed the phone and slammed it against the toilet paper dispenser.

"Fuck yeah I'm good. You know what? Now I do want that blumpkin."

Tony opened the phone and punched in the numbers.

"Charlene, it's me. There's no toilet paper in this shitter ... how do I know which one? Just try all of them."

He closed the phone and pounded out a vigorous tattoo on his knees, humming the melody to Chuck Berry's *Route 66*.

"Better hurry up, baby. I'm starting to get low on fuel."

I could see his arm sweep upward as he checked his watch.

"Fuck!" he said, bolting up from the seat and thrusting open the door, which knocked Charlene, bearing several new rolls of toilet paper, onto the ground. Tony picked up one of the rolls and threw it at her. "You're too late!" he screamed, before stepping over her splayed form and striding purposefully toward the ghetto of ramshackle tents, trucks and trailers that housed the extras and crew.

I extracted my head from the vent—more difficult than the original insertion—and leapt to my feet, staying low to the ground as I moved into the clearing, where I pursued with a combination of speed and stealth, tracking Tony the way a Masai warrior might stalk a gazelle out on the Serenghetti. My quarry quickly disappeared into the squalid below-the-line netherworld, and I hastened my pace to catch up, turning this way and that, tripping over various cables and conduit and jogging breathlessly down blind alleys. I feared I'd lost him when I noticed a small thin man with Latin features and long hair in a ponytail rounding the corner wearing a leather mail carrier's pouch slung over his shoulder. My instincts told me to follow him, and before long he led me right to Tony, who was pacing back and forth anxiously behind a grey box truck.

I hung back so that I could observe the interaction unseen. Tony was cautious at first, arms folded, eyes darting every which way, while the ponytail man calmly walked right up to him, then stopped and took off the mail carrier's pouch.

"You Angel?" said Tony. "I've been standing here like three minutes."

"Good things come to those who wait," said Angel.

"How do I know this shit is any good?"

"Best in the West," said Angel, showing a sandstone smile. "Ask anyone around."

"Just give it to me," said Tony, reaching for the bag.

"You have the money?" said Angel.

"I'm good for it."

Angel hesitated.

"What are you worried about? You know where to find me. My face is splashed across every billboard from here to Timbuktu."

"Unfortunately at this time we are unable to handle accounts receivables."

Tony pulled his t-shirt over his head and waved it under the man's nose.

"This is a five hundred dollar Hermes t-shirt," he said. "This is the very same shirt I wore in *Double Diamond*."

Angel held the shirt and studied the fabric.

"Sign it," he said.

"I can't do that," Tony said. "I have an exclusive deal with Silver Light Entertainment."

Angel handed back the t-shirt and slung the pouch over his shoulder.

"Gimme a pen," said Tony.

Angel patted himself down.

"I am sorry," he said.

"Jesus H Christ," said Tony, grabbing an empty bottle of Miller High Life and breaking it on the bumper of the truck.

He picked up a piece of broken glass and cut into his finger until it bled. He then spread out the t-shirt and slowly signed his initials with the bleeding digit.

Angel scrutinized the signature.

"Shoes too."

Tony handed him the sandals.

"And the shorts ... to complete the set."

Tony stripped off the shorts and handed them over to Angel. After a moment, Angel smiled and threw the bag to Tony. Tony immediately opened the bag, making a cursory inspection of the contents, then ran off shirtless, shoeless and pantsless into the heart of the cinematic ghetto.

"You know where to find me," said Angel with a faint tone of amusement.

Tracking Tony through the Bombay-like mean streets of this infernal slum proved to be no mean feat, and I was fortunate that he stopped a short distance away, where he stood in the shadow of a huge supply tent in a quiet lane. The instant he pressed the metal nipple to his lips, I was there with a fist full of flame to light the dull rock simmering in the bowl of the crack pipe, beating him to the punch, so to speak. He tucked his own lighter away, eyes growing wide, and sucked the flame into the bowl until he'd had his fill.

Once he'd had a chance to fully savor the crack, to take in the rich blend of coca and ammonia and note the peculiar complexity and balance, he coughed out a huge cloud of smoke.

"Thanks," he said, extending the pipe. "Want some?"

"So we meet again," I said.

"We do?" he said, eyes narrowing over the pipe as he took another hit.

"Our relationship—both personal and professional—has become, over the years, as I'm sure you are well aware, the stuff of legend."

"Relationship?" he said. "Are you a friend of my uncle or something? I don't have any money. All that stuff is now handled by the firm of Green, Green, Allen and Ortega."

"The *Vanity Fair* piece caused a near riot, and the reverberations were felt on both sides of the pond, both Pacific and Atlantic. Our little *tete-a-tete*, lubricated by fine spirits, too many cigarettes and the adrenaline rush of high speed driving along the winding causeways of oblivion, is currently inspiring a generation to take up arms against the mundane, step out beyond the edge of reason and cast their undeveloped fates into the existential abyss of romantic suicide and auto-erotic immolation. The experience changed my life in a profound way, and having exhaustively observed yours through the proverbial lens—both micro- and telescopic—of my shaman-like sensibility, I am sure that the impact has been no less cataclysmic for you."

"The reporter," he said, reloading the pipe.

"I like to think of myself as more of a seer. Although I make my bread in the skin trade known as entertainment journalism, the vocational categories of writer, journalist, reporter are far too constricting considering the near mystical depth of vision I have brought to bear in my work. Despite a career spent chronicling the lives of our most notorious luminaries, despite the brushes with nominations for Pulitzers, Cabots, Bergers and other awards too numerous to count, I consider the work that we have achieved together—this *sui generis* love child of worldly experience on the one hand and preternatural masculine beauty on the other—to be our crowning achievement."

"Wasn't there a restraining order?" he said.

"That edict is only binding in the United States of America," I said. "Besides, there is no legal instrument capable of separating two beings—subject and object—inextricably bound, who are essentially, ontologically, one."

"I thought we were in Arizona or something," he said.

"We spend our whole lives constrained by imaginary lines in the sand," I said. "The only true borders are the walls we build that separate us from our other true selves."

"I personally don't give a shit. That was my manager, PR rep, the studio. I keep out of all that. I'm live and let live."

"I see you have a fresh wound," I said, unsheathing a huge bowie knife, blade glinting in the rays of sunlight that pierced the tent poles and canopies of this ephemeral city. "Before we have it cleaned and dressed, let us not miss this opportunity to at last consecrate our spiritual bond and enter into the perpetual union of comingled flesh."

"You wanna be blood brothers?" he said.

"Something like that. What I have in mind is a more permanent and fundamental alteration of our physical geometries."

"You don't say. Well, you'll have to..."

Tony took another hit off the pipe.

"...you'll have to tell me more about that some time ..."

He coughed smoke.

"This is the worst goddamn crack I've ever had," he said,

checking his watch. "Shit, I gotta be in makeup two minutes ago."

He handed me the still smoldering pipe and ran off down the shadowy lane.

I took a hit, held it, blew smoke. In fact, it wasn't bad, wasn't bad at all.

# CHAPTER 41

"Stop it right there," said Dante, signaling with a lit cigarette. "Back it up two frames ... one more. There."

On the screen, the paused frame showed Tony (as the Gang Lord) in the process of stepping out of the black Rolls Royce limo. The door was open. One hand gripped the arm rest of the door. On the fingers of the hand gripping the arm rest were a number of large rings—Chinese dragon, skull and crossbones, black unicorn. He had his legs outside the car, about to stand up.

"Now back it up three more frames," said Dante.

Seated behind a laptop computer, Silvio rolled the clip back three frames until the shot of Tony getting out of the limo transitioned to a shot of the limo Driver holding open the door. The limo driver wore a black chauffeur's hat and a black and yellow suit made from gila monster skin. Except for the thin black mustache, he looked exactly like Nero.

"Between these two shots, we need a close up on that ring," said Dante. "The one with the bloody unicorn."

On another screen, Silvio dragged over the hand-on-car-door shot and zoomed in on the unicorn ring, until the image took up the whole screen. Then he dragged over the re-framed shot and dropped it right at the transition point between hand-on-car-door and driver-holding-door.

"Run it straight through," said Dante.

Silvio backed up the clip and ran it forward.

On the screen, the limo driver opened the door and held it. The camera cut to a close up of the unicorn ring, the sun glinting off the black horn, as the hand gripped the arm rest of the door. The camera then cut to a full view of the Gang Lord (Tony) stepping out of the limo. Silvio backed up the clip and paused it on the image of the Driver opening the door.

"See what I'm saying?" said Dante. "It looks good on paper, but when you see it up on the screen it's bull shit."

"The unicorn is a key symbol. It represents the crime lord's outward projection of what is essentially an illusion of potency," said Blow.

"Sure, sure it does," said Dante. "Except nobody gives a flying fuck about that. It distracts from a perfectly good scene."

"It takes just two, maybe three, seconds," said Blow.

"Three seconds is an eternity up there," said Dante. "In three seconds you count the champ out, in three seconds you count down to a nuclear blast. In this business, you can't lose their attention for an instant, or you're fucked forever. Every beat counts."

"I see what you're saying," said Blow. "But Nero made it clear he wants to emphasize the mythological subtext -"

"Then let him cut the bloody film. I'd like to see him get his hands dirty for once. His fingers are on everything and nothing. Don't let him get inside your head. You're the bloody writer. It's your vision, and it's my vision, and it's even bloody Tony fucking Billings' vision. We're the *creatives*, see? We're the ones actually making the bloody thing."

"An article recently hailed him as one of the new breed of super-creatives."

"Super-creative, my ass. He's just a glorified money man. Nod, smile, flatter him, tell him whatever the fuck you want, so long as he picks up the tab. It is your ethical duty to bleed him dry, drain him to the last drop. Just remember, no matter what they say, no matter what you read in the magazines, they're not one of us. They can't have it both ways."

"As long as we get a pick-up shot with the falcon standing on his shoulder," said Blow. "To represent the connection to Horus."

"As long as you shoot it yourself," said Dante. "I don't work with bloody animals. That's where I draw the line, unless it's a cock fight or a Tijuana pony show."

"I'm just honored to be part of the process," said Blow. "Usually my involvement ends when I turn in the script."

"Not every director is a dictatorial prick. I'm long past the point where I want to do every goddamn thing myself. I'll tap every piece of talent in stroking distance, whether they're on the payroll or not. Because when all is said and done, I still get the credit."

Bax ducked under the tent flap and entered the screening room, followed by Nick.

"Beautiful timing. You just missed my standard speech about the evils of money men."

"I always tell people I'm not creative," said Bax. "But they keep asking me to do their job anyway. Where should we put the sunset? Where should we put the rainbow, they ask? I just say the first thing that comes into my head. Put it over the mountain, at the end of the second act. Make it a reflection on a lake. Paint it on a child's face. I don't even have to think about it."

"I thought about being a creative type," said Nick. "Once upon a time. Thought about branching out from the money game and developing something from my own imagination. But I found it hard to come up with ideas while constantly getting blown by all these little actresses in my ninety thousand dollar car."

Dante looked up at the screen—*the paused image of the Driver (dead ringer for Nero) holding open the door of the black Rolls limo.*

"Jesus, fucker looks just like him, doesn't he?" said Dante.

"How do we know it's not?" said Bax.

"No way to be sure of course. Fucker never comes anywhere near the set. But this Victor St. Germaine hack has an actual verifiable track record; you can look him up on the Internet, credits far as the eye can see," said Dante.

"Just happens to look exactly like Nero," said Nick.

"Separated at birth," said Bax.

"Could be a fucking clone. I mean, it's possible, right? Fucker has the money," said Silvio.

"Fucker has the money for ten thousand clones. An entire mother fucking clone army," said Dante. "The man is a complete narcissist."

"Goes hand in hand with genius," said Silvio.

"You're thinking too much. Just say pain-in-the-ass and leave it at that," said Dante. "The only geniuses around here are those poor brainy bastards blowing up rockets out in the middle of the desert on a government allowance that barely covers a soda and a good jerk."

"You got anything?" said Bax, nodding toward the screen.

"We need something to report to the Japanese," said Nick.

"Roll it, Silvio," said Dante. "From the top."

*On the screen, Tony sat in the back seat, surrounded by black leather. The Driver turned around to face him.*

*"Drive me out between the two sides before I let the battle start. I just want to see for a minute," said Tony.*

*Tony sat calmly as the car took him out into the clearing. The car stopped. The Driver opened the door. Tony swung his legs out, grasping the handle of the door, and stepped from the car.*

*The Driver closed the door. Tony turned his head to the left, saw the men lined up with their guns drawn, ready for battle. He turned his head to the right, saw his own gang lined up in equal force.*

*Some distance away, the opposing gang leader sat on the hood of a black Mercedes AMG, with his hands in his lap, calmly waiting.*

*Tony raised the gun, poised to fire the opening shot. A moment passed during which he did not pull the trigger.*

*"What do you see?" said the Driver.*

*"On both sides, men who I have known my whole life," said Tony, lowering the gun. "Better that I should die here than unleash this carnage."*

*"Where does this cowardice come from?" said the Driver. "Have you forgotten yourself? You are a warrior. And the highest goal of a warrior is a good war. ... So get in there and fight. Do you think you were going to kill these men? They are already dead."*

*The Driver touched Tony's eye and Tony saw his friend transformed into a tremendous monstrous divinity with many mouths full of great tusks. As this vision expanded, Tony saw both armies flying into these mouths and smashing like grapes, and the blood pouring down like spilled wine.*

*"Who are you?" said Tony.*

*"I am black time, here for the end of the world. I am licking up mankind."*

*The Driver's appearance returned to normal.*

*"These forms that you kill do not exist. What was never born never dies. Rains do not wet it. Fire does not burn it. So get in there and seem to be doing*

233

*things. You can be the instrument of destiny itself."*

*Tony looked to one side and then the other. He raised the gun and began to squeeze the trigger.*

"That's probably good right there," said Bax.

"Just needed to give them a little taste," said Nick. "So they don't get their panties in a bunch."

"You're gonna miss the best part," said Silvio.

"Marianne's new tits," said Tina, looking up from her laptop. "They've been up there all morning."

"Two of southern California's most precious resources," said Dante.

"Well, if you insist," said Bax, opening a mineral water and taking a seat.

*On the screen, Tony squeezed the trigger by degrees, the hammer inching back. Suddenly, a black horse materialized in the distance. Tony lowered the gun and watched as the horse galloped toward him. The horse stopped a short distance away. Although there was no rider, the horse was pulling a sleigh. Tony and the Driver walked past the horse to inspect the sleigh. In the bed of the sleigh was a coffin. Tony opened the lid to reveal the Shared Bride (played by Marianne) lying naked and unconscious. The Driver put his ear to her chest and nodded. Tony removed one of the four wedding rings on her left hand and held it up high for his men to see. [We saw the ring through binoculars, from the point of view of one of Tony's lieutenants]. Tony's gang erupted in loud cheers. Tony walked away from the coffin and faced the opposing gang leader, then ceremoniously put the gun back in his holster. The opposing gang leader stood up and got into the car. The car backed up, circled around and drove away.*

*In the ornate dining room of Tony's palatial compound, Marianne was laid out nude on the ceremonial banquet table with all seven brothers seated around the perimeter. Armed guards stood at the doors and windows.*

*"How can we trust them? It could be a trap," said Brother #1.*

*"I searched her myself," said Tony, giving a wry smile. "No explosives."*

*"I still think it could be a trick. It is not like Drazen to back down from a fight," said Brother #4.*

*"You have my guarantee. She is pure, and ready for the child," said Tony.*

*"Before the child is brought in, I want to see for myself," said Brother #1.*

234

*"Me too," said Brother #3.*

*"It is the only way to be sure," said Brother #6.*

*"Then every one of us will go in turn," said Tony.*

*Tony nodded at Brother #1, who got up and approached Marianne's recumbent form. He kissed the wedding band on the index finger of her left hand, then leaned over and gently suckled her breast.*

*He nodded. "It is good."*

*Each brother got up in turn and suckled from Marianne's breast and each indicated that the milk was satisfactory. When it got to be Tony's turn, all eyes turned to him.*

*"I am satisfied," said Tony. "It is time to bring in the child."*

*A Wet Nurse entered the room, carrying a baby. She crossed the room, cooing to the child, which appeared quiet and lifeless. She then pressed its mouth to the naked breast.*

*Once the infant latched, it suckled hungrily.*

*"It's a miracle!" cried the Wet Nurse. "The child hasn't fed for six days."*

*The room erupted in loud cheers, as the brothers stood up, embracing and toasting the health of the infant.*

*When the infant finally broke off, it started to cry.*

*"Healthy now," said the nurse, rocking the baby in her arms.*

*"Quiet!" Brother #2 shouted. "She's trying to speak."*

*He lowered his ear to Marianne's lips and listened.*

*"My baby, my little boy," she murmured.*

*"The crying of her child has broken through her coma," said the elderly Doctor, in a thick German accent.*

*Suddenly, Marianne shot bolt upright in bed, her eyes popping open as she screamed bloody murder.*

*"My baby! My baby!" she screamed.*

*"Restrain her," said the Doctor, pinning her down onto the bed.*

*The attending nurses strapped her down to the table as she continued to scream.*

*"What has happened to this woman?" said Brother #1.*

*"She has gone mad," said the Doctor. "Look at her eyes. The striation, dilated pupils ... classic symptoms of LSD 69 intoxication."*

*"Will she be all right?"*

*"I'm afraid not. LSD 69 permanently rewires the brain, bringing about full blown insanity in less than eight hours."*

*"It was a trap," said Brother #2. "Drazen spiked the milk."*

235

*"I am afraid so," said the Doctor. "That is the only logical conclusion."*

*"What are we supposed to do?" said Brother #3. "Just sit here and wait to go mad?"*

*"There is nothing else to be done," said the Doctor. "There is no known antidote to LSD 69."*

*Tony walked to the front of the room.*

*"We must get our houses in order," he said. "While we are still sane."*


Silvio paused the image on the screen.

"How's that?" said Dante.

"The Japanese will love this shit," said Bax.

"The whole thing with the milk. They'll lap it up," said Nick. "They're real kinky bastards."

"It's not actually supposed to be kink," said Blow. "It's simply a device to blend the central feature of the Mahabharata myth—the idea of the shared bride with the Trojan Horse concept."

"That's what we'll tell the critics," said Dante. "It worked with Marianne. Amazing how quickly they'll drop their knickers for a whiff of gravitas."

"It's a courageous performance," said Blow.

"She's lying there with her eyes closed," said Tina.

"She's baring her soul," said Blow.

"A rubber fuck-doll could have done that," said Tina.

"Already thinking about the press kit," said Dante, giving Blow a wink. He checked his watch. "It looks like we have time for a quick drink before the magic hour."

"You should see the fuck dolls they got now," said Q, stepping into the tent. "Act the pants off some of these bitches."

"Amen to that," said Nick, twirling away from the bar with a bottle of mineral water and a Singapore Sling.

236

# CHAPTER 42

As Q entered the trailer, Tommy Boy, Antoine and DJ Trix were seated around the breakfast table playing cards.

"Sup, Q?" said Antoine, laying down a card.

"Yo Q wassup?" said Tommy Boy, looking up from his hand.

"Holla," said DJ Trix, raising his index finger up by his ear while remaining seated with his back to Q.

Q loomed in the doorway, the desert light singeing the outline of his silhouette.

"Girls just stepped out," said Antoine.

"Made a fresh batch of ice," said Tommy Boy. "Should be just about set. Used that primo oxygen water shit, shipped special from France, stainless steel trays, just the way you like it."

"Raise you," said Trix, throwing crisp bills on the table.

Q moved fully into the trailer, closing the door behind him. He stood in the narrow throughway that ran the length of the trailer and inhaled deeply through his nose.

"Lavender," he said. "Cinnamon. Undernote of ... cardamom."

Antoine and Tommy Boy's eyes met quickly over the table.

"The disinfectant," said Tommy Boy. "Lavender scented was the only kind they had left."

"Use white vinegar," said Q. "One part vinegar to four parts

237

water."

"I don't know about no cardamom," said Tommy Boy.

"Erica's perfume," said Antoine. "Smelled like cinnamon and ..."

"I told her not to wear that shit," said Trix.

"Blue Lady #9," said Q.

"That's it. She's got a whole bottle of that shit in her purse," said Antoine. "I've seen it. Must be 2-3 ounces."

"Notes of cinnamon, anise, cardamom," said Q, nose twitching as he moved through the trailer. "One thing I can't fucking stand is cardamom."

"Here it is," said Antoine, finding the purse buried behind some pillows. He searched through the contents and took out the bottle.

"What you want me to do with it? Throw it away?"

"That shit never works. She'll find it," said Tommy Boy. "Light it on fire,"

Antoine took out his lighter and started twisting the cap of the perfume.

"Not in here," said Tommy Boy. "Have to light the whole damn *trailer* on fire."

"Drink it," said Q.

"Drink it?" said Antoine.

"Drink the mother fucker," said Q.

"It's the only way to be sure," said Trix, taking a card from the pile.

Antoine looked to Tommy Boy, then to DJ Trix, then to Q, then back to Tommy Boy. Reluctantly, he removed the cap and raised the bottle to his lips. He checked the faces one more time—all eyes staring back at him intently—then tilted back the bottle and drank.

Once the bottle was emptied, he closed his eyes hard and shook his head.

"Not bad," he said, opening his eyes wide and looking down at the bottle. "No worse than Hypnotiq. Shit's 80% alcohol. That's 160 proof."

"Erica's gonna be pissed," said Tommy Boy.

"Don't worry bout Erica. Erica gonna be fine," said Q.

"When she sees that purse, what we supposed to say?" said

Antoine.

"Tell her I put my dick in it," said Q. "Put my dick in it and moved it all around."

"That's a nine hundred dollar purse," said Tommy Boy.

"That's a triple platinum dick," said Q.

"Bitch got more purses than a Alabama church choir got lips," said Trix.

"You strapped?" said Q.

"Not me," said Tommy Boy, shaking his head.

"Me either," said Antoine.

"Always," said Trix, hiking his shirt to reveal the butt of a snub-nose .38.

"From now on, I want everybody strapped," said Q.

"What for?" said Tommy Boy, shuffling the deck.

"I've seen the signs," said Q.

"Signs of what?" said Antoine.

"Enemy presence."

"Nobody out here but us, bro. And all these little magic-of-movies motherfuckers," said Tommy Boy. "Just rocks and sand in every direction, far as the eye can see."

"We're a thousand miles from all that shit back home, no East Coast, no West Coast, no coast of any kind, you know what I'm saying? No Bloods, No Crips, hell, I aint even seen no Cherokees, Chocktaws, Iroquois, whatever the fuck kinda Indians they got out here."

"What you see out there got you all spun up, bro?" said Tommy Boy.

"Alien life forms," said Q.

"You been watchin' too much Discovery Channel."

"I pay attention," he said pointing to his eye. "Read the lay of the land. Why I'm always one step ahead."

"Make you feel better," said Tommy Boy, removing a .44 from under the seat cushion and tucking it in his waist band.

Tommy Boy picked up a card, then looked up to observe a large tarantula crawling from the dome of Q's shaved head down the side of his face. Instinctively, Tommy Boy withdrew the gun and pointed it at Q.

"Holy shit! Holy shit!" he gasped.

Antoine looked up, then fell backwards out of his seat,

landing on his back and trying to propel himself across the floor with a series of frantic kicks.

"Shoot the mother fucker!" he screamed. "Shoot!"

"Shake it off, bro! Shake it off!" said Tommy Boy, pulling back the safety.

Slowly, the spider crawled down Q's neck and along his arm, eventually coming to rest in the palm of his hand.

From his position on the floor, Antoine rolled into the bathroom, grabbed a Tek-9 that was taped under the lid of the toilet, then rolled back into the throughway and pointed the gun at Q.

"Name's Tick-Tock," said Q.

"That thing real?" said Antoine.

"Real? How you know any mother fuckin' thing's real? How do I know your black ass real?" said Q, drawing a Smith & Wesson and aiming it down at Antoine's chest.

Q moved the gun from Antoine to Tommy Boy and back to Antoine.

"See you," said Trix, picking up a card. "And raise you."

Tommy Boy and Antoine put down their guns.

"Easy, chief. You cool with that creepy crawly mother fucker, we're cool too, know what I'm sayin'?"

"We cool, bro," said Antoine, holding up his hands. "Every mother fuckin' thing's cool."

"This is us talkin' here," said Tommy Boy. "Now, Erica and the girls see that thing, that's another mother fuckin' story."

Q lowered the gun, sticking it under the waistband behind his back. He set the spider on top of his head and covered it with a purple bowler hat.

"Where you find that thing, bro?"

"Came to me in a dream," said Q. "I woke up this morning out in the desert, standing there just like I am now, staring into the sun."

"Hope you were wearin' sunglasses," said Antoine.

"Same pair I'm wearing now, black wrap-around Guccis, 100% UV Protected. You can see, my eyes are completely fine."

He removed the sunglasses—revealing a fixed thousand mile stare that was chilling in its intensity—then put them back on.

"You sure you're all right, bro?" said Tommy Boy.

"I'm better than all right. I'm better than mother fuckin' ever.

240

I'm a new man. Hell, I'm a new mother fuckin' species. I'm mother fuckin' born all over again."

"You look like you got a little bit of sun, that's for sure," said Antoine.

"In the dream, I was in the middle of an enchanted forest, surrounded by huge jade plants, ferns and strange beautiful flowers. I was covered in brightly colored birds, you know, parrots and shit like that, standing on my shoulders, my shoes, on the top of my head. They were singing to me, the sweetest song you ever heard. I could have stood there forever like that, just listening to them sweet little things sing. When I woke up, the forest was gone, and I was in the desert. I started to walk on out of there, was just about to put my foot down when I saw it, a scorpion about as big as my hand. I turned and there was another, and another. They were all over the mother fuckin' place. Hundreds of them. I couldn't move a muscle. They was all staring right at me, with their claws up in the air, waiting to bum rush my ass. I thought I was toast. I couldn't jump over the mother fuckers. There was too damn many of them. I closed my eyes and tried to return to the enchanted forest, but every time I opened my eyes all I saw were them mother fuckin' scorpions. There were too damn many to shoot. I crossed myself, Hail Mary style, and put the gun to my head. Suicide's for chumps, but in this case won't suicide at all, just an alternate method of execution. No way this player's goin' out like that, slowly poisoned to death by an army of nasty lobster sized mother fuckin' little insects. About to pull the trigger when the bird hit, landed on my shoulder like the grim reaper his self, with a mother fuckin' tarantula in its mouth. Mother fucker dropped the tarantula right on my mother fuckin' head, then hopped down and started murdering all them mother fuckin' scorpions. When the other birds saw what was goin' on they started dive bombing those little mother fuckers, hammering the mother fuckers with their beaks and flying away with em in their teeth. Only took a few seconds before it was all over, and I walked outta there, over all them dead scorpion bodies like Moses walkin' over the Dead Sea. Forgot all about the tarantula until I showed up at make-up and the bitch freaked the fuck out."

"You gonna *keep* the mother fuckin' thing?" said Antoine.

"At least put it in a terrarium or something," said Tommy Boy.

"Maybe I put *your* ass in a terrarium," said Q, pointing the gun at Tommy Boy's head.

Tommy Boy held up his hands.

"Easy, chief. Just makin' a suggestion," he said.

"This my guardian angel," said Q. "Wherever I go, he goes. From now on we're inseparable."

"Thought you said that thing came to you in a dream," said Antoine.

"What I realized, soon after I woke up, was that the dream never really ended. This here," he said, waving the gun. "This all still the dream. Aint none of y'all mother fuckers real. I could waste any one of you right now and won't mean shit to me cuz all you mother fuckers already dead."

"Guardian angel can take any form," said Trix. "Bitch. Spider. Wolf. Even an actual angel with halo and wings and shit."

"This for real, chief. For sure," said Tommy Boy. "Ask any mother fucker around here."

"I know what I know. Only reason I left the enchanted forest cuz I heard the tick-tock of the old grandfather clock and knew it was time to wake up, but when I opened my eyes out in the desert, wasn't a tick-tock at all, just this loud crackling sound from some old yellow-and-black radio looking mother fucking thing sittin' on a rock."

"Radio? You're hallucinating that shit, G," said Tommy Boy.

"That's what I'm tryin' to tell y'all mother fuckers. All this shit just a hallucination."

"You up now, G. Feel this table and shit," said Antoine, knocking on the table.

"Everything chill for now. Don't wake up soon, though, gonna have to start shootin' my way out this mother fucker."

"See? That's a real mother fuckin' table," said Tommy Boy, erecting a small house of cards. "Can't do that on no imaginary table."

Q, wearing a single black leather glove on his left hand, ran his finger along the underside of the table. He held up the finger and inspected the white powder.

"That's some real mother fuckin' dust right there. For real." He raised the gun and pointed it at Tommy Boy. "Now clean that shit up."

# CHAPTER 43

The Land Rover rumbled across the rocky desert terrain as the sun crept over the horizon. Jerzy drove, with Dante riding shotgun. Barclay sat in the back, squeezed between Blow and Tina. Barclay attempted at first to write his notes on paper, the traditional way, but every time the Land Rover went over a bump his hat hit the roof and the pad bucked off his lap. The pen had actually left more marks on his safari grade khakis than on the leather bound notepad.

"I hate to resort to this," he said, taking a cigarette sized micro-recorder out of his vest pocket. "But do you mind if I record our conversation?"

"Okay by me," said Dante. "No secrets here, unless you ask me how I know about Tina's pervy new lower back tattoo."

"How *do* you know that?" said Tina.

"I must remind you that this conversation is being recorded," said Dante.

"I was actually interested in talking about theme," said Barclay. "I'm particularly curious about the role of the desert, and the mythological subtext that underpins the story."

"It's simple really," said Dante. "I can explain it in about thirty seconds, and then we can get back to Tina's naughty bits."

"Don't even think about it," said Tina.

The Driver, you know, the cat who looks like Nero, see, he

represents the gods Krishna and Seth," said Dante.

"Two gods," Barclay said.

"Hindu and Egyptian. The thing about Krishna is, even though he's like, you know, a god, he likes to hang out with regular mortals. Just for sport," said Tina.

"Like Tony," said Barclay.

"Tony's character represents the clan leader, Krishna's friend, from The Bhagavad Gita story," said Blow.

"He's a regular guy who commands a humongous Hindu army," said Tina.

"...also, Horus," said Blow.

"Horus," said Barclay.

"The god of the sky," said Blow. "That's why Tony's got the two-toned eyes."

"Thank God for colored contact lenses," said Tina.

"The blue eye on the right is the sun, and the dark eye on the left is the moon," said Blow. "Horus and Seth are brothers, see. They went to war over a big chunk of desert. Also, Horus was pissed off that Seth killed their father. When all was said and done, Horus lost an eye but got the real estate. Seth lost one of his nuts."

"Which one?" said Barclay.

"I'm not sure. It doesn't matter. Let's say it was the left," said Blow. "That's how Seth came to represent the desert and windstorms."

"He was the god of windstorms and the desert," said Tina.

"And infertility, because of the missing nut," said Blow. "At some point, before, I imagine, he lost the nut, Seth tried to rape Horus, but Horus caught his spunk and threw it in a river, then jacked off on a piece of lettuce which he fed to Seth. When the contest was ultimately adjudicated by the gods, they gave Horus credit for his stealth dietetic rape and declared him the winner."

"So Horus got the W, out raping his brother on a technicality," said Dante.

"I thought Horus was some kind of bird man," said Barclay.

"He had the head of a falcon," said Blow.

"Could he fly and shit?" said Jerzy.

"In the film, the sky represents the ocean. Tony's got this ridiculous cigarette boat, 40 feet long, 2000 horsepower," said Blow.

"Even though he's out in the middle of the desert, with no

water anywhere," said Barclay.

"He's got a whole fleet ... because, see, he's a superstitious type, and his whole life he's been waiting for the flood. Plus, he really loves boats, especially luxury yachts and cigarette boats," said Blow.

"Go-fast boats," said Tina.

"Can you imagine trying to rape somebody who has the head of a falcon?" said Dante.

"Can you imagine trying to rape your own brother over a land dispute?" said Tina.

"Eventually the whole thing was settled by a boat race," said Blow.

"They should have done the boat race before trying to out rape each other. That would have been a lot easier for everyone," said Dante.

"Seth is also considered the lord of the underworld," said Blow.

"After he lost the boat race, he gave up Egypt and went down into the hole to stir some shit up from beneath the earth," said Dante.

"Where'd you find the tits?" said Tina.

"Castaway. Had to comb through thousands of shots," said Dante.

"Shots of tits," said Tina. "They give Oscars for that yet?"

"Boring show. They need a Best Tits category," said Jerzy. "Marianne win for sure."

"She's got a lock on the Golden Globes," said Dante. "The Foreign Press loves American tits."

"Ordinarily, there's not a lot you can do with tits, except put food on them," said Blow. "We were all sitting around saying, hey, we've got these spectacular tits, what are we going to do with them?"

"You could lick them, of course. But how does that serve the story?" said Tina.

"What if they were full of milk?" said Blow.

"And everybody had to try some," said Tina.

"And the milk was laced with LSD," said Blow.

"Tony lost her to his cousins in a dice game. The one stipulation was, he had to turn her over alive," said Tina.

"But there was a loophole. Nobody said anything about she had to be awake," said Dante.

"So he slipped a mickey into her appletini and she went into a coma," said Blow.

"The problem was, the infant, the heir to the throne, so to speak, didn't thrive on the milk of the wet nurses," said Blow.

"Tony and his brothers were desperate to get her back and threatened to start a war," said Tina.

"The truth is, we shot the scene first, then backed into the reason," said Blow.

"Pure Kamikaze filmmaking," said Dante.

"What about the girl, does she also represent a god?" said Barclay.

"Snow White. And the seven brothers represent the seven dwarves. The infant represents Prince Charming whose magic kiss brings her back to life," said Blow.

"Wait, Tony's a dwarf?" said Barclay.

"It's a metaphor or something," said Jerzy.

"Stop the jeep," said Dante. "This is the spot."

The Land Rover slowed to a stop, and the four men got out. Dante formed a square with his thumbs and middle fingers and held his hands in front of his face, squinting through the make-shift lens, alternately squatting down, leaping up and spinning about. Jerzy was doing the same thing, only in a more nonchalant manner.

"It's gorgeous," said Dante. "Absolutely gorgeous. What do you think?"

"Yes, it is good," said Jerzy, dismantling his digital camera lens so that he could light a cigarette. "The color values, they are very ..." He paused to take a drag on the cigarette. "...very good."

"The good guys on that side, the bad guys over there, and the sun over our heads," said Dante.

"What about that?" said Blow, pointing to the huge dinosaur-like oil derrick bobbing up and down on a patch of high ground in the distance.

"It is no problem," said Jerzy. "You will never see it."

"Keep it," said Dante. "I want it in there."

"How are we going to explain it?" said Blow.

Dante gave him a big smile and patted him on the shoulder.

"I'm sure you'll figure it out."

246

# CHAPTER 44
*FREDERICK M. BARCLAY*

I woke up with the taste of whiskey on my lips, the morning sun boring holes through my eyelids deep into my reptile brain. The empty bottle was still in my hand. I pushed myself up from the sand and threw the bottle at a vulture standing watch nearby. The vulture easily side stepped the bottle, taking a short hop and spreading its wings before continuing its morbid vigil. I looked around, panning my gaze from horizon to distant horizon. There was nothing as far as the eye could see, nothing but rock and scrub and sand. The memories of the night before were a collage of transcendent ecstasies and soul crushing debasements that mingled in my aching skull like the charged particles of an atomic reaction. Through sheer force of will, I rose to my feet and set out into the desert, in what direction I will not bother to describe. Because I could not recall from whence I came, it hardly mattered in what direction I traveled now. I would either find my way back or I would not. There was nothing to be gained by staying here, wherever this was, this vast nothingness.

In my errant wandering I eventually came upon a team of scientists who had established an encampment on a particularly wind swept plain. With their numerous computers, their machines full of dials, switches and digital displays, and the myriad instruments sprouting shimmering air foils, spinning propellers and bouncing antennae, too the array of sleek and sophisticated weather balloons arranged in silvery clusters like decorations at a birthday party in space, I gathered that they were meteorologists of some kind. The balloons came in a variety of colors and sizes, from the standard silvery globe suitable for carrying a small bit of sensitive electronics up into the stratosphere to an almost entirely translucent orb to a balloon that appeared substantial enough to carry away a small car.

At the moment, a majority of the scientists sat at a cheap fold-up table playing a game of cards. As a group, the scientists had olive complexions and dark wavy hair and spoke in a language that I immediately recognized as French, a language oft associated with art and love but rarely with the cold facts of science. There was only one woman among them, a feral raven haired creature possessed of an earthy instinctual beauty. At the moment, she was engaged in an intimate *tete-a-tete* with the youngest and most handsome of the scientists. Although the table between them was littered with instruments, sheets of data and other technical detritus, their proximity (noses practically touching) suggested they were up to anything but science. I walked among them as a ghost, no one showing the slightest recognition of my existence until, at a loss, I asked—"So is there anything to drink around here?"

A coarse looking man with large sideburns uncorked an unlabeled bottle and poured several fingers of an amber liquid into a dusty snifter. He pushed the glass in front of me then poured one for himself. I raised the glass to my nose and inhaled deeply. From the initial *montant*, it was clear that this was a superior Cognac, probably a De Luze XO or perhaps even a Camus Borderies. I allowed the amber blondes to swirl around the crystal before once more raising the glass and taking a sip, letting the delicate fluid decompose on my palate—saying to myself (but in a voice loud enough to be overheard), "notes of *ugni blanc*, a distinct Limousin oakiness, a hint of *terroir* (just enough to remind one that the elixir, though divine, was of earthly origin) and more than a trace of chalk"—before raising my chin so that it trickled like nectar of the gods down my parched throat. I pursed my lips and nodded appreciatively at my host.

"It is shit," said the Frenchman, as he finished his portion in a single gulp and returned to his seat at the card table.

A strong gust buffeted the encampment. The raven haired

woman brushed her hair from her eyes as her young paramour moved in to light her cigarette, closing the space between them to protect the precariously dancing flame from the wind. It was then that I noticed the camera, a small hand-held movie camera to be precise. The man holding the camera was Jerzy Pavel, an obscure Eastern European cinematographer who was doing second unit work on the *Scorched Earth* project. The man standing just behind him— bearded, middle aged, moist lipped—was none other than critically acclaimed auteur (and close personal friend) Jack Dante.

With drink in hand, I walked up to Dante, making sure that I was just out of frame.

"I owe you an apology. I didn't realize you were shooting," I said.

"Neither do they, apparently," he said, nodding dismissively toward the French scientists. "We've been shooting for hours and they've barely shown any sign they know we're here."

"I experienced much the same sensation," I said. "It was quite alienating."

"Quite liberating in my opinion. I prefer it. We're getting some great shit."

"What kind of shit, if I may ask? Bonus footage, perhaps, for the *Scorched Earth* DVD?"

"Way bigger than that, my friend. What we're shooting here, this is a completely different movie."

"A documentary," I said.

"An art film," he said. "There. I'm not ashamed to say it. A good old fashioned art film. The kind nobody makes anymore. Not like that Tony Billings piece of shit over there."

"Tony Billings piece of shit?" I protested.

"And you know the best part? I don't have to ask for anybody's permission. I'm just doing it. Skeleton crew. Hand-held cameras. A handful of actors. Almost no script to speak of. The whole thing is basically improvised, just like the original."

"The original what?"

"*Walkabout.* I've been trying do a remake for decades. Came close with that *Fire Devil* piece of shit, until Ray Leo burst into flames."

"That was quite unfortunate."

"Every time I've come close, something happens. The money

backs out. Scheduling conflicts. A tornado catches on fire and incinerates one of the leads."

"I must say, that is surprisingly generous of Nero to allow you to work on a side project right in the middle of a major studio production, with, I'm assuming, borrowed equipment…"

"Allow? Nero's not *allowing* me to do anything. One thing I've learned, if you want something, sometimes you just have to take it. So we're borrowing a camera, a couple extras. Some sound equipment. He'll never miss it. And when all is said and done and that big budget Tony Billings spectacle over there explodes in his face, I'll be moonwalking my way across Cannes with this little gem."

"I must congratulate you on your boldness. This is guerilla filmmaking in the truest sense of the word. You are essentially using a big studio production—location, talent, technical resources—to stage a clandestine indie film.  As far as I am aware, an unprecedented act of subversion, both in an economic and artistic sense. Although I am certainly no lawyer, I can't help but wonder about the potential contractual ramifications."

"Who gives a fuck? What's he going to do about it? Sue me?"

"He could do worse than that."

"Let him try. Fuck him. By then it'll be too late. I'll have a bucket full of awards, a fat-ass distribution deal. He can't touch me. Just let him try to pierce my corporate veil, baby."

"*Walkabout* was set in the Outback, was it not?"

"A desert's a desert. I'm substituting an Indian kid for the Aborigine."

"The character who hangs himself from the tree?"

"This is his one shot with the girl, and he blows it. Once you get that close, there's no going back. There are no u-turns in this life, only forks in the road."

"Forks leading to forks," I said, somewhat redundantly.

"Take the scene here," said Dante. "Jerzy and I were just wandering around shooting miles of deserty looking shit: weirdly shaped rocks, huge gangly cactuses, the *sun*. And then out of nowhere, voila. All these Frog scientists playing with balloons. Can you fucking believe it? It's almost exactly like the scene from the original. I mean almost exactly. Like it was meant to be. Once you overcome your fears, your petty concerns, all the little things that are holding you back, it's almost like the universe just opens up to you."

"Almost uncanny, really, when you think about it," I said. "With any fortuitous coincidence I become deeply pessimistic, convinced I am walking into a trap."

"You've got to loosen up, take life as it comes, Freddy."

"There is nothing else for one to do," I said, leaving Dante's side and walking back into the frame.

I hovered over the card game, watching the men bluff and banter, laying down cards and money. And then all at once it hit me. I reached into my jacket pocket and pulled out the Queen of Spades I'd found in Tony's trash.

"I think I have something that belongs to you," I said, showing them the card.

The man with the sideburns looked up with a faint laugh.

"That card does not belong to us. See…"

He pulled a card from his hand and showed it to me. There was no doubt about it. It was the exact same card, down to the mole on the Spanish girl's left tit.

"Double … trouble," he said in his resonant French accent as he took the card from me.

He laid the twin Queens down on the table, tits up, and swept away the entire pot of, not Francs, or Euros, or greenbacks for that matter, but some strange currency the likes of which I'd never seen. Then the man cocked his head to the side, giving me a wink and saying, in what I swear was such a pitch-perfect Australian accent that I did an immediate double-take, "Thanks mate."

# CHAPTER 45

Except for the Raja's palace, the tee pee was the tallest structure in the camp. It was easily 40 feet high and 30 feet wide at the base and was made from fine Galuchat leather. Dante ducked inside to find Nero seated Indian style on a Tatami mat. Blow, also Indian style, was seated to his left. The style of the space was more Zen minimalist than Sitting Bull sweat lodge.

"Aren't there any chairs in this god forsaken hot house?" said Dante, pacing about in an agitated state.

"Please, join us," said Nero, beckoning with his hand.

Dante walked over and reluctantly joined the circle (which consisted of Nero, Blow, Bax, Nick and an Indian in face paint and full head dress), plopping on the Tatami mat with an exaggerated groan. He sprawled out, with his arms propped behind him.

"A pillow at least," he said. "I haven't sat on the floor since grade school."

"I find such things to be an unnecessary distraction," said Nero. "While on location, I prefer the most Spartan accommodations—no chairs, no bed, no television, no furniture of any kind, no toaster, no refrigerator, no refrigerator magnets, no coffee maker. This arrangement allows me to focus completely on the project. I subsist on nothing but nuts, dried fruit, raw vegetables, green tea, sushi and goose liver paté. You will notice there is no artificial light. When the sun turns down, so does the higher cortex of my brain. My body remains in the position you see now, persisting in a state of deep, almost trance-like, relaxation from dusk until dawn. By following this regimen, I am able, every six days, to stay alert and productive for stretches of up to 72 hours, without aid of any narcotic. ”

"If I sat Indian style all day you'd have to use the jaws of life to unknot my legs," said Dante. "And the only way I'm staying up 72 hours is if hour one begins with me snorting a line of Virgin Mary blow off some dirty little hooker's brown caboose, and each of the 70 hours after begins just like it."

"We wanted to discuss some changes," said Nero.

"What kind of changes?" said Dante.

"The Driver must always be shot from below," said Nero.

"From below," said Dante, appearing to mull it over. "From just how far below?"

"From the ground," said Nero. "Or below the ground, when possible."

"And what about the scenes that have already been shot?"

"They'd have to be re-done, of course."

"Don't you think it's just a bit on-the-nose?"

"Not at all. Merely sends the proper message."

"You want to know what I think? I think it's complete shit. I think you don't know what the bloody hell you're talking about."

"We anticipated this kind of reaction and took the liberty of moving forward with the pick-up shots. At this moment, the assistant director is shooting coverage with St. Germaine."

"It looks like you've got it all figured out. So what do you need me for?" said Dante.

"For the Japanese," said Nero.

"Why don't you put your own damn skin in the game? You've got more money than God."

"Only a fool invests his own money in a picture. My money's tied up in the cartels. We experienced record earnings last quarter from imports of marijuana and cocaine."

"Do they know you put yourself in the bloody movie?" said Dante.

"Any similarity is purely coincidental," said Nero.

"Actually, the Driver represents Krishna," said Blow.

"I know who he bloody represents," said Dante. "A goddamn money man with a messiah complex."

The Medicine Man attempted to pass Dante the peace pipe.

"Get that bloody nonsense away from me," said Dante, waving him away.

"Don't worry, there's no smoke," said Nero. "It's an e-pipe, just a few medicinal herbs and pure clean steam."

"You expect to seduce me with some kind of herbal inhaler?" said Dante.

"Going forward, the AD will direct all shots involving the Driver," said Nero.

"Over my dead body," said Dante.

He proceeded to storm out, but the bodyguard stepped in front of the flap, blocking his path.

"Don't think I don't know about your little side project," said Nero.

Nero gave a nod, and the bodyguard stepped aside, allowing Dante to leave the tee pee.

"Remember, I've got final cut. This is my goddamn movie, so fuck the lot of you," Dante said, giving the room the finger then ducking under the flap.

The Medicine Man extended the peace pipe to Blow. All eyes were on Blow as he took the pipe and considered it.

"Don't mind if I do," he said, as he inserted the pipe into his mouth.

With Nero nodding approvingly, he ignited the bowl of the e-pipe and took a nice long drag.

# CHAPTER 46

Q smoked a big fat blunt. There wasn't much light, just enough to see the smoke curling out from his lips. The wind kicked up and almost lifted off his hat. A single hairy arachnid leg extended from the brim of the hat before he smacked it down. With the huge dark glasses, the bowler hat and the long silk dragon jacket, he resembled the opium dream of a 19th Century Mongolian assassin. He stuck the blunt in his mouth and fanned out a thick stack of fifties. Erica Cash leaned against him, took the blunt from his mouth, took a long drag, then returned the blunt to his lips. She arched her head back and let the smoke rise out of her like the vapor trails of a demonic possession. Bodies moved about in the night, swirling, surging and ebbing like a human tide. Voices echoed and multiplied into a locust swarm of immaterial conversations that drifted in and out with the wind.

Q ripped off ten bills and handed them to Tommy Boy, who waded through the teeming bodies and handed them to Jimmy, a burly ex-Teamster who was gigging on the picture as the Best Boy.

"Put it on Old Dirty Bastard," said Tommy Boy.

"To in-it or win-it?" said Jimmy.

"To win the shit," said Tommy Boy. "Straight up."

"Two to one," said Jimmy.

"That's bull shit," said Tommy Boy.

"Bastard's hot," said Jimmy. "Little prick won the last two races."

"Mother fucker's tired as shit," said Tommy Boy.

"Don't take it personal. It's a formula and shit," said Jimmy.

"Fuck this. Give that shit back," said Tommy. "Put it in gold or pork bellies or some shit."

As Jimmy counted off the bills, Bax and Nick appeared. Bax handed Jimmy a neat stack of bills.

"800 on Scout Master's Delight," said Bax.

"To place," said Nick.

"That's chicken shit," said Tommy Boy.

"Yeah, grow some balls," said Jimmy.

"Okay, to win," said Bax.

"And here's an extra hundred," said Nick, laying the bills on Jimmy.

"Make it three to one," said Jimmy, nodding to Tommy Boy.

"Now we're mother fuckin' talkin'," said Tommy Boy. "Hold the money."

Jimmy turned to Bax. "Four and a half," he said.

"Cool," said Bax.

"Hot shit," said Nick.

Bax put his hand on Tommy Boy's back.

"Tell Q we're lookin' for a little something on the side."

"Just to make things interesting," said Nick.

Tommy Boy returned to Q and gave him the pitch. Q nodded, and Bax and Nick came over.

"What are we talkin'?" said Q.

"One on one," said Bax.

"Straight up," said Nick.

"Five g's," said Q.

Bax and Nick exchanged a look. Then Bax nodded.

"Signed and sealed," said Tommy Boy.

Nick pulled an envelope from his jacket.

"Don't worry bout that shit," said Q. "I get it one way or another."

Nick let the envelope slip back into his pocket. "Cool," he said.

The rich velvet voice of Victor St. Germaine came over the PA.

"Riders, get into starting position," said the Voice. "Three ... two ... one ..."

The count was punctuated by the sound of heavy machine gun fire. Out in the clearing, the rapid-fire blasts lit up the night, as the unseen gunman sprayed sparks over the heads of the crowd.

"Blanks," said Bax. "I think."

"No way to know for sure," said Bax. "Unless somebody gets hit."

"And they're off!" said the Voice.

The sound of machine gun fire was replaced by the pounding of hooves over the hard packed sand.

Nick turned around just as the spotlight powered on, projecting a beam of light from behind the crowd that lit up the tightly grouped animals as they streaked awkwardly across the sand. After about thirty yards, the group started to spread out, with Old Dirty Bastard and Scout Master's Delight racing neck and neck for the lead position.

"I never realized camels could move that fast," said Bax. "I thought they were strictly a walking animal."

"You're thinking of giraffes," said Nick.

"Giraffes can run, too," said Tommy Boy. "I seen it on Animal Planet."

"No shit," said Bax. "We should get some."

Nick punched some numbers into his cell phone and held it to his ear.

"Yo, Kool Keith," he said. "Far out ... yeah, we'll take some of that too ... giraffes, mainly ... how many you got? ... that's cool ... " He lowered the phone and looked around, then raised the phone. "Somewhere out in the desert ... Peace."

Nick dropped the phone back in his jacket.

"How much?" said Bax.

"It's on the house."

"Sweet," said Bax.

"Old Dirty Bastard hits the turn first, followed by Scout Master's Delight," said the Voice over the PA.

The spotlight followed the loping herd as the animals curled around the turn, the infield crowd turning in unison to follow the action.

"Why don't you go ahead and give me that money?" said Q.

257

"Save yourself some time."

"Sure," said Nick, pulling the envelope from inside his jacket. "That's cool."

Nick popped open the envelope and peeked inside.

"Woops, looks there's nothing in here but soiled teeny-bopper panties," he said. "Must be the one for the Japanese."

"Wait," said Bax, patting down his jacket. "I have one too."

He pulled out the envelope and opened it up.

"Looks like it's full of dirty greenbacks. Large denominations," he said.

"Large. Small. Don't matter to me. Could be a hearse full of dimes and nickels, far as I care. Long as I get paid," said Q.

"How about a hearse full of soiled teeny-bopper panties?" said Nick.

"That's got nothing to do with me," said Q. "I like to get my freak on now and again. But gotta have something to hold onto. Cartoon rabbits. Panda bears. Pokémons. That aint my scene."

"Old Dirty Bastard ahead by two lengths as Scout Master's Delight closes the gap on the final stretch," said the Voice on the PA.

"How bout we make this shit a little more interesting," said Q. "Throw in another couple G's and I give you two to one."

"Cool," said Nick.

"Sweet," said Bax.

There were only three camels left in the spotlight now, the rest having fallen back into the night. Old Dirty Bastard was out in front, with Scout Master's Delight right on his heels. In fact, with his neck craned out, his head reached the lead camel's forward hump. Old Dirty Bastard's jockey, a shirtless diminutive character actor named Ronald Helm, whipped the animal furiously with a cat-o-nine tails, while Scout Master's Delight, whose rider had just fallen off, continued to make up ground.

"It's coming down to the wire," said the Voice of Victor St. Germaine, booming over the PA. "They're almost neck and neck now. Old Dirty Bastard leads by a head, and it's .... Scout Master's Delight by a flapping gum. I've got the picture right here, folks. Unbelievable finish."

"That's bull shit!" said Tommy Boy. "We got to have a rematch."

"That's cool," said Bax.

258

"Yeah, sure thing," said Nick.

"Fuck that," said Q. "Those mother fuckers have to fight it out."

"The camels?" said Bax.

"Hell yes, the camels. Those mother fuckers need to fight to the mother fuckin' death," said Q.

"That can be arranged," said Bax, nodding his head.

Nick nodded as well. "They're not rented," he said. "We own 'em free and clear."

"Camels don't fight, unless it's over a female," said Tommy Boy.

"The winner can have Jackie-O," said Q.

"The fuck it can," said Jackie-O. "I aint gonna fuck no camel, with those nasty humps."

"You fucked Tron-A," said Tommy Boy. "Homeboy's a fuckin' hunchback."

"He aint a hunchback, he's just an old goat, and he's hung like a mother fuckin' horse," said Jackie-O.

"So's a camel," said Tommy Boy.

"What the hell are those nasty camels doin' here anyway," said Tammy. "Isn't this supposed to be Mexico?"

"The prop guy thought it was Saudi Arabia," said Bax. "Who knows, they might come in handy."

"Right. By the time we're done, this could be the Gobi Desert," said Nick.

"The Gobi Desert?" said Dick Pearl, a short middle aged man with a curly rim of hair and a pronounced paunch. "There's a slight problem there."

"The extras," said Bax.

Dick folded his arms and shook his head.

"Where the hell are we going to come with up with three hundred Mongolians?"

"Don't worry about it," said Nick.

"And what the hell are all the boats for?" said Dick, sweeping his arm across the darkness.

"It'll get worked out," said Bax.

"Blow's got some really strong ideas," said Nick.

"Wait, what was that?" said Blow, clutching a fistful of money and turning around in a shroud of dope smoke.

259

"Something about the boats," said Nick. "And the Mongolians."

"There's, like, you know, a shit load of them," said Blow.

"See that," said Bax, patting him on the back. "Cat never stops working."

"Where's Dante going with those Indians?" said Nick.

Just beyond the track, in the beam of the spotlight, a boy, a teenage girl and a bunch of Native American types climbed in Dante's Land Rover. The vehicle started, the lights went on, and the Land Rover crept quietly over the sand until it passed beyond the frame of the spotlight and vanished into the darkness.

"Must be shooting some coverage or something," said Bax, shaking his head with a laugh. "Cat never stops working."

# CHAPTER 47

The Medicine Man, in full head dress, wearing the full length deer-leather witch doctor outfit covered in tassels and totems, danced around the fire, issuing a deep rhythmic chant as he bobbed and weaved, ducking down then launching into an elaborate pirouette. Silvio circled slowly with the hand held camera, with the AD right next to him.

"I don't remember seeing anything about a witch doctor in the script," said Silvio.

"Just getting some behind-the-scenes shit, for the DVD," said the AD. "Nero wants to make sure there's plenty of footage, in case there's a documentary."

"What's he think's gonna happen, a complete meltdown like *Apocalypse* or *Fitzcarraldo*?"

"Who knows? Maybe we'll get lucky," said the AD.

"Why the hell not. I'll get paid either way," said Silvio.

Most of the crew was assembled around the Raja's palace. Six stationary cameras were set up around the palace, two up high and one on each side at ground level. The camera assistant was holding the black and white clapperboard and smoking a cigarette. On the clapper was written: "Take 1—Tornado destroys palace."

"How long have you been standing here like this?" said Nick.

"About four hours, give or take," said the camera assistant.

"What are you waiting for?"

The man nodded in the direction of the dance.

"For that little Injun over there to make it rain, and, you know, conjure a tornado…" He took a drag on his cigarette. "…so we can get the fuck out of here."

Suddenly, the Medicine Man's dance picked up intensity as he flung himself around the fire, leaping into the air and landing on all fours, turning cartwheels and somersaults.

The camera assistant heard the electric crackle of a voice booming over the public address system. He looked up to see a large translucent bubble floating high overhead the set, suspended from a large crane. Inside the bubble he could make out Nero, wearing a head set, seated Indian style on a Tatami mat. He looked calm and cool. There wasn't a drop of sweat on him. While down below, shielding their eyes from the klieg lights, the crew appeared disheveled and drenched in perspiration.

"Positions everyone," said the resonant electric voice of Nero.

The Medicine Man's dance quickly built to a frenzied crescendo, and then all at once it was over as he collapsed in a heap.

"Action," came the voice from the bubble.

After several long minutes nothing had happened.

The AD looked up toward the bubble.

"I don't think it worked," he said.

"What's with the bubble?" said Silvio.

"Made out of a special polymer used for weather balloons. Supposed to block out solar radiation," said Nick.

"It's night," said Silvio.

"Moon glow," said Nick.

"Hold your positions," said the voice of Nero.

Slowly, the bubble floated back down to earth.

"Where's Dante?" said Nick, looking around.

"No one's seen him," said the PA. "We turned the camp upside down. It's like he just disappeared."

Nero emerged from the bubble wearing a full length white sun suit and a pair of large convex space-fly sunglasses. He walked over to the Medicine Man, who was starting to pick himself back up.

"I thought you said this always worked," said Nero. "You came highly recommended."

"The dance always works," said the Medicine Man, emphatically.

"Then where is it?" said Nero.

"The ancestors work in mysterious ways," he said, giving a shrug and walking away.

Nero waved over Bax, Nick and the AD.

"It's time to move on to Plan B," said Nero.

"What's Plan B?" said the AD.

"Do I have to think of everything?" said Nero. "Just burn it down."

"How are we going to do that?" said the AD.

"Get a can of gasoline, walk into the palace and pour it all over everything," said Nero. "Then light a match."

"What about the sprinkler system?" said Nick.

"Yeah, that's a state of the art sprinkler system," said Bax.

"Why did you install a sprinkler system in a prop house?" said Nero. "A prop house that is scheduled to be destroyed at the end of the third act."

"It gave us a discount on the insurance," said Bax.

"In every room?" said the AD.

"In every room including closets," said Nick. "For the maximum discount."

"It'll put out that fire in no time flat," said Bax.

Nero addressed the Production Assistant.

"Disconnect the water supply into the palace," he said. "Reconnect it to the gasoline cistern."

"What happened to Dante?" said Bax.

"He's indisposed at the moment, I'm afraid."

"Indisposed?" said Nick.

"I suppose before we do this, we better make sure there's no one inside?" said the AD.

The PA checked the shooting schedule, flipping pages over the clip.

"Dante was going to be in there doing some pickup shots," he said. "But it got crossed off."

"There we go," said Nero.

"It's a shame about that tornado," said Nick. "That would have been something."

"You want to burn it down pretty bad," said Bax.

263

"It's in the script," said Nero, nodding in the direction of Blow.

Everybody looked to Blow. After a beat or two, Blow looked up from his gyro sandwich.

"Yeah, that's right," he said, then returned to the sandwich.


An hour later, the AD approached Nero, who had just gotten back into the bubble.

"Everything's ready to go," he said.

"I have to take care of some important business," said Nero, as the bubble began to rise.

"What about the scene?" said the AD, screaming through his hands at the rising bubble.

Nero's voice boomed down through the PA: "Make it so."

# CHAPTER 48

"Hello," said the man.

Blow didn't recognize the voice. It had a flat affectless tone that lacked a discernible accent. He looked up, instinctively shielding his eyes from the full moon, although he hadn't needed to because it was fully eclipsed by the man's head. Once his eyes had adjusted, he made out the smooth penumbral features of the narrow face looming over him. The skin was dark, the features seemed exotic, out of place. They were Indian, not Native American Indian but Indian Indian.

Blow reached up and shook the hand.

"Sal," said the voice.

"Blow," said Blow, adding (when he failed to detect a sign of recognition in the man's face), "The writer."

"Ah yes, Richard Blow. I have heard your name," said Sal.

"What brings you to tinsel beach?" said Bax.

"Just passing through on my way back from Mumbai," said Sal.

"Afraid we're going to jack your credit?" said Nick.

"Credits are good for business," said Sal.

"Are you one of the producers?" said Blow. "I apologize. I was brought into the project late."

"More of a partner producer," said Sal.

"Nero didn't tell you?" said Bax. "This wasn't an original

idea."

"Nothing ever is," said Sal.

"Nero picked it up from our man here for a cool quarter mil, full remake rights," said Nick.

"This here's the Remake Raja himself, Sal Khan, in full singing and dancing high-stepping Technicolor flesh and blood," said Bax. "Practically cornered the market on Bollywood originals."

"I'm sure Blow's seen the original a hundred times by now, studied it like the Koran or some shit," said Nick, giving Blow a nod.

"I hadn't realized..." said Blow.

"What do you think? Is it worth a look?" said Bax, nodding to Sal. "Blow's a very busy man."

"I never saw it," the man said, laughing. "I don't see many movies."

"There you go," said Bax. "He hasn't seen it."

"Me neither," said Nick.

"Can't think of anybody who has really, not off the top of my head," said Bax.

"Nobody's seen it," said Nick. "Except 800 million people in India."

"If you hadn't seen it, how'd you know it was any good?" said the AD.

"I was working with a producer on another movie and he mentioned a Hindi movie that he said had two really scary scenes, so I went out and got the rights. I go with what people tell me to go for," Sal said.

"Pure electricity," said Bax, the corner of his mouth curling up in a half-smile.

"You got any more hot properties you want to lay on us?" said Nick.

"*Car Accident*. It's a supernatural thriller about a boy in the slum who has to sell drugs to survive, supposedly modeled on some Hindu mythology thing about a boy entering somewhere and doing something. Maybe you could set it up for Justin James."

"Who wants the honors?" said the AD.

Everybody looked to Blow.

"Not me," said Blow, who was sprawled out on an alpaca blanket smoking a cigarette. "I'd love to, of course, but you know how the unions are. Overstepping of boundaries, that sort of thing."

As Blow looked up, Sal's face disappeared once more into its own shadow, an almost pure blackness that seemed to swallow all light and everything around it, and then, just as before, the features emerged by degrees from the darkness, only this time they were not the features of a man, but of a hideous beast. The face was dark and round, resembling a big cat, and surrounded by a collar of purple feathers, with a huge smiling mouth full of long razor sharp teeth, shocking white eyebrows swirling over blazing red eyes and a strange blue and red crown that sat atop the head like a pagoda.

Blow looked at the other faces, Bax, Nick, the AD, but none seemed to register what he was seeing. All at once, there was a loud explosion, like the popping of a giant balloon. In that instant, he had a flash delirium of his head exploding, a massive big bang sending shock waves across the desert.

"Don't be a pussy," said the monstrous voice.

The vision was as frightening as anything Blow had ever experienced, and he felt his hair literally stand on end. It took several beats before he realized that the cigarette had fallen from his mouth and was burning a hole in his shirt. Without giving it another thought, he picked up the cigarette and flicked the ash, sending the glowing end arcing out and landing at the edge of the pool of gasoline. He watched, transfixed, as the flame rose up and blazed a trail down the narrow garden lane, up the stairs and across the sprawling porch until it expired unceremoniously at the imposing front doors of the palace.

When Blow looked up, Khan had disappeared.

# CHAPTER 49

They were out in the desert, barely within sight of camp. DJ Trix leaned against the Escalade, admiring his nails through mirrored sunglasses. Antoine and Tommy Boy stood under the sun tent, drinking Arnold Palmers. Bax watched as Q, bare chested, wearing shiny black silk pants, squatted down before the full length mirror that was propped up against a large rock, his hands forming tight fists.

"What's he doing?" said Bax.

"What's it look like he's doing?" said Tommy Boy. "He's doing Kung Fu in a mirror."

Q sat down in the pose, with his legs apart and his back erect, his lap level with his knees, elbows tucked into his sides, fists turned up.

"What's that?" said Bax.

"Horse riding stance," said Antoine.

Q dropped his right leg back then swept it forward in a high arc.

"What about that?" said Bax.

"Striking roundhouse kick," said Tommy Boy.

Once his feet were re-set, Q spun completely around, ripping the back of his fist through the air.

"And that?" said Bax.

"Spinning back fist," said Antoine.

"Is this for real?" said Bax.

"What do you mean, *for real?*" said Tommy Boy.

"Does he really know Kung Fu?" said Bax.

"'course he knows Kung Fu. What the fuck's it look like? You can't fake that shit," said Tommy Boy.

"That shit is for real," said Antoine.

Q inhaled deeply, his eyes focusing like laser sights.

"Now you're gonna see some shit," said Antoine.

"Twisted," said Tommy Boy.

Suddenly, Q launched into an intense and acrobatic routine, moving through a series of robust stances, furious spinning punches, leaping somersaults and high soaring kicks.

"What do you call all that?" said Bax.

"Call that the Duan Chuan," said Tommy Boy.

"Dig that Essential Front Kick," said Antoine, wincing.

"Now that's what I call some serious Shao-Lin shit," said Tommy Boy.

"Dig that concentration," said Nick, joining them under the sun tent.

"Total focus," said Bax. "It's like he's not even aware that we're here."

"The whole mother fuckin' world disappears," said Antoine. "For real."

"Home boy's in the mother fuckin' zone," said Tommy Boy.

"Wanted to talk about a few changes to the contract," said Nick.

"A few minor tweaks," said Bax. "For compensation, naturally."

"For compensation, damn straight," said Antoine, donning a pair of reading glasses.

Nick dropped the contract on the table. Antoine leaned over the document and immediately went about giving it the red ink treatment.

Q continued doing the Kung Fu, out under the hot sun, when from out of nowhere Nero suddenly appeared in front of the mirror. Q, undisturbed, continued working through his routine, stepping into a single leg stance then delivering a devastating snap kick.

"Don't worry, they can't see me," said Nero, as Bax, Nick, Antoine and Tommy Boy continued with their business under the sun tent.

"Who's they?" said Q, bringing his hands together as he finished the routine.

Nero looked from Q to the very animated discussion taking place under the sun tent then back to Q.

"So, you're really serious about this acting thing?" said Nero.

"Hell yeah, mother fucker. Don't it look like it?" said Q.

"Come with me. I want to show you where it is," said Nero.

"Show me where what is?"

"The real action."

"The real action," said Q, seeming to savor the feel of the words in his mouth.

"Here's your assignment, should you choose to accept it," said Nero. "First, there's the matter of an escaped weather balloon. I want you to shoot it."

"You want me to pop a balloon?" said Q, incredulously.

"In a manner of speaking. Just be sure not to get too close. It could be radioactive."

"Easy as shake and bake," said Q.

"The second thing is, I'm assuming that if I provided the materials, you could put together some sort of bomb?"

"You could assume," said Q. "And assuming I do all this shit, what do I get?"

"Top billing."

"You're going to give me top billing? Over Tony Billings, Lee Montana, all those A-List mother fuckers?"

"If you do these things, there is nothing that I, or anybody else, could do to stop it."

Q picked up the gun from a nearby rock and stuck it in the waist band of the silk pants. Then he set the spider on his head and covered it with the bowler hat. As Q and Nero walked out into the desert, DJ Trix continued to admire his fingernails, holding up one after the other in the hot white light.

# CHAPTER 50

There wasn't much left really, a few weather balloons, the card table, some empty wine bottles, a collapsible chair tossed on the ground, few signs of the once bustling encampment and the French scientists who had inhabited it. The sun set low on the horizon, a smooth burnt orange dragging its light back over the edge of the world. The orange hues lit up Jerzy's face, cigarette dangling from the corner of his mouth, as he collapsed the tripod, breaking down the equipment and packing it away in the compartments of a waterproof soft-sided camera bag. Dante sat on a rock smoking a cigarette and staring at the sun.

"We got some good shit today," said Dante. "Some very good shit."

Jerzy gave a little laugh as he slung the camera bag over his shoulder and adjusted his hat.

"Yes, was good shit," he said. "Very good."

Dante looked over and noticed that one of the balloons—about the size and color of a silver Volkswagen—had inched a little closer.

"I haven't done one like this in so long, flying by the seat of my pants, going purely by instinct. It's a shame it has to end," said Dante, casually eyeing the balloon.

Jerzy loaded the bags into the jeep.

"I am on schedule tonight," he said. "Pick-up shots inside Raja's palace."

"I had a dream that he burned up in there," said Dante.

"Tony Billings?"

"Nero. His flesh turned to steam right before my eyes. It was almost spiritual. For me, that is. Poor Nero was completely destroyed, body and soul. Now Tony, Tony's a good kid, he's just useless."

"As tits on bull frog," said Jerzy.

"Speak for yourself," said Dante. "Tits are tits."

"You want ride back?" said Jerzy, climbing behind the wheel of the jeep.

Dante turned his head, looking first at Jerzy, then at the large silvery balloon, which had crept so close he could almost reach out and touch it.

"Go on," said Dante. "I'll wander back eventually."

Jerzy started the engine and drove out of sight.

As the sun began to dip below the horizon, casting long shadows on the sand, Dante noticed for the first time that the skin of the balloon was translucent and that there appeared to be something inside. At first he could only make out the shape, but as he drew closer, peering through the newly translucent skin, he was able to make out the identity of the thing in greater detail. It was a person. Live or dead he couldn't tell for sure. In a panic now, he shouted and clawed ineffectually at the balloon's tough, slick hide. Eventually he found a small seam in the side of the balloon, just long enough to get his head through, and then before he knew it he was all the way inside the balloon, with the seam sealing back up around him. He now found himself wrapped in a rubbery chamber (it reminded him of the moon pools used to enter in and out of an underwater station, themselves mechanized versions of the mammalian womb), a kind of balloon within the balloon where he found yet another seam. Inserting himself through this second seam, he entered into the interior of the greater balloon where he found himself staring down at the dead eyes of the face that stared right back up at him and which, with the beard and large twisted nose and wild thinning hair, he instinctively recognized as his own. He held this face in his hands. It was a familiar feeling. The skin felt like silicone drawn over a hard plaster core.

# CHAPTER 51

Q was way out there, at the outer perimeter, under the glaring midday sun, with his hat on his head, the camp a distant vision behind him, the gun leveled on the unseen enemy advancing toward them silently across the rocks and sand. His skin was dry in spite of the heat, except for a single bead of sweat that traced a path from the brim of the hat down his forehead and into the corner of his eye. He blinked, only once. His breathing had slowed to a deep steady rhythm until finally he ceased to breathe at all as his eyes zeroed down the barrel and his finger squeezed the trigger. The report cracked the overheated air like a pane of glass, sending out jagged lines of sound that traveled for miles in every direction. A moment later, you could still hear the report, like thunder from a jet plane fading toward the horizon. The bullet hit the bug flush, blowing it to pieces. Q held the scope to his eye. Next to the rock where he'd been aiming, only the stinger remained, slightly twitching.

"Now that's what I'm talking about," he said, blowing on the smoldering barrel.

Q took off the bowler hat, revealing the tarantula perched calmly upon his skull, and set the hat on a rock.

"They're all around us. I can hear them out there, thousands of them mother fuckers, creeping towards us, their little armored robot legs goin' clickety-clack over the rocks. They think I don't know they're there, they think they're rolling under the radar, but I can hear 'em, I can hear every goddamn last one of 'em. That's why I come all the way out here. Somebody got to take a stand before it's too late. Somebody got to draw a line in the sand, head these creepy crawly mother fuckers off. Otherwise, only a matter of time. They'll be in your boots, your hat, your bed. They'll be in your mother fuckin' corn flakes. Only thing between them and full on space invaders style invasion is you and me. You speak their language, you understand their customs and mother fuckin' tribal rituals. You know how to walk the walk, know what I'm saying. You got to read the terrain, you got to watch every mother fuckin' thing, know what I'm saying? When you see one of them creepy mother fuckers, just whisper into my ear..."

He held the gun with both hands, crouching down and slowly panning the barrel from left to right.

"There we go, that's it, now you're talking, sounds just like a lullaby," he said.

He squeezed off a shot … and another … and another …

"That's it! That's what I'm talkin' about," he said, as chunks of scorpion gore rained down on the sand.

A little white girl appeared at his side. Although Q didn't recognize her, she was the lead in the *Walkabout* remake. In the original, the girl was a teenager, but Dante had decided to go younger.

"What are you doing, mister?" she said.

"I don't rightly know," said Q. "My mind is open, like an antenna."

"I know who you are," she said. "You're a radio head."

"What you want, little girl?"

The girl pointed. In the distance, Q could see a soft silver sphere dragging along the sand. Eventually, the form came to rest between two rocks, where its body expanded and contracted in the wind, as if it were breathing.

"What is it?" said Q.

"Jellyfish," said the girl.

"That's a big ass jellyfish," said Q. "I aint never seen no jellyfish like that before. What kind of jellyfish you find floating around the desert?"

"They come from outer space," said the girl.

"Walk out there and tell me if it's still alive," said Q. "Me and

274

Tick-Tock hang back and provide cover, know what I'm sayin'?"

The girl walked out toward the silver jellyfish while Q watched through the scope of the gun. When she got close, she picked up a stick and prodded at the undulating silver body. The thing immediately jumped up into the air and skittered across the sand, then swirled around and began staggering back toward the girl, who held her hands over her eyes and screamed.

Q squeezed off three quick shots, stopping the advancing blob in its tracks and producing a violent pop. Grounded once more, the thing's loose silvery skin rippled in the wind. As its deflating body sank into the sand, Q, observing through the scope, made out a distinct misshapen patch of brick red on the silvery skein, what he immediately recognized as a blood stain, a kill shot at that, no doubt about it.

"Now that's what I'm talkin' about," he said, firing four more shots, as the girl continued to sob by the gradually deflating victim.

# CHAPTER 52
*FREDERICK M. BARCLAY*

It was in the neighborhood of 10:00 PM when Sherrill showed up at the door of his double wide trailer. She knocked, then waited. She knocked again, waited. She knocked four times hard and yelled his name. Music could be heard inside, something by James Brown, with a brisk funky beat and a high-wire guitar line. I was obscured behind a diesel generator, watching the scene unfold through the field glasses. She banged on the door four more times with an open hand. Finally, she turned the knob and opened the door. There was an immediate explosion of music and light from the trailer. Tony was clearly visible inside, on his knees, furiously doggie fucking a slinky little brunette wearing only a pig mask and an assortment of tattoos, including representations of Tweety Bird and Betty Boop as well as what appeared to be the death mask of the Romantic poet Keats. Tony quickly jumped to his feet and ran to the door, removing the cowboy hat and holding it over his nether regions.

"You got the shit?" he said.

"Fuck you, Tony. I can't believe I trusted you," she said.

276

"That?" he said, cocking his thumb behind him, as the woman in the pig mask stretched out on the floor. "Hey, I don't even know what she looks like. She was wearing that when I found her. For all I know she's just some butterface with a hot ass."

"You're disgusting."

"It doesn't mean anything. I told you, I don't even know this bitch."

"That's supposed to make me feel better."

"It's not like what you and me have. There's no spiritual connection. If you think about it, it's basically like jacking off."

"Except instead of jacking off, you're sticking your penis in some strange cunt in a pig mask."

"If you want to put it like that..."

"Good-bye, Tony," she said, turning to go.

"Wait," he said, grabbing her by the shoulder and lowering his voice to a hushed tone. "What about my shit?"

She opened the bag and turned it over, emptying all the drugs onto the ground—powders, mushrooms, blotters, hypodermics, pipes and hundreds of pills of every size and color that bounced off the stairs like raindrops—then dropped the bag.

"What the fuck?" he said.

Tony dropped to his knees and desperately scooped the scattered contraband back into the bag.

"I hope you drown in your own puke," she said, walking away.

"I'll call you," he said.

I followed her.

She went in every direction—straight ahead, side-to-side, diagonal; she careened around in the darkness, alternately wailing, cursing herself and laughing like a half-mad streetwalker. She picked up an open bottle of Bacardi rum sitting next to a trash can, guzzled most of it then smashed the bottle on the ground. She stumbled and fell to the earth, rolling onto her back and making angels in the dust ... while I lurked in the shadows whispering into the recorder, capturing every detail. I longed to step into the beam of the flood light and help her to her feet but somehow found the strength to resist, answering my higher calling as a chronicler of this dizzying gilded world we few were so privileged to inhabit. Sherrill would no doubt have appreciated my dedication implicitly, would have recognized our mutually dependent roles in this strange play, like two strands of DNA forever twisting into a tantric helix of symbiotic unity containing the blueprint of the whole universe, all the stars, comets, supernovas and brave new worlds.

She rolled over and got onto her hands and knees, hair hanging in the dust, then pushed herself to her feet. She was staggering badly now. She was a notorious pill head and the combination of pills and hard liquor produced unpredictable results. On the horns of an ethical dilemma, I continued to pursue my increasingly disoriented subject as she knocked over a moped before falling through the front flap of a large dimly lit tent where a conclave of Mexican roustabouts was playing cards and drinking Tequila.

I pressed my eye to a small tear in the fabric of the tent in order to observe the action inside. The men—a gruff risible lot—barely seemed to notice Sherrill as she sashayed clumsily about the table fondling each man in turn with a sensual hand to the chest, a haphazard cheek-to-cheek or a tantalizing caress from that perfumed auburn hair. It was as if movie stars dropped by so often that they had become entirely blasé. This seemed unlikely, however, because the men were hired locally, having been recruited out of a nearby dirt farm.

Failing to get the desired attention, she undid the top button on her blouse, insinuated herself between two of the players and bent over at the waist, affording a Peeping Tom's view of those delectable apple sized breasts.

"What are we playing, fellas?" she said, leaning over so that her elbows rested on the table, spilling several bottles of beer and scattering the various piles of cards into disarray.

A few of the men found the intrusion to be quite hilarious, while another contingent became extremely agitated, jumping to their feet and hurling obscenities in Spanish.

"Get that skinny ass bitch out of here!" said an old man with a face of cracked leather.

It was then that I realized the men had no idea this exotic interloper—this "skinny ass bitch" who had invaded their card game—was in fact a world renowned actress of stage and screen. Two of the laughing men got up and pulled Sherrill off of the table and carried her—one holding her under the shoulders, the other taking the legs—to the tent flap, whereupon they unceremoniously

278

threw her through the flap and out into the dusty lane. They returned to the table, slapping their hands together and laughing uproariously as if they'd just tossed some bum out of a saloon.

I watched silently for a moment as she lay there on the ground, trying with varying degrees of futility to pick herself back up, but those were real tears, not the lachrymose confections of Stanislavskian method. She was truly, almost existentially, alone, and I was, after all, first and foremost a man of the world and (naturally I was keenly aware on some level that I was witnessing something momentous in the annals of pop cultural *reportage*) so it was with a twinge of vocational regret that I broke the ontological plane between us and emerged from the shadows to help the distressed and surprisingly pixilated damsel to her feet. Initially, she made a sudden feint toward the very opening from which she'd just been ejected, requiring me to throw her over my shoulder and swiftly carry her away from that den of swarthy low-wage height-challenged temptation. Breathing heavily, my face dripping sweat, I moved with great labor and haste down the lane, and as I rounded the corner I became aware that I couldn't say for sure whether she was crying, laughing, alternating between the two or experiencing both emotions simultaneously. It occurred to me that I'd misinterpreted the abjectness of her state lying there alone on the ground and had unwittingly projected onto her my own sense of existential singularity.    Regardless, I had broken the fourth wall, observer entering the petri dish of the observed, and there was nothing to do now but to see the adventure through to its logical conclusion. I had, of course, planned to reveal myself at some point anyway. Sherrill and I had a bit of a history together, and, moreover, no matter how strenuously my editorial patrons insisted to the contrary, whether covering a summit to end world hunger (featuring some impossibly star studded panel, natch) or a child actor's personal train wreck, it was ultimately the author's own visage that reflected back from the glinting steel of the literary rapier. That is to say, sooner or later the spotlight always turned on me.

Ensconced behind the porta-potties, I held her hair as she vomited the evening's humiliation onto the dusky sand. This wasn't the first time, nor would it be the last. This was the type of relationship we had—she the damsel in distress and I playing the role of the guardian angel, watching from the wings and swooping in

279

unexpectedly in a moment of need to wipe drool, hold hair, or in extreme cases, provide CPR, and then exiting the stage as discreetly and unceremoniously as I had entered. No thanks were ever given, and none were expected. We had a mutual understanding. We had become central characters in each other's dramas, our fates inextricably intertwined, and in a very real sense, this was true for Tony as well, I felt that I had taken on the role of creator. This world that they inhabited was in whole or part the product of my invention, and I understood, instinctively, that if I were to close my eyes and turn away (to be honest the prospect terrified me more than anything) they would all simply disappear.

"Take me home," she said.

"Home," I said. "Is a long way away."

"Take me to my trailer," she said. "I want to take a bath."

Not wanting to remind her of the unfortunate turn of events, that due to her falling out with Tony she no longer had a trailer, was, to some degree, a vagabond among the flotsam and jetsam of this impermanent community, I stroked her hair and reassured her in hushed tones that everything was going to be all right.

There was only one place to go.

I was staying in an old abandoned camper at the edge of the settlement. It wasn't much, but it suited my needs for the moment. I had found it shortly after arriving. From the overall weathered and dilapidated condition—flat tires, rusted rims, broken lights and peeled paint—it looked like it could have been here for a decade or more. Of course, nothing worked, not the toilet, no electricity or running water, but there was a small bed and a table to do my work. It was anyone's guess what happened to the original occupants. Hippies. Indians. Sportsmen. Retirees. Meth cooks. Whoever they were, their luck had run out somewhere along the way and they'd vanished like one of those lost civilizations: Jamestown, Jonestown or the Anassazi. I looked for evidence of mass murder, cannibalism and other human depredation, but found nothing. It was almost as if no one had ever lived here at all. I found the lack of perceptible history to be both eerie and oddly comforting, as if I were inhabiting a sound stage built especially for me. It wouldn't have been the first time. Time and again, I sensed myself wandering the corridors of an elaborate maze designed by an invisible hand. There were clues of this design everywhere—unlikely coincidences, frequent bouts of *deja vous*, dream symbols infiltrating the waking world—but no matter how close I seemed to get I never made it to the center, which was forever melting away and reforming just out of reach. It had occurred to me naturally that what I was searching for, the grail of my knight's errand, was in fact my own annihilation. This possibility did nothing, however, to deter me from pursuing the sweet marrow of my quest.

I helped Sherrill up the steps and into the camper. I turned on the kerosene lantern just as she lurched down the narrow passage and retched into the sink.

"Do you have anything to drink?" she said. "To get the taste out."

There was a bottle of Macallan 12 year old Scotch on the table next to a small *terra cotta* coffee mug. I motioned for her to join me at the table. She slid into the seat across from me. I poured two fingers into the mug and pushed it over to her. She took a sip.

"Sure beats Listerine," she said.

She threw back the rest of the drink and set the mug on the table. I poured another two fingers, then raised the mug to my lips, inhaling the deep stringent bouquet, and took a long draught, closing my eyes and allowing the divine liquid to trickle down my throat and the taste to linger on my palate. I opened my eyes to discover Sherrill taking another draught, straight from the bottle.

"I don't usually drink Scotch," she said, lowering the bottle and wiping her lips with the back of her hand. "I could really go for a Mojito."

"I consider that more of a breakfast drink," I said.

"You only have the one cup?"

"I'm afraid the accommodations are somewhat meager," I said. "This is a bit of a guerrilla style assignment, you see. I guess you could say, in some respects, I'm not really here."

"What about food?" she said. "I'm starving."

"To my surprise, the cupboards are quite bare. I expected to at least find an old box of crackers or a can of beans. It seems there are a few details missing."

"I'm sorry about your sink," she said, slurring her words. "I'm not usually like this. Usually I'm a great deal of fun."

"What's a little retch between old friends," I said.

"Friends?" she said, lowering the bottle.

281

"We used to run in the same circles," I said. "For a time we were quite close. Surely you remember."

Her eyes strained to focus on my visage, but they were hopelessly lost, swimming in a sea of booze and pills.

"Years back, Tony, you and I went everywhere together. We formed a *menage* of sorts, a musketeers *a trois*, if you will."

She shook her head.

"Fred Barclay," I said. "The writer."

"Doesn't ring a bell."

"I wrote the profile for *Vanity Fair*."

"Oh yeah, the profile," she said, smiling for a moment, then narrowing her eyes. "The one that never got printed?"

"A huge injustice," I said.

"I can't remember," she said, her eyes searching the air. "Something having to do with ... I'm sure it'll come to me. Things are a bit fuzzy at the moment. You mind if I smoke?"

She had already taken the cigarette—a Kool menthol—out of the pack and stuck it between her lips. I parried by extending my pack of Pall Malls.

"The flavor is really quite superior," I said.

"I didn't even know they made those anymore," she said, lighting the Kool and taking a drag.

I withdrew the pack of Pall Malls, pulling one out and inserting it between my clenched teeth.

"There have been accusations that I delve into a story a little, shall we say, *too deeply*."

"Now I remember," she said. "There were a lot of personal details, things of the sort you could only know if…hey, is there a bathroom around here?"

She stood up quickly.

"I want to wash up," she said.

She tripped as she took the first step.

"Whoa," she said, catching herself. "I think I need to lie down for a bit."

I helped her down the corridor. She was staggering badly. With her arms around my neck, I lowered her to the bed and eased her in. I attempted to withdraw and leave her to her slumber, but her arms were holding me tight.

"Is there something I can get you?" I said. "A cup of hot tea?

Or a bucket?"

"Come here," she whispered, her eyes closed.

I lowered my ear to her lips, feeling her hot breath on my skin.

"There's something I want to tell you," she said.

I brought my head even closer, until her lips almost touched my ear.

"Julian," she whispered.

"Yes?" I said.

"Oh Julian," she said again, and then I felt her tongue like a hot poker, tracing the folds of my ear with her serpent's caress.

"I think you have me confused…" I said, trying yet again to pull away.

"Shut up, you fool," she said, pulling my face to hers.

I could still taste the bile on her lips, as her tongue hungrily probed the deep recesses of my mouth, squirming, darting and slithering about, what I imagined it must be like to swallow a live snake. She was consuming me like some great swirling vortex of animal heat. All at once, I realized resistance was futile, and I felt myself melting into her desire. Her fingers played at my zipper, pulling it all the way down and freeing my own libidinous snake from its sartorial confines, fingers delicately working their seductive magic up and down my stiffening pungi like a Delhi busker charming the indolent hooded serpent from an attitude of coiled repose to one of flared viperous erection.

And then all at once I was inside of her. I had taken the plunge, losing myself, losing all sense of dimension and time. It could have been an hour, an eon, a millisecond. An entire life flashed before my eyes, what I quickly realized was the life of the universe itself, from the explosive parturition of the big-bang to the infinite abyss of the final deadening collapse. Afterward, I shook uncontrollably and almost vomited, even though I'd barely had a thing to drink.

"That's all right," she said, patting my back maternally.

"It was more than all right," I said. "It was the Battle of Thermopalae, the music of the spheres, Apollo beheading Medusa…"

In the melee, my specs had fallen onto the floor. I reached down to retrieve them.

283

"You look…," she said, studying my eyes. "Gosh, that's funny. I really thought you were him."

"Who?"

"Julian," she said. "Julian Schnabel."

"The artist? No, I am not. Although we are frequently mistaken. We wear the same glasses."

"Congratulations," she said, lighting a mentholated cigarette. "Although I don't suppose it really matters at this point. I've had too much to drink, plus a lot of other stuff. Tomorrow I won't remember a thing."

"At least we have tonight," I said. "Before these precious moments turn to dust in the light of a new day."

"That son of a bitch," she said, shaking her head.

"Schnabel?"

"Tony," she said. "I came all the way out here to tell him."

"It must be important," I said.

"After the last time we got together, I went to the doctor. I didn't have a chance to talk to him before he left."

"You're pregnant."

"God, not that," she said, with a laugh. "It's just that I have, well, *crabs* … and the clap and … some other things." She blew a cloud of mint green smoke. "I guess he'll find out sooner or later."

"Undoubtedly," I said, as a light sweat broke out on my forehead.

She clutched my arm, holding it firmly.

"Thank you for understanding," she said. "I'm extremely vulnerable right now."

"Yes, of course—you wouldn't per chance know of a clinic in the vicinity?" I said.

"I heard there's a medicine man," she said. "They brought him in as a consultant. Tony says he's the real deal."

"Would this medicine man happen to carry penicillin?"

"Sure, why wouldn't he? It's medicine, isn't it?"

I left her smoking in the narrow bed and stepped out for some air. As I walked, carrying the open bottle of Scotch, with only the creeping night sounds to keep me company, I ran through the various scenarios in my head, trying to weave the disparate strands into something resembling a basic narrative. Time was running out. The events that led up to this moment had just about run their course. The party was winding down. I tried to anticipate how things would play out from here. Where was it all going? What did it all mean? What was missing, more than anything, was closure. Something on which to hang the final mark of punctuation. There were a number of possible endings, but there was one more than any other that stuck in my head, that lit up my imagination. I had to admit that it wouldn't be the worst thing in the world to, when I returned, find the camper on fire. It wouldn't take much. The weathered old carcass was as dry as kindling. The longer I delayed my return, I thought, as I watched the smoke gather like a shroud over her recumbent from, the greater the chance that events would take care of themselves.

# CHAPTER 53
*DON*

"Let's take a walk in the moon light," Maria said.

She smiled—I could see this even in the dark, in the warmth of her eyes—and we got out of the car. We didn't do much talking. We didn't exactly speak the same language. I tried to imagine her past, her history erased. We walked arm in arm, enjoying the warm breeze, the gentle caress of the night.

After a time, we stopped and I looked into her eyes.

"What do you want?" she said to me.

I ran my thumb across her cheek, brushing away her hair, then moved in and kissed her on the lobe of her ear. With the blush of the moon on her face, I laid her down on the sand. Her lips opened for me, and I met her there, my hand pushing the dress up along her thighs, and as I reached her panties and pulled them off, her legs parting around my fingers, she put her arms around me, holding me tight. I could taste the salt of her sweat, her hair damp and tousled. We made love in the sand. She let her arms fall to her sides, and her fingers slowly traced along the ground. She squeezed the sand and let out a sigh. It was the sound more than anything that took it out of me. I was letting go, melting in the night. We lay there silently under the stars, until we fell asleep. And then I was in the light. I was out of the car, walking toward this great house. I was at ground zero again, all the way down. I felt the earth beneath my feet, I was at one with the desert. I made my way up the steps and opened the door, and stepped into a dream. What I walked into was the most unexpected kind of gruesome scene. Bodies all over the place, sitting, fallen over, in varying attitudes of nightmare repose, what I assumed to be the great crime lord Quetzalcoatl's cousins, in a peculiar state of ghoulish decomposition, almost preserved in a way, not rotting exactly, skin cool and grey despite the presence of a palpable radiant heat, eyes bulging out, rubber straps tied off around arms, melting spoons, hypodermic needles hanging out of veins raised in grotesque bas relief, striated with traces of toxic heat. And then I saw it, a cool dark powder and a razor blade on the shimmering surface of a gilt framed mirror. Golden Triangle black tar heroin. This was some of the heaviest shit around. I could just imagine these common drug traffickers, saying, *This golden horse, this some heavy shit, man*, before shooting it straight into their hungry veins. Evidently they had never encountered anything so pure, so potent. How could they? You could hardly blame them. A substance like this was beyond their comprehension. It was on a completely different plane. I picked up the razor and cut a fat line, took a twenty out of my pocket and rolled it tight, curling the face of some dead Mesopotamian god. It had been some time since I'd truly scored. This was a long time coming. Who said I'd come to the end of the line? The intimations of the imagination ultimately left you high and dry. I knew I was living in myself. I'd never get out. I put the rolled twenty on the mirrored glass, at the beginning of the line, and leaned down. I was poised, the rolled twenty in my nose, ready to inhale. Then I heard a sound.

"I thought you were on your honeymoon," I said.

"I only had the room for an hour," Juan said.

Again I lowered my head, newly resolved, ready to plunge in.

"What the fuck you doing, man?" he said.

"I'm about to snort up all this heroin."

"It's bad shit, man. Look at these greasers."

"These people didn't know what they were doing. They're just a bunch of crazy ass spics. They couldn't handle it."

"Don't you hear that fucking sound, man? That's radiation."

"Now that you mention it."

I had barely noticed it, the crackling of a Geiger counter. It had become so familiar, like background noise.

"I don't think that's heroin, man. You know what I'm saying? I think it's uranium. You know, like it's radioactive."

"Uranium? That's pretty far out."

This was, after all, his field of expertise. I had to consider it.

"No, wait. That's not uranium," he said.

"Hey, you're the mad scientist."

He brought his face so close as to seemingly inhale the substance through the dark visor of his eyes.

"That's *plutonium*."

Wow, that was even further out.

"This must be some of the heaviest shit on the planet," I said.

"Man, this plutonium, man, I think it's really expensive."

My mind began to reel with the possibilities.

"Do you have any idea what the street value is for this shit? I have a feeling we're going to be very rich men."

Just then our heads turned toward a sudden commotion behind us. And then they appeared, passing through the doorway from an adjacent room. It was Priest and his henchmen. I recognized them from the Institute of Piscatorial Science. There was still a bitter taste in my mouth. Priest was dressed the same, all in black with the white banded collar. His henchmen were wearing white environmental suits, covered head to toe, and carried a wide variety of devices, one I recognized as a Geiger counter similar to the one from the cantina, and its electric crackle was exceptionally pronounced now. They also carried an array of firearms and brightly colored balloons. The only one not wearing an environmental suit was an unctuous Mediterranean type carrying a video camera on his shoulder, eye pressed to the lens, as if the camera alone would protect him from whatever it was that was out there.

Priest spoke first, his hand sweeping across the whole scene: "Unfortunately for these gentlemen they mistook our plutonium for their usual shipment."

Standing next to Priest was a hard looking black man wearing a purple bowler hat. He had on a pair of oversize black sunglasses, and a tattoo of a winged snake climbed up from his shirt collar and wound up around his throat.

"Big fan of your work," he said, nodding. "You and your cook."

I gave him a nod. The man looked vaguely familiar.

"Anyway, there's someone here I think you should meet," said Priest. "An old friend…"

I knew at that moment I was about to witness something I was in no way prepared to see. He materialized from behind the crush of environmental suits, wearing a black cape, holding a black cane, face obscured by the rim of a black hat. Then he raised his head. He had no face. Where a face should have been, there was nothing but a blur of skin, as if his features had been rubbed away by an eraser.

I noticed that Priest was waving his arms like a sorcerer trying to cast a spell.

"Allow me to introduce you to Orren," said Priest.

"I always thought you were a myth," I said. "The man without a face."

"You know, sometimes, when I look at you," he said. "I feel like I'm looking into a two-way mirror."

"Don't flatter yourself," I said. "A man like you, you're going to get us blown to bits and pieces."

"We're already bits and pieces," said Orren. "I'm here for the end of the world."

"You're an atomizer," I said. "Every man for himself."

"It's too late for that. We are the light or we are nothing. It all goes back in the smelter, all the golden hair, teeth as white as pearls, eyes that sparkle like diamonds. I found these in the sand."

Suddenly, I felt that my teeth were missing. I put my hand to my mouth. He showed me his hand, full of teeth and sand.

"Had you going there," said Orren.

He threw the sand at the floor, and the teeth exploded like fire crackers. I ran my tongue across my teeth. I could feel them again. At that moment, one of the henchmen handed him a balloon. He put the valve to his lips and breathed half of it in.

"You recognize me now? This is the voice of God."

He now sounded like Donald Duck, a familiar sound indeed.

"Helium," I said. "That's an old trick."

One of the balloons popped on the ceiling. It didn't startle me a bit.

"Get used to it. It's how everything sounds in the ether," he laughed.

"What are a couple of high priests going to do with all this plutonium?" I said.

"This is about what happens at the end of the good book. God is the bomb, Don. And he made each one of us in his image."

"You still have those dice on you, those loaded dice?" asked Priest.

"I don't believe so."

"See, here they are," said Priest, raising his hand and pulling them from behind my ear.

"More tricks."

"What kind of holy man can't perform a little sleight of hand?"

The dice were connected by a long strap of leather. He wrapped one of the pair tight around his left arm. The other he stuck to his forehead.

"You're a conjurer," I said.

"These are funny dice all right. They're phylacteries. No kidding. You can crack 'em like a couple of eggs and see what comes out."

He shook the dice in his hand and threw them down on the table.

"Look at that. The sun and the moon," said Priest.

One of the pair was white, the other black. So the values came up one white dot on black, and one black dot on white.

"You get the message?" he said.

"Explain it to me."

"Follow the sun," said Priest

"Not your dick," Orren cracked.

He scrutinized me for a moment.

"You really shouldn't wear those inside. Haven't you heard? Sunglasses are a narcotic."

"They take the edge off," I said, adjusting my shades.

With a sweep of the hand Orren drew our attention to the other side of the room.

"Let me introduce you to the bomb."

I'm not sure why I hadn't noticed it before, hanging right there in plain sight. The infamous golden horse: a piñata.

A thin stream of silvery powder bled from a slit in its underside. Orren addressed it with that long black cane and with a single precise blow obliterated it, the *papier mache* carcass blowing apart, exploding in a shower of golden confetti. The whole lode of plutonium dropped to the floor in one concentrated mass, not a poof or a cloud, not a single scattered grain.

That phone conversation I overheard, what seemed like a lifetime ago —"down in Tierra del Fuego ... a phaeton with junk in the trunk hitched to the Golden Triangle pony express." It was never heroin at all. In the argot of our tong, a phaeton with junk in the trunk could mean a car load of drugs, but when combined with Golden Triangle and Pony Express it was a reference to the mythical charioteer Phaeton and his cosmic cargo, the sun, the symbolic union of chariot and sun in turn representing the ultimate payload, plutonium.

"Of course that's just the raw material," said Orren, bringing the cane back to his side. "These gangsters thought they could hide it inside a piñata like a bunch of cheap smack."

"You have to do better than that to fool a Geiger counter," said Priest.

"Now once more, let me introduce you to the bomb," said Orren. "Gentlemen, the colossus."

He pointed with his cane as several of the henchmen wheeled in a statue made out of the same silvery white metal that leaked from the piñata. On closer inspection, it was a life-size statue of me.

"Do you worship the Helios?" said Priest. "Do you like to stare at the sun?"

"Only when I've had too much of the local tea," I said.

"It's not about blowing everything to bits and pieces," said Orren. "It's about coming together. For all practical purposes, fission *is* fusion. They're two sides of the same coin. I put the sun in a box. By detonating a fission bomb in a sea of hydrogen, four atoms are fused into one—Helium. The release of energy at that instant is almost beyond belief. That's the secret of the sun, Don, the well from which all life sprang. Evolution happens like a heart attack. It's when you give birth to a monster. Life as we know it ends now. The earth is soiled, Don. It's time to clean house. Through fission we can achieve the unification of all those lost souls, turn the world's oceans into one great big desert. Would you like a match?"

I had pulled out a cigarette and held it between my lips.

The flame parted my hands, rising to the tip. He flipped the top down and handed me this familiar object, the lost lighter.

"I believe you dropped this," said Priest.

I turned it over and caressed the Zippo's polished steel casing, something real, a genuine artifact from that vaguest and blackest of memories.

"That's all I get?"

"You get your life back. You get a second chance."

I took in the whole scene and noticed that everyone was smoking now. I looked at them one after the other. Juan was smoking. Priest was smoking. Orren was smoking. I was smoking.

"See, we're all smoking now," I said. "Isn't that nice?"

"We've got a little surprise for you," said Priest.

Maria was led in by two henchmen. I could tell it was Maria, even with the brown paper bag over her head, by the way she looked in that dress. From that bag over her head came a muffled litany of profane and indignant sounds.

"She spotted us and started to cause a fuss. So we had to tie her up. She was trying to warn you," said Priest.

"She's one of the missing persons," said Orren. "Your little Arab woman."

Arab? I hadn't thought of that. I looked at the bagged face with new eyes.

"Come on, do it for Don," said Priest. "I'm trying to get her to ululate. You haven't lived until you've heard that."

Behind the bag, her indignation reached a furious pitch.

"You shouldn't let your woman drink," said Orren. "I can smell it on her. I asked her about that bottle of yours, with that little worm in it. She wouldn't talk. But let me tell you, you eat that and you're an atomy."

"I'll take my chances."

"To paraphrase from the book of Deuteronomy, thou have had so many gods before me," said Orren.

"It's like a count-down," said Priest. "Three ... two ... one ..."

"That's why they call me the high priest of MOAB," said Orren.

"Takin' more brothers to the promised land than Moses," said the black man in the bowler hat.

Juan frowned coolly, nodded.

"How you know these *putos?*"

"From a bad dream."

"Follow the sun," said Orren. "Return to the Helios and remain in the everlasting light."

"Good catching up," I said, tipping my hat and turning to leave.

"One more thing," said Orren, slipping off the necklace with the otherworldly black pendant and handing it to me. "You remember the black bullet. It was made out of a tektite. Fanta left it in his eye all those years, refused to have it removed so he'd never forget. That car fire didn't leave much in the way of forensic evidence. By the time we found it, all the hair and flesh, the glass, rubber and steel, had burned to ash. This was the only thing left."

"How does this work?" I said.

"I gave you something, now you give something to me," said Orren.

"What could I possibly have that you'd want?" I said. "A man who has everything."

"You know what I want. I want that bottle."

"The one with the worm in it," I said.

"Those things don't grow on trees."

"It's in the car," I said. "Be right back."

He took an hour glass from inside his cape and turned it over in his hand.

"You have a hot second," he said, as the grains of sand dusted the bottom of the glass.

I grabbed Maria by the arm and we went out the door.

"Time to split," I said, giving Juan a nudge. "Time to blow out."

"Snap out of it," she hissed. "Can't you see what's going on?"

I ignored her, dragging her along.

"I parked over here," said Juan, heading off in the opposite direction.

I pulled the bag off her head and received the look of the wounded lamb, as if I were responsible somehow. We got in the car and I crouched down, untying her hands and scoping it out. I slipped the necklace over the rear view mirror where the dice had been, leaving the black bullet swinging dreamily before my eyes. Maria snapped her fingers in front of my face. I blinked. I couldn't have come this far for nothing. My mind raced as I tried to figure how to get my skin out of the game. And then it hit me, the sound of a locomotive thundering down the tracks. I could feel the earth shake. The winds blew about violently, almost blinding us with sand. But through it all I could make out the undulating form of the twister, a gargantuan of destructive power. When the winds died down and the sand and dust had settled, I could scarcely believe my eyes. The entire estate was gone, ripped right off the foundation. I scanned the horizon. It was nowhere to be seen.

I got out of the car and walked to where the house had been. There was only an outline now, the jagged excrescence of foundation. Not a scrap remained. It had all been stripped cleanly away. I searched around. Only the colossus remained, standing like a sentry before an invisible city. And that made me feel somehow very lasting and very heavy, too magnificent to be blown away. But there was something else. The whole lode of plutonium, it too was still there, not a single grain missing. And when I found that cool dark powder, undisturbed and intact, the proverbial main vein, at that moment I knew, this was truly some of the heaviest shit on the planet. I scraped the bulk of it into the brown paper bag. Who knew how much was enough? There was something else. Sitting next to the plutonium was a purple bowler hat. I raised the brim and a large spider crawled out.

By the time I got back to the car, now wearing the purple bowler, Juan and his bride were already waiting for me.

"We have to take your car, man. Mine got taken away by the tornado."

We piled into the car, just like old times. The sun set low on the horizon. The moon burned bright.

"What that greaser say? You're supposed to follow the…"

"The sun."

"Yeah, the sun. That's right, the sun," he laughed, finding the whole thing hysterical.

I awoke to find the girl looking down at me.

"Don," she said. "You were having a dream."

"It's okay. I'm awake now," I said.

"You were talking while you were asleep," she said. "What is it, this golden horse? Is it what I think?"

"What do you know about it?" I said.

"I have heard other men speak of it," she said. "Shipments

from Indo-China."

"Can you help me find it?" I said.

"There is a man. He will be here tomorrow," she said. "His name is Quetzalcoatl."

"The so-called crime lord I keep hearing about."

"Do not underestimate him. He is like a snake. He may have introduced himself to you and you don't even know it. He has the answer to what's in your dreams."

We got up and walked back to the car. Juan and Ana were leaning against the hood sharing a cigarette.

"We're gonna tie the knot," Juan said, holding the girl's hand.

We got in, Maria slipping into the seat beside me.

"Where do we go now?" said Juan.

I stared out the window.

"We must find Quetzalcoatl," said Maria. "At La Casa del Sol."

"I must warn you," said Ana. "You are in grave danger. The Quetzalcoatl does not like to lose. And if you do not find him first, he will find you."

For certain, the end was drawing near. For the first time, I felt I was onto something truly heavy, and the feeling ticked inside me like a bomb.

At the chapel, Juan and his bride had a simple ceremony presided over by an old Mexican priest, who performed the rites in Latin. Even though I was not, strictly speaking, Catholic, I joined in the communion and had several cups of sangria during the ceremony, not to mention what I had at the reception that followed during which Juan and I did shots of Mezcal in the church parking lot.

The happy couple drove off in a black El Dorado, trailing an assortment of beer cans and liquor bottles as they disappeared into the afternoon sun.

In a way, it was hard to believe that a woman like Maria could have the kind of information I needed, be the key to something this big, but one never knew who might turn out to be a major player.

We got into the car and went on our way. I was on a quest now, a search for something truly heavy, maybe some of the heaviest shit on the planet. It was a feeling I had, a longing. The pressure at my back, the black hole that lay ahead. I couldn't wait any longer. I wanted it now. The wheels burned over black top. It was good to be on the road again, the big car knifing through the desert wind at over a hundred miles an hour. No obstacles in our way, all foreign matter fallen by the wayside in a crude outline of detritus—road kill, tumble weed, plastic wrappers, beer cans, shoes, blown out tires, and the expanse of the desert closing in around us, swallowing us alive.

# CHAPTER 54
*FREDERICK M. BARCLAY*

I had just discovered a can of gasoline lying next to one of the generators when I noticed the orb. At first I mistook it for the moon, thinking it had come unmoored from the sky and was now bouncing along the earth. The orb pulsed and shape-shifted as if it were made of mercury then picked up speed, skipping across the sand until it disappeared in the darkness. I picked up the gas can, bidding adieu to the mysterious orb as I made my way back to the camper. I knew my way in the dark, knew exactly where I was going, and could have easily found the camper even without the light of the moon to guide me. Imagine my surprise when I came to the place where that dilapidated camper had been parked for eons—I knew for sure this was the spot because it was situated at the base of a large precariously balanced rock (the narrow base of which made it appear that it would tip over at any moment)—and found that there was nothing there. In fact, less than nothing. Not only had the decrepit motor home vanished without a trace but where it had once been there was now a vast absence, a deep dark hole that, when I peered down into it, seemed entirely without a limit. The earth had opened up and swallowed her whole. Oh what a dark and lonely fate. I couldn't tell if the tears I wept were for the undermining of my dark designs or for the loss of my beloved Sherrill. I turned up my breast to the heavens and emitted a mighty baleful howl that peeled like thunder across the vast empty desert. So distracted was I by grief, it took a moment before I noticed the electric crackle. At first, I was sure it was a Geiger counter, a device I had only seen in movies but whose sound was unmistakable, but when I picked it up it became clear it was an old black and yellow transistor radio tuned to dead air. The device had a leather strap that allowed me to hang it over my shoulder. For certain it was a gift—whether from the gods above or some middle-earth deity remained to be seen—but it was not enough to slake my desire for revenge. I picked up the gas can and marched steadfastly and with an almost fanatical  purpose toward the set. Initially there was no specific target for my rage; I would have lashed out at anything within reach, from the exalted studio head to the lowly desert toad. As I walked through the fetid sweltering blankness, a specific image began to take shape, forming by degrees in my mind's eye. It didn't take long to find it, the Raja's palace, rising out of the desert like some architectural kraken, swallowing the night and everything. Though displayed to stunning effect by the looming kliegs, like some luminous celestial body floating in deepest blackest space, and despite the brilliant color values (thrilling reds, stunning mauves, verdant ashes) it was still the darkest thing around, darker even than the impenetrable fabric of the night that shrouded it. Though well lit, and though there were little flurries of activity all around, there was nary a sign of life inside, so I barely attracted any attention at all as I began pouring gasoline over the elaborate front staircase and then splashing it joyously and with increasingly reckless abandon about the façade of the great house. It wasn't the people I was interested in, it was the edifice itself, which had all at once come to embody the human sins of this carnival of greed and vice and myth making, the colony itself like some flash Sodom and Gemorrah with the Raja's palace the center of gravity, the dying sun at the heart of a collapsing solar system, the instantiation of all our decaying hopes and dreams.  Hunching over the gas can as I backed down the marble stairs, I poured a trail of gasoline that ran from the imposing and ornate front doors out to a point on the stone walkway that I considered (perhaps naively) to be a reasonably safe distance away. I paused for a moment to fully appreciate the gravity and symbolic significance of what was about to happen then struck the match off the side of my boot and dropped its flaming timber into the limpid moon glossed headwaters of the gasoline trail. The burning match made a gentle splash and I watched transfixed as the flame quavered lazily in the wind, the calm before the storm, before suddenly, and without warning, swelling out pregnantly in an almost Da Vincean figure of impending combustion and then, right at the very cusp, just as suddenly, and without ceremony, expiring—not with a bang, but a whimper—in the unexpectedly impotent fuel. The thought occurred to me that the petrol was not after all gasoline but was instead perhaps a less combustible fluid like diesel. I searched my pockets desperately for another match and was on the verge of ripping my jacket to shreds when I saw the approaching headlights and then, caught within the headlights' crazed glare, the terrified expression of a creature desperately running for its life. As the headlight beams bounced along the sand, alternately illuminating the creature and veiling it in dismal night, I began to make out the shape of the vehicle—the shattered windows, the rusted hull, the naked wheel rims, bumper hanging by a thread—eventually recognizing it as the very same camper that had heretofore served as my temporary abode, and even more, as the headlight beams slashed across the expression of naked terror, recognizing this desperate pathetic running animal as the iconic actor Tony Billings. As the camper drew near, rapidly closing the gap with Tony and drawing him toward his inevitable devouring beneath the wheels, I caught sight of the driver's eyes, which blazed more radiantly than the headlights; they were, unmistakably, Sherrill's eyes, and they were burning with murderous intention. With the prow of the camper nipping at his heels Tony sprinted up the marble stairway toward the front doors. When the camper hit the stairs, the prow dropped suddenly, as if the frame were about to separate from chassis, whereupon the entire vehicle launched upward, tires bounding violently over the stairs, camper top bucking like a *howdah* on a wild bull elephant. Reaching the top of the stairs the broken motor home seemed to instantaneously pick up speed, taking off like a shot across the ornate sprawling porch on a collision course with Tony and the impenetrable façade of the palace. In the same moment that the great rattling camper eclipsed Tony, who completely vanished from my line of sight, it collided with the enormous front doors, the concussive impact sending up a huge fireball that rose heavenward for the duration of a single bated breath before collapsing back to earth and quickly spreading over the blanket of fuel that coated the front of the palace, covering everything (and, presumably, every*one*) with a thick skein of hot crackling fire. In an instant the entire palace was a blaze as the tendrils of flame crawled up the walls and through the open windows like some febrile strain of poison ivy. For a time I was so transfixed by the conflagration that I almost forgot about the enormous black hole that had just opened up in the center of my universe—the sudden premature absence of Tony Billings creating a void in my life—and in lives everywhere—so profound that once the realization hit, I very nearly blacked out. There was some comfort in observing Sherrill being tended to at the perimeter of the blaze. By some miracle she'd been thrown clear. As much as Sherrill had meant to me over the years, without Tony she was, this perennial object of my obsession, practically a stranger. Our once inviolable *menage* had burst asunder, scattering our purposeless deracinated bodies to the farthest reaches of this alien space.

As more bodies were drawn to the mushrooming structure fire, and even more to the fallen starlet, I retreated into the gloom of the night. Clutching the old black-and-yellow radio as I staggered out into the desert, I began turning the dial in search of some voice, some sign of life out there to keep me company on my travels. I stumbled on a pile of rocks, picked myself up, and kept walking with no destination in mind. I wasn't even running away really. I was moving toward something, something that would reveal itself to me in the elusive sounds that carried on the wind and the strange shadows that played in the spill of moon light on the misshapen landscape. The mission to which I'd dedicated the last act of my life had finally come to an end, leaving me a free agent, set adrift amidst the galaxies of itinerant bodies that swirled aimlessly about the cosmos like sand in a wind storm, another lost soul amongst the hapless meteors, comets, cosmic dust and assorted space junk. In spite of the jarring turn in my fortunes, I remained hopeful as I searched the dial. And when I glimpsed the silver orb up ahead, revealing itself in the moonlight as it wafted on a current of air, I knew I was on the right path. So I was not at all surprised by the sound of a voice emerging from beneath the white noise. The voice seemed to grow clearer with each step then all at once broke up in static. I turned this way and that, taking several steps back and several more forward and then just as mysteriously the voice returned, crystal clear. In fact it couldn't have been clearer if it had been coming out of my own mouth. I listened intently to the voice, all the while keeping an eye on the orb as it drifted out toward the horizon on a receding tide of moon light. It sounded like an old RKO radio program, with each character played by a different actor. I hadn't heard one of these in some time. The main character, a hard sounding fellow who also served as the narrator, delivered his lines in a deliberately dry world-weary tone no doubt intended to convey experience beyond his actual years. Despite the affected quality, the actor possessed a rich voice full of nuance and insinuation that practically begged one to not only read between the lines but to curl up inside them, wearing the lush cadences like a blanket or a second skin. The voice belonged to Tony Bllings. The other voice (rich, deep, velvety) belonged, unmistakably, to the veteran character actor Victor St. Germaine. I found myself becoming increasingly transfixed, letting the rippling words lap over me like sea foam as I sank ever deeper into the warm resonant depths of these inscrutable enunciations. The more I lost myself, the nearer I came to finding that thing that I had lost and that the world had determined forever to deny me. And yet here it was, this voice, so instantly familiar, yet strange as a visitor from distant space.

A reasonably faithful transcript of the program follows:

Tony: "I always thought you were a myth."

Victor St. Germaine: "You know, sometimes, when I look at you, I feel like I'm looking into a two-way mirror."

Tony: "Don't flatter yourself. A man like you, you're going to get us blown to bits and pieces."

Victor St. Germaine "We're already bits and pieces. I'm here for the end of the world."

Tony: "You're an atomizer. Every man for himself."

Victor St. Germaine "It's too late for that. We are the light or we are

301

nothing. It all goes back in the smelter, all the golden hair, teeth as white as pearls, eyes that sparkle like diamonds."

And then it was gone, the signal lost, that golden voice plunged into a raging ocean of static. I swung about, to the left, to the right, frantically turning the dial as I sprinted into the moonlight, trying to chase it down, a blip here and there giving false hope, but after a time I resigned myself to the certainty that whatever this transmission was, wherever it came from, it was lost forever. There was something about that voice—familiar and strange at the same time—that haunted me. I was certain that now, if I hadn't been before, I was truly alone in the world.

The orb had come to rest a short distance away, caught on a jagged rock. I knelt down beside it, putting my ear to the orb's palpitating skein. I listened intently, but soon realized that the sounds of life I believed I'd heard within were but mere echoes of ambient noise, the old trick of the sea shell. There was, to be sure, absolutely nothing inside.

As I drew near enough to reach out and touch the orb, I realized that it was—rather than some Jungian archetype let loose in the vast desert of my unconscious—merely an escaped weather balloon from the French scientists' open air lab. What had in the glaring light of day appeared gauchely futuristic now took on, in the vague murmuring darkness, an intensely metaphysical aspect. I ran my hand over the surface of the balloon, finding to my surprise that it was tethered to a harness, such as one might wear while rappelling down the side of a cliff or, perhaps, into a cave. So absorbed was I in this new discovery that it took me more than a moment to notice, standing just a short distance away, a man in a space suit.

"Pardon me," I said. "I was just admiring your balloon. It is quite magnificent."

"It better be," said the voice, which I immediately recognized as Nero's. "It took a team of elite European scientists and more American dollars than you can count to develop it."

I was able to make out Nero's increasingly occult features in the dull smear of moon light that coated the landscape, his human sized head swimming in the comparatively oversized space suit. The helmet, sitting on a nearby rock, was not yet attached.

"Are you alone?" I asked.

"I assure you that I am, in more ways than you can imagine. Hand me the helmet, please."

I lifted the helmet from the rock and handed it to him. He set it down on top of the suit and locked it on.

"Are you planning to go somewhere?" I asked.

"Quite," he said, voice echoing out from behind the visor of the helmet. "And there is not a moment to lose."

He picked up the harness that was connected to the balloon and put it on like a jacket, fastening it to a heavy belt that wrapped around his waist and down between his legs.

"You're going up there?" I said, nodding up toward the heavens.

"I told you of my post-career plans," he said.

"I do recall your mentioning that you saw ballooning somewhere in your future, although I must admit to some surprise at how quickly you've taken it up. Moreover, considering that you are midway through production on a major motion picture that you alone appear to be driving, the current moment hardly seems to qualify as post-career."

"My career, such as it is, and this film, are converging on a terminus that is far closer, and far more cataclysmic, than anyone could have ever expected. Since I have anointed you as the chronicler of this soon to be infamous story, I will share with you some intimate details of the plot. The real story is not what's happening in the movie, but to it. By the time this balloon reaches the ionosphere, carrying me with it, this entire production will have fallen under a cloud of toxic radiation so lethal that no one will leave this place alive, neither cast nor crew, bird nor beast."

"Surely you jest," I said.

"Do I look like a jester to you?" he said, voice echoing from within the space helmet.

"Not in the conventional sense," I said, eyes traveling the length of the space suit.

"Everything has been arranged. The dirty bomb will detonate tonight. There is nothing that can be done to stop it now."

"But why?" I asked, dumbfounded.

"Revenge, for one. And so many other reasons that I won't bore you with now. My days are numbered with the studio, this studio that I built from the ground up, that I made the Titan that it is today. At some point the accountants will come for my head. Those bloodless line-item assassins. It will happen quickly, without warning. Only I will not be there to hand it to them. And when I am gone, there will be nothing left of this studio but ashes. Nothing to salvage but waste and misery."

"Although I am reluctant to ever judge a source—or a patron for that matter—I must ask you to reconsider and call a halt to these diabolical machinations, if only to protect the innocent."

"Name one," he said, penetrating me with his eyes.

I started to speak, then stopped, my parted lips breathing the dead smoke of silence.

Nero smiled, perhaps the first time I'd seen him form this expression.

"Forget them and focus on the story," he said. "That is your destiny. You have been chosen. Should get you a Pulitzer, or worse."

"I must admit, until running into you just now, I thought the story was over."

"Not by a long shot," he said. "Now kindly do me the honors of cutting the cord."

He handed me a utility knife. I crouched down and sawed at the nylon cord that fastened the balloon to a stake in the ground. The strands of nylon parted easily and when the cord broke, the balloon rose into the heavens like a shot, carrying the spaceman with it. I watched the ascent until balloon and balloonist vanished into the nullity of night.

I sat down on the sand and rested my back against the rock. Setting the radio on my chest, I continued turning the knob, searching up and down the dial for any traces of that phantom voice I'd heard earlier, quickly at first, then more and more slowly, until I was able to perceive, in vivid detail, even the finest, most minute grain of noise.

# CHAPTER 55

From the back, the magnificent Raja's palace looked less than magnificent. The shots had all been designed from the front and the sides and the blueprint for the palace followed suit, toning down the ornamental and architectural flourishes that characterized the rest of the building. In fact, the back served mainly as a staging area, used for moving props and equipment in and out of the house, and for these reasons—architectural and logistical—the rear of the palace maintained a somewhat disheveled and utilitarian appearance that made it seem not obviously connected to the rest of the structure. In fact, from the posterior vantage, the palace more resembled the loading area of a warehouse than anything that might be inhabited by the mythical beings of Oriental antiquity. Coincidentally, from the back there were few signs yet of the nascent blaze that had just consumed the front of the palace, other than the intense flickering light that seemed to give the whole structure a vaguely incandescent halo. The two crew members having a smoke next to the cable coils and crate stacks seemed to barely notice when the door opened and the star of the picture, Tony Billings, emerged in a discomfited state with his hair and pants on fire and proceeded to run away from the set at a breakneck pace until he disappeared in the darkness.

# CHAPTER 56

It was a long way down, a lot longer than he expected, by a long shot. Every once in a while Tommy Boy struck the lighter to get some sense of how far he'd come and how much farther he had to go, but all the small pocket of illumination revealed was what he already knew, that he was in one deep dark mother fucking hole. Within the intimate radius of flickering match light was blackness and beyond that, where the bubble of light attenuated to a fine sliver of incandescence, was utter insensible oblivion. It was a shaft of some kind, like one of those old mine shafts, carved out of bed rock. Lacking any point of reference, he wondered how far he'd descended, it could have been a couple hundred feet or a couple miles, he'd lost all sense of perspective and time. The rope was already there when he found the hole, anchored by a spike in the rocks. Next to the spike, there were a couple harnesses, the type used by rock climbers. He suited up, hooked the carbine to the rope and dropped right down without thinking twice about it. The way he found the hole—in truth, he damn near fell in—was the electric crackle from an old yellow and black radio sitting on a big rock by the climbing gear, the craziest sound, not like the usual thing you heard with dead air. It was like a beacon. As much of a struggle as it was to get down, feeling his way in the dark, never having done anything like this before, he didn't even want to think what it would take to get back up, with gravity working against him, pulling him down into the earth. When he finally reached bottom, it caught him off guard, the unexpected sensation of hard ground beneath his feet, and he went right down on his butt.

"Anybody down here? Hello?" he said. "Yo, seriously, what's up with this?"

His questions meeting with silence, he struck the lighter and slowly moved it around in the darkness, squinting through the small red flame. He moved it to the left, nothing, and then back to the right, even more slowly so as not to miss anything, sighing in frustration—"I can't believe this shit"—when a face suddenly appeared in the muted light, its unexpectedness causing him to scream and leap backwards.

"Holy shit!" he said, dropping the lighter.

He quickly picked it back up, striking the flint.

"Hey, is that you?"

The face looming over him, cast in the dim amber glow of the flame, slowly revolved toward the source of the light, revealing the identity of the shadowy being to be Q.

"You decided to follow me," said Q.

"I'm in it all the way, no turning back."

"You sure about that?" said Q.

"I'm ready for anything," said Tommy Boy.

"It's not too late," said Q.

"I came this far and shit."

Q reached down, grabbing Tommy Boy's hand and pulling him to his feet.

"You ready for this?" said Q.

Q struck a huge gunmetal torch lighter that seared the air like a jet flame. He swung out the blue cone of flame, illuminating the surprisingly capacious cavern. The first thing that struck Tommy Boy was that it looked like some abandoned coal mine or copper mine or whatever the fuck it was they dug up out here, like the kind they'd show on TV whenever a bunch of poor hillbillies got trapped underground for weeks or forever. It looked like it had been abandoned long ago. The second thing was all the heavy metal— stack after stack of these big metal rods, as far as the eye could see.

"That what I think it is?" said Tommy Boy.

"You got eyes," said Q. "What you think it is?"

"Spent fuel rods," said Tommy Boy. "*Nuclear*, know what I'm saying?"

"That's what I'm talkin' about,' said Q.

"What we gonna do with it?"

"We gonna move some mother fuckin' weight."

"One thing I gotta ask, how you fall into this shit?" said Tommy Boy.

"It went down like this. Nero chose me, you see. Cut me a deal. I do him a favor, he give me top billing."

"Whatever that cat wanted, had to be heavy," said Tommy Boy.

"Supposed to go down like this. Mother fucker left an old camper at the top of the mine shaft, filled up with straight diesel. Plus a shit ton of fertilizer. A whole bunch of other shit."

"He want you to make a bomb," said Tommy Boy. "A *dirty* bomb."

"Wire the whole thing up, then push the camper down the mine shaft."

"So it hits the bottom and blows up all this nuclear waste, send a huge fire ball up into the sky, a black cloud of radiation raining down over everything."

"I show up, ready to do this shit," said Q. "No fuckin' camper."

"Somebody stole that bitch," said Tommy Boy. "Driving around in a hot wired dirty bomb and they don't even know it. Imagine their surprise when -"

"Imagine my surprise when I crawl down into this hole and find all this premium atomic shit. Up to that point, I don't know what's down here. A man wants me to do a job, price is right, I don't ask questions. He wants me to drop a bomb in a hole, I drop the bomb. That's the way I roll."

"Sometimes you don't wanna know."

"Don't know, don 't care, just do the job, dig? 'cept there's no camper. No camper, no bomb. I aint the type of cat runs away when shit gets tight, you know what I'm saying. This shit never go down easy. I figure I go down the hole and see what's up, improvise and shit. That's when I found all this heavy metal, and I think, hell yeah, this some pristine hundred percent grade A shit."

"Fuckin' beautiful shit," said Tommy Boy.

"You know what this shit worth?" said Q.

"I got an idea."

"Fuck movies," said Q. "Fuck music. Fuck all those mother fuckers. We gonna move this mother fuckin' weight."

"A fuckin' dirty bomb," said Tommy Boy. "That's some cold shit. What the fuck he want to do that for anyway?"

"Insurance. Had to be."

"Everybody gonna get radiation poisoning. Their hair gonna fall out. Fingernails. Teeth. That some nasty shit."

Up on the surface, Tony continued his desperate flight into the darkness, every so often turning his head to look behind him. His face was dusty and streaked with sweat, his hair shooting out in all directions as if electrified. He stumbled, almost fell, then got his legs under him and kept going. And then, just like that, he disappeared.

Down below in the mine shaft, Tommy Boy and Q slowly circled each other in the glow of the cigarette lighters.

"Only thing is, isn't this shit, you know, radioactive and shit?" said Tommy Boy.

"What you worried about? You for real or you a little bitch?"

Tommy Boy swallowed hard.

"Yo, I'm for real, Q, there aint no doubt about that, all I'm sayin' is, there was this thing on TV about the, you know, the mother fuckin' radiation and shit…"

"Fuck TV. You see any TV down here? You see any whiney ass bitches down here? You hang down here, before long you be a mother fuckin' super hero."

"Long as I don't grow two heads and shit."

"You don't get to choose what happen to you, that's just the way the game is played. Maybe you grow two heads, then again maybe you grow two dicks, know what I'm sayin'? You damn lucky either way, a man with two heads? Shit, you could watch two different TV shows at the same time, talk on two different phones, got your subprime bitch talkin' into this head, your bottom bitch talkin' into this head over here, while a couple a day-glow bitches from Venus suck both your big fat mutant dicks. How you like them super powers now?"

"I hear you, Q, I'm in it, you know what I'm saying? I'm just thinking we could, you know, put on some of those big ass rubber suits and shit, with the breathing tubes?"

"You ever see a super-hero breathing through a tube, walking around in those big rubber boots? You wanna step up, you wanna be a man? Shit, you wanna be a *giant*? You got to put your ass on the line. No turning back, baby. You got to exceed the lethal limit."

"Got to be a mask or some shit around here," said Tommy Boy, moving his lighter around in the darkness. "At least some goggles, know what I'm saying?"

Tommy Boy heard it first—the screaming, faint at first then growing exponentially louder. He raised his lighter and peered up into the mine shaft. Q raised his lighter too, both of them standing there silently staring up into the mine shaft, waiting. And then there he was, right between them—Tony Billings hanging upside down, the rope wrapped around his ankle. He hung there for a moment, gently swaying, before suddenly dropping to the floor of the cavern with what seemed like a mile of rope falling from the upper reaches of the shaft and piling up around him.

Tony looked up and said, "Hey, you guys have any chronic?"

Q and Tommy Boy exchanged a look as the rope slithered down endlessly between them into the mounting pile. When at last the end of the rope sailed past and landed with a slap of finality on the pile, which resembled an enormous heap of spaghetti, Tommy Boy said, "Guess we gonna be down here for a while."

"Speak for yourself, mother fucker," said Q. "My ass gonna turn into Spiderman and crawl right the fuck on out of here."

"Speaking of spiders, where is that freaky thing?" said Tommy Boy, suddenly looking around frantically.

"Some place safe, don't you worry 'bout that," said Q.

"Crack, meth, zombie, whatever you got," said Tony. "I need something to take the edge off."

"Let's say this super-hero thing don't exactly work out, what we supposed to do then?" said Tommy Boy.

"Look around," said Q, casting the glow of the blunt-torch on the stacks of gleaming fuel rods. "I'm gonna build my ass a time machine."

# CHAPTER 57

In the screening tent, smoke hung languorously in the air, like a sultry twilight mist. Bax and Blow were drinking hundred year old Scotch. Nick roasted a bowl, taking a big hit then passing the pipe to Silvio.

"That's good shit, man," Silvio said, jets of smoke squirting out between his teeth.

He passed the pipe to the AD, who reloaded it from a plastic baggie of vibrant green buds.

"Where'd you find hundred year old Scotch?" said the AD. "That shit is, like, impossible to find."

"Got it off a dead man," said Bax.

"He wasn't dead when we found him," said Nick.

"Blow killed him," said Bax.

"Then copped the bottle," said Nick. "Stuck it on his hip and ran a bootleg around the whole damn side show."

"You see, Blow killed him because he has a freak for vintage shit," said Bax.

"Can't get enough.," said Nick.

"The hell of it is, cat was barely hanging on," said Bax.

"He was knocking at death's door," said Nick.

"Blow couldn't wait. As soon as he found out about the Scotch, he had to have it," said Bax.

"Cut him to the quick. No hesitation," said Bax.

"Iced him like the abominable snowman," said Nick.

"He died of natural causes," said Blow. "He was 99 years old. The Scotch was a gift to the man's father on the day he was born."

Up on the screen, there was something going on. If you weren't paying close attention, it was hard to tell exactly what. There was the sound of general commotion, then screaming. Smoke poured out of the Raja's palace, from every opening. A man hung out of a window, then let go. Another man jumped out after him. Inside, bodies ran aimlessly through smoke filled corridors. A woman fell over and was quickly trampled by a stampede of cast, crew and extras. A statue of Shiva lost an arm. A vase shattered against a wall, leaving a stain of water and pollen.

"How's it taste?" said the AD.

"Smooth," said Blow, considering the amber liquid swirling around in the bottom of his glass. "But old as shit."

"Sort of dusty-like," said Bax.

"Not bad," said Nick.

"Personally, I like newer shit," said Bax. "Eight year old is okay. Twelve max."

"18 is my sweet spot," said Silvio. "Year after year, I gotta have the 18. No more, no less."

He re-packed the bowl, raised the pipe to his mouth, lowered it, then, after turning to the console to pause the image on the screen, raised the pipe back up and took a big hit.

"I once had some thousand year old shit," said Nick. "It was down in the catacombs. I was wearing a mask and a cape. It wasn't Scotch. I don't even think they had Scotch back then. It was some kind of medieval shit—mead or sack or some shit. I can remember what it tasted like. It tasted like shit. I was drinking it out of a skull or a silver goblet. There was a body, bloated and hairless, and candles all over the place. Everything smelled like melted wax."

"He lived in my building," said Blow. "I only talked to him a couple times. I think he was an extra in some of the DW Griffith pictures. I wish I'd had the chance to hear some of his stories."

"Survived by a bottle of hooch and a… what was the name of the cat?" said Nick.

"Yeah, what happened to the cat?" said Bax.

"I have no idea," said Blow, taking a leisurely sip of Scotch.

Up on the screen was the paused image of a face: one of the brothers (Brother #6) played by the Australian actor Rod Markle. Surrounded by smoke and twisted in fear, the face was screaming, a silent blood curdling scream. It was an interior shot of the Raja's palace, the same room where the brothers had sampled Marianne's LSD tainted milk.

"He was hot shit as the junkie car thief in *Outbound*," said Nick.

"Lost 50 pounds for that part," said Bax.

"I can't remember why he's screaming," said Tina.

"It's because he's been driven mad by the LSD-69," said Blow. "And because of the fire."

"I see your point," said Bax. "It's not specific. It's just a scream. He could be screaming about any damn thing. I don't think he even knows why he's screaming."

"It's coming back to me now," said Silvio, watching the smoke that streamed from his mouth admiringly. "I completely forgot about the fire."

"I can't believe nobody got killed."

"Nobody that we know of," said Tina.

"It turned out the second unit *was* in there shooting pickup shots," said the AD. "I saw the schedule. It was crossed off."

"Stroke of luck," said Silvio. "Got some brilliant reaction shots."

"They could have all died," said Tina.

"Mostly just second degree burns," said Nick. "And some, what's the worst kind, first or third?."

"It doesn't matter. He's got policies on all of us. The insurance company doesn't give a fuck because they've covered the losses on the derivatives market. They win either way," said Bax.

"It looks real as shit," said Silvio.

"It's blind terror," said the AD. "I was there."

"That doesn't make it authentic," said Nick.

"You could tear out a guy's fingernails with pliers," said Bax. "That doesn't mean he should get an Oscar."

"I always think it's better when it's completely fake," said Nick. "Raw emotion is always a little on-the-nose."

"How do we know that nobody was still in there," said Tina. "What if everybody didn't get out?"

"We'd know by if somebody was missing," said Nick.

"So far I can't think of anybody," said Bax.

"There are like a hundred extras," said Tina.

"I suppose we'll find out for sure when they go through the rubble," said Nick.

"Who's going through the rubble?" said Tina.

"Figured somebody would," said Nick. "Maybe the insurance company."

"Has anyone seen Dante?" said the AD.

Everybody looked at Bax and Nick.

"Last I heard," said Bax, "he's out in the desert with a hand-held."

"Shooting rocks and cactuses and shit," said Nick.

"Last I heard," said Bax.

"What's happening there?" said Tina, pointing to the screen. "In the background, down there in the corner? What's all that about?"

Silvio highlighted the section of the image she was referring to and expanded it out until it filled the screen.

"Run it through," said Bax.

On the screen, the hunched figure, wearing a Drivers cap, seemed to blend into the shadows as it moved along the wall with a combination of stealth and wraith-like immateriality until finally exiting the frame like an apparition.

"Looks like Nero," said Bax.

"Can't be," said Nick.

"Did anyone see him?" said the AD.

"Gotta be St. Germaine. You can tell by the cap. Poor sap never takes it off," said Nick.

"He's very deep into the character," said Blow.

"He's carrying something," said Nick.

"Back it up, slow it down this time," said Bax.

Silvio rewound the scene then ran it through at quarter speed.

"He's running off with the goddamn baby," said Silvio.

Everybody turned to Blow.

"Is that supposed to be in there?" said Nick.

"Hey Blow, what's that all about?" said Bax.

Blow looked at them blankly.

Just then Sal Khan entered the tent. All eyes turned to Sal.

"It's his baby," he said, gravely.

"The Driver's secretly a chick?" said Bax.

"Tony's character is impotent," said Sal, shooting a glance at Blow.

"Tony's character didn't want his brothers to find out," said Blow, who appeared to suddenly snap out of his reverie. "So he had the Driver step in to fill his shoes, so to speak."

"That's bull shit," said Tony from the couch, interrupting his cell phone conversation. "If the Driver is supposed to represent Seth, *he* should be impotent. That's how it is in the myth."

"Our story turns the myth on its head," said Blow.

"You're going to hear from my agent," said Tony.

The phone rang. The AD put it on speaker.

"I thought Tony was supposed to be the Superman," said super-agent Mort Klondike on speaker phone. "Not the one from the comics, the one from philosophy."

"It turns out the infant is the Superman," said Blow. "That's the twist."

"The infant," said Bax.

"Because it's half-god," said Sal.

"A half-god baby with a head full of LSD," said Nick.

"I thought the LSD permanently scrambled their brains," said Bax.

"It's true. The infant is insane," said Blow. "As the Driver intended."

"And as he carries the infant in his arms, the Driver says to him," said Sal, moving fully into the room. "*One day, we will rain terror on the world.*"

"What I want to know," said Tina. "Is what we're going to do about the palace."

"It's a total loss," said Nick. "In my opinion."

"Don't worry about it," said Bax. "We got it covered. Insurance will take care of everything."

He took a hit, blew smoke and smiled.

"After all," he said. "It was an accident."

"That's right," said Sal, giving a sinister little laugh. "It was an accident."

"What I want to know," said the voice of the agent, on the speaker phone. "What I want to know is how can the kid be half

315

god?"

"That's a good point," said Tina. "It's inconsistent with the genre."

"Crime drama," said the AD.

"This was supposed to be a realistic story," said Mort Klondike over the phone.

Sal looked to Blow. All eyes turned to Blow.

Blow said, "The Driver is an alien."

# CHAPTER 58

It was still hot in the tent, but not too hot. Bax and Nick sat across from each other. They had their shirts open and sleeves rolled up. The safe was out on the table, the door open, stacks of bills piled up between them. The man entering the tent wore tea colored aviator sunglasses, a crisp white Oxford shirt and a blue and red striped power tie.

"Hi," said Brad, all tan skin and brilliant white teeth. "I'm the adjuster. From the insurance company."

Brad extended his hand.

"Welcome to the money tent," said Bax, as he slipped a rubber band around a fat stack of fifty dollar bills.

Bax reached up to shake hands. Brad held the grip, showing an intense, bright smile. Without looking up, Nick gave a nod of acknowledgment as he counted out a stack of big bills.

"What up?" he said.

Bax made a notation on the ledger then stuck the pen between his front teeth, where it twitched around like a hot cigarette. He held out his hand, offering Brad a seat at the table. Before sitting down, Brad laid a copy of the policy on the table.

Brad said: "According to the terms of the contract, Fortress is responsible..."

"Due to certain individuals going AWOL," said Bax.

"…due to abandonment of production, for indemnifying the principal investors," said Brad. "The Saudis."

"Check," said Bax.

"The Albanians," said Brad.

"Check," said Nick.

"The Japanese," said Brad.

"Check check," said Bax.

"Et cetera, et cetera," said Brad.

"Ditto," said Nick.

"Double ditto," said Bax.

"As a condition of accepting the claim, Fortress assumes ownership of the project and reserves the right to terminate said project and settle any outstanding financial obligations," said Brad.

"You want something to drink?" said Nick.

"Lemonade, thank you," said Brad.

"Hard … or soft?" said Bax.

Brad looked from Bax to Nick, then back to Bax.

"I'll have a mineral water," he said, smiling fiercely.

"Good choice," said Nick, setting the bottle down in front of Brad. "Mineral water is hard by definition."

"Hard *ipso facto*," said Bax.

"We've been drinking them all day," said Bax.

"They're fortified with oxygen and vitamins and a lot of other shit," said Nick.

"Trace amounts of bioavailable helium," said Bax. "And xenon."

"It's the latest thing," said Nick.

"They go down like water," said Bax.

"However," said Brad. "In this particular case, Fortress has decided to continue with the production."

"That would be highly unusual," said Bax.

"…under the circumstances," said Nick.

"We believe, after reviewing the data, that the best decision, taking into account all future cash flows, discounted at the standard rate, natch, and considering the salient risks, is to get this baby in the can in time for the Toronto Film Festival."

"They're your dice," said Bax, closing a fan of bills into a neat little stack.

"It goes without saying that all personnel attached to the

318

project would retain their current roles, except, obviously, for the director and the studio head, who seem to have gone missing. I have one request. The actress who plays Wet Nurse #2. Sara. I was hoping she could be given a small speaking role, say, Gang Moll #3?"

"Done," said the voice from the back of the tent.

Brad turned around in his seat.

"I don't think we've been introduced," said Brad.

"That's the writer," said Bax.

"Name's Blow," said Nick.

Blow was kicked back in a teak wood and canvas recliner, marking up an old racing form.

"Pleased to make your acquaintance," said Brad.

"She shows a lot of promise," said Blow. "I hadn't really noticed her on the set. Nobody had. But she really came through in the dailies."

"I took the liberty of putting together a director list, experienced individuals who will likely be available on short notice," said Brad, setting the list down on top of the policy.

"Start over," said Bax, shooting a quick glance at the list.

"There are a lot of balls in the air," said Nick. "By the time you bring somebody in, get them up to speed, it's too late."

"Crash and burn," said Bax. "Big time."

"What's on your mind?" said Brad. "Silvio? The AD?"

"What about Blow," said Bax.

"Kid's an up and comer," said Nick. "A real mensch."

"Been carrying the picture on his back the last eight weeks," said Bax. "What was I saying just a second ago?"

"Said it was a total loss," said Nick.

"And what did Blow say?" said Bax.

"Tell him what you said?" said Nick.

"It's not as bad as it looks," said Blow.

"You ever directed anything?" said Brad.

"A few small things," said Blow. "Nothing on this scale."

Brad looked to Nick and Bax, whose attention had returned to the money, then back to Blow.

"Done."

He finished the bottle of water and started to leave, then sat back down in his chair.

"I couldn't help but notice, a number of line items can't be accounted for," he said. "I guess what I'm trying to say is, well, a big chunk of the budget seems to be missing."

"Must have fallen into a hole," said Bax, as he slipped the rubber band over another big stack of cash. "Out in the desert."

# CHAPTER 59

Outside the tent, the AD and the PA were having a cigarette as Sal Khan got off a call.

"What's the low-down?" said Khan, putting away his phone.

"Jack Dante..." said the PA.

"The director," said Khan.

"Missing, presumed dead," said the PA.

"And..."

"The infamous head of a major studio, MIA since Friday," said the AD.

"No doubt he felt the heat," said the PA. "The vultures were circling back in L.A."

"Interpol, the NSA, the FBI," said the AD.

"The Board of Directors," said the PA.

"They were starting to climb his trail of slime," said Khan.

"It was only a matter of time," said the AD.

"Appears he's slipped from their grasp yet again," said Khan.

"Only a matter of time before he turns up, somewhere," said the PA.

"You can't kill what isn't there. You can only hope to contain it," said the AD.

"Bottled like a genie. One moment," said Khan, raising his hand as he took the call.

# CHAPTER 60

Everybody was there. Bodies pressed together in the tent. Tony. Marianne. Bax. Nick. The AD and the PA. Silvio. Tina. Most of the cast (those with speaking roles) and the key members of the crew. A number of cast and crew wore bandages—on the side of the head, the upper arm, the leg. A number leaned on crutches. They looked like casualties of war. Blow stood in front of the group, with his hands on his hips. He wore wire rim glasses, which made him appear slightly older and, it had to be admitted, a shade wiser. He also had on a New York Yankees baseball cap, a faded surf shop t-shirt, cargo shorts, three days of stubble and Prada black leather sandals, an ensemble that, he believed, gave him a directorial air. He took a seat on a shipping container, resting his foot on a small speaker, so that he was slightly lower than the faces that looked back at him.

"I wanted to start by thanking each of you for your hard work and perseverance," he said. "Without your dedication, we never would have made it this far. I'd also like to thank Fortress Indemnity for believing in this project and committing the resources necessary to see it through to completion."

Cut to – the Movie:

*Exterior. Desert. Night. Looking through night vision goggles, the Rival Gang Leader surveys the graveyard of ships strewn about the desert.*

*Rival Gang Leader: "Why do they have so many boats?"*

*Attendant: "Perhaps they are planning to move their operation to the coast."*

*Rival Gang Leader: "It troubles me."*

Back on the scene:

Blow held out his hand, palm up, out-stretched fingers directing their eyes to the man standing at the back of the tent. Brad gave a razor glint smile, lowering his head slightly, arms folded tight against his chest.

"As most of you know, Fortress has done me the honor of allowing me to fill the role of Director for the remainder of the production. I intend to do everything I can to live up to the confidence they've shown in me, and I'll be relying on all of you to make this dream a reality that can be shared with billions of people around the world."

Cut to – the Movie:

*Interior. Raja's Palace. Night. The Gang Leader (Tony) paces about the great room, a fire roaring in the background. His expression is bitter, twisted, desperate. He turns around and sees his reflection in the mirror over the fireplace mantle.*

*Tony (addressing his reflection): "Everything has been taken from you. Your brothers. Your son. Your bride. Even your sanity. You have been betrayed by your kin, by your gods, even by your most trusted confidante. Meanwhile, your enemies are massing on all sides, moving closer by the hour, patiently waiting for the opportunity to deliver the death blow as you hide in this crypt, stewing in self-pity, the walls of your empire crumbling at your feet. There is no other choice. Not another moment can be wasted. The time has come to release the black beast."*

Back on the scene:

Blow scanned the faces in the tent, looking from one to the next until he found it: on the face of the new Gang Moll #3 (Sara), a glimmer of raw unmeasured enthusiasm. As Blow resumed, he felt the heat from all those eyes, except for those of Bax and Nick, which, concealed as they were behind dark sunglasses, just seemed to go straight through him as if he wasn't even there.

"As most of you know, I worked closely with Him right up to the very end to develop a story that reflected His powerful and singular vision. His sudden absence, not to mention that of veteran director Jack Dante, has left a gaping hole at the heart of this production, one that no amount of hard work or inspiration will be able to entirely fill. As we move forward, we will continue to remain faithful to His vision … However, the events of the last several days have led us to reconsider certain aspects of the plot, so you can expect to see a few changes as we begin setting up to shoot the final scenes. Some of these changes will be minor, for instance, Tony's impotence…"

Blow gave a subtle nod to Tony, who, seated in the back, talking on his cell phone, shot a quick nod back.

Cut to – the Movie:

*Exterior. Desert. Twilight. Up on the mesa, the oil derrick hammers the earth rhythmically, like a lover, backlit by a sliver of orange sun melting below the horizon.*

*Several hundred yards away, the Gang Leader (Tony) pushes the T-plunger into the ignition box, then covers his ears.*

*Up on the mesa, there is a huge flash and a concussive shock wave, as the billowing smoke swallows the broken carcass of the derrick. Tony watches as the smoke swirls around the derrick, slowly spreading out, and then he sees it, a trickle of black crude running down the hill, and then all at once the trickle is a river, and then a cascade of pure viscous black.*

Back on the scene:

"…Tony's rise from the ashes," continued Blow, "…and a

few other things, but the most salient feature of the new direction, which came as a kind of revelation, will be, on both a narrative and thematic level, a kind of return to order."

He held out his hand, indicating the craft services table at the back of the tent.

"Help yourself to coffee and pastries."

Cut to – the Movie:

*Exterior. Desert Valley. Night. The rival gang's army, a full force of armed men and weaponized Land Cruisers and Hum-Vees, are positioned along the perimeter of the valley. The full moon looms overhead, and, after several beats, begins to reflect on the surface of the desert. The Rival Gang Leader crouches down and puts his hand in the shimmering silver reflection. He raises his hand, rubbing his fingers together in the moonlight. The fingers drip black crude.*

*Rival Gang Leader: "Oh shit".*

*Cut to: Exterior. Desert valley. Night. Machine gun fire lights up the darkness, punctuated by screams of agony and terror. The valley lights up with each incendiary flash, revealing a massive armada of armed sport boats and pleasure cruisers advancing across a lake of black oil, as the rival gang attempts with futility to navigate their terrestrial vehicles through the thick crude.*

*A cigarette boat engages a Hum-Vee, mired in the rising tide of oil. Two men crawl out the window of the Hum-Vee and onto the roof. They attempt to fire on the cigarette boat, but it's too late. The boat's gunners mow them down with ease, like shooting ducks in a barrel.*

*The Gang Leader (Tony) watches from the mesa, fire reflecting in his sunglasses. He takes a drag on a cigarette, savors the smoke, then flicks the ash, watching as the glowing end drifts down onto the lake of oil, transforming it, almost instantly, into a roaring lake of fire, consuming everyone and everything.*

*Tony watches it burn.*

Afterward, the AD and the PA stood outside the tent and had a smoke.

"Can you believe there were only a dozen casualties?" said

the AD.

"And not a single fatality," said the PA.

"Mostly flesh wounds. I was standing right next to Silvio when the bullet grazed his head," said the AD.

"Good thing actors are terrible shots," said the PA.

"How you figure all that live ammo got mixed in? And those unmarked AKs?" said the AD.

"I'm surprised it doesn't happen more often," said the PA.

"I think it happens more often than you think."

# CHAPTER 61

A number of people were standing around looking on. Brad drove the Landcruiser up as far as he could, then got out and walked to the edge. Down in the ravine, in the middle of the arroyo, was a man's body. Nobody had touched it yet. The body was lying face down. It looked broken and rumpled, like the life had gone out some time ago. Brad steadied himself as he made his way down the incline. At the bottom, he hiked his slacks and crouched down next to the body. He took a silver Mont Blanc pen from his breast pocket and poked at the skin at the back of the neck. Then, he put his hand on the far shoulder and rolled the body toward him. It was, unmistakably, the face of Jack Dante. There were bullet holes in the neck and torso.

"Should we call it in?" said the man in the stylish priest's outfit, standing at the top of the ravine.

"One more thing," said Brad.

He took the corner of the corpse's mustache between his thumb and index finger, and, with a quick flip of the wrist, ripped it completely off.

"It's a counterfeit," he said, throwing the mustache down onto the sand and wiping his hands. "The face is made out of rubber or something. Looks just like him."

"The FX department used us as models for the body-prop

corpses in the oil fire scene," said Blow. "They made life-casts of our faces."

"Looks like Dante is still a missing person," said Brad.

"It makes perfect sense," said Blow, walking around the body and running his hands through his hair didactically. "Nero wants to make an example of Dante without leaving behind the actual body or anything that would connect him. That's his MO, like with the head. He impacts things at a distance, without touching them."

"Or getting his hands dirty," said Brad.

"Whether Dante's alive or dead is, when you think about it, entirely immaterial," said Blow.

"The god-like creator who pulls invisible strings," said the man dressed as a Priest, laughing. "You don't know jack shit."

"It's a theory," said Blow, massaging his chin and looking off into the distance.

# CHAPTER 62

As the 747 nosed over the Rocky Mountains, the tranquil blue skies belying the geological violence that gave birth to the colossal snow-capped peaks and jagged valleys below, the pervasive low hum of the jet's engines enveloped the passengers in a medium of dreamy narcotic white noise. Sherrill sat by the window, with the two first-class seats next to her empty. Even with the oversize baseball cap, the too-dark oversize sunglasses, a few passengers still recognized her, although not as many as she assumed. An even greater number figured that, what with that getup she was wearing, she must have been somebody but couldn't quite put their finger on it. Sherrill turned the pages of the latest *Vanity Fair*. After scanning through the party pictures and not finding any of herself, she closed the magazine and took out her phone to check her messages. She was expecting a call from her agent. She started to dial and then stopped and put away the phone. She glanced around the cabin furtively. The bathroom door opened and the stewardess stepped out. Sherrill stood up and quickly made her way to the vacant bathroom, shutting the door behind her. She removed the baseball cap and hung it over the smoke detector mounted above the mirror. She opened her purse and removed a pack of cigarettes and a round silver compact of blush. She set the compact on the sink and flipped the top. The compact began emitting a whirring sound, like a small vacuum cleaner. She set the cigarette between her lips and lit it, taking a long drag and blowing the smoke at the whirring compact, which rapidly sucked it in. Sherrill smoked the cigarette hungrily, burning it halfway down in just a few drags and dropping the smoldering butt into the toilet. The little electric compact was so efficient that not even the faintest ribbon of smoke remained in the air. Sherrill flushed the toilet, then picked the baseball cap off the smoke detector, returning it to her head, and made her way back to her seat. The compact had been given to her by a billionaire airline mogul who guaranteed it would work on any of his planes. He was a smoker and used the device himself (the male version appearing to be a tin of pomade) every time he flew on one of his commercial planes, which he did more often than he liked for PR purposes. It would have been much easier to simply smoke an e-cigarette, which produced vapor rather than smoke, but e-cigarettes didn't do the trick. It wasn't just about the nicotine. She needed the burn and the taste of the smoke.

As Sherrill took her seat, the flight attendant gave her a little look, like yeah I know what you did in there but no-blood-no-foul sister. Most people just wanted to get through the day and wouldn't make waves as long as you didn't put them on the spot. That was the secret that so many of her friends never learned, that discretion was a form of etiquette and making a big display of doing whatever the fuck you wanted was a violation of the social contract and was always met with heavy official censure, from the police, the studio, the press. Being a celeb you could get away with practically anything as long as you didn't make a show out of it. She knew she slipped up every now and then but for the most part she knew when to keep her mouth shut.

The nice thing about buying a whole row of seats was you didn't have to talk to anyone, and you didn't have to worry about pissing anybody off when you closed the shade on the window right over a breathtaking view of the Rockies. Just as she started to lower the shade, she noticed something out there, like a balloon, yes it was definitely a balloon, floating in the clear blue air miles above the mountains, and as the plane passed the balloon she could even make out what had to be, even though she couldn't really believe her eyes, an astronaut, or a man in a space suit anyway, suspended beneath the balloon. Whoever it was, they were still going up, up and away by the time Sherrill finally got the shade down, lowered her cap and closed her eyes on the world and everything.

# CHAPTER 63
*DON*

This Quetzalcoatl was a notorious blood-thirsty gangster, so it was with no small amount of trepidation that I idled at the mouth of his lair. It was impossible to tell for sure what might lay ahead. The long road down was difficult to gauge from this *coign of vantage*, winding as it did through hills and scrub and disappearing in a series of sharp twists and turns. I gripped the wheel and shifted into gear, kicking up dust as the nose of the car went over the side of the road and dropped down.

I was beginning to feel some nerves now, a trace of anxiety. And Maria could sense this, this foreboding I had, and she gave me a wary sidelong glance. At last we came to within view of their compound, and I slowed to a stop a safe distance out. It looked like an ancient manor house that had seen better days. But I could smell death in there. Dust devils swirled about in the half-light. The tension mounted. A real fear gripped me. Was I to take the plunge at last, become swallowed up by the abyss? The old house was disarming enough, but I knew there was none of the right kind of light, like a negative. The world turned inside out.

"You know, baby, I could really use something to ease the tension," I said, my finger tracing along her lips.

She took my finger into her mouth, closing her lips around it and sliding back to the tip. She took my hand and placed it in my lap.

"Work first," she said, smiling. "You take care of …" She pointed down, toward the house. "And Maria will take care of … everything."

"Tell me how you're going to do it."

"I'm going to say, where's my little boy? I want to take him out and play. Then I pull down the zipper. So big now, my little boy, so big now for Maria. Are you hot for Maria? Are you hard for me? So big now, my little boy, all grown up, like a fat man." She laughed. "Don't worry, baby, Maria will take care of you. Feel my mouth on your skin, all the way down, all the way down, taking you all the way in. It's okay, baby. You can stay, you can stay inside as long as you like, you can stay inside forever."

Her lips were wet as she said this, her eyes full and heavy. She smiled deliriously, the smile of sweet, immaculate sex.

"You like the way Maria take care of your little boy?"

"Blew my mind."

She pressed a roll of bills into the palm of my hand. I dropped the bills in my pocket without looking.

"Wait in the car. I'll only be a minute," I said, as I opened the door.

Even coming up on it from the back in the dark, I could tell the house was really something. Lit up the way it was by the security lights it resembled a figment from an exotic fever dream—the centuries old palace of a Brahmin prince, perhaps, transported to the middle of nowhere by a rich and powerful sociopath who indulged every whim, no matter how extravagant. One thing I knew for sure, they could see me coming from a mile away. There was nothing else around. There was no point skulking in the shadows, so I kept my head up and walked with a steady gait across the sand until I reached the door. If they'd wanted to kill me, I'd have been dead a good way back. I smelled the smoke as soon as I turned the knob, opening the door. Inside, the palace was full of gloom and creeping shadows and flickering orange light. Once my eyes adjusted, I quickly made him out slouched in a giant Hindu throne at the end of the room. Moving down the strip of red carpet that ran from the door to the throne, I took deliberate carefully measured steps such as one might make not wanting to rouse a giant. As I drew closer I could make out his features—a black man with a hard jaw and a muscular build. He wore a purple bowler hat tilted on his head like a crown and dark sunglasses, black leather pants and a loose fitting red and gold silk shirt adorned with all manner of Far East ghouls and dragons. A tattoo of a winged serpent climbed up from the collar of the shirt and wrapped around his neck.

There was a moment of *deja vous*, a fleeting recognition, like the glimpse you get of another life or a long-ago dream.

I stood there before him a moment without saying anything.

"Are you Quetzalcoatl?" I said.

"I am now," he said.

The way he said it, without moving a muscle, you wouldn't have been sure he was even alive.

"I should probably explain why I'm here."

"I know why you're here, mother fucker. You got something for me?"

I handed him the wad of bills I'd received from Maria. As he flipped through the bills, it gradually dawned on me that these weren't greenbacks, or Euros or yen for that matter, or any currency I'd ever seen before. The sepia toned paper was covered with Sanskrit symbols, Arabic lettering, Roman numerals. One bill was impressed with the face of a woman, a young queen or princess who bore, it must be admitted, more than a passing resemblance to Maria. From the look on the dealer's face, as he stowed away the bills, they clearly weren't counterfeit, more likely the latest black market currency, of the type printed by a fugue state and backed by space rock and heavy metal.

"I was told this was some heavy shit," I said.

"You were told right. This is the heaviest shit on the planet," he said.

He took off the bowler hat, turning it over and presenting it to me. Inside the hat was a brick of dark powder.

"What's this?" I said.

"It's a magic hat."

"Why do you say that?"

"If you take it, there's no bottom."

"You look familiar," I said. "Like from a dream."

"You don't know me," he said. "Not anymore. You don't even know yourself."

I took the hat.

333

"Show yourself out," he said.

The room had become filled with smoke. As I took the hat, seating it on my own head and turning to walk back down the red carpet, the flickering orange light I'd noticed upon entering had become a raging conflagration, coating the doors, tapestries, wall hangings and window treatments with a thick swirling impasto of fire that spread through the room so quickly that by the time I finally reached the door and exited the palace I was enshrouded in a roiling penumbra of flame which, the instant it threatened to completely devour me, shed from my moving form like a dead skin, leaping outward then recoiling back toward the palace like a whiplash. With the purple bowler on my head, I walked away from the palace in the same steady gait that had carried me there, while behind me the great house erupted in a violent orgiastic blaze.

# CHAPTER 64
*DON*

We drove straight up into the mountains and by midnight had reached the lake of fire. We took off our clothes and slid into the burning bath, reclining against the rocks, the hot gases swirling around us like ghosts, like opium. Maria handed me the bottle of Mezcal. I pulled the cork out and drank greedily until the great homunculus swirled down the neck of the bottle and then, finally, into my parched mouth. One more swig to wash it down. And readied myself for my moment of death. I could feel it coming on, the temperature rising inside, burning out my eyes. I prepared myself for descent. I was going down, down into the hole. To crawl over the dark underbelly of the earth, down, down, deep down into Marianas, at the throne of Neptune. Follow the sun? I'll be my own blinding light. My eyes burned, boring into darkest night. I spilled the hot powder out onto the rock then leaned over and snorted it all up, feeling the heat behind my eyes, behind my sunglasses. For once, my eyes aglow, I didn't need them anymore. For once it was truly hotter inside than out. So hot, hotter than a blackout. I could hear Juan now, his voice barely audible over the sound from the yellow-and-black radio (the old torch song having broken up into a torrent of hard crackling static), saying, "Hey man, don't Bogart that plutonium." I raised the brim of the bowler hat and felt the spider crawling down my face and then the sting of the fangs sinking into my neck, sucking up the hot radioactive blood. I was immediately struck by the gravity of the gift I'd just bestowed. One day, in the not too distant future, this lowly spider would possess superhuman powers. I took off the sunglasses and thought once more about the sun. What of it? I'll see the brilliant fucker when I come back up. Because baby...Because baby, I'm the bomb.

# ABOUT THE AUTHOR

Morgan Hobbs was born in Tidewater, Virginia and graduated from the University of Wisconsin – Madison with a degree in English and History. He has worked as a day laborer in Austin, Texas, a commercial fisherman in Kodiak, Alaska, and a reader and story editor for several motion picture production companies in Los Angeles, California. He currently lives in Tokyo, Las Vegas and Washington, D.C.

Made in the USA
San Bernardino, CA
05 August 2016